Stacey's Flyer

Stacey's Flyer

PATRICIA BURNS

St. Martin's Press
New York

Library of Congress Cataloging-in-Publication Data

Burns, Patricia.
  Stacey's flyer.

  I. Title.
PR6052.U664S7   1985   823'.914   85-11811
  ISBN 0-312-75483-3

First published in Great Britain by Corgi Books.

First U.S. Edition

10 9 8 7 6 5 4 3 2 1

To the staff of the special care baby unit, Rochford General Hospital, and Princess Alexandra Hospital, Harlow.

Stacey's Flyer

Chapter One

Death did not ride a pale horse, Simon Wynwood realized with detached fascination. He drove a mud-splattered Suffolk Punch and sat hunched and unheeding whilst hoof and wheel crushed the life out of his victims. He watched with a growing sense of unreality as the huge beast plodded ever nearer, his numbed mind unable to accept that this was actually happening to him, that his fine body and agile brain had finally let him down. Clearly through the pain hammering in his head, he could hear the clump of the iron-shod hooves, the rumble of the wheels, and breathing of the horse.

How long he had lain in the dirt of the Breckland track, Simon had very little idea, but it must have been several hours now, for the bitter grey of a February morning coloured a sky that had been night-black when he was attacked. They had been no ordinary footpads, he was sure of that. Chance thieves would not lurk in this lonely lane, and even if they had, they would merely have knocked him unconscious and fled, no doubt amazed by the amount they had netted. No – this had been a warning. He had been too successful, trodden on some important toes. Just whose toes he could not be certain. It could have been any one of a dozen rich and powerful men, but of all the possible names, one stood out: Henshaw. The events of the last few months became blurred and confused in his memory as he tried to follow a logical train of thought, but amongst the jumble there was one scrap of comfort in the fact that Perdita had not been discovered. If her existence was known, she would almost certainly have been used as a weapon against him. So she at least was safe, though still without the security he wanted to give her. Three thousand pounds was not a fortune, but enough to ensure her future. And now that was gone. While a chilling intermittent rain raked across his bruised and broken body, he hatched wild plots of revenge, and waited. He was still alive, that was the important thing. He had been in many tight corners before and always managed to bounce back, though admittedly none had been quite as bad as this. Eventually someone would find him.

But this time it seemed that fortune had firmly set her face against him. The senseless chawbacon on the cart sat head down, huddled against the cutting wind, the reins bunched loosely in his cold-stiffened hands. He was just about as alive to his surroundings as the iron-bound wheels. It was too late now for Simon to move out of the way. He had tried moving earlier, before the chill had gnawed into his bones, and it had been bad enough then. With his last reserves of strength, he raised an arm and gave an inarticulate croak, and placed his faith in the innate sense of the equine race.

The huge muddy legs stopped inches from his face, the hooves half-hidden in the mire. From miles above, it seemed, a long chestnut head came down and blew gently at him, brown eyes mildly enquiring. Simon touched the velvety muzzle with grateful fingers. It was only then that it came home to him just how close an escape he had had.

The carter, coming slowly to life, slapped the reins on the horse's back, urging it on. When the animal refused to move, he saw at last that there was an obstacle in the way, and a human one at that, and climbed laboriously down to see what was ado. A bowed figure in hobnailed boots and leather gaiters, a couple of old sacks draped across his smocked shoulders as an ineffectual protection against the rain, he stared at the prone man.

'Well now,' he said, whether to himself or the horse, Simon could not make out, 'what be this?'

Unhurriedly, he took in Simon's fine broadcloth coat, heavy riding cloak, quality buckskins and topboots, and equally his ugly injuries.

'Looks like someone's given you a right hammering,' he commented.

Simon inwardly commended his brilliant powers of observation and waited patiently for him to finish his train of thought.

'Best get you on the cart, I reckon,' he concluded, and bent down to grasp Simon under the arms.

A shattering explosion of pain was followed by the merciful black of unconsciousness which lasted the length of his undignified journey amongst the yellowing remains of yesterday's load of turnips.

When he surfaced reluctantly and unsteadily to awareness again, Simon became sensible first of a blissful warmth permeating his body. For a while he lay quiescent, grateful just to be out of the weather, then gradually began to take stock of his surroundings. Above him was a low, smoke-blackened ceiling, the uneven beams harbouring waving cobwebs, and he seemed to be lying on a greasy wooden table. The air was thick with a smell of tobacco smoke, unwashed bodies and stale beer. A tavern, and a pretty low one at that. And as he came to this conclusion, he realized that somewhere nearby his future was being decided.

'Sammy!' a woman's voice shrilled. 'Sammy! Drat the boy, where's 'e gone? Never here when 'e's wanted. Sam! There you are. Where you bin? Listen, you run to the sawbone's house – not Price the apothecary, mind, but Armatage the surgeon – and tell him to come quick, there's a gentleman hurt real bad. You got that?'

The message was repeated back, a draught whistled across the room, a door slammed.

'Reckon I done you a good turn today, Moll,' Simon

11

recognized the carter's voice. 'Worth a drink on the house.'

'Good turn?' The woman was contemptuous. 'And how do you figure that out, might I ask? I got enough to do running this place single-handed without bloody gentry taking up table space in my taproom.'

The carter was roused to truculence.

'Ain't you got no sense in your fat 'ead? You see to 'im and 'e's going to be grateful, ain't 'e? Stands to reason. Now where's that pot of ale? Come out of my way, I have, bringing him here.'

There was a thump of pewter on wood.

'There you are, then,' the woman said ungraciously. 'But if you ask me, you brought me nought but a pack o' trouble.'

The carter snorted.

'Look, you daft besom, you got a spare room upstairs, ain't you? And by the look of 'im, 'e ain't going nowhere for a fair space o' time. That means you got 'im paying for bed and board till 'e's fit to move on. Make your fortune, you will, and all because of me bringing 'im 'ere instead of somewhere else.'

Simon's respect for his rescuer's intellect increased considerably.

'If 'e's bin robbed, 'e won't 'ave no money to pay, will 'e?' the woman objected.

''E's got kin, ain't 'e? Everyone's got kin. They'll pay. Pay handsome too, I shouldn't wonder.'

'Ah – well—'

The woman stumped over to where Simon lay and loomed fatly over him. The stale smell of her assailed his nose. He kept his eyes resolutely blank and unfocused. He was not going to plead, even in his present helpless state. Wheezing slightly, she examined him as the carter had done, but her reaction was different. Her work-roughened fingers smoothed his once white neckcloth, strayed over his mud-caked hair. When she spoke, her

12

voice had softened by several degrees.

'Aye, someone'll pay for him all right. Look at them curls – pretty enough for a maid.' She leaned over Simon, her bloated face swimming into his view. 'Gawd, someone's made a right mess of you, ain't they? Looks like you bin walked over with hobnailed boots. But never you fear, Moll will see you right. Soon have you good as new.'

Simon turned his head slightly to look her full in the face, then gave a slow and deliberate wink. Against all the odds, he had fallen on his feet yet again.

Pale spring sunshine filtered through the dust as Barty Brown, pocket watch in hand, checked the arrival time of the Lord Nelson from Yarmouth. Ten past four, dead right. He raised his hand in cheerful salute to the coachman, acknowledging his accuracy of timekeeping, and watched critically as the passengers and luggage were dealt with and dispersed, the guard disappeared into the booking office with his waybill, the coachman into the bar for a drink with one of the passengers and finally the Lord Nelson itself was led away into the back yard by the horsekeepers. All was running smoothly at Brown's Coaches.

Barty dropped the heavy gold watch into the pocket of his broad-striped waistcoat and stood in the yard, hands on hips, surveying his kingdom. Once again he blessed the moment that had moved his late lamented father to leave the Crown to his brother Noll and the coaching business to himself. The two enterprises had grown hand-in-hand during the twenty-six years since he had taken over in the turbulent days of 'ninety-four. He had not realized it at the time, but he had inherited the business just at the start of its expansion, when coaches and roads were being improved, the middle classes were caught with an altogether admirable itch to imitate their betters and travel about the country, and

13

the wars made whole sections of the population more mobile. The inns needed the stagecoaches to bring travellers to their doors, the coaches needed good hostelries at which to change horses and lodge their passengers overnight. And the trade grew, much to the delight of innkeepers and coach proprietors alike, but of the two Barty was certain he would rather be in coaching. It was a risky business, he reflected, and he had feather-edged it a few times, come close to overturning the whole show on occasion, but by Harry it beat running around seeing to folks' beds and bellies at all hours of the day and night. Noll was welcome to the Crown, to its three stories of galleried bedchambers, its spacious and comfortable public rooms and its prime position in the centre of Norwich under the lee of the castle.

The stagecoach company and its vast assortment of employees, a hierarchy reaching from swaggering dragsman to scrawny stableboy, were all ruled with the firm benevolence of a patriarch. Barty knew every one of them, their families and their difficulties. Brown's Coaches were an extension of the Brown family, that close-knit and self-interested web that spread itself over half the mercantile life of the city. Which brought Barty to the two problems most exercising his mind at the moment: his nephew Oliver and his daughter Stacey. Running a last critical eye round the yard, he nodded, satisfied with what he saw, and made his way to the booking office. His best thinking was done behind a four-in-hand team, his next best in the office with the help of a pipe.

From inside the booking office, brightly painted in company colours of royal blue and brown, the lowliest clerk saw his master's approach and sprang to open the door. Barty stumped in past the counter shared by the two juniors and paused at the fortress of Amos Burgess, chief clerk and cashier. From his high desk in the corner, two steps up from the floor and guarded by the three-

14

inch wooden balustrade all round its edge, Amos kept his myopic eyes on the doings of the outer office.

"Afternoon, Amos,' Barty greeted him. 'How's the owd rheumatics these days?'

Amos's face, grey and lined as the ledgers he habitually pored over, broke into the nearest he ever came to a smile.

'Not so bad, thanking you Mr Brown sir,' he replied in his prim, old-womanish voice. 'This warm weather helps to ease the joints considerably, I am happy to say.'

'Good, good, glad to hear it. Nought like a touch of sunshine, eh?'

'Quite so, Mr Brown sir.'

'Takings all right today?'

Amos pursed his lips and shook his head.

'Not what one would hope for, Mr Brown sir. It's this competition from Pymer's.'

Barty snorted his contempt of the rival coaching firm.

'Piffling bunch of jumped-up carriers! Don't you be fretting about them, old friend. I'm just waiting for the right moment to push 'em off the roads.'

The two juniors exchanged gleeful glances. The Gaffer had something up his sleeve, that was for sure. Amos was similarly convinced.

'I'm certain we shall, Mr Brown sir.'

Having soothed his cashier's worries, Barty let himself into his inner sanctum and plumped down behind his scarred desk. He was a queer stick, was old Amos, he reflected as he unlocked a drawer and fished out his long churchwarden pipe and a jar of tobacco. Dry and dull and utterly humourless. Stacey laughed at him, calling him a shrivelled monkey, but Stacey did not appreciate what a rare bird old Amos was – a man whose sole interest in life was keeping the company's books balanced. He would be hard-put to replace Amos.

When the pipe was drawing to his satisfaction, Barty swivelled his chair to look out of the window and across

15

the yard, and saw to his annoyance that one of his problems was striding in under the archway. Oliver Brown, his nephew. Try as he might, he had never quite taken to his brother Noll's eldest boy. At twenty-four he was as honest and upright a young man as could be found in the city of Norwich, but there was a stiffness, an intolerance about him that Barty found hard to swallow. And over the last couple of years, since he had become a convert to those damned Methodists, he had grown into a positive prig.

All this would have been quite possible to tolerate, had it not been for two factors: as Barty had no sons, Oliver considered himself natural heir to the coaching company, and even more alarming in Barty's view, he had his eye on Stacey. If there was one thing that Barty was not going to countenance, it was a union between his merry scamp of a daughter and his dour nephew. But how to say so without touching off a family row of monumental proportions? He would have to stall Oliver until Stacey came home, then trust to her refusing the boy. Then he would go around shaking his head and saying things about girlish fancies – it was well known throughout the family that he spoilt his daughter shamefully. And then he would have to look about for a suitable match for her, which was another problem.

Oliver was making his way purposefully towards the office. With resignation, Barty turned back to his desk and shuffled a few papers around. When the inevitable knock on the door sounded, he barked, 'Come!' and kept the young man waiting while he frowned over a letter he had answered two days previously.

'Ah,' he said at length. 'Ollie. Sit down, my boy.' He was about to say, 'And what can I do for you?' but changed course at the last moment, preferring to keep the ball in his court. Instead he said, 'I'm glad you've turned up, there's something I'd like to discuss with you.'

16

Oliver sat on a high-backed wooden chair, his hat held loosely between his knees. Taller than most of the Browns and massively built, he had earned a reputation as a fighter before his new-found convictions taught him to keep his temper in check.

'And what might that be, Uncle Bart?'

Barty leaned forward, his forearms on the desktop.

'Seems to me you've been getting a raw deal lately, one way and another,' he started, earnest and friendly. 'There you are, out at the coachworks, taking most of the responsibility and not getting near enough reward for it.'

Oliver's expression showed that he was in complete agreement with this, but Barty gave him no space for speech.

'Now you might think that I don't know what's going on at the works,' he swept on, 'but in fact I keep a pretty close eye on things. I have to – a business neglected soon runs to seed. But more that that, I like to run a happy ship, see? Now you ain't said nought, because you ain't the type to complain, but I know what's going on in your head. You see owd Jem Forbes dozing in that little office of his with 'Foreman' written on the door and doing nought but wander round the place two or three times a day and have a word with the men. And there's you doing all the work and getting no recognition for it. Ain't that so?'

'You could say that, Uncle Bart, but I dare say you have your reasons.'

Oliver's tone suggested that whatever Barty's reasons might be, he still felt hard done by.

The time had come, Barty decided, to appear to take his nephew into his confidence, to make him feel he was in the know.

'Well now Oliver,' he said, 'I'm in a difficult position over this, you understand. If Jem was an ordinary employee, I'd have pensioned him off a couple of years

17

ago. But the fact is that when I bought the coachworks from him at a knock-down price back in 'sixteen, it was on condition that I kept him on as foreman. That suited me very well at the time. Jem had no head for business, but he was a very good craftsman and that was what I needed. And since then, of course, the coachbuilding side of the firm has come on very nicely. Now, what I'm thinking of doing is this – you'll be made assistant foreman and get a nice raise in your wages to go with it, and then in a year or so if you're doing all right, we'll have a talk about bringing you in as a partner, which means you'll get a cut of the profits at the works. How does that sound to you?'

Barty leaned back in his seat and regarded his nephew. Would that be enough to satisfy him, or would he see that it fell a long way short of a promise of a share in the whole company?

'That sounds very fair,' Oliver agreed, and Barty, perversely, was disappointed. He should have fought back, have bargained for more. He was in a strong position with his claims of kinship and skill as a coach-builder. He should have sold himself dearer, insisted on becoming a partner now. It confirmed Barty's long-held view that Oliver was not the man he wanted to take over the reins as he grew older.

'Capital,' he said, taking up his neglected pipe. 'I'm glad we understand each other so well.'

His gaze strayed to the heavy clock over the mantel-piece. Where the devil was the Eclipse? It should have been in five minutes after the Lord Nelson. He would have a word or two to say to Ned Shears on the subject of timekeeping when he did arrive. Bringing his attention back to his nephew again, he held his hand out, to draw the interview to a friendly conclusion. But Oliver was not so easily deflected from his original purpose. Refusing to take the hint to be gone, he sat on stubbornly in his uncomfortable chair.

18

'What I came to ask you Uncle Bart,' he said, 'was whether you'd had a letter from Stacey today.'

Stacey. There was no getting away from that problem. There was nought for it but to pack the child off to her Aunt Eustacia's when she came home, Barty decided, which was a great pity for he had been looking forward to her company after a year at that fool academy place he'd been talked into sending her to.

'Aye,' he said, affecting not to read anything out of the way into the request, 'and she's as mad as fire at being kept in quarantine, I can tell you. It was damned bad luck, this measles outbreak coming at Easter.'

'She's not gone down with it?'

'No, no, not our Stacey. Fit as a flea.'

He looked out of the window, knowing that the next question would be whether Stacey had sent any particular messages, and determined to get rid of Oliver as soon as he had answered it. He was not going to give him any chance of raising the subject of what Stacey would be doing when she came home in the summer. And as if to help him out of the corner, a scratched and battered stagecoach came limping under the archway and into the yard. Barty leaped to his feet.

'God's teeth!' he growled, leaning forward and peering out in disbelief. 'What the hell's happened to the Eclipse?'

And with Oliver in his wake, he strode out of the office to find out.

A few miles outside Thetford, Simon Wynwood stopped at yet another turnpike and paid for the four horses in his possession. Just as he was leading them through the open gate, the deep quiet of the wide countryside was shattered by the brazen call of a key bugle.

'Thass the Eclipse for Norwich,' the pikeman remarked, spitting to show his contempt of all travellers who used his road. 'Mad bugger's got 'ere before the

Commodore today. Thinks 'e'll get me to open the gate orl ready for 'im to spring 'em down this 'ere straight stretch.' He banged the gate purposefully shut behind Simon and made for the door of his tollhouse. 'Anyone'd think I was put on this earth just to serve the bloody stagecoaches. Think they're lords o' bloody creation.' Still muttering, he went inside.

Simon smiled and gathered up the leading reins of his charges. It was good to be back in the mainstream of life again, to feel his weakened muscles tightening up. The long weeks of recovery had hung intolerably heavily on his hands, even after he had escaped from Moll's rough brand of care. The chance of a long stretch of time with Perdita had been welcome, of course, but the enforced idleness had been purgatory. He could waste his days as well as the next man when he chose to, but he resented the restrictions of having his right arm out of action, of having his concentration ruined by recurrent headaches. But now at last he was free, and on a fine spring day which matched his optimism, with scudding clouds in a rainwashed sky and the countryside trembling with the promise of things to come.

Perdita had clung to him and begged him not to go, but even the memory of her tears could do very little to mar his good spirits today. It suited him that he had no definite plans beyond setting his enquiries into his attackers into motion and selling his horses at a handsome profit. All four he had picked up very cheaply, and he had an almost certain market for the two hunters in an acquaintance about ten miles further down the road. The carriage horses he would probably be able to get rid of by the end of the day, too. They were neither of them much to look at, but he would no doubt find some horsing contractor to the stagecoaches in need of fresh animals. Perhaps the proprietor of the Eclipse, now pounding up the road some way behind him.

A fresh blast on the bugle and the sound of hooves and

20

wheels and loud cursing told of the coach's arrival at the gate. Simon looked back to see the infuriated coachman berating the piker for his tardiness. His need for haste soon became clear – another horn sounded in the near distance. The rival concern, perhaps, eager to catch up and overtake on the tempting stretch of road ahead. Simon edged his horses over onto the grass verge, not wanting his stock-in-trade frightened or injured by two mad devils of dragsmen racing past him. He turned again in the saddle to watch the fun.

The Eclipse was away, the coachman whipping the four horses into a gallop. It thundered past with the outside passengers clinging to their seats and the guard blowing a defiant volley on the bugle. One of Brown's, Simon noted, recognizing the royal blue and brown of the Norwich proprietor. Brown's were crack coaches, well horsed and well maintained, and Simon laid a bet with himself that the rival outfit would find it impossible to catch up, let alone overtake. But by the time the Eclipse left the gate, delayed by the recalcitrant piker, the challenging Commodore had reached it and money changed hands with the speed of light.

With a roar at his cattle and a mighty flailing of the whip, the coachman set off in hot pursuit. Screams could be heard from the terrified female outsiders as the Eclipse held the crown of the road and the Commodore strove to get by, first on the outside then, changing tactics, on the inside. As Simon watched, the Commodore began to inch up, kicking up mud from the grass verge. The Eclipse came over to the left-hand side of the road, effectively blocking the other coach, and for two long minutes it seemed that the Commodore's bid for supremacy was over, for a bend in the road was drawing near and the lathered horses were tiring. And then it happened – the Eclipse swerved violently off the road and the front nearside wheel hit a pile of stones. The passengers were shot forward and the coachman and boxseat passenger tossed like rag dolls into the air. As the Commodore swept by in a garish blaze of orange and black the Eclipse meandered erratically on and off the road for another fifty yards before running into the hedge at the bend.

Simon set spurs to his mount and raced up the road, the spare horses jostling beside him. One stomach-turning glance at the coachman told him that there was nothing to be done for him. He must have fallen between the horses and been crushed by the iron-bound wheels of the coach. Simon saw in his mind's eye the farm cart rumbling inevitably toward him and tore his sickened gaze away from the body. The living had need of him.

The young man who had been riding on the boxseat had fared better, for he had fallen onto the grass, clear of danger. Simon tethered his horses to a nearby gate and ran to see how badly he was injured. White-faced and shaken, the young man was already struggling to sit up.

'I'm all right,' he assured Simon, cautiously testing his limbs. 'Nothing broken, thank God. Lead rein snapped. Leave me – ladies on the coach. Be along in a minute.'

Simon took him at his word and sprinted up the road to where the coach rested at a crazy angle with one wheel in the ditch. The guard was assisting a hysterical matron to climb out of the body of the coach, much hindered by a man who appeared to be her husband and kept telling her to shut her row and sit down. Simon promptly took her other arm and heaved her out.

'The lady will be better outside, sir,' he told the husband, 'and we'll need everyone out of this vehicle if we're to get it back on the road again.'

The man's already florid features turned an unhealthy crimson.

'I'll have you know, young man, that I have paid for an inside seat to Norwich and inside I intend to stay. Nothing, sir, is going to make me stir from here.'

A third inside passenger, a sharp-faced old lady with her bonnet askew, advised him shortly to go to the devil, and climbed out after the hysterical woman, whom she proceeded to calm. By mutual unspoken consent, Simon and the guard left the choleric husband to decide his own fate.

'My thanks to you, sir,' the guard said, casting a distraught eye over the wrecked coach and nervous horses. 'Would you be so kind as to see to the outsiders while I get the cattle free? They'll be kicking the pole to splinters in a minute.'

'Of course,' Simon agreed. 'How long will it take for help to arrive from the next village, do you think? I take it the Commodore's coachman will send some asistance back.'

The guard snorted in derision.

'You'll wait till Doomsday if you expect them to help us,' he said. 'That lot from Pymer's wouldn't lift a finger for a Brown's coach, not if we'd bin swept away in a flood with a load of women and babbies, they wouldn't. The only person they'll tell is Pymer hisself, and he'll get it all puffed up in the *Norwich Mercury* as our fault.'

'Then we'll have to see to it ourselves,' Simon decided. 'As soon as we've made sure that all the passengers are safe. There must be someone round here who can be entrusted with a message.'

The guard hesitated a moment, assessing the extent to which the use of the word 'we' was going to undermine his authority. Then, deciding that any competent help was to be welcomed in an emergency, he said, 'Right you are, sir,' and went to see to the struggling horses.

The outside passengers were in a far worse state than their wealthier travelling companions.

'Hey, guard, bear a hand aloft here,' an aggrieved sailor demanded. 'We may be only outsiders but we're bloody human creatures all the same.'

Simon climbed up by way of the rear wheel.

23

'Curb your tongue, Jack Tar, and I'll see what can be done,' he said. 'What's your trouble?'

The sailor's manner became decidedly less truculent.

'Here's this lass stove her head in when we went over them stones,' he explained. 'I tried to move her, but I've gone and put my shoulder out.'

The girl in question lay slumped awkwardly across the narrow benches, only saved from slipping off the tilting roof of the coach by the sailor's firm grip on her arm. She moaned faintly as Simon lifted her into a safer position, and he found that she had caught her head against the corner of a trunk projecting from the pile of luggage on the roof. Her cheap straw bonnet was split and beneath it the mousy hair was dark with blood. An unprepossessing creature, he noted. Pudgy features, neatly and plainly dressed. The type of girl much sought after as a maid by mistresses with growing sons or erring husbands. He called to the guard and passed her down to be consigned to the care of the sharp-featured old lady, who had appointed herself as being in charge of the injured and was dispensing brandy and lavender water to great effect. The sailor scrambled down and Simon climbed across the shifting pile of luggage to see to the last passenger, a small middle-aged man with the pale, soft look of an indoor worker. He had been thrown against the back of the boxseat and was sitting rigidly, clutching his chest.

'Can you move?' Simon asked.

'No sir,' the man whispered, sweat breaking out on his ashen face. 'If I move a muscle, I get a terrible pain here.'

'Sounds like a cracked rib,' Simon diagnosed.

Hope dawned in the stricken man's face.

'Are you a physician, sir?'

'No, no—' Simon smiled at the idea. He could not picture himself as a healer of ills. 'I just happened to have suffered from the same thing myself recently,' he

24

explained. 'The problem is, how are we going to get you down without shifting the bone? I'll have to strap you up with something.' He looked about for suitable material, and decided on the tarpaulin covering the luggage. The guard, however, was doubtful.

'Cut up the tarpaulin?' he repeated. 'Dunno about that, sir. Company property, that is.'

Simon was about to argue that it was the company's fault that its passengers were injured, when he had a better idea. Jumping down, he went to the sorry collection of people sitting by the road. The old lady regarded him sharply.

'I do not know who you are, young man, or where you have sprung from, but you and I seem to be the only people present with any grain of sense,' she said, sweeping her charges with a disdainful eye. 'Has a messenger been sent for assistance?'

'Not yet, ma'am, but it will be done as soon as I have everyone off the coach,' Simon assured her. 'Which is what I came to consult you about. I suspect that the man still on top has a cracked rib or two and I need something to bind him up before I move him down.' He gave her a conspiratorial smile, drawing her further into the idea she had started as to their being the responsible pair amongst a crowd of fools, consciously using the charm that seldom failed to persuade females of all ages to do his bidding. 'I thought a petticoat might make a useful bandage, if you or one of the other ladies . . .' His speculative gaze wandered over the matron and the whey-faced girl and, finding nothing to arrest his interest, returned to the old lady. She at least had claims to character.

'Petticoat!' she said, with a repressive look that turned by degrees into a roguish twinkle. 'I can do better than that. And so could you, I shouldn't wonder.'

Calling the guard, she demanded that her trunk be brought down, which was accomplished after a good deal of grumbling and effort. A crisply-ironed sheet was produced.

'Say what you will about the improvement of inns,' she said, snipping at the hems with a pair of embroidery scissors and ripping off long strips, 'but I prefer to travel with my own linen. When some of these places say "clean on", they mean "clean on last month".'

Simon could only agree with becoming gravity.

By the time the clerk was wound up in sheeting and safely on the ground, help was arriving from other quarters. Two labourers who had seen the accident had sent a lad pelting to the farmhouse, and the farmer himself duly arrived with men and hurdles and ropes, together with his wife and her maid and a bundle of bandages. The sailor, the clerk and the young girl were dispatched to the farmhouse to await the surgeon with promises that Brown's would pay their fees and any other expenses incurred. The young man from the box-seat insisted that he was perfectly well, though Simon suspected he was suffering from concussion. The biggest problem was what to do with the body of the coachman.

'Poor owd Ned,' the guard sighed, shaking his head over the crushed and mutilated corpse. 'What a way to go. One minute up on the box, right as ninepence, tooling the owd Eclipse like a good 'un, and the next, bang! under the wheels. He were a rare fine waggoner, were owd Ned. The Gaffer's going to be fair cut up about this.'

'Did he live in Norwich?' Simon asked, more concerned with the immediate practical difficulties.

'Aye, and thass another thing. There's his owd woman and five children left.'

'We cannot take him in the coach. Could he be left at the farm until a cart can be sent to bring him home?' Simon suggested.

The guard and the farmer agreed to this, and the old lady donated her torn sheet to cover him.

'Though he was driving much too fast,' she commented.

Attention was turned to setting the Eclipse to rights. The near lead horse was found to be lame, but the draught gear and harness, except for the broken rein that had caused all the trouble, were still intact. The horses were put to, with one of Simon's replacing the leader, and with the help of the farm labourers and lengths of timber, the Eclipse was hauled out of the ditch. The guard walked round it, shaking his head despondently over the cracked panelling and scratched paintwork.

'Lord help us, what a sight,' he said gloomily. 'I dunno what the Gaffer's going to say about this.'

'Your Mr Brown's a tormentor, is he?' Simon asked, crouching by the heels of the wheelers to examine the splinter bar. 'This is somewhat shaky, but I think it will hold. The coach must have been well built to come out of it so lightly.'

'The Gaffer? Christ, no! A real trump, he is,' the guard maintained. 'But a saint 'ud hardly be happy seeing a crack stage roll in in a state like this.'

'He's lucky to have it rolling in at all if his harness is so bad that the reins break,' Simon commented. He called to the men holding the horses' heads. 'Move her forward a little so I can see how the wheels set.'

The Eclipse rumbled along the turnpike, and as far as Simon could see, the wheels appeared to be safe enough.

'I think it might limp into Norwich,' he concluded.

The farmer, though not asked his opinion, agreed. But the guard pointed out a further problem.

'We ain't got no coachman,' he said. 'I never learnt to handle the ribbons myself.'

The prospect of a turn on the box opened up before Simon, and all thoughts of selling the hunters were postponed at least until the next day.

'Fear not,' he said, 'I shall bring you all to Norwich

27

with no further alarms or excursions.'

The guard looked doubtful.

'Begging your pardon, sir,' he said warily, conscious of the debt he owed Simon for his assistance, 'but the Gaffer don't allow amateurs to take the ribbons. 'Gainst company rules, it is.'

'Amateur be damned,' Simon told him. 'You are talking to the one-time co-owner-driver of the Brighton Expedition, so stop havering and get your passengers on board. And make sure the young gentleman with the blow to his head rides inside. The way he's looking, he'll drop off if he goes on top.'

The guard dithered for a moment or two, then finding that he really had very little choice in the matter, went and did as he was bid. Whistling, Simon hitched his three remaining horses and the lame leader to the back of the coach, retrieved the dead coachman's whip from the side of the road and walked round to the front to see what could be done about the broken rein. What he found caused him some surprise.

'What do you make of this?' he asked the guard, passing him the broken ends, sliced cleanly two-thirds of the way through, and frayed the rest. 'I'll wager your Gaffer will be interested to see them.'

The guard looked at the sabotaged leather with gathering rage.

'Christ, I'd like to get my hands on the bastard as did this!' He flung the rein down and turned away, his face dark. 'I'll lay my life it was one of Pymer's rats! Murdering bastards! They killed owd Ned by this, they did.'

Simon laid a hand on his shoulder.

'I think you might be correct, my friend, but you've no proof whatsoever, so for God's sake don't go spouting your theories in every tavern in Norwich. If you are right, this fellow Pymer might well think it wise to send a couple of bully boys to shut your mouth for you.'

The guard turned on him truculently.

'I'm not letting those murdering swine frighten me! Ned was a good friend of mine. I'll not stand by and let them get away with it scot-free.'

'Your loyalty does you credit,' Simon temporized, 'but rushing in like a bull at a gate won't bring Ned back. What we need is solid evidence. You see what your Gaffer says.'

'Aye, well—' the guard hunched a shoulder. 'Mebbe I will—'

'Good. Now listen, I used to keep a short strap with a buckle at each end about me for just such emergencies as this. Do you have any such thing on the Eclipse?'

'Might well have,' the guard said, and stumped off to see what could be found. He returned with just what was needed, plus a bradawl to make a hole in each of the broken ends. Two minutes' work and the rein was functional again. The passengers settled, rather dubiously, into their places, and the luggage was roped down. Simon thanked the farmer for his help, took up the ribbons and the whip and climbed onto the box.

'All right behind?'

'All right, sir!'

'Let 'em go, and many thanks!'

The labourers released the horses' heads, Simon dropped his rein hand and the Eclipse moved off at a sober walk, an odd spectacle with its battered bodywork and spare horses tethered behind. Simon was glad for the first time that it was his right arm that had been broken. If it had been his left, he would not yet have had enough strength in it to handle a four-in-hand team. He whistled as they plodded sedately along. Those had been good times, the months on the Expedition. They had not made a fortune, of course, with just the one coach, particularly amongst the cut-throat competition on the Brighton road, but that year had been one of the most enjoyable in his varied life. There were few things finer than rattling along on a fine summer's day with four good horses and a full complement of passengers, the road busy enough to demand real skill in handling the ribbons but clear enough in places to get a good speed up and keep ahead of the nearest rivals. Even in winter, there had been a grim pleasure in keeping the service going in all weathers. And the useful people one met. Many a profitable deal had he made through a carefully casual chat with a boxseat passenger. It was a pity, looking back on it, that he had ever given up his share in the Expedition, but he had been struck with one of his periodic fits of restlessness and moved on to the more lucrative and risky world of horseracing. The ache in his whip arm reminded him just where that little enterprise had landed him.

While the horses were being changed at Attleborough for the penultimate stage, Simon arranged for an ostler to bring his two hunters and the unused carriage horse into Norwich. The one which had taken the lame leader's place he decided to sell sight unseen to the Eclipse's proprietor. B. Brown, whoever he might be, owed him a good sale at the very least.

The leisurely journey ended all too soon, heralded by the imposing bulk of the Norfolk and Norwich Hospital. The Eclipse rattled into the city along St Stephen's Street, where its battered condition excited a good deal of comment from passers-by. Small boys trotted alongside demanding of the guard what had happened, a question which he steadfastly refused to comment upon. Simon, though having to keep his wits about him in the city streets, still had time to look around and appreciate what he saw. He liked Norwich and had several useful contacts in and around the town. Perhaps, he decided, he would stay for a few days and see what opportunities might happen along. Arriving at last in Crown Lane, he summoned up his skill for the tricky corner under the narrow archway, pointing the leaders and shooting the wheelers to ensure a controlled turn, and was happy to find that he had not lost the knack during the two years since he gave up the road.

He pulled up in the yard of the Crown, the guard jumped down and the horsekeepers ran forward to hold the cattle. Flexing his right arm, Simon looked about the yard over the heads of the inn servants and the gawping spectators, and saw two men advancing on him from the direction of the booking office. The younger of the pair was tall and powerfully built, but it was the older man who caught Simon's attention. He was dressed in breeches and top-boots, a silver-buttoned blue coat opened to reveal a broad chest swathed in a waistcoat of striped magnificence. Short and bald-headed, with ferocious sprouting eyebrows and a pug-nacious swagger to his walk, he exuded the air of a none-too-genial bulldog. This, Simon decided, must be the Gaffer. He swung down from the box just as the two men reached the Eclipse.

'Good afternoon,' he said with cheerful ease, holding out his hand, 'do I have the honour of addressing Mr Brown?'

The coach proprietor's shrewd eyes assessed him, taking nothing at face value. Simon met his gaze stead-ily, aware of a desire to find approval in the other man's expression.

'Aye, that's me,' the Gaffer agreed grasping the prof-fered hand in a huge paw. 'And who might you be, bringing my coach in in a mess like this?'

'Keating – Simon Keating.'

He felt a curious hesitation in using an alias with this man, an urge to deal straight that was marred by start-ing with a deception, but the impulse to hide his origins had become such a habit over the years that it had grown into a necessity. To cover his misgivings, he swept on to answer the second part of the question.

'As to the Eclipse, I just happened to be in the right place at the right time.'

He was interrupted by the bad-tempered husband, complaining bitterly about his experiences.

'Are you the proprietor of this coach?' he demanded, waving his walking stick at the Gaffer. 'You ought to be ashamed, sir, of running a service to the public in such a fashion! Drunken, incompetent coachmen, impertinent guard, faulty harness – it's a disgrace, that's what it is! I'll tell you this, sir, I shall never ride in one of your coaches again as long as I live!'

His wife dithered in the background, not daring to put in a word. But the old lady had no such inhibitions.

'You, sir, are excessively tiresome, aye, and ridiculous with it. Pray see to your wife and leave off your complaints,' she commended, and while the man spluttered in impotent anger, she took advantage of his temporary loss of speech to strike in herself.

'The coachman was not drunk, but he was driving too fast,' she maintained, addressing Barty. 'This young man,' she nodded at Simon, 'acted with considerable resource, and the guard did his duty competently, but I would advise you to ensure that your equipment is in good repair in future, or more lives may be lost.'

Barty handled them both with the skill of a diplomat, contriving at least partially to convince them that in spite of the unfortunate accident to the Eclipse, Brown's was still the best run and most efficient coach service in East Anglia. As he did so, the luggage was brought down, and when the passengers finally dispersed, the guard, waybill and purse in his hand and bugle under his arm, came round to face his employer. Barty drew him to one side, out of earshot of any interested bystanders.

'What happened, Dick?' he asked. 'And where's Ned?'

The guard launched into his own version of the truth.

'It were murder, Mr Brown sir. Some bastard of Pymer's cut the rein and the Eclipse went over a pile of stones and shot poor owd Ned under the wheels. Didn't have a chance. Someone's got to pay for this, sir, and I don't care who knows it.'

Barty's broad, good-humoured face darkened.

'Ned went under the wheels?' he repeated.

'Aye, back on the galloping ground. Dead as mutton he is, poor owd sod.'

'I can't believe it.'

With sagging shoulders, Barty looked up at the vacant boxseat, as if expecting to see Ned Shears still sitting there. Simon, watching from his station by the front wheels, realized with surprise that genuine shock marked the proprietor's face. He seemed to age by ten years.

'He was a good man, was Ned,' he said heavily. 'A loyal friend and a fair waggoner, too. In his prime. It's a terrible thing.' He stared unseeing at the Eclipse while Oliver and the guard nodded in silent agreement. 'I'll have to go and tell his missus,' he said finally, 'let her know she'll not go wanting. It'll be a nasty blow for her. Ollie,' he turned to his nephew, 'have we got something down at the works we can fetch him home in?'

'I'll see what I can find, Uncle Bart.'

'Good lad.' Barty made a visible effort to pull himself together and his voice regained something of its usual incision. 'And what about the damage to the Eclipse? How long will that take to put right?'

Oliver had already run an experienced eye over the coach.

'About ten days, Uncle Bart, with the repainting. It will have to be given a thorough check, of course.'

'Aye,' Barty gave an approving nod. He looked at the guard again. 'What's all this about a broken rein? My reins don't break.'

'This 'un did,' the guard maintained. 'Just you take a look at this, sir.'

He led the way round the horses and caught hold of the mended section. 'You see, sir? It's been cut, then left

33

to break, that's what. 'Twas Mr Keating here first found it. He thinks it's passing queer as well.'

Barty stood frowning at the evidence, unspeaking, then unbuckled the rein in question, passed it back through the terrets and neatly coiled it.

'All right, boys,' he said to the waiting horsekeepers, 'take her along to the works, then get the cattle seen to. And not a word about what you've heard, mind, or you'll answer to me.'

The battered coach moved off, accompanied by Oliver. Barty turned to the guard, and laid a heavy hand on his shoulder.

'Now see here, Dick,' he said, 'it does look passing queer, as you say. But there's better ways of catching a cat than yelling your head off and blasting at it with a blunderbuss. You follow me? You leave this one with me, and if anyone's responsible for Ned's death, I'll see they're brought to justice, never you mind.'

'I see, Mr Brown sir.'

Quite clearly he did not.

'That crowd down at Pymer's are as crafty as a boatload of politicians,' Barty elaborated. 'Let them smell a rat and they'll make sure we find nought to prove it, but just you keep a still tongue in your head and we might well find the culprit, see?'

'I see, Mr Brown sir,' the guard repeated, but this time he sounded convinced.

'Good,' Barty was satisfied. 'You cut along now and see Mr Burgess, then have a drink on me in the coach-men's parlour. You deserve it.'

The guard went off to take his money and waybill to the booking office and the crowd of spectators began to move away, now that the fun was over. Barty turned to Simon, who had been admiring the way he handled the situation.

'I've not yet thanked you properly for bringing my coach in,' he said. 'Had some time on the road yourself,

34

have you? Old Ned couldn't have come round that corner neater than you did.'

The praise, from a man who knew what he was talking about, brought an unexpected glow of satisfaction.

'I part-owned a coach on the Brighton road once,' Simon explained.

'Ah.' There was new respect in Barty's expression. Simon guessed that he had risen in the Gaffer's scale of values from meddling gentleman amateur to nearly professional status. Nearly, but not quite. Dabbling with one Brighton coach was hardly in the same category as an enterprise like Brown's. 'Lucky for me you came along when you did,' Barty said. 'We'd have been in a rare owd state else. Will you come and take a drink with me, Mr Keating?'

'I'd be delighted,' Simon responded, for the first time in months accepting an invitation not because it might be useful to him, but simply because he liked the Gaffer and enjoyed his company.

They walked across the yard towards the main door of the inn, but before they reached it the ostler from Attleborough came trotting under the archway with Simon's three horses, reminding him of what had been his day's business.

'I was taking these to be sold when the Eclipse came to grief,' he explained to an interested Barty, and signalled to the ostler to bring them over. 'There was another one, an eight-year-old piebald gelding, but I used him to take the place of one of yours that went lame in the crash. I left him behind in Attleborough as I was sure you'd want to buy him as a replacement.'

The gloom lifted miraculously from Barty's shoulders at the scent of a round of bargaining. He chuckled appreciatively and walked round the remaining three horses, running a hand over their quarters, looking at their legs.

'You were, were you?' he said, enjoying the joke. 'And what the devil have you heard about me that makes you think I'd buy a horse as I've never clapped eyes on?'

'I heard you were a fair and reasonable man,' Simon improvised. 'A man who'd realize that twenty guineas for a horse that has already shown its worth in getting your coach out of difficulties was a proven bargain.'

Barty was patently unconvinced. He continued to examine one of the hunters, peering at the animal from behind to see if its hocks turned inwards. 'Now if you asked me twenty for this fellow here, I might well be interested, but for an unseen piebald jade—' he shook his head doubtfully. 'What's it worth? Ten?'

Simon looked vaguely offended.

'He's a good strong coach horse, no vices, sound in wind and limb. Not very beautiful, maybe, but he'll give you three or four years good service,' he expanded, saying no more than the truth for once. 'In fact he's worth twenty-five guineas of anyone's money, but I'll let you have him cheap because—'

'Because you like the look of my face?' Barty concluded for him, laughing.

Simon grinned back at him, acknowledging their mutual enjoyment in the game.

'Let's say because I was happy to be given the privilege of driving one of your coaches,' he said. 'Look, just to show you that I mean it, I'll throw in this one for another tenner.'

He held the two hunters and told the ostler to lead out the remaining carriage horse, a dun mare. She had been practically given to him by a harassed coachman who could do nothing with her.

Barty looked at her critically as she was trotted up and down the yard.

'How old?'

'Nine.'

36

'Sound? No vices?'

'At that price, Mr Brown, you can't expect me to give a written warranty.'

'At that price, Mr Keating, there must be something wrong with her. Where's she from?'

'Property of a gentleman till yesterday, but she didn't suit. Put her in front of a heavy coach, though, with three steady 'uns, and she'll be as good as gold.'

Barty snorted.

'I heard that one before, laddie,' he commented.

He checked the mare's age and looked her over for any physical defects. Finding none, he fell back on instinct. 'There has to be a catch somewhere,' he concluded, 'but seeing as I owe you a favour, I'll take her off your hands. Shall we say twenty for her and the other one together?'

'Make it twenty-five and you've got a deal,' Simon offered.

'Done!'

They shook hands on it, each admiring the other's style, but both satisfied that they had got the best of the bargain. The ostler from Attleborough was paid off, two from the Crown took the hunters and the dun mare in charge and a porter picked up Simon's belongings.

'Are you planning to stay in Norwich?' Barty asked, looking at the travelling bag.

Simon hesitated, looking round the prosperous inn with an odd sense of belonging. His gaze came to rest on the coach proprietor's broad, open face, and the decision was already made.

'I think I might well do,' he said.

Chapter Two

The Rose Inn at East Dereham was in the midst of its mid-afternoon doze. Drowsing in the heat of the summer's day, the place might have been abandoned for all the activity it displayed. Even the washing on the line in the neat vegetable garden hung limp and static. In the yard, a dog lay sprawled on the dusty cobbles, a broom had been left where it had fallen across the door of one of the stables, and in the sunniest corner an ostler sat slumped in a broken Windsor chair, arms folded, head drooping forward over his chest. Only the flies moved, dancing above the reeking midden.

But the tranquil scene was fated to be shattered, for over the stones of the street outside came a dust-filmed travelling chaise, a dashing vehicle with two liveried postillions and a deal of luggage strapped on behind. Turning briskly into the yard and stopping precisely before the principal door, it jolted the Rose into life. The dog barked, the ostler jerked awake and ran to the horses, calling to the stable boys to stir themselves, and inside the inn Turnbull the landlord rubbed his face blearily as his middle son, sent to rouse him, shook his shoulder. Before any of these people had gathered their wits, however, the door of the chaise flew open and a tall girl in a blue pelisse and a plain blue bonnet jumped down and turned to call back to the remaining inmate of the vehicle.

'Goodbye, goodbye, and thank you so much for taking me up! Promise faithfully you'll write every week!'

The gushing farewells were somewhat spoiled by her obvious joy at being let down, and the impatience with which she waited for the postillions to unstrap her luggage. Brown eyes dancing beneath the brim of her bonnet, she exchanged vows of eternal friendship with her travelling companion and watched anxiously as a trunk, a valise, two bandboxes and a portfolio were lowered to the ground.

Turnbull, barely awake and his hair standing up in a crest, hurried through the doorway and stopped short in surprise, his professional expression of welcome turning into a genuine smile.

'Well, Miss Stacey Brown, as I live and breathe! What in heaven's name are you doing here? Is your friend alighting as well?'

'Mr Turnbull! How are you? Are you not surprised? No, no, the chaise is going on, my friend only stopped here to let me down—' Already the postillions were remounting. Torn between two worlds, Stacey gave her distracted attention to the pretty girl who was hanging out of the window of the chaise. 'Goodbye, dearest Annabel,' she cried, reaching up to kiss the proffered cheek. 'Remember me!'

'Always!' her friend responded fervently, and as the carriage moved off she blew kisses out of the window, much to the amusement of the inhabitants of the Rose.

The sorrow of parting choked Stacey's throat at last as she waved the departing chaise farewell, and for fully two minutes she stood in the empty yard, tears blurring her eyes as the dust settled. It would probably be months, if not years, before she saw Annabel again, or any of the friends with whom she had shared the last nine months. But with this thought came its corollary: that she was done with Miss Hester Haveringshaw's Select Academy for ever.

'Freedom!' she cried, flinging her arms wide to

39

embrace the glorious feeling of release. 'Freedom, freedom, freedom!'

Dancing round the frenzied dog and gaping ostler, she finally caught hold of the astonished Turnbull's arm, gasping with laughter.

'You feeling quite the thing, Miss Stacey?' he asked anxiously. 'Come along in and sit down, and the missus'll get you something.'

'I never felt better in my life, Mr Turnbull,' Stacey assured him. 'I could jump the moon! You cannot imagine how wonderful it is to be almost home! I shall love Annabel Harthwaite for ever for offering to bring me this far. But yes, I should love to come in and meet Mrs Turnbull and the family. I shall take a place on the Tantivy when it arrives. It does still reach here at half-past three, does it not? Is there a seat available, do you know? Just think how dreadful if there isn't . . .'

The landlord ushered her, still talking volubly, into the family parlour of the inn, where the entire tribe of Turnbulls had duly gathered to meet her. They had known Stacey since she was four years old, when Barty Brown had brought her along with him to negotiate the horsing contract that had heralded a new era of prosperity at the Rose. Since then she had grown from a stout and sturdy child to a long-legged coltish girl and now, after three terms at school, she had changed again into the semblance of a young lady. A tall, strong-featured young lady though, able to look Mr Turnbull and most other men in the eye, with the added disadvantages of a wide, mobile mouth and a gap between the front teeth.

As Stacey dutifully asked after the health and well-being of every member of the Turnbull family, she proceeded to do justice to the best the house could offer in the way of tea, cold meats, pies and pastries. Excitement did nothing to dull her appetite. When at last she had finished her social duty to her hosts in enquiring after their affairs, she started on the subject that lay closest to her heart – getting home as soon as possible.

'Is there an outside seat on the Tantivy today, Mr Turnbull? I shall die of disappointment if I have to arrive at the Crown in a hack chaise.'

The landlord's cheerful expression drooped somewhat.

'There's places a-plenty, Miss Stacey, and that's fact. Inside or out, take your pick.'

Stacey made a worried face.

'Pymer's?' she asked. 'Pa did say they were running on all our best routes now.'

'Just so, Miss Stacey. They started up on this road about four months ago, changing horses at the Black Dog.' The contempt in his voice told what he thought of the rival inn at the other end of town. The rest of the Turnbulls nodded and made sounds of agreement. The smaller ones pulled rude faces. 'They even have the sauce to call it the New Tantivy,' he went on. 'It's made a difference to our trade, I can tell you.'

'I should think it has,' Stacey said thoughtfully. It must be making a hole in Brown's trade as well, she realized, but she said nothing of that. Confidence in Brown's must be maintained at all times, that was what her pa said. 'Never you fear, Mr Turnbull,' she said. 'Brown's will get rid of them, just you see. My pa will have a trick or two up his sleeve to show Pymer's.'

'I'm sure he will, Miss Stacey,' Turnbull agreed heartily, but it was with his professional voice that he spoke.

His wife covered up what might have been an awkward pause.

'Your pa'll be passing glad to see you home again, my dear. I expect he'll see quite a change in you. Proper young lady you are now. Real gentrified.'

Stacey gave a simpering smile, and assumed her best

41

Hester Haveringshaw accent.

'Why thank you, ma'am. My Aunt Eustacia will be exceeding glad to hear that.'

She laughed at their expressions, helped herself to another slice of veal pie, and lapsed into her usual racy style, growing more strongly tinged with Norfolk by the minute. 'It was my Aunt Eustacia's idea that I should be sent to that stupid school,' she explained. 'I didn't want to go at all at first, but it wasn't all that bad really, once I got used to it.'

Her father had been dead set against her going when the idea was originally mooted, but later he changed his mind. He never did tell her why. It was certainly not because of any argument Aunt Eustacia might have put forward. Her aunt had a bee in her bonnet about Stacey being brought up properly, and considered it her personal responsibility as a godmother to see that everything Stacey's late mother would have wanted should be done. Unfortunately, Barty's views of what his wife's wishes were and Eustacia's tended to differ, and Barty always had the last say, much to his daughter's relief. So the about-face over the school came as something of a shock to Stacey. She was not used to having her wishes overridden. But none of this did she reveal to the Turnbulls, for the Browns never paraded their family differences in front of the rest of the world.

'I'll say this for my aunt,' she said. 'She did pick a very good school, or rather, a school that everyone said was the best in Scarborough. There were always more applicants than places. Not that they taught us anything useful. I mean, what on earth will it profit me to be able to recite the names and dates of the Kings and Queens of England? Or speak French, for that matter. And all those silly accomplishments! I suppose it will be useful for the other girls to be able to net purses or make filigree baskets, but I cannot see myself spending hours at it. I shall have something better to do with my time.'

Mrs Turnbull gave an arch smile, which Stacey found rather irritating.

'We'll see you walking down the aisle with some lucky fellow soon, I'll warrant,' she prophesied.

It was a remark calculated to raise a blush and a simper in most seventeen-year-old girls, but not Stacey. She had long made up her mind what her role in life was to be, and even nine months of whispered secrets and giggling surmises at Miss Haveringshaw's had not changed her resolve.

'Oh no!' she declared. 'Not I. Just think how dreadful to be at the beck and call of some self-important man all the time, and have nothing more exciting to occupy one's time than housekeeping and paying morning calls! That wouldn't suit me at all.'

Mrs Turnbull and her daughters could not conceal their amazement at such a sweeping condemnation of the marriage state. Indeed, it was a cherished and quite impossible dream of the landlady's to have nothing but housekeeping and morning calls to occupy her time.

'But you don't want to die an old maid, surely?' the eldest girl asked.

'No—' Stacey conceded. Her ideas about the distant future were rather hazy, her conception of an ideal husband coloured by the romances that had been eagerly passed from hand to hand at the school. She had quite enough common sense to realize that such fantastic heroes were not for the likes of her, but the everyday young men who came her way hardly seemed an adequate substitute. 'I expect I shall be married one day, when I meet someone I like,' she said, 'but not yet. I shall be too busy helping Pa with the company.'

The assembled Turnbulls gaped at her.

'Well—' said Turnbull weakly, long practice in humouring customers coming to his aid. 'Your pa'll be glad to hear that, I'm sure.'

Stacey could not understand them.

43

'I don't know why you're so surprised,' she said. 'I would have thought it was the obvious thing for me to do. If I had brothers, it might be different, but as it is, Pa's only got me, and I know he's relying on me helping him. Brown's is becoming a large concern, you know. We have coaches running six days a week to every part of East Anglia, and to London.'

'Quite so, quite so,' Turnbull temporised, anxious not to bite the hand that fed him. 'Brown's is a fine company, and no mistake.'

His eldest daughter lacked his professional tact.

'Running a stagecoach company is no task for a lady,' she stated, managing to imply that Stacey's coming upon them in state from her select school in a fine carriage was all a show put on to make them feel inferior.

Stacey resented her tone.

'I don't see why,' she retorted. 'You help in your father's business about the inn, do you not?'

'That's different,' the Turnbull girl insisted.

'At the Saracen's Head in London, Mrs Maintain runs coaches and a coachbuilding business even bigger than ours,' Stacey told her. 'And I'll warrant nobody ever told *her* that it was no task for a lady.'

It was fortunate that at that moment Stacey's sharp ears caught the sound she had been waiting for, and what threatened to become an argument ceased abruptly. Along the main street of the town a bugle was playing a hunting call – tantivy, tantivy, tantivy! Stacey sprang up, the dispute forgotten.

'It's coming!' she cried. 'You must excuse me, but I simply have to see it arrive.'

Infected by her enthusiasm, the younger Turnbulls tumbled in her wake as she scampered down the stairs and into the road to watch for the coach. The quiet town shook itself awake, and a stir of excitement brought faces to the windows and children and idlers out into the street. Without realizing it, Stacey held her breath. Over the stones it rumbled, accompanied by a froth of shouting boys and barking dogs, top-heavy with luggage, dead on time. A glow of pride swelled inside Stacey, until she could hardly stop herself from jumping and yelling and waving her arms. There was nothing, nothing in the world that compared with the power, the magnificence, the glory of a Brown's stagecoach.

Guided as always by the expert hand of Harry Cox, it rounded the corner faultlessly and pulled up in the yard. Stacey, following it in, gazed ecstatically at the Tantivy. The four tired, sweating horses hung their heads, their necks lathered and harness dusty from the dirt of the road. The coach itself, well-sprung and comfortable, had been built in Brown's own works under her cousin Oliver's supervision, and was finished in the company colours of royal blue and chocolate brown. On the front and rear boots the names of the towns at each end of the route were emblazoned in letters of black and gold, and on the door, above the licence plate, the words Tantivy, Prop. B. Brown were surmounted by a picture of crossed whips and a fox's mask.

Mr Turnbull advanced to open the door, asking the inside passengers if they would be pleased to alight, and an ostler placed a ladder for the outsiders to descend. The guard busied himself with parcels stowed in the depths of the boot, whilst porters waited hopefully for a job. The horsekeepers started to unharness the team, an enormously corpulent man began gingerly to climb down the ladder, a crowd of spectators appeared seemingly from nowhere to witness the scene, the coachman . . . Stacey looked, and looked again, disbelieving, for Harry Cox was on the passenger seat of the box, he had given up his place to a stranger, a gentleman.

With a sinking feeling of disappointment, Stacey realized that her first day back with the company was going to be marred by having to issue a rebuke, and to Harry Cox too, one of Brown's most trustworthy coachmen. With choking indignation, she watched as the interloper jumped down from the box with easy grace, called. 'Fifteen minutes, if you please, ladies and gentlemen, fifteen minutes,' to the alighting passengers and pocketed tips from those who had reached their destination. Harry descended more awkwardly, spied Stacey amongst the spectators and rolled over to greet her, a thick-set figure in a low-crowned beaver hat, drab coat, breeches and top-boots.

'Hang me if it ain't little Miss Stacey!' he cried, and his broad face with its red mottled complexion peculiar to coachmen creased into a grin of welcome. 'By George, you're a sight for sore eyes and no mistake! Where did you spring from? Gaffer's not expecting you home for three days yet.'

'I took advantage of a ride in a friend's carriage,' Stacey explained briefly, and before Harry could comment on this, went on reproachfully, 'but Harry, how came you to hand over the ribbons to an amateur? You know what company policy is on that point, the Gaffer's always very strict about it.'

Harry laughed uproariously.

'Lor' bless you Miss Stacey, that's no amateur. That's Mr Keating, new General Manager, and a fair waggoner he is, too, for all he's . . .'

But Stacey was not listening.

'*General Manager?*' she shrilled, watching the culprit as he strolled into the parlour of the inn. 'What does Pa want with a General Manager?'

'Ah well now, he ain't getting any younger, your pa ain't,' Harry pointed out, 'and the business is getting bigger.'

'But he's got me!' Stacey declared, flushed with indignation. The revelation had knocked all the brightness out of the day. She could not, would not believe

46

that her father would put someone else in the position that was hers by right, and that someone not even a member of the family. It was insupportable. There must have been a mistake.

Harry shifted uneasily.

'You'll have to talk it over with your pa when you get home,' he said. 'And now if you don't mind, Miss Stacey, 'tis only the bare quarter of an hour here and my throat's passing dry.'

'Yes, yes of course,' Stacey said absently. Then gathering her wits together she went on, 'Let us go inside, by all means. I should like to meet this Mr Keating.'

He was standing chatting to the three inside passengers, tankard in hand and looking very much at his ease. Stacey's first impression was of a crop of exuberant dark curls and a pair of eyes as blue as sapphires and every bit as hard. On seeing Harry and Stacey enter the parlour, he strolled over to join them, giving Stacey an appraising look that made her conscious of her height, her nose, the gap between her teeth. She flushed slightly with annoyance. As if it mattered. She was going to help run the company, and this intruder was standing in her way.

'You've stolen a march on me today,' he said to Harry. 'Won't you be so obliging as to introduce me?'

''Course,' Harry said, but there was a slight reluctance in his voice. 'This here's Mr Simon Keating, Miss Stacey, and this is Miss Stacey Brown. Gaffer's daughter,' he added, unnecessarily, in Stacey's opinion.

'Your humble servant, ma'am,' Mr Simon Keating said, bowing. Even Miss Hester Haveringshaw would have found nothing to criticize in his manners.

Assuming her Academy accent, Stacey sketched a curtsey and trotted out a conventional reply.

He was a good two inches taller than her, she realized, so that she had to look up slightly to speak to him. He

47

had a broad-cheekboned, narrow-chinned face, and the blue eyes were fringed with lashes far too long and dark to be wasted on a man. The girls at school would have swooned over him, she thought, but at the moment she was only interested in finding out how difficult it was going to be to dislodge him.

'So this is little Miss Stacey,' he said, with just the slightest emphasis on the 'little'. 'I have heard a great deal about you.'

'You have the advantage of me, sir,' Stacey replied, frigidly correct, 'for I did not even know of your existence until five minutes ago.'

'That is most fortunate, Miss Brown, for anything you might have heard of me would almost certainly have been to my disadvantage, whereas I have heard you spoken of only in terms of glowing praise.'

Stacey felt this conversation was getting her precisely nowhere, but at that point they were interrupted by Mr Turnbull bringing Harry's tankard with his own hands, whilst his wife made sure that the passengers wanted for nothing. For the remainder of the short break, they talked of their surprise at seeing Stacey, and the state of the roads. Stacey, trying to get the measure of her rival, decided upon reflection that her case was by no means as bad as it first appeared. For Mr Keating was undeniably a gentleman, and young gentlemen frequently succumbed to the fascination of the road. The coachmen on the Cambridge route in particular made a vast amount in extra tips for allowing undergraduates to take the ribbons, whatever company policy might state. To be sure, they did not usually go so far as to take up posts as general managers of coaching firms, and Mr Keating was older than the average undergraduate, but she felt reasonably confident that his stay with Brown's would be a short one. The long hours and hard work involved in running the company would soon put an end to his flirtation with the world of trade.

Having come to this conclusion, she was extremely glad she had not immediately challenged his right to a place at Brown's, as had been her first intent. Pa always said that one must first weigh up one's opponent, and Pa was always right. She had but to make herself useful and bide her time. But just as she had come to this happy state of mind, Mr Keating caught her studying him, which threw her into some confusion, for she could not help but assume that he must think her dazzled by his excessive good looks. Flustered, she said the first thing that came into her head.

'I hope you will be able to find a seat for me. Nothing in the world would induce me to ride home on a Pymer's coach.'

Mr Keating regarded her gravely.

'My dear Miss Brown, if I thought there was the least danger of that happening, I would turn off poor Harry here, or even one of the passengers. Nothing is going to prevent me from claiming the distinction of bringing the Gaffer's daughter home.'

Stacey thanked him, uneasily aware of having been put at a disadvantage. She should not have given the impression that it was his place to make arrangements for her. She was just about to say that on no account should any passenger ever be turned off, when the guard appeared in the doorway, timepiece in hand. Mr Keating embraced the parlour with a sweeping glance, reminded the company of the necessity to get on, and stood aside for Stacey to precede him out of the room.

In the yard, the new team had been put to and the entire Turnbull family assembled to bid Stacey farewell. The inside passengers climbed on board, and the outsiders appeared from the kitchen and clambered up onto the roof, puffing and complaining of the hurry. The guard, consulting his waybill and checking the newly-loaded goods, finally mounted at the rear and Stacey said goodbye to each of the Turnbulls and hopped nimbly up to take a seat directly behind the box.

Whilst everyone was sorting themselves out and disposing of scarves and hand-luggage, Mr Keating walked all round the team checking that each horse was properly harnessed, the collars sitting correctly and each buckle securely done up. He pointed out a loose pole-chain to one of the horsekeepers, reminding him that the mare in question took fright at anything banging at her heels. Finally, having satisfied himself that all was safe, he took up first the lead-reins then the wheel-reins and pulled them to ensure that they were running freely, then caught up the whip and climbed onto the box. Even Stacey had to acknowledge that his approach to driving was thoroughly professional.

'All right, Turner?' he called back to the guard.

'All right, Mr Keating!'

'Let 'em go, and look to yourselves!'

The horsekeepers jumped clear, and at the slight yielding of Mr Keating's rein hand, the horses began to pull. The Tantivy was off.

Stacey, turning in her seat to wave to the Turnbulls, glowed with the thrill of being back on a stage again. It was a perfect summer's day, warm and sparkling, the motion of the coach making just the right amount of breeze to prevent her from feeling uncomfortably hot. Once they were off the stones and through the first tollgate the glory of the Norfolk countryside was spread out before her, the hedgerows bright with wild flowers, the young corn scattered with poppies. Labourers stopped to watch them pass, children waved and shouted, heads craned out of open windows. Even the fact that she was not seated on the box with Harry only slightly dulled the enchantment of the swaying coach, the four powerful horses pulling at a steady eight miles an hour, the cheerful bray of the hunting call from the guard's bugle, the pride of being part of the swiftest,

50

most efficient, best turned out coaching company in East Anglia.

It was some time before even the conversation on the box penetrated Stacey's jubilation, but once it did, she joined in with enthusiasm. They were talking of horses, and Stacey, after years of Barty Brown's expert tuition, considered herself something of a judge of horseflesh.

'If I knew I was going to have to drive that dun, I'd have thought twice about selling her to the Gaffer,' Mr Keating was saying, sending the whip out to flick the mare in question on the haunches and catching it up again with the dexterity of an expert.

The mare flung up her head and snorted, upsetting the other leader, and was brought sharply back into line with a lash on the neck.

'Ah, she's a rare handful, that one,' Harry commented, 'but she goes well enough so long as she's in the same place and you don't let her get away with aught.'

'You have to expect a few difficult ones on the middle ground, Mr Keating,' Stacey struck in with a faintly patronizing air. 'Brown's cannot afford to run top-class horses all the way.'

Harry laughed, and turned in his seat to talk to her more easily.

'That ain't just a difficult 'un, Miss Stacey,' he told her. 'That is a dud what the Gaffer paid a fiver for.'

'Stuff!' declared Stacey. 'Nobody ever sold my pa a dud.'

Why, her pa was known all over Norfolk as a canny buyer of horseflesh. Dealers considered it a game to try and pass useless animals onto him, and laid bets as to who would succeed in doing so. But however cleverly the faults and vices of a creature might be disguised, they had never yet managed to get the better of her pa.

'Oh yes they did,' Harry chuckled. 'And you're looking at the man what did it.'

51

Stacey found it impossible to believe that Barty Brown would be taken in by the likes of Mr Simon Keating.

'Impossible,' she commented.

'True as I sit here!' Harry asserted. 'Moved freely, she did, answered nicely when she was led out, backed into place as sweet as a nut. But when she was asked to work she just lay down. Lay down, she did, in full harness! You never saw such a mess. The Gaffer, he nearly laughed hisself daft.'

'She may have been a dud when I sold her, but she's not now,' Mr Keating pointed out. 'I don't know any other man who could have got her going the way your father did, Miss Brown. It was quite remarkable.'

Praise of her father never came amiss with Stacey, but the incident of the sale aroused some misgivings in her mind. Whilst a detailed account of the taming of the dun mare was related for her benefit, she reflected that anyone who could successfully hoodwink her pa was sure to gain his admiration. On top of that, she had to acknowledge that Mr Keating was a very fair waggoner, handling an indifferent team with quiet skill. When a chicken pursued by a dog darted across the road right under the leaders' noses, she gleefully hoped for trouble, but was disappointed, for though the dun mare reared and her team-mate shied, still Mr Keating kept them together and sent them on with hardly a check in pace.

Stacey knitted her brows over this, for though she was no lame hand herself, she knew she lacked the strength and expertise that made a really good coachman. But then it occurred to her that there was more to being general manager than driving the coaches. After all, that was what the coachmen were hired to do. She knew every aspect of the business inside-out, for her father had allowed her to accompany him from a very early age into the yard and on purchasing expeditions. The sight of Barty Brown with his little daughter on his saddle-bow, or later on a sleek grey pony, was a familiar sight round the inns and farms and dealers' yards of the county. And on top of that was her trump card: her facility with numbers. Rapid mental arithmetic or painstaking checking of accounts were a challenge and a pleasure to her. Without undue pride, she was sure that Mr Keating could not equal her there.

She began to feel more confident again, to the point of complimenting him on his driving. Affecting not to notice her patronizing air, he replied that he was honoured to receive the approval of a lady who had been taught by Barty Brown, and that he hoped she would repeat her opinion to her father. Finding herself neatly defeated, Stacey asked Harry how it was that Mr Keating was obliged to take over the ribbons for this journey. Harry explained that he had hurt his shoulder in an accident and had been staying with his sister in King's Lynn for the past week, but expected to be back at work within a couple of days.

'An accident, Harry!' Stacey exclaimed. 'But that's most unlike you, you have the best record for accidents in the company. And in summer, too. How did it happen?'

''Twas a dray, Miss Stacey. Backing into the road, as I came round a blind corner. Caught the wheelers and the front of the coach before I could get us out of trouble. Very nasty. One lady was flung clean off the top and broke her arm and the rest was tossed about and bruised. And as for the horses, the near wheeler had to be shot on the spot.'

Stacey was appalled.

'But how dreadful, Harry! Such bad advertisement for the company. Did we have to pay out much in compensation?'

'Two hundred guineas in all, promptly paid,' Mr Keating told her, raising his voice slightly for the benefit, Stacey realized, of any passengers who might be

53

listening. 'Brown's are never backward in shouldering their responsibilities.'

'No indeed,' Stacey responded. Then after a moment's thought, she asked, 'Did you say *backing* out? With nobody on the opposite side of the road to give warning?'

'Quite so. Most unfortunate, was it not?' Mr Keating said blandly.

'A sight more than unfortunate, if you ask me,' Harry muttered.

'Hold quiet,' Mr Keating ordered tersely. 'There's no need to air your suspicions here.'

Aflame with curiosity, Stacey leaned forward.

'Pymer's?' she questioned, low-voiced.

'Possibly,' Mr Keating replied, and changed the subject.

Had anything else been under discussion, Stacey would not have allowed herself to be diverted, but she was well aware of the inadvisability of reviewing the rival coach company's skulduggery in public. She made a mental note to bring the matter up with her father at the first opportunity. The whole question of the accident had a nasty smell to it.

They changed horses at Honingham, picking up one of the crack teams for the last stage into Norwich. Brown's always made a show of their best horses at the main arrival and departure points, matching the animals as nearly as possible for colour and stride. They set off in fine style therefore along the Tud valley towards Easton. Stacey strained for a first glimpse of the cathedral spire, the church towers, the grim bulk of the castle. And then behind them came the sound of a post horn, tinnily mocking their own call: tantivy, tantivy!

'Anyone for Easton, Turner?' Mr Keating called back to the guard.

'One to put down, two to take up.'

'Damnation!'

54

Mr Keating dropped his hand and the fresh horses broke into a gallop along the straight level road. Turner blew a defiant reply, and Stacey twisted in her seat to see the Pymer's coach half a mile behind them and going at a tremendous pace. Two ladies of nervous disposition on the rear-facing top seats squeaked with fright and clung to each other, but any thought Stacey might have had of upholding the company policy on racing flew right out of her head. It was unthinkable that Pymer's should beat them on the home stage.

'Come on!' she cried. 'Oh come on, they're gaining on us!'

The whip lashed out, urging the four bays to greater efforts, and a cloud of dust rose from the dry summer road. Cheers were torn from wayside spectators as they thundered by. Gradually, they drew away from the rival coach, but their triumph was short-lived. Already Mr Keating was slowing to a decorous trot as they approached Easton, finally drawing up in front of the inn.

'Perhaps Pymer's will have to stop here too,' Stacey said hopefully, as Turner busied himself with the luggage, and new passengers and the fares, checking each meticulously against his waybill, chivvying his charges like a demented sheepdog.

'Rush, rush, rush,' a ponderous middle-aged man complained as he heaved himself up the shaky ladder onto the roof. 'It's nought but hurry these days. Ruled by the clock, that's what we are. T'ain't natural—'

And as he spoke, the New Tantivy swept past them at a hand gallop, the horn braying derisively and the coachman flourishing his whip. Unwary idlers in the village street leaped out of the way, children screamed with fright and mothers shrilled abuse. A duck was discovered to have met a mangled death beneath the flailing hooves.

'Racing,' the new outsider grumbled as he settled into

his seat beside Stacey. 'Ought not to be allowed. It's a danger to man and beast, that's what it is, and what's more, it ain't natural, flying along like that.'

He settled his carpet bag between his feet, still muttering. Stacey was struck with inspiration.

'I do so agree with you,' she replied. 'A well-bred young lady hardly dares travel on the roads these days, what with racing and accidents. I tell you what I think, I think that coachman ought to be reported for furious driving. That would teach him a lesson.'

'Oh aye,' the man agreed, but his tone was non-committal. He rapped Mr Keating on the shoulder with his walking-stick. 'I trust you know better than to go haring about the country like a bat out of hell, young man.'

Mr Keating turned round, catching Stacey's eye for a second with a conspiratorial glint.

'Brown's are renowned for the safety and promptitude of their services,' he informed the man gravely. 'You can rest assured that there will be no alarms and excursions on board one of our coaches. All right, Turner?'

'All right, Mr Keating.'

The Tantivy set off again at a smart trot, the horses still steaming slightly from their gallop. Stacey returned to the attack.

'I have heard tell,' she said, 'though I may be incorrect, that anyone laying information against a coach-driver before a magistrate is entitled to a percentage of the fine if the case is proved.'

'Is that so?' the man said, interest stirring in his voice.

'It is indeed,' Mr Keating assured him. 'And quite right too. The dangerous element are a disgrace to the profession.' His foot came down surreptitiously on Harry's.

'Fines can be as high as three guineas,' Harry put in, dead on cue. 'Especially if you deal with Mr Engleton. He's very hot on dangerous driving, he is.'

56

'Ah, that so?'

The man digested this information, whilst Stacey sat rigid, sucking in her cheeks to stop herself from laughing. A three-guinea fine was nothing to Pymer's, of course, but coaching firms in trouble with magistrates were always newsworthy, and the *Norwich Mercury* was sure to publish a piece about it. And once it was in the newspaper, the entire network of Browns, Jupps and Maddoxes would go into action, making sure that the matter was chewed over in every shop, tavern and coffee house in the city, until the whole of Norwich knew that Pymer's employed wild and irresponsible coachmen. It was certainly worth the sacrifice of pretending not to know Harry and Mr Keating for the rest of the journey.

They passed the last tollgate and clattered onto the stones of streets where every ten yards brought a familiar landmark to Stacey. She fumed with impatience as the traffic forced them to slow to a walk, could scarcely contain herself when a recalcitrant team slewed across the road held them up for fully five minutes.

But at last, at long last, they arrived in Crown Lane, and there spanning the road in wrought-iron letters a foot high was the legend 'Crown Inn and Posting House', surmounted by a huge gilded crown. With a final blast on the bugle, the Tantivy turned into the yard and pulled up. The horsekeepers ran to their charges' heads, porters and waiters converged on the coach, Uncle Noll advanced to assess the new arrivals, Turner started to sort out the luggage. Stacey stood up in her seat, anxiously surveying the seething, milling crowd. Was he here today? Surely he was not out on business? And then she spied him strolling out of the booking office, a burly foursquare figure with tufts of grey hair sprouting from beneath his low-crowned beaver hat. Stacey waved wildly.

'Pa!' she yelled. 'Pa, I'm home!'

Barty caught sight of her and broke into a rolling trot.

'Stacey!'

Abandoning every pretence of ladylike restraint, Stacey scrambled halfway down the ladder then flung herself into his arms. Laughing with surprise and delight, Barty caught her as if she were seven years old instead of seventeen and half an inch taller than himself, and swung her to the ground.

'Stacey – what a grand surprise – three days early!' He held her at arms' length and surveyed her while she gazed back, laughing and breathless. 'Well, well, that high-nosed old hag did well by you, didn't she? Quite the young lady. Aye, we got our money's worth there right enough.' He turned to his brother, fairly bristling with pride. 'Hey, Noll, look who's turned up to plague me! My little girl, and more bonny than ever!'

After that everyone in the company pushed forward to add their welcome, from Amos Burgess and the head yard porter to the lowliest stableboy. Harry Cox and Turner the guard related to anyone who cared to listen how they pulled into the Rose at East Dereham and found Miss Stacey waiting for the Tantivy. Brown's usual efficient handling of incoming coaches would have broken down entirely if Simon Keating had not been on hand to organize the dispersal of horses, passengers, luggage and goods.

Barty paused briefly before leading Stacey into the Crown to meet her aunt and cousins.

'Simon!' he roared above the confusion, and the new general manager shouldered his way through the throng. Barty clapped him cheerfully on the back. 'Ah, there you are. You made good time. How's that dun mare going?'

'Like a dream, sir. The best bargain you ever made.' The hard blue eyes lost their calculating look and the grin was genuine.

Barty guffawed at the joke against himself.

'Just for that, you impudent young beggar, I'll make

you drive her on a night run in January,' he threatened. 'Look here, just take over for the rest of the day, will you? I'm going to have my hands full.'

Stacey was too intoxicated by the joy of being home even to notice their easy familiarity, let alone read anything sinister into it.

Chapter Three

Home! And back to stay this time. Stacey leaned out of the window and looked over the cool green of the garden, dappled in the late afternoon sunlight. The greenhouse was rather sparse this year, and some of the shrubs had grown, but otherwise nothing had changed. It was the same indoors as well. Particularly the smell. As soon as she stepped over the threshold, Stacey noticed the faint aroma of wax polish and lavender and Pa's tobacco smoke, and was reassured. The sojourn at Miss Haveringshaw's was over, and now the real business of life could begin. She turned away from the view and looked round her bedchamber with equal satisfaction. The mahogany bedstead, the flower-patterned rugs, the blue-sprigged paper had been her friends ever since she had graduated from the night nursery. The jug on the washstand bore a crack from the time she had knocked it over in a fit of childish temper. In every other room of the house the same air of familiar solidity prevailed, for very little had been altered from the time that the Browns moved from rooms at the Crown to their own house here on All Saints Green. Elizabeth Brown furnished and decorated it in comfortable good taste, as befitted the home of a successful coaching proprietor, and since her death it had not occurred to either Bart or Stacey that any alteration might be for the best. The only new additions were examples of Stacey's amateurish attempts at watercolours and embroidery, and hand-tinted copies of a series of prints of Brown's coaches that had been published by a Norwich printer a few years ago.

A housemaid appeared with a can of hot water and asked which dress Miss would like laid out. Stacey went over her small wardrobe with a frown of concentration between her brows. All the dresses she had brought back from Miss Haveringshaw's were plain, schoolgirlish affairs, not at all in tune with her need to look grown-up this evening. She riffled through them, hanging limp and crumpled from the journey, and longed for something flounced and beribboned, such as she and the other girls had sighed over many a long winter's evening. It was important that Pa should think of her as a responsible adult, not just his little girl, especially now that this new threat to her position had so suddenly appeared on the scene. In the end she picked out a white sprigged muslin gown and sent the maid off to press it. The final effect was not at all what she had hoped for. Even with her only piece of jewellery, a garnet necklace that had been her mother's, she was not transformed into a poised and confident lady of twenty-five. It did not help that her thick, heavy hair was already threatening to come unpinned and hung, rebelliously smooth and straight, down her back.

'Oh well,' she remarked to the maid. 'It'll just have to do, I suppose.'

The secret of success probably lay in her behaviour rather than her dress anyway. With which thought she walked downstairs with more than her usual dignity to join her father in the dining-room.

Stacey thought she managed very cunningly over dinner. It was no use, she decided, jumping in with two feet and demanding that Mr Keating should be dismissed in her favour. Subtlety was needed. She had to find out just how firmly entrenched the newcomer was and then determine her course of action. So she started by discussing all the family gossip. She had, of course, heard most of what had been going on through letters during her time away, but it was not the same as going

61

over everything in leisurely detail. The whys and wherefores of every birth, marriage and death took most of the two courses, and lulled Stacey into a false sense of security. Like the house, it was familiar, well-trodden territory. But with the dessert, and the change by way of Ollie and the coachbuilding works to business matters, she became steadily more uneasy. Whatever was under review, be it the threat from Pymer's or the possible cost of winter feed next year, there was no escaping from Mr Keating. It was Simon this and Simon that at every turn. It was not going to be as easy as she had anticipated.

She reached for an apple and began to peel it very daintily, in best Miss Haveringshaw manner. Barty was telling her how Simon had reorganized some of the staging-posts on the London route.

'He sounds quite efficient, considering,' she said with a faint air of superiority. 'And he's been here an amazingly long time, for an amateur. I wouldn't be surprised if he goes back home once the winter comes, though.'

But Barty was far too old a hand to be caught like that by his own daughter.

'Now, it's a funny thing,' he remarked, leaning back in his chair and lighting up his churchwarden pipe. 'Nobody actually knows where that young man does come from. Turned up last April, he did. Drove the Eclipse home when poor owd Ned went under the wheels. Told you about that, didn't I? Nasty business. Very nasty. Never did get to the bottom of it. Sent Simon out to Thetford the next day to look into it and he found they'd had a new horsekeeper by the name of Platt who'd disappeared only half an hour after the Eclipse left, but that was all he could ferret out. Couldn't find hide nor hair of Platt. But that's beside the point. I was talking about the Eclipse, wasn't I? Lying in a ditch it was when along comes young Simon, puts it to rights then sells me a dud. God's truth!'

Stacey was obliged to listen again to the tale of how her father had been persuaded to part with five guineas for a horse that lay down in harness. She cut her apple into four, then eight, then sixteen slivers and arranged them in a flower pattern on her plate.

'. . . So we had a drink or two and it turned out he'd run a coach on the Brighton road once and wasn't doing aught in particular at the moment, so I offered him a job. One of the best moves I ever made. He's a rogue, of course, but a likeable one, and he's not tried to pull a fast one on me yet, that I do know, 'cause I been watching him and I know every trick in the book. He even asks before taking company time to do a spot of dealing on the side, and that is unusual. Real stroke of luck, it was, him happening along when he did.'

Thoroughly alarmed, Stacey stared with unfocused eyes at the fruit on her plate. Inside her head, she could hear just the right note of confident unconcern that should be used. She cleared her throat.

'It's curious,' she said, and try as she might, she could not quell the quaver of petulance, 'that you did not mention him in your letters. Three and a half months is a long time to forget to say anything about such a paragon.'

Furious with herself, she fought to keep her expression bland. It had come out all wrong. What should have been a mild joke had turned into cheap sarcasm and exposed her hand completely.

'Ah well,' Bart explained. 'I didn't say nought because you might have got the wrong idea, see? Thought it best to leave it till now, when you was home to see for yourself how things were.'

For a moment, hope flared again.

'So he is only here as a temporary measure?' Stacey fixed eager eyes on her father. 'I thought as much. After all, he doesn't really belong here, does he? I'm sure he was very good as a stop-gap,' she conceded generously. 'With the company growing bigger, you must need someone reliable to help you, someone who knows every part of it. But now I'm back, he can be dispensed with, and we'll all go on as happily as bugs in a bed.'

'It's real nice having you back again, and that's a fact,' Barty said, sidestepping the issue. 'I can see now that your Aunt Eustacia was right, for once. That school was just the place. But it was a sight too quiet round here without you and no mistake. Real lonely at times. Still, it was worth it to see you come back looking so fine, and now you're here you'll have to buy yourself some new dresses. Something fancy, proper for a young lady. Your Aunt Eustacia is coming over for a few days so you can get yourself fitted out. Nought but the best, mind! No expense spared.'

'That will be splendid,' Stacey said, suspicion clouding her enthusiasm. 'I was thinking only an hour or two ago, when I was changing, that I needed some more fashionable gowns. But there's no need for Aunt Eustacia to trouble herself. I can manage perfectly well without her, in fact she would be rather in the way. You know how she does dawdle about, and I'm going to be busy—'

'You'll soon get used to it, chicken,' Barty interrupted. 'After all, she is the most suitable person, being your mother's sister and your godmother.'

'Suitable for what?'

'You know – chaperon—' Barty waved a vague hand in the air. 'Take you round to assemblies and suchlike. I can't do that sort of thing. Obvious.'

There was a long moment of silence. Bart blew a perfect smoke ring, and watched as it drifted lazily upwards, distorting and fading and finally dispersing against the yellowed ceiling.

'Pa—?' Stacey spoke with great care. The time had come for things to be stated clearly. 'Pa, you are going to take me into the business, are you not?'

Barty looked straight at her.

'No, chicken,' he said gently. 'I'm not.'

'But - but - you promised! Right from when I was tiny, you always took me with you. I've been learning the trade since I was a baby. It's not that I don't want to go to parties and suchlike, but not with Aunt Eustacia and all her boring friends, and not all the time. There's no point in that, no fun at all. I want to be a help to you!'

Reaching across the table, Barty patted her hand.

'That's a nice thought, Stacey love, but it ain't practical, see? It was all very well taking you along when you was a little scrap of a thing, but it's different now. You can't go traipsing about the yard like you used to. Why do you think I sent you away to that school?'

Stacey looked back at him, her ambitions fading like so many smoke rings.

'I really do not know,' she said miserably. But she was beginning to have a suspicion of an idea. Miss Haveringshaw's, much patronized by the daughters of newly-rich mill owners, was dedicated to the turning of sow's ears into silk purses, and all to one purpose: marrying the said daughters off to the well-bred but relatively impoverished sons of the landed classes. This, of course, was never openly acknowledged or even obliquely alluded to by Miss Haveringshaw and her refined staff, but the girls had no such scruples. They not only knew their future role in life but welcomed it. Talk of beaux and prospects abounded, and those who had no likely candidates in their immediate neighbourhood were obliged in self-defence to invent one or two. They all lived for the day when they would be released from Miss Haveringshaw and let loose to practise all she had taught them on the unsuspecting male population.

Stacey always considered herself rather above these designs, both because of her desire to be an active partner in the coaching business and because she saw clearly her own disadvantages. She knew she was, if not

65

plain, certainly not pretty, and that Barty's fortune was a mere pinch compared with the amounts amassed during the wars by the fathers of her schoolfriends. To make the kind of match envisaged by the other girls, one needed either looks or money. She had neither, and that lack had been a comfort rather than otherwise, for it meant that her hopes of assisting her father were even more firmly based. Until now.

Putting down his pipe, Barty reached across the table and took her hands between his two paws.

'Now look at it this way, pet. I've always wanted the best for you. You're all I've got and nought else'll do for you. So what do I do? When you were little I thought you might as well have some fun playing around the stables and the inn, and I liked taking you with me on business trips. You were good company, and you brought me luck. My lucky talisman, you were. But that was when you was a child. Working all hours at the yard and haggling with rogues of dealers and competing with the likes of Pymer ain't the life for a young lady rising eighteen. Best leave that to me and—' he stopped himself on the point of saying Simon Keating, recovered with the rapidity of long practice and went on with hardly a break '—get on with what you can do best for the good of the company.'

Despite her disappointment, Stacey's interest was captured, just as her father had hoped.

'But what can I do for the company apart from work in it?'

Barty, as usual, did not answer directly.

'You think, chicken. Think back to what we was talking about earlier.'

Stacey wrinkled her brow.

'Pymer's?'

He was not going to suggest that she married into Pymer's?

'No, no, before that. While we was eating.'

'But that was just family gossip.'

'Just so, family gossip. And did aught odd strike you about any of it?'

'No – should it have done?'

Barty released her hands and took up his failing pipe.

'Intermarriage,' he pronounced between puffs. 'Inbreeding, that's the trouble with this family. We all go and wed with cousins and suchlike. What we need is new blood, new interests. I thought that when I married your mother, and that was the best move I ever made. Cut above the rest, your ma was. She wouldn't have wanted you in the yard.'

It was then that Stacey knew she had really lost the battle. Once her mother was brought into an argument, there was no more to be said. Elizabeth Brown's word, her views, even her lightest opinions, were sacrosanct and prevailed over those of the living with an autocracy they would never have carried had she been there in person to enforce them. And if, over the years, her beliefs had shifted to concur with Barty's, it was not so much a matter of expediency on his part as a genuine conviction that they had agreed on all matters of importance.

Stacey waited for her sentence.

'What would she have wanted, then?'

'Not to have you wed to some journeyman shopkeeper or tradesman, that's for sure,' Barty asserted. 'Not that she ever turned up her nose at 'em, don't think that. Oh no. After all, she married me, didn't she? And I was still making my way in the coaching then. Didn't even have this house. But in spite of that, I know she wanted you to get back among her own folk. That was why I put up with your Aunt Eustacia, and why I sent you away to that school.'

So her fate was to be no different from the other girls at Miss Haveringshaw's after all. Elizabeth Brown had been the daughter of a Hussar officer, himself the fifth son of a country squire so that he had breeding but little income, a misfortune compounded by his addiction to gaming. The family was in particularly low water when they came to stay with friends in Norwich, so much so that Barty's origins and his low profession had been overlooked in the relief of not only getting a daughter off their hands, but some of the debts paid into the bargain. Not that Elizabeth looked on it in that light. As Barty had told Stacey, she never despised the people amongst whom she found herself. In the Browns in general and Barty in particular she found a haven of warmth and dependability that made a welcome contrast to the life she had led up till then. Gentility she gladly traded for love and a feeling of usefulness.

'Does that mean,' Stacey asked, feeling for the extent of her doom, 'that Aunt Eustacia is coming to live with us?'

'Ah well, that wouldn't work, would it? All your aunt's friends are out in the country. She don't have much to do with life in the city.'

Exile!

Stacey leaned her chin on her hand and sighed. A profound gloom was settling over her volatile spirits and turning her bright future a depressing shade of grey.

'You're sending me away to Raston?' The prospect was lowering in the extreme. 'Pa, I've only just come home. You said just now that you were lonely here without me. Surely you'd rather I stayed?'

''Course I would, chicken! You know that. But Raston's not the moon, you know. It's only a couple of miles outside the city.'

But in Stacey's view it might just as well have been the moon. It was not so much the distance as the completely different way of life that she objected to. She had stayed with Aunt Eustacia in the past and knew exactly what it entailed: long boring mornings spent being polite to her aunt's tedious friends and endless hours wasted on useless pieces of embroidery, reading aloud from improving books and banging away at the spinet. She would have to be meek and quiet and obedient, with nothing more exciting to do than go for a walk or make a weekly expedition into Norwich. No cheerful bustle of the inn yard, no problems to be solved, no decisions more taxing than which hat to wear, nobody asking her opinion and listening with respect as she gave it. And to what end? To get herself married to some insipid young man who hardly knew a pole-chain from a coupling-rein, and whose only claim to distinction was that he came from a genteel family. Stacey drooped in her chair, her expressive face showing exactly how she felt.

'Cheer up, chicken!' Barty said, just a shade too heartily. 'You'll enjoy yourself, just you see. A lot of your aunt's friends have young folk of their own and there will be plenty of parties and what-not.'

Unconvinced, Stacey heaved a great sigh. She could just imagine what those parties would be like. Very different from the splendid noisy affairs the Browns organized. And more than that, she would be on display all the time. Stacey Brown, the coach proprietor's daughter, with her height and her teeth and her lack of a really tempting fortune. What she really feared was failure. Having to marry some nondescript squireling was bad enough, but far worse was the prospect of not achieving that undesirable goal. Supposing nobody offered for her? But she could not bring herself to admit to that possibility even to her father.

Instead she tried another tack.

'But Pa, I still do not see how this is going to benefit the company. What's to happen when – when you're not as fit as you are now? If I go and marry some gentleman, he's not going to want to soil his pretty hands with a coaching company. You're not – you cannot be thinking of retaining that Keating man as manager?'

'It's early days yet, Stacey, I've not made any firm

plans. And in any case, I'm good for another ten years. Die in harness, I shall. I took Simon on 'cause the company's getting too big for one man to run properly.' Barty studied the ceiling thoughtfully, avoiding his daughter's aggrieved gaze. 'And very useful he is too,' he went on, 'seeing to all the routine jobs and little emergencies. Take today, for instance. There's Harry Cox off work because of his shoulder, and one of the relief drivers already on the Cambridge run and the other got his nose broken in a mill last night. We might 'a been in a bit of a fix if Simon hadn't been here to take the Tantivy out. This evening, too. I wouldn't be here chatting cosily to you now if I didn't have someone to take over at the yard.'

'You always managed in the past,' Stacey objected. 'Everyone knows their jobs. They don't need constant supervision.'

'Well now,' said Barty. 'And what is it you've got against Simon Keating?'

Stacey found that difficult to answer directly. She did not like the way he seemed to sum her up at a glance. She did not like the way he made her feel ungainly and ignorant. He was altogether too smooth and self-assured. He was an intruder.

'He's not one of us!' she burst out finally. 'He's an outsider. If you must give my place to someone else, why not one of the family? There are enough of them to choose from, heaven knows.'

'It might seem like that, but when you come down to it, there's nobody just right,' Barty said.

'What about Ollie?' Stacey suggested. 'He's the natural choice. I should think he's mad as fire at having a stranger put into the company.'

'I've nought against your cousin Ollie,' Barty placated her. 'He's a first-rate craftsman, and one day I'll make him foreman of the coachbuilding business. But why is it that your Uncle Noll is training up young Joe to take over the Crown instead of Ollie? Ollie's the elder, after all. It's because he ain't got the head for it, that's why. He's steady and reliable, but he's not sharp enough. You could run rings round him any day.'

This Stacey knew was perfectly true, so she abandoned Oliver's cause and scouted round for another candidate. But to every protégé she brought forward, Bart had some sound objection. One was too young, another already helping with his father's business, another not reliable, a fourth Barty simply did not like. In the end, Stacey ran out of possible contenders.

'I suppose you're right,' she conceded. 'But I still do not think it's fair. Pa, you're not going to cut me off from the company altogether, are you? I couldn't bear it.'

''Course not, chicken!' Glad to be able to agree with her over something, Barty hastened to sugar the pill as best he could. 'Look, how would it be if you was to come to dinner once a week, every Saturday say, and we'll have a nice comfortable chat, you and me. You tell me all you've been up to, and I'll let you know what's been going on. How'd that suit you?'

'Oh, I'd like that! I'll look forward to it all week!' Stacey jumped up, ran round the table and dropped a kiss on her father's bald head. And seeing that she had the upper hand now that he was trying to please her, she tried for one more small concession. 'We don't have to call Aunt Eustacia in straight away, do we? After all, I am home three days early. Can I not go down to the yard tomorrow? Just for one day? Please!'

And because he liked to see her happy, Barty agreed.

Chapter Four

The last of the day coaches, the Trafalgar for Great Yarmouth, rolled out of the yard at nine o'clock sharp, carrying a full complement of passengers and a carefully stacked load of excess baggage. The Trafalgar was one of Brown's best bread-and-butter runs, even with Pymer's operating the same route at a lower fare. And if Pymer's could be put out of business, Simon Keating thought, so much the better. The profits would then look very healthy. He glanced round the yard, checking that everything was in order while he turned over a few of the ideas he had for making life difficult for the rival company. When the Gaffer came in today, he would find time to discuss them with him. If he was not too tied up with that daughter of his, that was. He smiled to himself. She was an odd mixture, that girl. The veneer of Young Ladies' Academy manners on top of the Brown brand of open-hearted good humour was incongruous enough to be comic, and she had not the looks to carry it off. He had experienced great difficulty in keeping a straight face when she had tried to tell him his business over the middle-ground horses. But he had to admit that she possessed a degree of her father's native cunning. The attempt at getting the coachman of the New Tantivy reported for furious driving was well done, and might have succeeded if she had not ruined it with the enthusiasm of the family reunion. There was, too, the remote possibility that the disgruntled passenger was grasping enough to claim his cut of the fine, even though he did know he was being used by the Brown organization. And remembering the cut he was hoping to make on a deal he had set up, Simon took a last look at the stableboys sweeping up after the early morning activity, and strolled into the Crown for breakfast.

Inside the best parlour it was relatively quiet, as the Trafalgar passengers' meals had been cleared away and the next influx of customers was not expected until later in the day, when the build-up to the midday rush began. A couple of middle-aged men were half-hidden behind newspapers in one corner, and a large family group was sitting over a late breakfast. Simon exchanged a joke with one of the waiters and sat down by a window overlooking the yard. From here he had a clear view across to the booking office and could keep an eye on what was going on. He reminded himself that he must look through yesterday's accounts again. Last night he had only run a quick eye over the daybook, and it appeared to balance all right, but he had an odd feeling that there was something wrong with it. It seemed hardly possible, since old Amos Burgess worked with terrifying efficiency, but still it ought to be checked. He should have gone through the figures properly last night, of course, but due to the Gaffer's unexpected absence he was already three hours late for an appointment with a certain lady in King Street. And a fine scene he had been treated to when he did arrive. Tears, reproaches, accusations – though she had made up for it afterwards, he had to admit. Nevertheless, as he attacked the loaded plate that the waiter placed before him, he considered his position there and decided it was time to make a break. It was a pity, as she was ideally situated with her husband often away, and just his type, small and blonde and curvaceous, but once they started making claims on you and thinking they had rights of possession, it was a question of either ending it or running the risk of becoming involved. And that he always avoided.

Harriet Brown came tripping through the parlour at this point, humming carelessly to herself, studiously avoiding seeing him until almost level with his table, then pretending to realize who it was with an overdone start of surprise.

'Oh, Mr Keating! Fancy you being here! You're very late today. I thought the parlour was quite empty. Mama just sent me on an errand and I thought I might as well come through this way.'

Simon affected to be taken in. He liked Harriet, and her transparent acting afforded him endless amusement. He rose punctiliously to greet her.

'A fortunate chance, Miss Brown. I expect you are looking forward to a visit from your cousin this morning?'

'Oh yes! Such a surprise, her coming back yesterday! It was quite delicious, seeing her again. Stacey and I are the greatest friends. She is almost dearer to me than my sisters, in fact we were brought up like sisters when we were little. And now she's back and we shall have such fun, except that she's always saying she going to help Uncle Bart run the company, but I don't think she really means it, and anyway, you're doing that now, aren't you?'

'Quite so,' Simon agreed, noting this piece of information. 'And I suppose it is in Miss Stacey's honour that you are wearing a new dress this morning?'

Harriet giggled in delight, blushed, bit her lip.

'Oh Mr Keating, fancy you noticing! Yes, I only had it from the dressmaker's yesterday. It's quite the latest thing. I wonder if Stacey will like it?'

She waited breathlessly for his approval and Simon obliged her by saying that it was very pretty, throwing in for good measure that blue ribbons suited her.

'Do you think so? Well, I want to look nice for Stacey, after all—'

She broke off, colouring a deeper shade of pink as she saw the door open to admit the unwelcome presence of her eldest brother.

'Ollie! What are you doing here at this time of day? I was just passing through on an errand for Mama and—'

She trailed off into a guilty silence under her brother's accusing glare.

Oliver's eyes travelled from his sister to the general manager and back again with undisguised disapproval. 'You'd best be off, then,' he stated.

'Oh – yes – of course,' Harriet stammered, and thinking at the last moment that she might as well be hanged for a sheep as a lamb, switched her fluttering gaze to Simon. 'Good day, Mr Keating.'

Simon bowed.

'And good day to you, Miss Brown.'

Oliver watched her out of the room, then turned his attention to Simon, who promptly sat down and resumed his cooling breakfast.

'What were you talking to my sister about?' Oliver demanded.

'Just passing the time of day,' Simon said. 'Won't you sit down?'

He harboured a reluctant admiration of Oliver, a regard that he was well aware was not returned. To be a strict Methodist in a family of innkeepers required a considerable strength of character. That they all still lived together without any violent disagreements said a great deal for the tolerance and solidarity of the Browns. But tolerance was a quality Oliver found almost impossible to extend to Simon.

'No thank you,' he said stiffly. 'And what's more I'd be obliged if you'd leave my sister alone in future.'

Simon affected mild surprise.

'I beg your pardon, but I was always taught that it is extremely impolite not to answer a lady if she addresses one first.' Irritation showed clearly on Oliver's heavy face, and Simon could not resist stirring the situation a little more. 'I wonder you do not warn me off your cousin while you are about it,' he said. 'Since we were introduced yesterday and already on speaking terms, she might try to talk to me unless I'm very guarded.'

'You know very well what I mean,' Oliver growled, goaded by this deliberate misunderstanding.

Humour, Simon reflected, was not part of Oliver's

character. And as always when confronted with the pompous or the moralizer, he felt an irresistible urge to present himself in the worst possible light, to say something calculated to shock.

'Indeed I do,' he agreed equably. 'You believe my intentions, as the common phrase has it, are entirely dishonourable, which is very acute of you. However, you need not put yourself about in this instance. Young girls of respectable families do not particularly interest me, unless they happen to be very rich. No – I find that bored married ladies of about ten years' standing are far more to my taste. They are always so anxious to have a little adventure before their looks fade.'

Oliver's face betrayed a battleground of reactions: disgust, anger, a desire to show this sinner the error of his ways. Finally, unable to express any of these adequately in the best parlour of his father's inn, he announced, 'I shall pray for you,' as if it were a threat, and marched out.

He left unaware that he had scored the last point, for if there was one thing calculated to annoy Simon, it was being prayed for.

'Damned sermonizing hypocrite,' he muttered. 'Best look to your own life first. Envy is one of the seven deadly sins as well.'

And at the side of his head, the unevenly-healed scar he had collected on the Breckland track began to throb. That was another cause for frustration. His efforts to find out who the instigator of the attack might be had got nowhere. He had not been naïve enough to expect immediate results, but he had hoped for some sort of a clue by now. He was beginning to wonder whether the very lack of information was in itself a lead, for he had met with the same wall of silence in the past when he had tried to interfere with the business of a certain Mr Henshaw. Added to this was the possibility that Job Watkins and Will Page might be working for the same man. He was not at all certain that it was they who had been his assailants, for all he had been able to make out in the dark was that one was far smaller than average and the other quite the opposite, an ox of a man. If he could just get hold of them, preferably one at a time, he would find some way of prising the truth out of them.

As he turned over this agreeable prospect, a slight, nervous young man in fashionable blue coat and buckskins came through the outer door of the parlour. Arthur Harris, eldest son of a local squire, hesitated and peered myopically about the room. On seeing Simon, his anxious expression cleared a little and he hurried over to the table by the window.

'Keating! For a moment I thought – but you are here after all,' was his unconventional greeting.

Simon felt the predator's stir of excitement at scenting the quarry. The next quarter of an hour promised to be one of unalloyed pleasure. He gave a friendly, reassuring smile.

'Yes, here I am, Harris, just as I promised. Won't you sit down? Coffee? Drink?'

The young man sat tensely and declined any refreshment with a nervous twitch of the hand.

'No no, nothing. My digestion – terrible – can't swallow a thing before noon. But what of the horse? Did you find one?'

Simon maintained a steady gravity of expression.

'It's no easy task, you know, locating a three-year-old strawberry roan filly at just the right price,' he stalled, 'and at such short notice.'

'I know, I know, I tried myself before ever I was recommended to your good offices.' Harris ran distracted fingers through his limp brown hair. 'I'm at my wit's end. I don't know what made me go into such detail. I don't know why I said I owned a racehorse at all . . .'

Waiting till he trailed off into a dejected silence, Simon said, 'However—' and Harris's face lit with hope. 'As it happens I did manage to get hold of the very thing. As neat a little filly as ever you saw, and with quite good form, though she hasn't actually won anything yet.' He paused to let his companion express his unbounded delight before letting slip the bad news. 'Of course, it was a tricky job persuading her owner he might want to part with her, but I succeeded in the end. For a price. I'm afraid I had to offer rather more than you stipulated.'

'No matter, no matter. You have her, that's all I care about. My dear Keating, I am infinitely obliged to you, I don't know what I would have done – the relief! You cannot imagine!'

'Oh, I think I can,' Simon sympathized, one man of the world to another. 'Women! What we do to gain their favour, eh?'

Harris nodded and gave a wan smile, grateful not to be considered a complete fool, whilst Simon reflected that though he might in extreme cases be driven to inventing racehorses, he would never be such a weak-witted idiot as to actually buy one. There were plenty of other expedients to be tried before resorting to that.

'There's just one problem that still worries me,' Harris said. 'The name. The name cannot possibly be the same.'

'That's easily overcome,' Simon assured him. 'Quite a number of thoroughbreds have a stable name and an official one. The one you gave will do very well for common use. I'm sure the horse won't mind. All you have to do now is contact the trainer and get your colours registered at the Jockey Club. Everything is fixed. You can arrange a visit to Brighton during the races and bask in your friends' envy and the lady's admiration. You'll make a pretty penny on the filly, too, if she wins, since she'll be rated an outsider.'

He allowed the thankful Harris a minute or two to contemplate this happy picture, then embarked on the second part of his project.

'Of course,' he said thoughtfully, 'if you really want to

complete the effect, you ought to consider your carriage horses.' He paused to make sure he had his victim's full attention, and went on, 'Now, you know and I know that those bays of yours are a very fine team, but the female eye does not see that. There's hardly one woman in fifty who appreciates the finer points of a horse. What they like is a pretty colour. Bays are too dull to impress. What you need is a showy pair of greys.'

'Ah – well – I'm sure you're right – but it's the cost—' Harris floundered. 'After buying the thoroughbred, I really don't think I can afford – and there are so many other expenses involved. You do understand?'

'But of course, nobody's made of money these days. There are limits to everyone's funds,' Simon assured him. He looked absently out of the window, and went on almost to himself, 'It's a pity, though, because I could have fixed you up with a couple of beautiful silver greys, practically pure white. Lovely creatures. Might even have got rid of the bays for you, with a modicum of luck, so you would not have had to go to a vast amount of extra expense. But not to worry. Ten to one the lady likes a bay just as well.'

Harris's thin face was a picture of indecision. He twitched in his seat, gnawed at his knuckles, looked short-sightedly about the room as if searching for an acceptable answer. Simon felt almost sorry for him. But not quite enough to let him off the hook.

'I must be off, if you will be so kind as to excuse me,' he said, pushing back his chair. 'I'm a busy man. It's been a pleasure to be able to be of use to you. Any friend of Corby's is a friend of mine. Give him my warmest regards when next you see him, won't you? And if ever there's anything else I can do, just say the word.' He extracted his pocket book and produced a folded piece of paper. 'There you are,' he said, handing it to Harris, 'the bill of sale for the filly. I'm sorry about the extra fifty guineas, but between you and me, I think you've got a bargain even at that price. Never mind about that now, though, if you're pushed. Any time you like. There's no hurry.'

Predictably, Harris was overcome by this careless generosity.

'Oh no, I couldn't possibly let you – and after all the trouble you have been to – I'll write you a draft directly.'

'No trouble at all, I assure you,' Simon replied, catching the waiter's eye and sending him for pen and ink. 'What are friends for, after all?'

Harris drew out his bank book and sat flicking the pages with his thumb, his face puckered with anxiety. Simon idly watched the arrival of a smart barouche in the yard. 'Neat team there,' he commented. 'Very pretty.' The waiter came back bearing writing materials and placed them on the polished table, deftly removing the remains of Simon's breakfast.

'Look here,' Harris burst out, 'about these greys – you've done so much for me already, I cannot possibly put you to any more trouble. I'm deeply indebted to you.'

Any further display of disinterested assistance, Simon decided, would lead even this greenhorn to smell a rat. The time had come for a little honesty.

'To tell you the truth,' he said, with an ingenuous smile, 'I shan't be the loser by the deal. I happen to know of someone who wants a matched pair just like yours.'

Harris relaxed visibly.

'In that case – yes – by all means – if you really think they would be such an improvement.'

'Sure to be, my dear fellow, you take it from me,' Simon gave him a knowing look. 'A very wise decision on your part, if you will allow me to say so. I'll bring 'em round to your place within the next two or three days for your approval.'

'That soon! You really are – but if there is ever anything I can do for you, anything at all, just say the word,' the unfortunate Harris begged.

'As a matter of fact, there is something,' Simon said slowly, considering just how far he could trust this saphead to act with a degree of circumspection. Harris leaned forward, eager to be of use. 'It's not much, but I would be obliged to you if you would just keep your eyes and ears open when you're at the racecourse. There are two men I particularly want to get in touch with.'

'Yes, yes, of course. I'll do everything in my power. Who are they? Would you like me to deliver a message?'

Simon's fingers crept involuntarily to the scar beneath his crop of curls.

'No, there's no need for you to approach them at all. Just send me word that they are there, that is all. They may not be, but if they are, I would very much like to know. One is a rat-faced, shrivelled individual, an ex-jockey named Will Page, and the other is Job Watkins, a failed bruiser with the inevitable broken nose. If you do see them, stay clear of them, they're not to be trusted an inch, and Watkins can still pack a punch like a steam hammer.'

Harris looked suitably impressed, and agreed to be on the look-out for these characters. Simon, reassured by the fact that even if the idiot did let something slip, he was not known to them by the name of Keating, was satisfied that one more small wheel had been set in motion.

He listened with great patience to the younger man's effusions of thanks, pocketed the banker's draft and finally rose to take his leave, struck anew with the happy conviction that there was one born every minute. In the yard he paused to take a deep breath of the mid-morning air, taking in the city smell of cooking, rotting garbage, dust and overwhelming all else, of horses. The galleried inn yard, with its rows of bedchambers, its well-appointed public rooms, its cavernous coach house and innumerable stables wore an especial charm for him as it basked in the summer sunshine. If he failed to clear two hundred guineas on the combined deals, Simon decided, he deserved to take holy orders. And with this unlikely thought, he breezed into the booking office.

In the outer room the two junior clerks on their high stools were busily scratching away at letters and accounts, whilst Amos Burgess in his fastness in the corner was counting up the day's takings so far.

''Morning, Burgess!' he said cheerfully. 'How's business today? Bring in yesterday's daybook, would you? I didn't have time to look at it properly last night. We don't want the Gaffer to think I'm slacking, do we?'

He already had the door to the inner office half open, and hardly listened to the chief clerk's hurried attempt to apprise him of something important, before he marched in. He found the place already occupied. Barty Brown was seated at his desk with a ledger open in front of him, and beside him was his daughter, studying the rows of figures with every appearance of appreciating their exact meaning. They both looked up as he entered, Miss Stacey arrested in the act of pointing something out, her expression changing from one of eager enthusiasm to profound annoyance.

'This is an unexpected pleasure,' Simon said, ignoring the fact that his arrival did not seem a pleasurable event to all concerned. 'I did not think to see you here so early today, sir, and let alone with Miss Brown as well.'

'Just you try to keep Stacey away,' Barty laughed. 'She's a rare head for figures. Been trying to persuade me to put the fares down, she has.'

'Oh yes?'

Simon just managed to instil the right degree of interest into his voice. He had realized some time ago that however good a judge of character the Gaffer might be in most cases, he was apt to eulogize his daughter's talents with unashamed prejudice.

But as Stacey unfolded her idea, he began to listen with proper attention. She was not advocating a wholesale reduction of fares with the risk of starting a price war that might land them in the bankruptcy courts, but instead suggesting that the system should support much lower fares on one or two routes, with the intention of pushing Pymer's coaches out of business one at a time. With growing respect, he watched her chase figures up and down the columns of the various accounts until she worked out which of the coaches it was best to start on. Simon had to admit that she was far quicker and more accurate than he. He found small numbers tedious, preferring to work in round sums, but Stacey could calculate the cumulative effect of odd pennies taken on or off and come up with results at a speed that Amos Burgess would have found difficult to match. After half an hour's discussion, they finally decided to try the scheme out on the Tantivy.

'What d'ye think, eh?' Barty demanded of Simon. 'Bright little thing, ain't she?'

'Amazing,' Simon agreed. 'As quick as Amos Burgess and much prettier.'

Stacey leaned forward and shut the Tantivy ledger with a bang. A small cloud of dust danced up into the shaft of sunlight from the window.

'What was that you were saying about the daybook when you came in?' she asked.

'Ah – yes.' Simon had not realized they had overheard that. 'I just wanted to check it through again.'

Sensing a fresh field of combat, Stacey became helpful.

'I'll take a look at it for you,' she offered. 'It will hardly be more than a moment's work.'

And within a couple of minutes she found what she was seeking.

'Here,' she said, pointing to the fault. 'That eleven had been written as a one, and repeated over here in the debits, so that though it actually does balance, the whole thing is ten shillings out.' She looked at her father, aghast at the implications of the discovery. 'Pa, you don't think Amos Burgess has been cheating us? Surely not – and yet—'

'Never in a month o' Sundays.' Barty was emphatic. 'Just a simple error, that's all. I'll lay you anything you'd like to name the money'll turn up in the petty cash or something. All be cleared up in two shakes of a lamb's tail.'

But he did not want to question the integrity of his oldest company servant in front of the office juniors, or even in the presence of his daughter and the general manager.

'Why don't you show our Stacey that new team of chestnuts we bought for the Albion?' he suggested. 'It's their rest day today, ain't it? I'll join you in a minute when I've seen to this.'

It occurred to Simon forcibly that had the Gaffer been blessed with a son instead of a daughter, he would have been out of a job.

Amos Burgess was in the habit of taking the long way home each day, his reluctance to return winning over the weariness of his spare, hunched body. Many years ago, he had started going round by way of St Faith's Lane because the gardens and orchards were a welcome breath of the country after hours spent cooped up in the booking office. Now, apart from the effect it had on his rheumatic joints, he hardly noticed the change of the seasons, let alone his surroundings. Hobbling along past the neat market gardens, his head poked forward like a worried tortoise, he mulled over the day's incidents, prolonging the time in which he held a responsible place in the world, holding off the moment when the barrage on his self-respect would begin.

At Brown's he was a figure of importance. The guards waited anxiously while he checked waybills against the day's takings, the clerks dared not be discovered making a spelling mistake or a slip in an account sheet, even the coachmen, self-appointed lords of creation, had to refer to him if they wanted to see Mr Brown when he was shut

84

away in the inner office. Most of all, Mr Brown relied on him to see that efforts at cheating were foiled, every farthing accounted for and accounts both owing and owed were brought to his attention at the right time. 'The place'd fall apart without you, Amos,' Mr Brown would say, clapping a meaty paw on his thin shoulder. Amos knew that this was so. He was the Gaffer's right hand. And in return for this knowledge he gave to the company in general and Mr Brown in particular the devotion that other men might spend on their wives or their children or the gaming table.

Amos had been with the company ever since it separated from the business of the inn at the death of old Mr Brown. A much younger Barty, given the reins at last, had found a tangle of disorganized paperwork and worse, a plethora of customs and agreements that stood by word of mouth only. It was no basis for the sort of business he envisaged.

The dreadful weeks before Barty found him were etched with acid on Amos's memory. After the disgrace of being dismissed from the counting-house of Hendry's bank, and all over a misunderstanding, came the slow realization that nobody wanted him, a man of forty with a black mark against his name. Desperately he eked out his scant savings, but all too soon the day came when the landlady would wait no more and he was threatened with being turned out on the streets. And all the time he dared not admit to his wife what had happened. She despised him when he was employed, berating him for his lack of ambition, his inability to stand up to his seniors. Even now, twenty-six years later, he could still taste the fear that possessed him at the very thought of having to confess to her that there was nothing left. So through the bleak spring of 'ninety-four, Amos kept up the fiction of being still at work, leaving home at the same time each morning, spending the day scouring the city in search of a post, anything that was within his capabilities, huddling miserably in the dark corners of churches waiting for the time when he would have to go back again, face his wife and pretend that all was well.

And then, just as he knew that the play had to come to an end and all was lost, he met Barty. Desperation had forced him into an act entirely out of character. He went into a tavern, and bought a pennyworth of gin. As he sat sipping dubiously at the raw spirit, putting off the dreaded moment of truth, he overheard the conversation of two men sitting near him.

'It's a rare mess and no mistake,' the one was saying. 'I hardly know where to start. All written down on different bits o' paper, half of it with no date, and a lot not written down at all.'

His companion made noises of sympathy.

'Must make it difficult,' he commented.

'Difficult! Well-nigh bloody impossible. Fact is, my old pa weren't really interested in the coaching side of the place. He put all his efforts into making the inn a prosperous concern. The Crown, that was all he cared about. The coaches was just a sideline. And another thing, he was a rare one for keeping things in his head, was my old pa. He didn't trust folks not to have a poke around when his back was turned.'

'He had a point there.'

'Aye, mebbe he did, I'm not saying as he didn't,' the first man agreed. 'What I need is someone I can trust, to look after the books and the routine side of things while I go about setting the thing up.'

In Amos's fear-ridden brain a flicker of hope dawned. The glass of gin clasped unheeded between his trembling fingers, he eavesdropped unashamedly on the rest of the conversation. The man doing most of the talking – Barty, he learnt – was full of imaginative plans for starting an efficient coach service from Norwich to all parts of East Anglia, and to assist him he needed a clerk to attend to all the tedious details. This clerk, Amos realized in a rare moment of insight, would be a key figure as the enterprise expanded, and the more he listened, the more certain he became that he could fill that position. It was potentially far superior to anything he had applied for in the last few weeks, and the prospect of having his fortunes changed so radically on so slight a chance as an overheard conversation filled him with misgiving. After so many failures, he felt totally unequal to convincing the coach proprietor that he was the man for the job. Who would believe him?

Barty rose from his seat, clapped his companion on the shoulder and bade him farewell. Seeing his last hope of salvation slipping away, Amos panicked. Knocking over the gin in his haste, he pursued Barty to the door.

'Sir!' he gasped, grasping at the broadcloth sleeve. 'Please, wait, I beg you—'

And to his infinite relief, the coach proprietor stopped in the doorway and listened patiently to his gabbled recital of his qualifications, the reason for his dismissal, even his difficulties of the last dreadful weeks. The floodgates open, Amos could not stop talking. He never said so much without pausing before or since.

Barty, an optimist by nature and confident in his new venture, made the first of many snap judgements that were to fill his company with loyal and proficient servants.

'Come on a month's trial,' he said. 'Start tomorrow – six o'clock at the Crown.'

All that, Amos reflected as he hobbled along St Faith's Lane, had been twenty-six years ago. Many things had changed since then. Together, he and the Gaffer had survived the ups and downs of Brown's Coaches, the wartime uncertainties and shortages, the improvements in roads and coach design, the fluctuations in prices, the acquisition of the coachbuilding works, the expansion of the system and now the threat from Pymer's. At times the Gaffer took risks that terrified Amos, keeping him awake at nights worrying over the looming horror of bankruptcy, but the crash never came, the gambles paid off, and Amos was secure behind his wooden fortress in the corner of the office.

Until, that is, the coming of Simon Keating.

From the first, Amos feared and disliked Mr Keating. He carried with him the unmistakable aura of the governing classes, an unspoken power to make or break his inferiors with a casual wave of the hand. Though always polite, even friendly, towards Amos, still he managed just by his easy confidence, his charm and above all the equal footing he achieved with the Gaffer, to pose a threat to the chief clerk's security. A threat that gathered force with frightening speed. Within a week of his coming, Simon Keating had a desk in the inner office, an elevation that Amos had never dreamed of, let alone expected. But this stranger had walked straight in there, as if by right. The inner office had always been the Gaffer's sanctum, and Amos guarded it zealously for him. Now Mr Keating breezed in there at all hours, without so much as a tap at the door. Amos could hear them laughing in there together and jealousy stirred within him, mixed with irrational fear; were they laughing at him? And to his over-sensitive mind it seemed that the Gaffer confided in him less, no longer discussing future plans or pressing problems, but merely asking for the appropriate figures and closeting himself with Mr Keating, firmly shutting the communicating door.

Amos hardly dared name the nature of their relationship to himself, but inside he knew it: the Gaffer and Mr Keating were like father and son.

Through his growing anxiety, Amos clung to a bright certainty – Miss Stacey was soon to come home. Miss Stacey, the light of her father's eyes, would soon displace the upstart Mr Keating. And if, as all the company servants expected, she married Mr Oliver, the threat would be safely extinguished.

But then came the humiliation of this morning. Amos threaded his way round the back of the cathedral closes, and finally emerged through an alleyway into the bustle of Tombland. Try as he might to banish it from his mind, Amos could not help reliving the dreadful moment when the Gaffer pointed out the mistake in the daybook. To have made a slip was bad enough, shaking his faith in his own abilities, but the circumstances behind its discovery were far more sinister. For Mr Keating had first seen that something was wrong, and though the Gaffer did not say so, Amos was certain that it was Miss Stacey who had actually tracked down the fault. Miss Stacey, whom he had taught to cast up accounts accurately, to make rapid calculations in the head, to understand the double-entry system of book-keeping. She had joined with Mr Keating to discredit him.

He stood on the flagstones, blinking at the press of traffic. Through a cloud of choking midsummer dust, brewer's drays, delivery vans, handcarts and flat waggons were making their various ways home for the evening, while a single landau, hoods raised against the dirt, was setting our early for a night's entertainment. Amos hesitated, the scene blurring alarmingly before him. He took off his wire-rimmed spectacles, rubbed his eyes, then settled them again on his nose. That was better. It was his eyes, that was the trouble. The Gaffer had put his finger on it straight away.

'You been using the same pair o' specs all the twenty-six years I've known you,' he said. 'Why not try a new pair? Might make all the difference. If you can't see properly, it's no wonder you missed a figure.'

And Amos, profoundly grateful at having such a neat face-saver handed to him, agreed. He even believed it. His eyes were giving him cause for concern. The Gaffer reached into his breeches pocket and produced a guinea.

'Here,' he said, 'that should get you a good pair. Buy them on the firm. If you've worn your sight out working for Brown's, it's the least we can do. And set about it straight away, mind. We can't have you cracking up – I can't manage without you.'

Reassured, Amos went back to his desk. But away from the Gaffer's ebullient presence, the words rang hollow. Brown's could still function without him, now that Mr Keating and Miss Stacey had joined forces. He was dispensable, and he was sixty-six years old. This time there would be no last-minute rescue from destitution.

Wretchedly, he picked his way through the traffic and rounded the last corner, feeling as he did so the usual depression on reaching Hungate Street. He spun out the last stretch, dawdling to look blindly at shop windows that held no attraction for him. But in spite of it he came all too soon to the haberdasher's and the malodorous alleyway leading to the side door.

A haberdasher's, in his wife Martha's order of values, was an acceptable establishment to live over. A butcher's or a grocer's was not.

Amos stumbled over a dead cat and grazed his hand against the rough brick of the wall.

'Oh Lord,' he prayed, without conviction, 'let her be in a good mood this evening. Just this once, oh Lord.'

He lifted the latch and stepped into the dark, stuffy interior, groping for the stair rail. From above came a whiff of cooking fish that grew stronger as he slowly ascended the bare steps. Amos's stomach heaved. She was boiling the cats' fish again, and she knew how it affected him. As his head drew level with the top of the stairs, a shrill voice issued from the cramped parlour.

'Burgiss? Is that you?'

Well did he know that particular tone. God had been deaf to his prayers again.

'Yes,' he confirmed, 'it is I.'

Chapter Five

In the ancient lanes of the city, only a few yards from the comfortable redbrick houses occupied by the middle classes, half-timbered dwellings still leaned together for support over reeking alleys. The street lamps did not penetrate these regions, and neither did the respectable part of the population. By daylight it was subdued, inhabited by dull-eyed women and gangs of half-wild children, but with the twilight that came early under the overhanging eaves a change came over the area. The daytime inhabitants faded into their overcrowded rooms. Darkness drew a veil over all but the worst decay. Lamplight spilling from unshuttered windows gave an air of cheer and good company. The nocturnal creatures appeared, and began to make ready for the night's entertainment. Barmen set up rows of smeared tankards, pie-shop keepers stoked up their ovens, whores put on their tawdry finery and leaned in open doorways, eyeing the passers-by for likely customers. In ones and twos and small groups, the pleasure-seekers trickled in, apprentices, day-labourers, sailors, draymen, horse-keepers, failed professional men, the occasional young gentleman out on a spree. And the taverns and bawdy-houses began to fill.

Sauntering up one of the lanes, hands in pockets, came a group of three men dressed in dirty breeches and woollen stockings, with jerkins slung over their shoulders and brightly coloured kerchiefs knotted round their necks. Straw still clung to their hobnailed boots and about them hung the reek of the stables.

One of them, a heavily-muscled, bullet-headed man in his early forties, paused at a corner and jerked his head towards a tavern.

'Thass the place, Sam,' he said. 'Thass where you'll find 'em most nights o' the week.'

The man addressed as Sam, the tallest of the three, surveyed the scene with interest. A black patch covered one of his eyes and a wide-brimmed hat was pulled down over his forehead, obscuring a face already darkened by a day's growth of beard.

'Good man, Josh,' he said, his gaze travelling to the upper storey of the building in question. 'There's a way out through the back, you say?'

'Aye,' Josh nodded vaguely towards the rear of the building. 'Leads you into the tanner's yard.'

'Right. You both know what you're doing? Scroggy?' Sam turned to the third member of the group, a wizened little man with the bandy legs that had given him his nickname.

'Aye, just give me the nod when you're ready.' Scroggy's face creased into a gap-toothed grin.

'Good, let's hope they're there tonight. And remember – no letting slip where we're from. We don't want to go starting a blood feud, we just want a little fun at their expense, right?'

'Aye, we got it,' Scroggy agreed. Josh merely grunted.

'Come on, then. Let's to it.'

Whistling, Sam shouldered his way into the tavern and threaded between noisy groups of drinkers to the bar. A serving-wench, seeing the new customer was young and handsome in spite of his raffish appearance, stopped swapping backchat with a couple of sailors and scurried back behind the bar.

'And what might I do for you, my fine sir?' she asked, tucking a stray lock of fair hair into her cap.

Sam gave her a knowing smile, teeth glinting white against his dark stubble.

'You can fetch us three tots of Blue Ruin to start with, sweetheart. And later on I might see what else you've got to offer, if you're lucky.'

'Oo, hark at him!' she cried, pretending offence. 'If

I'm lucky, indeed!'

She filled the glasses of gin from a cracked jug and thumped them in front of him, slopping some in the process.

'You got the money to match your tongue, then?' she demanded, hands on hips, head to one side.

In answer, Sam fished a shilling piece from his pocket, tossed it in the air and before the girl had time to protest, caught it and tucked it down the front of her dress.

'I'll come and find the change for myself shortly,' he promised, and sliding the glasses along the counter to his companions, turned his back on her. The girl, seeing she would get no more for the present, went back to the sailors, who were loudly demanding her company at their table.

Sam leaned against the bar and studied the customers from under the black brim of his hat. His one eye ranged round the smoke-filled, low-pitched room, taking in the filthy, peeling walls, the sawdust-covered floor, the men lounging at the greasy tables, silent, convivial or truculent, depending on the effect the warm ale or raw spirits had on them. One group in particular caught his attention, half a dozen men more smartly dressed than the general crowd in topboots and breeches, huge coloured kerchiefs knotted about their necks and two of them with nosegays of wilting flowers thrust into the buttonholes of their coats.

Sam made a slight movement of the head in their direction.

'They the ones?' he asked Josh.

'Aye, thass them.'

Taking up his drink, Sam strolled over to the men in question and leaned a shoulder against a blackened oak pillar that supported the sagging ceiling.

'Now here's a group of fellows after my own heart,' he said. 'Swell dragsmen one and all. Allow me to stand you a round.' And calling the serving-wench over, he told her to fetch whatever the fine gentlemen wanted.

His new companions eyed him with veiled suspicion, but did not refuse his offer. 'To the road,' he said, raising his glass, 'and all of us who drive on it.'

They looked at him with a degree more of interest.

'You don't look like no coachy to me,' one of them remarked.

'Appearances are deceptive, my friend,' Sam told him. He nodded towards an empty space at one end of a bench. 'May I?' And without waiting to be invited, sat down. 'Had a spot of bad luck I did, up in the north country. Thought I'd come and see what the roads were like hereabouts.'

'Ah,' the first man said, 'I thought you didn't sound like no Norwicher.'

'Don't sound like no northerner,' one of his companions remarked. 'More like bloody gentry.'

Sam gave a slight shrug.

'Started off in private service, I did. Rubs off after a time, the way they talk. But it's no life for a man of spirit, being a wap-john. Ordered here and there, always got to act respectful and drive steady, no tips and perks. No – there's nought like driving the stages. Best life there is, I reckon.'

His listeners, warming to his theme, made rumbles of agreement. Stories of profitable sidelines, generous amateurs, famous races were related, many of them grown to epic proportions through numerous retellings. One man boasted of the occasion when he raced Brown's Eclipse right off the road, leaving it in a ditch.

'Brown's,' said Sam, 'that's a middling big company, ain't it? D'you think they're short of a good waggoner?'

'Brown's!' One of the coachmen spat on the floor. 'Right-on particular bugger owd Barty Brown is. Wouldn't take on no one-eyed dragsmen, he wouldn't.'

Sam half-rose and leaned across the table.

'Now just you look'ee here, matey,' he said. 'I can tool three blind 'uns and a bolter through the night and get there dead on time, see?'

The man next to him laid a heavy hand on his shoulder and pulled him back to his place.

'Surely you can, friend. Never said you couldn't, did we?' He turned in his seat and called for the serving-girl, sending her for another round. Sam allowed himself to be placated. He told a couple of tales about driving between the raw Yorkshire mill towns. The others capped them with stories of floods in the fens and snowdrifts on the Breckland. Glasses were refilled, cigars were handed round, the mottled complexions of the coachmen grew steadily more claret-coloured.

'You fellows all working for the same proprietor now?' Sam asked.

Around the table, heads nodded in affirmation. One man answered for all.

'Thass right – Seth Pymer at the sign of the Three Tuns. You must've seen our stages – bright orange and black, they are, nationly smart!'

'Pymer. Aye, I've heard of him. Decent gaffer, is he?'

The reaction was non-committal. Most of them agreed that they had known worse.

Sam appeared to be thinking.

'Ain't he got an uncommon pretty daughter? Nice little thing with flaxen hair?'

'Daughter? Thass his missus, bor!'

'And not so little, neither, and all in the right places.'

An appreciative chuckle went round the table.

'I tell you summat,' one man said. 'If I had a missus like that, I'd make damn sure I knew where she was, specially if I was an ill-favoured owd sod like the gaffer. Always out gadding about the town, she is. Never home.'

His neighbour leaned forward, addressing the rest of the table.

'Trouble with owd Ned here, he thinks he knows everything about women, just because he's got a missus at each end of the run.'

A shout of laughter greeted this.

'How d'ye know what one's doing when you're with t'other 'un?'

'After I've finished with 'un, she ain't got naught left for no-one else.'

In their corner, the sailors were waxing lyrical, their slurred voices raised in ragged song.

The coachmen gave a bellow of derision.

'Call that a song? Where's Tommy? C'mon, Tommy, on your feet. Give us "Butter and Cheese", bor.'

The man they called Tommy rose unsteadily and thrust his thumbs into his waistcoat pockets. Half singing, half chanting, he launched into the popular comic song, his companions roaring out the choruses. Unnoticed, Scroggy moved round the room until he faced Sam across the table. The performance ended in a cheerful discord, to the accompaniment of glasses thumped on the table.

'Hey you, wass y'name, Sam. You got a voice, bor?' one of his new friends demanded. 'Give us a song, or pay for the next round.'

More than ready to oblige, Sam got up and rested one foot on the bench. In striking contrast to Tommy, his voice was light and tuneful, carrying easily across the tavern without having to bellow. The song was new to his audience, and he delivered it with deliberate understatement, leaving his listeners to catch the double meanings.

'. . . She said unto me, Sir, I'm sure I don't know,
But under my apron they say it do go,
So if your powder is dry and your bullets play fair,
We'll both go together to find the bonny black hare . . .'

Grinning, the coachmen sat riveted, drinks forgotten as the song progressed to its inevitable conclusion. A shout of approval rewarded the singer, with demands for more and a call for another round. As his neighbour thumped him enthusiastically on the back, Sam briefly caught Scroggy's eye and gave a scarcely discernible nod. Scroggy replied with a change of expression. The coachmen wrangled over who was to pay next as the serving-girl slopped yet another jugful of gin into their glasses. In the middle of the confusion, Sam jumped to his feet, hands groping in his pockets.

'My watch! It's gone – my silver turnip! Some bastard's prigged my silver turnip. Give to me by my old pa, that was.'

Turning, he swept the smoke-filled room with an accusing glare, aggression in every line of his lean body.

'Which of you thieving bastards has prigged my watch?'

His one stony blue eye fell on a foxy-faced cheapjack on the next table, within reaching distance. Lightning swift, he dragged the man to his feet.

'You – turn out your pockets.' And over his shoulder to his drinking companions, 'Open up his pack.'

Two of the coachmen obliged, grabbing the greasy canvas pack and shaking it out onto the floor to shouts of encouragement from the surrounding drinkers. The cheapjack twisted and fought ineffectually against Sam's grasp, protesting his innocence.

'Weren't me, master! Never laid eyes on your turnip, I didn't! Honest! Never prigged a thing in my life, I ain't!'

The crowd howled its disbelief and jeered as knives, scissors, coins, cooking utensils, wire snares and a dead rabbit fell to the floor and rolled in the filthy sawdust. The cheapjack looked desperately from side to side, seeking a friendly face, a means of escape. But cheapjacks, like gipsies and tinkers, were easy scapegoats. Practically everyone there had been cheated at one time into buying a knife that broke at first using or a gold ring that turned out to be brass. The man's voice rose to a whine. 'There ain't nothing there what ain't mine, master. Them's my stock-in-trade, honest! Look!' Struggling to point, he managed to indicate the coach-man who had been sitting next to Sam. 'Look at him! He's got it!'

Reluctant to believe him, the eyes of the crowd focused unwillingly on the coachman. Bewildered, he looked down at his coat pocket and there, dangling out, was the end of a silver watch-chain. Sam let go of the cheapjack with an abruptness that sent the man sprawling amongst his possessions and turned on the coachman, catching him a blow on the jaw before he had time to gather his senses. One of his cronies caught him as he staggered backwards, and the others got to their feet with growls of protest. The mood of the crowd swayed, undecided. While the victim was a cheapjack, they were all behind Sam, but coachmen were a respected fraternity, imbued with the dash and romance of the road.

'Goddam lousy thieving swine! Play at making a man welcome then prig his old pa's watch,' Sam accused.

The largest coachman, a man with a broken nose and the build of a bruiser, swaggered between his friend and Sam.

'Shut your bloody clack-box afore I shuts it for you, one-eye.' The rest of his cronies gathered silently behind him.

Anticipating blood, the crowd moved back, giving them room.

'Gi' it to 'un, coachy!' a voice encouraged.

'Five to one on the coachy,' another offered.

Out of the throng, Josh materialized and lined up at Sam's side.

'This muck-spout giving you a spot o' trouble, bor!'

The loyalties of the spectators began to divide, the regulars backing the coachman, the casual customers favouring Sam and Josh. Fists at the ready, the front coachman took a step forward. At the same moment, Sam dodged under his reach and wrenched the watch from the thief while Josh dealt the bruiser a crashing blow on the side of the face. All thought of a fair fight dispelled as the coachmen piled into the brawl. From behind, Scroggy jumped up on a table, brought a tankard down on an unwary head and slammed his hobnailed boot into another before being brought to the floor.

'Hold hard, matey, we're with you!' one of the sailors yelled, and he and his shipmate lurched into the fray.

As benches toppled and glasses and tankards crashed to the floor, the cheapjack crawled beneath milling feet to retrieve his goods and the landlord tried in vain to eject the combatants into the street. Sam parried a blow from the coachman he had accused, only to catch another square on the side of his head, blurring his eyesight and opening an old wound. Righting his battered hat with one hand, he aimed a savage kick at his attacker and backed to where he had last seen Josh. The horsekeeper was felling a flailing carter, lips stretched in a brutal smile as the man's teeth crunched before the force of his fist.

'Find Scroggy and get out,' Sam hissed.

But Josh was already wading into the next opponent.

'Get out yourself bor, I'm jest beginning to enjoy meself.'

Sliding between Josh and a pillar, Sam stepped over a prone coachman and climbed onto a table, stamping on hands that grasped at his ankles. In the middle of the fray, lamplight flashed off the blade of a knife wielded by one of the sailors, confirming his opinion that it was time to cut and run. And on the far side of the room, he spied Scroggy scuttling behind the bar. He took the most direct route, jumping from one table to another, sending the last one flying as he launched himself onto the top of the bar. Skidding on the slippery surface, he fell and rolled down into a pool of spilt drink while a tankard aimed at him flew harmlessly over his head. With the resilience of a jack-in-the-box, Scroggy popped up beside him.

'You all right, bor?'

'Never better. Come on, time to leave 'em to it. They're getting the knives out.'

The two of them made a bolt for the room behind the

bar, only to find their way blocked by the massive bulk of the landlord.

'You,' he growled, grasping Sam by the throat. 'You started it.'

Grabbing a jug of gin, Scroggy aimed it at the man's head with all his puny strength. The heavy earthenware smashed against his skull and the spirit plastered his close-cropped hair and trickled down his face. For a moment he swayed, dazed, and in that moment Sam grasped Scroggy's arm and dragged him into the back room and through to the scullery. By the time they erupted into the back yard, the landlord had roused a hue and cry and was shambling after them.

Outside, the darkness was total after the smeary yellow lamplight of the tavern. Sam tore off the black patch, revealing an eye as perfect as its twin.

'That's better,' he said, peering about him, trying to get his bearings. 'Where's the way into the tannery?'

Scroggy nodded towards the bottom of the yard.

'This way, over the privy and them sheds.'

But even as he spoke, shouts were heard from the side alley and the landlord, at the head of his band of avengers, was silouetted in the scullery doorway. Figures swarmed over the fence from the alleyway and cut off their line of escape to the tannery. The third boundary to the yard was the blind wall, two storeys high, of a rickety wooden store.

'Up!' Sam hissed. 'Up onto that lean-to and into the first floor. Move!'

He swung up onto the woodshed built against the scullery, the rotten timber splitting beneath him, and climbed catlike onto the scullery roof, only feet from the landlord's head. Driven by fear of the mob behind, Scroggy followed, though it seemed to him that they were set on a course of certain disaster. He lay full length on the curling pantiles, hands clamped over the ridge of the roof, while below him in the moving darkness men milled about like penned hounds, searching the outhouses for their quarry. Sam, astride the ridge, got cautiously to his feet. The tiles shifted and clicked, but mercifully stayed in place. Reaching into his pocket, he produced a penknife and inserted it into the gap between the ill-fitting casement window and its frame. With infinite care, he moved it downwards until it met the tongue of the latch. The rusty metal refused to move. Cursing under his breath, he braced his knees against the wall and forced the knife down with both hands. The latch gave, Sam's foot slipped and a tile went crashing to the ground. Startled pale faces jerked upwards, a howl of triumph rose from the hunters, Scroggy whimpered with fear. But the window hung open.

'Come on, man, move!'

One long leg already inside, Sam leaned down to grasp his accomplice by a wrist and haul him up. Headfirst, he dragged him into the room, only to have his ears rent by a piercing scream. Dimly in the darkness a white shape glimmered, and from it came a shattering shriek.

'Forgive us for omitting to introduce ourselves, madam,' Sam apologized. 'But we do find ourselves somewhat pressed for time.'

Still holding Scroggy's wrist, he groped for the door, wrenched it open and stumbled onto a landing. From below, shouts could be heard, and footsteps on the bare wooden stairs. Sam thrust through another door and felt his way to his goal – the window giving onto the street. The pursuers burst into the chamber they had just left, to a renewed bout of screaming.

'Now, my friend,' Sam said, opening the casement and climbing through, 'there are two ways out of here – down, where you'll break a leg at the very least, or across, which is tricky. Make your choice.'

The building opposite, just eight feet away across the narrow lane, had once been the warehouse of a prosperous woolmerchant. A stout wooden beam still projected from above the upper window, from which a rope and pulley used to haul woolsacks into the first floor storeroom. Sam stood precariously on the window-sill holding onto the mullion, judging the distance. Unconsciously he held his breath, poised – and sprang. His hands touched and clung on to the beam, the force of his jump brought his heavy boots through the window with an explosion of glass. Scarcely heeding the jagged splinters, he swarmed through and once inside turned to knock out the rest of the glass with the handle of his knife.

'Come on!' he yelled to Scroggy. 'Jump, while you've still a chance!'

Perched on the windowsill, cheered and jeered at by fascinated spectators in the street, Scroggy was frozen.

'I can't!' he babbled. 'I can't do it! I ain't no bloody squirrel.'

Behind him a head appeared at the window.

'Jump, you bastard!' the newcomer jibed, and pushed him. With a yell of terror, Scroggy pitched forward, missed the beam completely and fell face down in a heap of rotting garbage to the accompaniment of a roar of derisive laughter. Always on the side of a clown, passers-by unaware of the brawl in the tavern picked him up and dusted him down. Dazed and bruised, but still with his instinct for self-preservation unimpaired, Scroggy bolted down the lane.

Relieved of responsibility for his accomplice, Sam turned to get out of the building he found himself in, and was brought up short by the sight that met his eyes. By the flickering stump of a candle a half-dressed whore and her client were revealed, locked together, frozen in mid-flight, their astounded faces turned towards him. Fighting back laughter, Sam swept them a mocking bow.

'Do please continue,' he begged them. 'Don't mind me, I'm about to take my leave.'

With which he made for the door.

Luck and a sense of direction brought him safely into yet another back yard, over a fence, down an unsalu-brious alleyway and finally into a respectable thorough-fare. He looked about, taking his bearings. Cook Street. Now he was back on familiar territory. But as he set off up the street, the exhilaration of the chase began to wear off. By the time he reached Tombland he was conscious of raw knuckles, cuts on his legs and arms, bruises all over and a relentless throbbing pain in the side of his head. And over half a pint of gin was rebelling violently. He recalled clearly now that raw spirit always had an evil effect on him. Never again, he vowed, never again, as he threw up the entire contents of his stomach. For a while he leaned helplessly against the wall of St George's churchyard, oblivious to his surroundings, until roused by the hoarse cry of the watch: 'Two o'clock and a fine night, all's well!' Two o'clock, and there was still work to be done. He heaved his full weight onto his shaking legs, made for the nearest pump and sluiced cool water over his head. He emerged gasping, his exuberant dark curls plastered to his skull, stone cold sober, and went on his way.

By the small hours, the Crown Inn subsided into sleep. Even Uncle Noll contrived to be in bed by one on most nights. But a skeleton staff stayed on duty, their presence declared by a lamp burning in the yard and another in the small parlour. Roused by the ringing of footsteps under the archway, the night yard porter emerged, lantern in hand. On seeing the newcomer, he was about to warn him off. There was no room at the Crown for disreputable ruffians such as this. But then the stranger took off his battered wide-brimmed hat and the porter stopped short in amazement, his manner turning from truculence to solicitude.

'Lord help us, Mr Keating, I never recognized you. You been mixed up in a baubery, sir?'

'If that means a common tavern brawl, Munnings, then the answer is yes. But I'm only a little the worse for

103

wear, considering. Be a good fellow and ask Jenson to bring over a pot of strong black coffee to the office, would you? Oh, and hot water to wash in as well. I've some paperwork to do.'

With the ease of long practice, the porter concealed his surprise and did as he was bid. Simon made his way across the yard to the office, lit the newly-installed gas light, dropped into his chair and put his feet up on the desk. He could quite happily have fallen asleep. But the scent of coffee, produced with the usual miraculous speed of the Crown, revived him. He washed the night's accumulation of blood and grime off his hands, took out writing equipment and a pile of paper and drafted a handbill.

'The proprietor of Brown's Coaches begs to inform the travelling public that seats are available, both inside and out, on coaches to London, Ipswich, Cambridge, King's Lynn, Yarmouth, Cromer, Lowestoft and all towns in between. The most marked attention and accommdation is guaranteed, at very economical rates.'

He read it through. It would do. There was no need to go into fulsome details, particularly as one copy for each of the potential passengers was needed by the morning. If, with very good luck, three of Pymer's coaches were out of action, with say twelve travellers on each – thirty-six! Why had he not thought of getting a printer to strike them off earlier today? It was very poor planning on his part. With a sigh of resignation, he dipped a freshly-cut pen into the inkstand and set to work.

Two hours later, his body aching and eyes gritty with fatigue, Simon finished the last copy. He was definitely not cut out to be a pen-pusher, he decided. He glanced at the clock. Half-past four. In another hour and a half the inn would be alive again, and he had to organize the extra coaches, horses and men, not to speak of arranging for the handbills to be discreetly distributed to the disgruntled passengers he hoped would be found at the Three Tuns. There was no point in going back to his room now, he would never be able to get up again once he fell into a proper bed, so he left orders with the night yard porter to send his daytime colleague over to the office the moment he came in, and dozed off with his head amongst the scattered handbills.

The scheme was every bit as successful as he had hoped, much to the delight of everyone at the Crown. Across the town at the Three Tuns, Seth Pymer was forced to take the ribbons of one of his London coaches, which did nothing to improve his uncertain temper, particularly in the mornings. And of course it was his wife, Deborah, who had to bear the first edge of it.

'Shift yerself, you fat cow' he grunted. 'I got to take the bloody Magnet out again today.

Roused by a violent shove in the small of her back, Deborah obeyed, cursing under her breath. She knew better than to voice her protests out loud.

'Ill-tempered swine,' she mouthed at her husband's broad back as he pulled on his breeches. 'Ugly pig.'

Not bothering to wash, she scrambled into an old print dress and replaced her nightcap with a slightly soiled morning one, covering curls that might have been blonde if they had been clean. Running downstairs ahead of her husband, she prayed that the cook had breakfast ready prepared. There would be hell to pay if it was not on the table, and she would be blamed. But at least Seth was going to be out all day again, for which she was inordinately grateful. She sent hasty silent thanks to whoever had started the mill that put three of their coachmen out of action. It had put Seth in one devil of a temper, but it did get him out of her way.

To her relief, the kitchens of the Three Tuns were busily turning out hearty breakfasts, and by the time Seth reached their table in the corner of the public parlour he had vented the worst of his temper on an unfortunate waiter who had dropped a tray. Over the meal, he told Deborah of his suspicions. He was sure

Barty Brown had been behind that fight. There was no proving it, but it was just the sort of thing he would do. Deborah humoured him by agreeing. She never argued with him to his face. She simply pretended to go along with him and did what she liked behind his back. It was the only way to make her life with him tolerable.

When Seth Pymer's second wife died, leaving him with no regrets and a tidy little legacy, he was in the happy position of being able to follow his fancy in the matter of her successor. And his fancy fell on Deborah, nineteen, blowsily pretty and generously proportioned, the daughter of a nearly bankrupt harness-maker. A round of negotiations with her hard-pressed father resulted in Deborah being traded for payment of most of the bad debts. Her family were delighted, for the Three Tuns was a prosperous inn, and Deborah's objections to Seth himself were totally ignored.

For a while Seth was delighted, and basked in the envy of his friends, but after a time he realized that having a young and desirable wife was little compensation for her being lazy, unco-operative and totally incapable of running the domestic side of the Three Tuns. At first he put it down to lack of experience, but time and practice brought no improvement. Service at the Three Tuns became slovenly, and trade suffered. So he began running stagecoaches, starting with one or two local routes and gradually working up to challenge his old rivals, the Browns of the Crown. Deborah was pleased. His preoccupation with the coaches drew his attention away from her shortcomings and left her time to indulge in her favourite pastimes of shopping and gossiping.

And now with his having to drive the Magnet a third of the way to London and bring back the return coach in the late afternoon, she had all day to while away just as she pleased. Deborah lingered for a time in the kitchen, chatting to the cook and pretending to supervise the meals, wandered round the inn and passed the time of day with some of the guests, then retreated to her bedchamber to make ready to go out. Six years of easy living at the Three Tuns had changed her from a well-rounded girl to a decidedly plump young woman. In another six she would be fat, but Deborah did not think ahead. She did not think at all if she could help it. She got a chambermaid to lace her into her whalebone corsets, put on a flounced dress that served to emphasize her proportions, tied a straw bonnet over her hair and set out, a basket over her arm.

She sauntered round the shops, trying on a pair of gloves here, buying a ribbon there, and then called on her mother. This was a mistake, for her mother could talk of nothing but the new baby that had been born to one of her cousins. Babies were a sore point with Deborah. She dearly wanted one or two of her own to dress up and show off, and a son would silence all Seth's complaints. He wanted an heir to the business, something which neither of his previous wives had been able to produce. If Deborah could but present him with a baby boy, it would compensate for all her inadequacies as a housekeeper. Depressed, she left her parents' home over the harness workshop and wandered along peering aimlessly into shop windows. What had started as a splendid free day had turned into a space of time to be filled in.

She was looking at a particularly pretty bonnet trimmed with pink ribbons and wondering whether she dare buy it and risk Seth's anger, when it happened. Two youths came yelling down the street, shoving and scuffling, and cannoned right into her, knocking her off her feet and scattering the contents of her basket. Deborah gave a squeal of fright, and sat helplessly on the dirty flagstones looking at her possessions. Another minute, and she would have been up and hurling abuse after them, but before she could do so a young gentleman was at her side, offering assistance.

107

'Allow me, ma'am. Please take my arm – that's right – can you stand?'

And in a trice she was set on her feet again, as if she weighed no more than a feather. Her rescuer was solicitous. Was she hurt? Had the young ruffians stolen anything? Deborah's backside was bruised, but she could not admit to that.

'My things—' she said, gazing at the half-dozen little packages flung about the street.

The gentleman snapped his fingers at a passing urchin.

'Pick up the lady's shopping, boy.'

The lad obeyed, and was rewarded with sixpence. Deborah's purchases were restored to her. She looked up to thank him, and found him gazing at her with frank admiration in his sapphire blue eyes.

'The pleasure is mine, ma'am,' he assured her, sweeping off his hat and bowing, exposing a mane of dark curls. 'I am happy to have been of service to you. But I am afraid you must be sadly shaken. I cannot possibly leave you to go home alone. Will you permit me to escort you? Where do you live?'

Charmed by his attention, Deborah told him.

'The Three Tuns!' Her rescuer was much struck. 'How foolish of me not to have recognized you. You must be Mrs Pymer.'

Amazed, Deborah admitted that she was.

'How do you know?' she asked, half expecting him to make some excuse and leave now that she realized she was the wife of an innkeeper, and not a lady at all.

'I had not been in this city three days before I heard of Seth Pymer's beautiful wife.' Smiling into her eyes, he drew her arm through his. 'How very fortunate that I should happen along just now,'

'Yes—' Blushing with delight at the compliment, she gazed back at him. Men had often looked at her in that way in the past, but always there had been her father or Seth in the background to stop any further developments.

108

With a thrill of excitement, it occurred to her that no-one knew of this unexpected meeting. It was her own adventure. And as if he understood the need for secrecy, he led her home the long way, through all the back streets, all the while drawing her out on the subject of her life at the Three Tuns. By the time they arrived at the corner nearest the inn, he knew all her grievances.

Here she stopped, not wanting to risk spoiling her new acquaintance by being seen by anyone at the inn.

'I'm all right now,' she said, looking about anxiously. 'Really. I'll go the rest of the way myself.'

'Of course. I quite understand.'

'It really was very kind of you—'

'Not at all, ma'am. It has been the greatest pleasure to be of service to you.'

He bowed, and Deborah, enchanted, sketched a curtsey then hastened along the street to the Three Tuns. At the main entrance, she turned and looked back. He was still there, watching her. He was really quite the most handsome and gallant gentleman she had ever met.

It was only as she made her way up to her room that she realized she knew not the smallest thing about him, not even his name. Tears of disappointment filled her eyes. For a brief moment romance had touched her existence, and now it was gone. The loss made her sulky and irritable. She snapped at the inn servants and hardly bothered to answer Seth at all when he came in late and tired from the strenuous journey. She compared him with her handsome young stranger and found him totally wanting. The night dragged by sleepless, with Seth snoring beside her.

And then, halfway through the next morning, a bandbox arrived at the inn from a milliners she never patronized. She told the delivery boy that there must be some mistake, but he insisted it was for her. Mystified, she carried it to her room, thankful that Seth was busy in the yard. The coachmen were back on duty today, so she had to watch what she did. Once the door was safely locked behind her, she untied the strings and carefully lifted out a bonnet trimmed with pink ribbons. With a cry of delight, she recognized it – it was the one she had been looking at when she was knocked over yesterday. And there, at the bottom of the box, was a calling card. Fingers trembling, she fished it out and sat staring at it, not knowing whether she was more pleased or afraid. She knew his name now – Simon Keating. But his address! The Crown Inn. The enemy camp.

Footsteps sounded in the passage outside and Deborah jumped up, heart beating, thrust the card inside her dress and looked around for somewhere to hide the bonnet. Without knowing it, it was then that she made the decision to go on. And later that day, after she had made sure that Seth was not watching her, she slipped out, wearing her gift. He was there at the corner, waiting. Drawing her out of sight of the Three Tuns, he took her hands in his.

'I just had to see you again,' he said.

Chapter Six

After nearly two weeks at the Red House, her Aunt Eustacia's home at Raston, Stacey was suffering from a sense of being stifled. Life was every bit as tedious as she had feared. The round of visits, the humiliation of being inspected and found wanting by her aunt's well-bred friends, the lack of anything demanding or challenging to do and the strain of always having to watch what she was saying weighed heavily on her. As for the young men that her aunt considered suitable, Stacey could not find any quality in them that would compensate for her loss of freedom. Added to this was the suspicion that while she was exiled out here at Raston, Mr Keating might be thinking up new and spectacular ways of disrupting Pymer's services. The only circumstance that made her life at all bearable was her father's promise to find her a riding horse to keep at the Red House, so she felt as if a siege had been lifted when the maid came into the tiny morning-room and announced that there was a man riding across the green leading two horses, and that he was likely to be coming to the Red House.

'It must be Pa!' she cried, and ran joyfully to the drawing-room to peer out of the window.

But she was disappointed, for the man on the middle horse of the three was not the familiar thick-set figure of her father. If it had been her cousin Oliver, or even one of the ostlers from the inn, she would not have minded so much, but to send *him* – whatever was Pa thinking of?

'Well, here's a pleasant surprise,' her aunt said, following her into the room. 'We don't often see your papa out here.'

'It's not Pa, it's that Mr Keating,' Stacey told her, her voice gruff with resentment.

111

'Is it indeed? Well, you run along and change, Stacey, and leave him to me.'

Stacey looked sharply at her, recognizing that tone of voice. For some reason, Mr Keating was on her aunt's list of Unacceptable Persons. It was quite likely that her aunt's dislike stemmed from something beyond Stacey's comprehension, but at the moment she cared little for causes. The effect was enough.

'Very well, Aunt Eustacia,' she agreed, and galloped upstairs to her room.

Once there, she took another look outside, this time to see what the horses were like. She was torn between dawdling to make Mr Keating wait and take the full force of her aunt's disapproval, and hurrying to try the animals out. The horses won. She scrambled into her wine-coloured riding habit in record time, pausing only to make sure that her hat was at the correct angle. Had she any skill at all in discerning what became her, she would have been pleased with the glimpse that she saw in the looking-glass. The tailored habit suited her far better than the closet full of flounced dresses she had ordered during her shopping forays in Norwich. The severely cut jacket and full skirt made her appear statuesque rather than just tall, the dark colour flattered her complexion, the saucy hat with its curled feather made it impossible to maintain a Miss Haveringshaw primness. But none of this made any impression on her. She was too concerned with choosing her new horse, and finding some way of setting Mr Keating down in the process.

In the drawing-room, her aunt was standing stiffly on the hearthrug, whilst Mr Keating, apparently blissfully unaware that in not being invited to sit down he was being snubbed, was making conversation. Neither betrayed relief at her arrival. Stacey suppressed a giggle, and in the moment it took to do so Mr Keating took the initiative and spoke first, presenting her father's apologies for not being there in person.

112

'He had to go out and see about a hay crop,' he explained. 'He knew you would understand. So as I was responsible for finding the beasts, he thought I had better bring them here for you to see.'

Put like that, Stacey could only agree to be reasonable. To do anything else was to show that she did not comprehend the importance of making a good deal over the supply of winter feed. So after an exchange of meaningless expressions of gratitude and pleasure, the whole party moved outside.

Here the groom, Hopkins, was holding the three animals in question. One, a neat brown cob, was evidently intended for his use. It was between the other two that Stacey had to make her choice. A cream-coloured mare and a dark bay gelding awaited her perusal, and well worth looking at they were, too. Only a lifetime spent watching her father complete hundreds of deals in horseflesh prevented her from expressing her wholehearted admiration. Restraining her natural enthusiasm, she copied her father's opening gambit when presented with a particularly inviting proposition and walked round the horses, giving them a cursory inspection.

'Hm,' she said, as if trying to think of something remotely good to say about them. 'Not bad, on the whole.'

It heralded the start of a lively round of bargaining, for Simon soon realized that here was a worthy opponent. They played an enjoyable game of bluff and counter-bluff, much to Aunt Eustacia's disapproval, for a good ten minutes before Stacey even consented to try each horse's paces. She decided, with pretended reluctance, that the gelding was the one she wanted, and they were about to settle down to the serious business of arriving at a price when they were interrupted by the arrival on the green of a shining blue curricle drawn by an attractive pair of matched greys. Stacey's attention was distracted by the impressive rig, but her aunt's predatory eye fell on its driver – Arthur Harris, top of her unwritten list of Eligible Gentlemen.

He drew up in front of the Red House, much to Aunt Eustacia's delight. But her satisfaction was short-lived, for it soon became clear that it was Mr Keating, not Stacey, he had stopped to see.

'My dear fellow, this is unexpected,' he said, after bidding them all good day. 'What are you doing in this part of the world? You're coming over to the Hall later, I hope?'

'Yes, I am, as it happens. I want to have a word with one of your grooms, a man by the name of Platt.'

Arthur looked vaguely puzzled.

'Platt? Would that be the new one? What do you want with him?'

'Oh, I just want to ask one or two questions.'

Stacey suppressed a cry of recognition as the name registered. The Thetford horsekeeper who had disappeared on the day of the Eclipse accident. A warning glance from Mr Keating told her what she already knew: that this was not to be spoken of in front of non-company members. He had already changed the subject, saying that he was engaged in selling Miss Brown a riding horse.

'When it comes to finding horses, you'll not meet anyone better at it than Keating,' Arthur Harris told Stacey. 'He has a positive genius for discovering just what one wants. Found my greys for me – do you like them? – my sisters all admire them excessively. They say they're much finer than the ones I had before.'

'They're very pretty,' Stacey said, with sincerity. She omitted to add that in her opinion they were too narrow across the chest and unlikely to stay for more than a few miles.

Aunt Eustacia, who had been itching to enter the conversation, praised them with such appalling lack of knowledge that Stacey unconsciously looked at Mr Keating, provider of these pasteboard paragons. He

114

caught her eye with a twinkle that told her he was well aware of the greys' deficiencies, abandoned the unfortunate Harris to Aunt Eustacia and re-opened negotiations on the dark bay gelding, Ballyfein.

'What do you think, Miss Brown? You've a capital Irish-bred hunter there, seven years old, top condition and jumps as cleverly as a cat. Shall we say two hundred guineas?'

Without a thought as to what her aunt might say, Stacey plunged gaily into battle.

'Two hundred? For that? Why, he's only half-broken and—' she looked at the horse's teeth '—scarcely five years old. He'll take a vast amount of work before he could even look at a hunting field without losing his head.'

And while her aunt desperately tried to distract the bemused Mr Harris's attention with minute enquiries into the health of his large family, Stacey cut the price down by fives and tens until Simon called her bluff and started changing saddles in order to ride the gelding back to the Crown. They finally settled on one hundred and sixty guineas. Stacey held out her hand, but to her consternation, Simon burst out laughing.

'Excellent! Capital! I hope you were listening carefully, Harris, you might have learnt something. You'll have to take Miss Brown along with you next time you buy a horse. She'll see you don't get sold a pup. That really was a first-rate performance, Miss Brown. Your father would have been proud of you. Mind you, he got me down to one-fifty, but then he's been at it a good deal got a bargain, even at one-sixty.'

It took several seconds for the meaning of this to sink in.

'You mean – are you saying that you and Pa have already agreed on a price?' Stacey spluttered. 'But—' For once, words failed her.

Even Mr Harris was moved to protest.

'I say, Keating, that was a trifle – I mean—'

'Well, perhaps it was a little unfair,' Simon admitted. He turned his most persuasive smile on Stacey, seeking to charm her into accepting an apology he had only half given. 'You did very well, you know. You would have got a bargain, even at one-sixty.'

Stacey knew this, but she was not going to be mollified. Her dignity was too badly wounded.

'You might have told me,' she protested.

'What, and spoil the fun? You must agree that you did enjoy yourself.'

She had enjoyed herself. It had been the best piece of entertainment she had had since arriving at the Red House. Stacey patted Ballyfein's neck.

'He's a good horse,' she admitted, and watched with reluctant admiration as Mr Keating extracted his friend from her aunt's clutches, bade them good day and rode off beside Harris's curricle on the cream-coloured mare.

Cheated of her prey, Aunt Eustacia dispatched Hopkins the groom to the stables and ordered her niece inside, her tone ominous. Stacey was obliged to sit through a lecture on the probable disastrous effects of her disgraceful performance, and the dreadful possibility of never making a decent match if that was the way in which she was going to behave. Stacey listened with all the appearance of humility, then escaped to try out her new acquisition.

Riding along the dusty summer lanes, Stacey put all thought of husband-hunting out of her mind. Let the Mr Harrises of the world be put off by a clever bit of dealing, it mattered not a straw. In Ballyfein she had found a challenge and a way to elude her aunt, and she meant to make the best of it. She even acknowledged that here was something she would not have time to do if she was tied to the Crown. Country life she found boring in practically every respect, but she could not deny that fields and open spaces were necessary for schooling a young horse. Six months' concentrated work on Ballyfein, and she would be able to sell him at maybe fifty guineas' profit, and then she could buy another young horse or perhaps two, and start on them. The idea rapidly took hold of her imagination. She saw herself running a successful business supplying all her aunt's list of eligibles with expensive mounts. Just as she had conjured up this happy picture, she arrived in the lane leading round part of the perimeter of the Upthorpe Hall estate. Plantations bordered the land, but beyond the trees lay open grass, and Stacey drew up at a gateway, tempted by the prospect of trying Ballyfein's speed. She had been introduced to the Harrises, she reasoned, and anyway, with a bit of luck they would not even know if she took a short gallop across the park. So she spent an absorbing ten minutes teaching the horse how to assist in opening gates, and rewarded him with a brisk canter down the track towards the park.

From the edge of the trees, the ground dipped to where a stream had been dammed to make a small lake, then rose again to the ugly yellow brick façade of the house. Ballyfein danced and snorted, eager to race down the gentle slope, but Stacey held him back, riveted by the scene unfolding itself before her. Two figures on horseback came hurtling towards the stream at full gallop, plunged across without a check in pace and turned to hare along the edge of the lake. From the quarter mile's distance, Stacey could not recognize the man in the lead but the pursuer, about fifty yards behind him, was clearly Mr Keating, his legs too long for the cream mare. At first she thought it was a race, and gleefully hoped that Mr Keating would lose, but as the man in front suddenly changed course and headed across the parkland towards the plantation she saw that he was not Mr Harris or any of his friends, but a groom from the Upthorpe stables. It was Platt, making his escape on one of the Harris hunters.

With a yell of excitement, she gave the prancing Ballyfein his head and joined in the pursuit, galloping to head him off before he reached another of the back

117

gateways. The wind snatched at her hat and crackled through her full skirts as the powerful horse ate up the ground. Platt's head jerked round as he found another rider coming for him, but seeing a woman and therefore no threat, held his course. With a surge of triumph, Stacey urged Ballyfein to greater efforts. She would catch him single-handed, before Mr Keating could reach them on the tiring mare. The gap between them closed, and she leaned forward, heedless of the warning cry behind her, of the vicious snarl on Platt's face as he saw what she was about.

'Clear off, lady,' he yelled at her, but Stacey only kicked Ballyfein on to cover the last few yards between them, gathering the reins in her right hand ready to catch at the other horse's bridle.

Too late she spied the hunting crop he carried, too late to do anything but fling up her free arm to ward off the blow. She yelped with pain as the thong hit her forearm and lashed her cheek and neck, and struggled to pull Ballyfein up, half blinded by tears of rage and pain.

'Swine!' she screamed at him.

But Platt had already wrenched his horse's head round and plunged into the woodland, crashing through the trees and heading for the track to the gate.

'Stacey!' Simon Keating had reached her now, his mare flecked with foam and panting like a bellows. 'Stacey, are you all right?'

'Yes, yes. Get him. Quick!'

Taking her at her word, he sped off in Platt's wake, crouched over the mare's neck as he weaved between the trees. Stacey brushed a sleeve over her eyes and followed. The young oaks and birches seemed to spring out at her as she threw her weight from one side to the other, steering the horse through the gaps. Her knee jarred against a trunk and branches reached down to sting her face. She gained the track in time to see Platt sailing over the gate into the lane. Simon steadied the mare, set spurs to her for the last two strides and practically lifted her bodily off the ground, but the height was too much for her. Her forelegs crashed into the top rail and she twisted sideways, throwing Simon off and landing heavily on her back. Stacey pulled up, afraid of landing on horse or rider if she tried to jump, leaped down and wrenched the gate open. Dodging the mare's flailing hooves, she dragged Ballyfein behind her to where Simon was getting to his feet.

'Good girl,' he panted, with a swift smile, and before Stacey could protest took the reins from her and mounted Ballyfein, awkwardly astride the side-saddle.

Stacey was left helplessly watching as he pounded off, a good way behind Platt now, but gaining with every stride. The narrow lane ran almost straight for nearly a hundred yards before disappearing round a bend, the plantation on one side and a thickset hedge on the other, too high to jump. Stacey turned to the sweating, trembling mare as she struggled up, thinking to get back in the chase, but the horse's near foreleg was swelling visibly. Stacey patted her drooping neck, then looked back up the lane and gave a yell of triumph, for round the bend came a huge farm waggon, drawn by two ponderous Shires, almost filling the road.

Platt dragged his horse back onto its haunches in an attempt to stop it charging into the waggon, Simon caught up with him whilst he was still off-balance, took a flying leap and knocked him clean out of the saddle. As the two men fell under the noses of the Shires, Stacey gathered up the hampering folds of her skirts and hared up the lane after them, stumbling in the deep ruts. The loose horses milled about in the confined space, obscuring her view, so that all she could see was a confused tangle of struggling men and trampling animals. With the breath rasping now in her lungs and a stitch in her side, she arrived in time to see Simon haul Platt up off the ground and knock him spinning into the carter's arms.

'Hold him!' he ordered, and the carter, a burly young man eager to break the monotony of his day, caught Platt in a well-muscled grip.

'Right.' Simon brushed the worst of the dirt off his coat, all the while regarding Platt with ominous intensity. Stacey caught the now quiet Ballyfein and leaned against his shoulder, suddenly nervous at the turn of events.

'Now, my reluctant friend, we shall resume our conversation,' Simon said. 'Tell me who put you up to it.'

Platt tried once more to get away from the carter, and failed.

'Dunno what you're talking about.'

'Then let me remind you. We already agreed that you were working at the Sun at Thetford last April. What we are talking about specifically is the murder of one Ned Shears, coachman of the Eclipse.'

Platt glowered at him from under his jutting brow.

'I never murdered no-one.'

Simon took a step forward. Platt flinched.

'Yes, you did, as surely as if you used that knife to stab him, instead of to cut the rein. You know it and I know it. Why else did you bolt from the Sun the moment the Eclipse left, and from me the moment you realized what I was after?'

Platt glared at him in sullen defiance.

'That don't prove nothing.'

'I can prove stealing a horse from Upthorpe and assaulting a young lady. How much were you paid for cutting that rein?'

'I tell you I don't know nothing.'

Platt's head jerked back as Simon's fist drove into the side of his face. Blood trickled from the corner of his mouth.

'You're in trouble whichever way you turn, you idiot. Tell me who put you up to it before I make you regret you ever saw a stagecoach.'

His pale eyes casting desperately for a way out, Platt drew breath as if to speak, then changed his mind. Hoofbeats sounded on the baked mud of the lane. Arthur Harris and two of the grooms were coming to find out what was happening.

'Tell me before they arrive or I'll see you hauled up before the beak for theft and assault, and then it will be Botany Bay for you at the very least.'

Platt's gaze flickered from Simon to the red weal on Stacey's cheek, and down the lane to the approaching riders.

'Clayton,' he blurted out. 'It was him, he made me. He said he'd get at my missus if I didn't—'

'And who is Clayton?'

'I dunno, honest. I only seen him once. He just sends messages. You got to do what he says, everyone knows that.'

Sickened, Stacey ran forward and caught at Simon's arm.

'He's telling the truth, can't you see? Let him alone.'

Simon looked at her for a moment as if he had forgotten her existence, then gave a slight shrug and considered the battered horsekeeper.

'You may well be right,' he agreed. 'It's this Clayton we have to find, though it will probably prove a difficult task. His sort are somewhat elusive, try to catch them and you come up against a wall of silence.' Then he switched his whole attention to her in a way that made her acutely conscious of her scratched, tousled appearance. 'You were splendid,' he said. 'Quite terrifying. I thought you were going to ride him down at one point. Did he hurt you with that crop?' He held her chin gently and examined the livid mark of the lash.

Stacey shied away like a half-schooled pony. 'Not much,' she muttered.

Arthur Harris arrived with his henchmen.

'I say, Keating,' he called. 'What the devil's going on?'

121

'Nothing of any importance,' Simon told him, with an easy smile. He nodded in Platt's direction. 'Take him away, he's of no use to me. Whether or not you want to keep him on after he's risked breaking the knees of a valuable hunter is your affair.'

'But—' Arthur looked from Platt, still in the grasp of the carter, to Simon, and finally to Stacey.

'Just a little misunderstanding,' Simon assured him. 'Miss Brown unfortunately happened to get caught up in it.' And seeing that Arthur was still on the point of asking awkward questions, he sought to divert his attention. 'I wonder if you would be so good as to accompany her home. She's less likely to get into a scrape with her aunt with you as an escort. I'm sure the two of you can think up some plausible reason for her appearance on the way.'

Arthur was left with no alternative but to comply, and Stacey, though she was loath to admit it, was forced to see that it was the wisest move. Not without misgivings, she left Simon to get what further information he could out of the wretched Platt.

At the end of each week at the Red House, Stacey was always longing for the respite of Saturday and the uncritical welcome of her family. But each time she went back to the Crown, she was conscious of a slight restraint in her relations' attitude. She was not at a loss as to know why: her Aunt Peg considered Barty's plans for her foolish, and wanted her to marry Oliver, and Harriet was downright jealous of what she thought was an idyllic life at Raston. Oliver, when she saw him, was clearly worried that her head was being turned from mixing with Aunt Eustacia's well-bred friends. She spent some time each week assuring them all of how bored she was and how utterly hopeless the young men she had met were, and in exchange caught up with all that had been going on at the Crown in her absence.

There was no getting away from the influence of Mr

Keating. Family opinion was sharply divided on him. Uncle Noll thought him a sharp young devil, just what his brother needed for the expanding business, and Harriet would hear no wrong of him, but Oliver considered him a bad example who was having an evil effect on the morals of company servants and Aunt Peg had her doubts about him.

'I wouldn't trust him further than I could throw him,' she declared. 'You don't want to be taken in by that smooth manner and gentry ways. He's naught but a jumped-up horsedealer with a gift for play-acting. And I'll tell you another thing, Keating's not his real name, either. There have been men in the yard a couple of times asking for a Mr Wynwood, and it turned out to be him they wanted. And only yesterday a right-on rough-looking cove came marching into my parlour – the best parlour, mind you, and full of respectable folk and regular customers – and demands to see a Mr Gregory Ward. "No-one here of that name," I told him, and I sent for a couple of porters to throw him out. Didn't want that sort in my best parlour. Then in strolls your Mr Keating, cool as you like, and lays claim to him. "Pray don't put yourself about, Mrs Brown," he says to me in that soapy way of his, "I'll deal with this." And if that don't look odd, I don't know what does. It beats me what your pa's up to, Stacey, keeping him on.'

'It beats me too,' Stacey agreed.

Towards the end of the month, though, it seemed as if she was a little nearer her goal of getting rid of him, for Barty took her into his confidence over the matter of the accounts.

'Would you mind looking over the books for me, chicken?' he asked, as they sat in the front parlour at All Saints Green waiting for dinner to be announced. 'I've an idea old Amos's eyesight is beginning to go. I don't want him to know that I'm looking over his shoulder, of course, so I thought I'd bring the books home for you to check over. If he really is getting past it, he'll have to go,

123

but I don't want him upset about it beforehand.'

Secretly delighted, Stacey could not help taking a small shot at her rival.

'I wonder you don't ask your general manager to do it,' she said.

Barty leaned forward and patted her knee.

'You're better at it than he is,' he told her, 'and we want to keep this in the family, don't we?'

Happy to have her talents appreciated, and even happier to keep a toe-hold in the running of the company, Stacey could scarcely contain a smile of triumph. She settled herself at the writing-desk and ran rapidly down the rows of figures, lips parted, tongue curled over her top teeth in concentration. She finished just as the maid put her head round the door and announced that dinner was served.

'That's all correct,' she said, closing the leather-bound ledger with a thud.

She took her father's arm and walked through into the dining-room with him, Barty liking to preserve the formalities that his wife had insisted upon. A steaming sirloin was brought in to crown a well-laden table. Barty started to carve whilst Stacey cut into the pigeon pie.

'They're not good, those figures, are they Pa?' she said. 'It's August now, and we should be running to capacity, and yet there are empty seats inside and out on practically every coach and the parcels are down on last year. If things are quiet now, at our busiest time, what are they going to be like in winter?'

'That's what bothers me,' Barty admitted. 'Fact is, there just ain't enough traffic for two large coach companies in this town. Last year, Pymer's were only running one London stage and a few slow coaches and they didn't poach on us too much, but now they've fast coaches on all our main routes and they're getting our custom.'

'But our coaches are faster and cleaner and more comfortable,' Stacey pointed out. 'You would think people would prefer to ride with us.'

'But we're not cheaper, and when you get down to it, that's what counts. Folks will put up with a bit of discomfort if it means they can travel for less, and that's what Pymer's are giving 'em - lower fares. They're undercutting us on every route now, and we're suffering for it.'

Stacey hesitated before stating the obvious, as she was certain her father had already thought of that. Instead she put it as a question.

'It's no good trying to undercut them in turn, I suppose?'

Barty cut a generous slice off the joint and dropped it onto her plate with a flourish.

'Tell me, chicken,' he said. 'What do you think Pymers'd do then?'

'Go lower still?'

'And what'd be the result of that?'

'We'd still be losing passengers and be making even less money into the bargain.'

Barty nodded, approving.

'That's it, so undercutting ain't the answer.'

'It's working on the Tantivy,' Stacey pointed out, always ready to advertise the success of her own ideas. The scheme she had proposed on the first day of her return had been put into action and now they were winning back the custom that had been lost to the New Tantivy.

'That's only one route,' Barty objected. 'We got all the others still running on the old fares to support it.'

Stacey helped him to a large portion of runner beans, fresh picked from the garden.

'So what do we do?' she demanded. 'Just sit here and watch them take over our business?'

'What we don't do is rush in blind,' Barty told her. 'You got to use your head first, lay the ground carefully. We got to work out just how long we can last out with only a slender profit, or even a loss. And more than that we want to know how long *they* can last out. That's the unknown quantity, and that's what our survival depends upon.'

'A spy,' said Stacey. 'That's what we need – a spy in their camp.'

Her father merely smiled and nodded, applying himself to his dinner. The wiry tufts of grey hair on the sides of his bald head quivered as if bristling at some private joke.

'Pa, you've got something up your sleeve.'

The faded blue eyes met hers steadily.

'Have I?'

'Come on, Pa, tell me. Have you found a spy? Who is it?'

But Barty only shook his head.

'The trouble with you is, you're too impatient, chicken. You want to know everything and say the first thing that comes into your head. You got to learn to wait, and watch, and listen, see? For all we know, Pymer's might already be in a shaky state from cutting the fares as much as they have. We just ride it out a few more weeks and see. Come the autumn, we'll hold a council of war and see what we come up with. Now then, what's all this about you going to some grand ball or other? You going to tell me about that?'

And Stacey found herself deflected into relating all the details of the dance to be held at Upthorpe Hall, the first affair of the kind that she had been invited to, and a minor triumph for Aunt Eustacia.

126

Chapter Seven

On a fine summer's morning, a hack chaise drew up at one of the back entrances of the Upthorpe Hall parkland, and a dishevelled passenger got down, defeat written in every line of his weary frame. With the very last of his borrowed money, he paid off the postboy and stood in the lane as the chaise rumbled off, trying to summon up the courage to walk in at the gates. Arthur Harris had come home.

For several minutes he leaned against the palings, trying to frame in his mind what he had been struggling with all through the night-long journey from London in the Mail: a plausible reason for being four thousand pounds in debt. Once again he came to the inevitable conclusion. It was all due to his own criminal stupidity. He would have to confess to the whole story, and beg his already hard-pressed father to pay up. The prospect terrified him. At length, the appearance of a couple of estate labourers set him in motion. Not wanting to be seen, he pushed open the gates and plodded through the plantation and across the parkland. Ahead of him, the ugly yellow facade of the hall looked out across the shallow slope towards the small artificial lake. Instead of heading for the dam at one end or the little Italianate bridge at the other, Arthur shambled into a group of trees growing picturesquely at the water's edge, and stood gazing into the dark depths.

The still, murky waters held him fascinated, tempting him with an easy alternative to facing the consequences of his mistakes. Just a few minutes of pain, of struggle and then – a lifetime's instruction taught him that then he would have to face a far greater judge and account for himself, but his mind veered away from that. Just blackness, and the sticky depths of the lake's bed. He could almost feel it closing around him, so real that he did not hear the thud of hoofbeats on the leafmould, the cracking of twigs, a cheerful voice bidding him good morning and chattering about the beauty of the day.

'Oh well,' the voice became hurt, offended, 'I'm sorry if I disturbed you, I'm sure. I'll take care not to ride over your land again, seeing as it's such a dreadful crime. I'll bid you good day.'

He jerked back into life.

'No,' he said, his voice oddly high-pitched, as if he had gone back ten years and it was breaking again, sliding out of his control. 'Stay. Please.'

He recognized her now. It was Miss Stacey Brown, on the dark bay horse she had bought from Keating. She looked at him a little oddly, but evidently decided not to comment on his crumpled, unshaven appearance.

'I expect it's as busy as an ant's nest indoors today, is it not?' she said. 'What with the ball and everything. Not that I've ever had anything to do with organizing one, but I should think there's a vast amount to be done on the day.'

'The ball?' he echoed.

The coming-out ball for his second sister. He had forgotten all about it.

'Oh my God,' he said. 'Is it today?'

'But of course. Surely you cannot have forgotten?'

She slid down off the horse and laid a hand fleetingly on his arm.

'Is there something wrong?'

'No, no—' he lied. When everything was so utterly and disastrously wrong, what else was there to do but deny it? 'No, nothing,' he said.

She gave him another odd look, but did not press him. Instead she chattered for a while, something about the horse, not waiting for any answers much to Arthur's relief. But at length she trailed off into silence.

'Well—' she said, looking about as if trying to think of

some way to extricate herself from the one-sided exchange.

Arthur found that he wanted her to stay. The quality of sympathy in her voice aroused a faint gleam of hope.

'If,' he began, 'if you—'

'Yes?'

'If you had done something very – stupid, who – what would you do?'

'I'd go and tell my pa.' Without hesitation.

'Even if it were something that would – disappoint him a great deal?'

'Oh yes, even then. I suppose I would feel dreadful, because the very last thing I would ever want to do is to disappoint him, but if I didn't – didn't go to him, I mean – then that would make it twice as bad. I mean, there would be whatever I'd done, *and* hiding it from him. That would hurt him more than the other thing, if he thought I couldn't confide in him. And he'd say, after I'd told him, he'd say, "Never mind, chicken, write it down to experience," and he'd do his best to put things right.'

Arthur had not thought of that, of his father being hurt by his not feeling able to confide in him. With the toe of his boot, he dislodged a pebble and sent it rolling into the water. As the ripples spread outwards, he turned the idea over in his tired mind.

'Yes,' he agreed at last. 'I think you're right.'

He looked across the water to where the hall stood basking in the sunshine.

'If you wish, I'll walk up to the house with you,' Miss Brown offered.

'No—' With a great effort, he pulled the muscles of his face into the semblance of a smile. 'It's very kind of you, but I must go by myself.'

'If you're really sure—?'

'Yes, really.'

'Then I must be going. My Aunt Eustacia will be anxious. She doesn't know I'm out alone like this.' She swung up onto the tall horse again, as nimbly as a boy.

'Goodbye, and – good luck.'

'Thank you,' Arthur said, and it sounded ridiculously inadequate. 'Thank you for – for everything.'

She smiled, a kind, friendly smile, turned the horse and trotted out of the copse, breaking into a canter across the turf of the parkland. Arthur watched her out of sight, then plodded the last few hundred yards up to the house.

And, as is often the way with ordeals, the anticipation turned out to be worse than the event. His father listened to his recital without comment, almost without expression, which was nerve-racking, but once he had started it was almost a relief to tell someone about it. Stumbling to begin with he related how he had first seen Fleur, in the corps de ballet at Covent Garden, how he had gone to every performance, just to catch sight of her again, and how a friend had taken him along to a party to which some of the dancers had been invited. He paused, remembering how overwhelmed he had felt just to be in the same room as her. He had hovered near her, dying to speak to her, too nervous to frame the words, until someone had rescued him and thrust them together with a casual word of introduction. The next part he glossed over, his dogged, devoted pursuit, the presents he sent, the promises he made, and all for the occasional reward of taking her for the odd ten-minute drive round the park or a half-hour's shopping expedition between other engagements.

Then came the day when she mentioned that she enjoyed racing. She loved the excitement of the horse-race, she said, she adored to gamble, especially when she knew the owner of a particular horse. Without stopping to think, he told her that he possessed a racehorse. At once she was interested, for the first time giving him all her attention. Intoxicated, he invented details. He invited her to come to Brighton with him for the next meeting. She accepted. He was the happiest man alive, until he realized that he now had to give substance to his tale. The days of frantic, fruitless searching and then miraculously a friend – he forebore to mention Keating by name – found him just what he wanted.

Brighton. The terrifying nights at the gaming clubs when if he did not lose, Fleur did, by the hundred. The late-afternoon promenades round the Steine, torn between pride at his beautiful partner and fear lest some other man might try to take her away. The ecstatic, delirious days in bed, far exceeding anything he had ever dreamed of. Five days in which he lived more fully than in the whole of the rest of his life put together. And then came the first day of the races. His horse, his strawberry roan, was to mend his failing fortunes. He borrowed from a money-lender, put the lot on the filly. If she had won, he would have made enough to finance Fleur for a year. But she lost. And he was back home with everything sold, even his clothes, and still four thousand pounds in debt.

There was a long minute's silence, then his father told him what he knew already, that agriculture was in a poor way these days, that the estate was already partially mortgaged, that there were eleven of his brothers and sisters to provide for. He was contrite. His sentence was pronounced.

'The only way to redeem your fortunes respectably, my boy, is to marry money. You will have to look about for a rich wife.'

Arthur was willing to do anything to atone.

'I don't think I know of any heiresses, though,' he said anxiously. 'Not in this neighbourhood. Perhaps in town—'

'Oh no.' His father was adamant on this point. 'No more junketing off to town. You've sown your wild oats, my boy. Now you're going to settle down. I'll tell you where you'll find money in these hard times – in trade. That's where the fortunes are.'

Arthur promised to do what he could, and was released. Avoiding the rest of the family, he crept up the back stairs, fell into bed and slept till the evening.

By the time Simon arrived at the ball, there was only an hour to go before supper. He was not expecting a particularly entertaining evening, but had put in an appearance because there was always the possibility of making the odd useful contact. He was received somewhat frostily by the Harrises and strolled into the two drawing-rooms that had been opened out to make a ballroom for the occasion. It was the usual sort of affair, he noted, as he ran an eye over the assembled guests and nodded to a few acquaintances. Indifferent music, hired chairs, ditto waiters, everyone beginning to wilt a little in the heat. Most of the older men and a fair number of the younger ones were in the card room, resulting in the usual surplus of women in the ballroom. Round the walls, growing steadily more uncomfortable, were the chaperons and the unchosen girls, envying the lucky ones on the floor who were circling to the lastest waltz tune.

He was surprised to see that Arthur Harris was there, until a few moments' observation told him that all had not gone well at Brighton. Arthur looked as if he had been through an emotional mangle, a state not improved by his present unenviable task as host of dancing with all the otherwise overlooked girls. Not much likelihood of any profitable deals in that quarter for a while.

Stacey Brown was there, he noticed, sitting with her dreadful aunt and most unsuitably dressed in a preposterous gown of pink and white adorned with rows of ruffles. On someone else, perhaps a petite girl with a simpering smile, it might have been pretty, but it made Stacey look like an animated bridecake. Behind the set smile, he could see that she was hating every minute, and with an unusual burst of philanthropy he decided to rescue her from obscurity.

Not that she seemed very grateful for being rescued.

'Thank you, I'm having a very nice time,' she said stiffly in answer to his enquiry.

'Is this the first affair of this kind that you've attended?'

'Yes.'

'And does it live up to your expectations?'

'Perfectly, I thank you.'

She was a good actress, he decided. She must have put that dress on in a flurry of excitement, hoping at least to dance the night away, if not to be swept off her feet by some eligible suitor.

'I hope I am not too late to claim you for a dance?'

'Oh – well – I don't think—'

Simon could see that the aunt was about to put her oar in.

'Come now,' he coaxed, turning his winning smile on Stacey, 'you're not still angry with me over Ballyfein, are you? How is he coming along?'

This had the desired effect of annoying the aunt and thawing Stacey. When he left them, having arranged to dance with Stacey after supper, he was amused to hear the aunt reproving her for agreeing to stand up with 'such a person' and Stacey replying with dignity that her pa would expect her to be civil to company servants. He was so taken with eavesdropping on the exchange that he did not notice a young man nearby staring fixedly at him, and was too late to avoid him when he jumped up with an exclamation of recognition and clasped Simon by the hand.

'Wynwood, my dear fellow! By Harry, it must be twelve years! Fancy seeing you again!'

Conscious of Stacey's curious ears but a few yards away, he looked steadily back at the unwelcome ghost from the past. He could not quite place the man.

'Sorry to disappoint you, but you must be mistaken,' he said easily.

'Oh come on, Wynwood, I'd know you anywhere. You remember me, surely? Talbot mi.? Harrow? What have you been doing with yourself since you tried to burn the place down?'

Talbot minor. Simon did remember him. An objectionable boy, always hanging on the fringes of his set.

'People change a good deal in twelve years,' he said.

'I'm a Rugby man myself. The name's Keating.'

He held out a hand, which Talbot took, confused.

'Keating. Yes. How d'you do? People do change of course, as you said. Changed a lot myself since I was fifteen.'

'Naturally. It's easy to make a mistake. Now, if you'll excuse me—?'

Without any appearance of undue haste, Simon made his escape and whiled away the time until supper by winning a few guineas at whist.

For Stacey, the ball had been a crushing disappointment so far. After the fun of choosing the dress and basking in her cousin Harriet's envy, she had expected great things, but instead she had sat with Aunt Eustacia almost the entire evening. Only Arthur Harris had danced with her, and he was so distracted by his own mysterious troubles that he was hardly the perfect partner. He had, though, thanked her for her help that morning, and said that things were not quite as bad as he had feared. She was more grateful to Simon Keating than she cared to admit. At least she would start off the second part of the evening with a partner. She greeted him with a sunny smile.

'And what's happened to cheer you up?' he asked, leading her onto the floor. 'Sold a dud for a hundred guineas?'

'One does not talk business in a ballroom,' Stacey informed him.

'Does one not? And who told you that, your Aunt Eustacia? Don't listen to a word of it. I've just met someone who wants to find a couple of good hunters. Should be a tidy spot of commission there for me if I can fill the bill.'

The dance was a waltz, which disconcerted Stacey. She felt she wanted to keep Simon Keating very much at arm's length. And besides, dancing in a proper ballroom was quite a different matter from practising with the girls at Miss Haveringshaw's or capering around with her cousins. She need not have worried, though. Simon was easy to follow and let her concentrate on her steps without distracting her with one of his double-edged remarks.

'You move very well,' he said, after a while.

'So do you,' she replied, not wanting to be patronized.

'If you answer all your partners like that, my girl, you'll never catch a husband,' Simon retorted in admirable imitation of Aunt Eustacia.

'I'm not out to catch anyone,' Stacey snapped. 'I would not do anything so vulgar.'

'Well spoken, Miss Stacey.'

'Miss Brown to you.'

'My profound apologies. I was merely making use of a privilege I thought extended to all company servants. Can it be, can it possibly be, Miss Brown, that I am now accepted as an equal?'

'Only here,' Stacey stipulated, 'seeing as all these people accept you as such, however misguidedly.'

'These people.' Simon swept the room with a contemptuous eye. 'Petty gentry, a field of contented cows. I wonder at your wanting to join them. You no more belong here than I do.'

Stacey looked at him in some surprise.

'You always seem to belong everywhere.'

'Oh, I fit in everywhere. I belong nowhere. We ought to start a combination, you and I, the United Brotherhood of Misfits against the Forces of Respectability.'

Annoyed at himself for having let an unguarded thought slip out, he silenced her by executing a complicated series of steps. Her face stiff with concentration, Stacey managed to follow without falling over his feet.

'If you really want to succeed, though, you'll have to do something about your dress,' he told her. 'I'm surprised at you, letting your aunt overrule you in such an important matter.'

Stacey flushed angrily.

'Overrule?' she repeated.

'Why, yes, it's patently obvious. That is the provincial matron's idea of what a girl's first ballgown should look like. You, of course, would have chosen quite differently. You would not have been seen dead in pink and white, since green or russet suits you so much better, and you certainly would not order a thing covered with flounces. Elegance rather than prettiness is what you would aim at. But then, your Aunt Eustacia must be formidable opposition.'

Infuriated, Stacey forgot what she was doing and trod on his toes.

'You are the arbiter of taste round here, I take it?' she blazed. 'The Brummel of Upthorpe Hall?'

Sarcasm rolled unnoticed off Simon's back. He was wondering if there was any truth in the old saying that a woman with a gap between her front teeth had a passionate nature. And if so, who was going to get the benefit of it? An empty-headed squireling in need of a fortune, or Bible-bound Cousin Oliver?

'But naturally,' he said. 'Can you not see that my coat is the best cut in the room? And for what it's worth, my taste in partners is fairly well attended to. One dance with me and they'll all be asking for the pleasure.'

Stacey could hardly keep her voice from rising.

'You are unbearably conceited.'

'On the contrary, I'm amazingly considerate. I'm saving you the effort of having to like me.'

When at last the conclusion of the dance released her, Stacey did not know whether to be pleased or annoyed that Simon's prophecy came true. She actually had more prospective partners than she could fit in. One of them was Mr Talbot, who questioned her closely about Simon Keating. Stacey gave away nothing but the bare facts of his working for Brown's Coaches. Infuriating he might be, but Mr Keating was part of the Brown organization, and as such was entitled to protection from inquisitive strangers. Or so she reasoned to herself.

With the many events of the day spinning round in her

head, it took a long time for Stacey to get to sleep that night, tired though she was. Longer still for Arthur Harris. Simon, adept from long practice at shaking off guilt, worry and useless speculation, slept soundly with a protective arm around a delighted chambermaid.

Chapter Eight

'Burgiss! *Burg*iss! Are you listening?'

Amos Burgess shivered in the cold of the autumn morning, his bony legs protruding from his flannel nightshirt, feeling for his slippers.

'Yes, my dear.'

Oh Lord, strike her dumb. Just for ten minutes, Lord, until I leave.

'Burgiss, them curtains is in a terrible state. All holes. They won't last the winter, that they won't, and I've got Mrs Vennor coming to drink tea next week. *They* don't have holes in their curtains. Oh no, not the Vennors. But then he's got a good post, has Vennor. He's got the sense to ask for a living wage. Not like some I could name.'

Gasping as the cold water hit his face, Amos washed in a perfunctory manner. He always shaved before going to bed, to cut down the time in which his wife could attack him in the morning. Today she was in a particularly virulent humour, finding a new theme to her continual complaint that her husband was a shiftless, weak, stupid, craven creature wished on her by an unkind fate. She had long ago forgotten the single-minded tenacity with which she, a plain and prospectless spinster of twenty-nine, had pursued him when he seemed to be her last chance of matrimony. She had forgotten that within six weeks of the wedding. Amos tried, as he tried every morning, to deafen his ears to her voice. Pulling on his clothes with fumbling haste – his rheumatism was troubling him now that the weather had turned – he set his mind on the day ahead. But her voice pervaded his every thought.

'. . . were a proper man, you'd see I was housed in a manner to what I was accustomed. No living like a pig in rooms above a haberdasher's, with holes in my parlour curtains . . .'

A pig, yes. She looked like a pig, with her fat bloated face and her snout of a nose, red and damp. She sounded like a pig, squealing, squealing. Oh Lord, let her have an apoplexy and die. Let her die slowly, Lord, so she knows I have her at my mercy. It would only be justice, after all these years.

Making for the door, he tripped over the cat, which yowled and scratched his leg. His wife lumbered out of bed, screeching at him for a clumsy oaf, scooped the creature into her arms and murmured sweet baby-talk to it. Amos made his escape.

It was a bad beginning to a bad day. Travellers argued over fares, two of the waybills did not tally with their takings, he found a corn chandler's bill that had unaccountably been overlooked, and Mr Brown was out all day, leaving Mr Keating in charge. Whenever this happened, Amos waited with irrational hope for something to go wrong, something for which only Mr Keating would be to blame. But as usual, he was disappointed. Worse, Mr Keating strolled in just as one inside passenger was becoming really abusive and smoothed over the trouble in half a minute with his charm and easy authority. Amos seethed with impotent fury. The injustice of life closed in on him from all sides, and there was nothing he could do to combat it. He bullied the junior clerks unmercifully, but found no pleasure in it. Not while the intruder was sitting in the inner office with his boots on the desk.

The last coach had come in and Mr Keating gone by the time Mr Brown returned. Amos was lingering, tidying an already precise desk, delaying the moment of departure.

'Ah, Amos. Still here? You'll work yourself into an early grave one of these days.'

Mr Brown was as friendly and jovial as ever, but Amos, knowing him of old, sensed that there was something brewing.

'Now off you go home,' Mr Brown insisted. 'What'd I do if you went down with an illness through tiring yourself out, eh? Company'd fall apart without you.'

Amos let himself be persuaded. In all the years he had worked for Brown's, he had never let slip a word about his private life. Outside in the yard, a closed carriage was waiting, such a common sight that Amos hobbled straight past it, but he had hardly gone ten yards before he heard something that stopped him in his tracks.

'Hey, Jemmy!' Mr Brown was calling one of the stableboys. 'Run along up to Mr Keating's rooms, lad, and see if he's there. If he is, ask if he'd please to come down to the office.'

Hidden from his master by the carriage, Amos was rooted by envy and fear. So something was afoot, something so secret that Mr Brown sent him off home before setting about it. Sent him, Amos Burgess, his oldest servant, home, and asked for Mr Keating. It confirmed everything that he had been most afraid of these last few months. The carriage door opened. In a low voice, Mr Brown asked whoever was inside if he'd be pleased to step down now. Without conscious thought, Amos moved as stealthily as his aching bones would allow to where he could lurk in the shadows and see who the newcomer was. And what he saw, with the aid of his new spectacles, gave him a further shock, for it was Mr John Hendry of Hendry's Bank, the man who had dismissed him from his post in the counting-house all those years ago. Confronted with the ghost of his desperation at that time, together with the threat to his present security, Amos was jolted right out of his usual pattern of behaviour. Instead of turning a blind eye and a deaf ear to what was obviously not meant to concern him and going home, he stayed hidden in the shadows, intent on finding out all he could about what was going on.

A few minutes later Mr Keating appeared, which surprised Amos somewhat as he had always imagined him going out of an evening after work. All three men went inside and the key turned in the outer door. The shutters had been closed in the inner office, and only a thin crack of light between them betrayed the fact that someone was inside at this late hour. Amos looked about him. The yard was fairly quiet, just a group of men with good dinners inside them parting with laughter and a private carriage disgorging its passengers, attended by the indefatigable Mr Noll Brown. Trembling with fear and guilt at what he was doing, Amos drew his own set of keys out of his pocket and slowly, stealthily, turned the lock and eased open the door. Inside, luck was with him, for the inner door had been left slightly ajar. The murmur of voices fell softly into his receptive ear.

'. . . ordinary journey, nobody will have cause to suspect.'

'But supposing news of this leaks out, what of the danger to our passengers?'

'It will not leak out, gentlemen. Besides myself, only my two senior partners know of this plan, and now you two gentlemen. It is not in the interests of any of us to let fall a word of what is said tonight.'

'Might I ask why this charade is necessary?' Mr Keating was speaking. 'Surely the bank has methods of its own for moving coin from one branch to another?'

'Certainly, sir, certainly. But these are lawless times. Twice our guarded vehicles have been attacked, and in broad daylight. This time we have a mind to catch the felons, but to do so we will use our own waggon as a decoy, whilst the coin travels in one of your coaches.'

As Amos listened, the plan unfolded. Surplus gold and notes from the Cromer branch, which did little business during the winter months, was to be moved in to the head office. He took in all the details, filing them into his orderly mind, but all the time it was the first remarks that occupied his imagination. Only five men were party to the arrangement, three from the bank, Mr Brown and Mr Keating. And himself. Obviously the integrity of Mr Hendry and his partners went without saying. Mr Brown

141

too was above suspicion. So if – *if* – information were to get to the wrong ears, on whom would the blame fall? The idea danced like a fiend, tempting him.

There was a scraping of chairs in the other room. The meeting was coming to a close. Amos jerked into life, making all haste through the outer door, locking it as the three men exchanged handshakes and expressions of mutual confidence. This time he did not stay to spy on them, but hurried across the yard and out into Crown Lane. There, instead of taking his usual route home, he set off in the direction of the market. He had the means to engineer the downfall of Mr Keating, and the feeling of power that the knowledge gave him carried him along.

A while ago, back in the early summer, a seedy, wizened man with a face as crafty as a stoat's had fallen in with him on his solitary homeward journey. He had tried, very cleverly as if in passing casual interest, to elicit information about Brown's financial state, but had found Amos unforthcoming. Undeterred, he hinted that if Amos ever did want to pass on anything of importance, he might be found at one of several taverns in the city. He also made it clear that it would be to Amos's advantage if he were to do so. The thought of the reward meant little to Amos. What mattered was disgracing Mr Keating, the one overriding credit against which a number of debits were set – the possibility of harm coming to the passengers of the Cromer coach, the dent in the company's good name, his own disloyalty, the danger of being found out. But none of these seemed as important as getting rid of Mr Keating.

In the taproom of the second of the list of taverns, he found the man he was seeking. His small greedy eyes lit up when he saw Amos, and he immediately made him welcome, ordering brandy and water.

'Well met, my friend. I didn't expect to see you again. It's taken you a nationly long time to think over my offer.'

Amos ran a dry tongue round his thin lips.

'When – when you spoke to me, you seemed uncommon interested in the money Br— my company was making,' he began.

The other man helped him on, encouraging him to sip his drink, reminding him of the reward to come. Piece by piece, Amos told of what he had overheard, not meaning to spill all of it, but succumbing to his contact's skilful hints and questions and suppositions.

'That's interesting, very interesting. I never thought you'd come up with something like this.' The man dug into his pockets and slid a small pile of coins into Amos's hand under the cover of the table. 'Keep it up, my friend, and there'll be more golden guineas like those 'uns. Once you've started, you'll be surprised how easy it is. Just a few words and clink! rhino in yer pocket. Simple as kiss yer hand.'

And then it was done. Amos stood outside the tavern, shaking. There was no unsaying it now. In a daze, he hobbled home, and it was only as he mounted the stairs that a hitherto unthought-of aspect of his treachery revealed itself. He cut through his wife's welcoming complaints with a contempt she had never before heard him use.

'Here,' he said, clapping the five guineas on the table. 'Buy your tarnation curtains.'

'I've got my doubts about this business of Hendry's,' Simon said, the day before the plan was due to be put into effect.

He and Barty were watching the departure of the Cromer Retaliator, which in winter went out one day and back the next.

'Cold feet? You? You're getting old before your time, bor. What can possibly go wrong?'

'I don't know. I just don't like the idea of all that money rolling along the turnpike unguarded in the boot of the Retaliator.'

'Put it out of your head, laddie. No-one knows it's going to be there 'cept us and Hendry's partners. There's no danger.'

143

'You're right, of course, but all the same—' Simon frowned thoughtfully after the stage as it rumbled out under the archway '—with your permission, I'd like to ride out to Cromer later today and come back on tomorrow's Retaliator. We can say I'm going after some horses.'

'If it makes you feel easy,' Barty agreed 'Mind, if it was Newmarket, I'd think you were up to something, but you can't come to much harm in Cromer at this time o' year.'

Against his better judgement, Simon rose to it.

'Why Newmarket?'

But Barty just gave a knowing grin.

'Can't keep nought to yourself round here, bor, not even where you set off to of a Sunday.'

The remark nagged at him, on and off, all the way to the coast, however often he told himself that he covered his tracks far too carefully for anyone to find out anything. The next morning, though, he had other things to distract him. He saw the decoy set off from Hendry's Bank, then strolled into the Swan Inn just in time to witness a diffident, quietly-dressed gentleman consign what looked like a sea-chest to the care of the Retaliator's guard. The coachman and guard welcomed him. Yes, of course there was a seat for him, though not much choice. They were running pretty full today, with all the insides taken.

Bowling along the Norwich road in the sunshine of a crisp early autumn morning, Simon surveyed the outsiders, anxious behind an impassive expression. Two portly matrons, and old man, three schoolboys yelling with the excitement of the journey, a girl of about eighteen – not at all attractive, with a white, pinched face and the eyes of a scared rabbit – all of them liabilities should trouble occur. Looking at the quiet golden countryside spread out beneath the high blue of the East Anglian sky, it was difficult to imagine the Retaliator being attacked by armed robbers. The day of the highwayman was long gone, the hazards of the road now being far less romantic

– accidents, breakdowns and reckless drivers out for a race. But all the same, Simon reflected, two thousand pounds in coin and notes was a temptation, should anyone know of it. Someone at Hendry's for instance, with long ears and a grudge. Simon checked with the guard that his blunderbuss, standard issue to all Brown's coaches, was loaded and ready to hand.

'You expecting owd Dick Turpin?' The guard had not used the gun in all the years he had travelled on the Retaliator.

'That's right, he'll be dropping by on his way to York, ready to pick the diamond rings off this lot,' Simon grinned. But his hand strayed to the hard outline of the pistol in his pocket.

The journey followed its usual course, passengers got on and off, parcels were delivered, pikers argued over the tolls. At Aylesham, they changed horses and took a quarter of an hour's break. The Retaliator out of season had no pretensions of being a fast coach. When they set off again from Norwich, the six inside seats were full, and of the original outsiders only the boys and the whey-faced girl remained. An unshaven man with a grim set to his mouth took the place beside her opposite the guard, and in front there was a new passenger in the prime seat beside the coachman, a man in his thirties as far as Simon could judge, broad across the shoulders.

He began to relax, discussing prizefights with the guard, who had seen all the great pugilists and was a keen follower of the fancy. Suspicion had become a habit with him, Simon realized, seeing plot and counter-plot where none existed. And he decided to let Deborah Pymer wait in vain for him this afternoon. That was an intrigue he could well do without, and the sooner it bore fruit and could be dispensed with the better. He had had misgivings about it from the start, preferring to keep his affairs as a welcome respite from living off his wits, but he had let Barty convince him of the necessity of recruiting a spy in Pymer's camp. Now that he knew Deborah, though, he doubted if she was going to prove very much use. She passed on some gossip and a great many complaints, but she probably did not know a ledger from a songsheet, let alone was able to read one.

'. . .and he went down in the twentieth round,' the guard was saying, 'you never— Hellfire! What the devil—?'

The coach swerved off the turnpike and plunged up a muddy track into a sheltering patch of woodland. The girl screamed and in front the schoolboys yelled with excitement.

'A gun, he's got a gun!' one of them shrilled.

The unshaven man's face broke into a glittering grin.

'Don't move cully,' he snarled, pointing a pistol at the guard. 'Jest sit nice and still till I gives the word. And you—'

Before he had time to finish his threat, Simon sprang, catching his right wrist and forcing it up and back. The gun fired, ripping harmlessly through the autumn branches, and the two men swayed on the lurching, dipping roof of the coach, each seeking to throw the other off. The guard lunged forward to help, but at that moment the coach jolted to a halt and he cannoned into Simon, pitching him and the robber over the side. Down they fell, turning in flight, and landed with a force that knocked the breath out of Simon's body and sent him rolling helplessly till he fetched up against a tree. Gasping, he struggled to his feet and found his opponent already making for him, dazed and swaying still from the fall. Simon started forward, hit him in the stomach, caught a feeble return blow on the shoulder and finished him off with a hook to the jaw, watching with satisfaction as the man's head jerked back and he collapsed.

For a moment he stood looking down at him, lungs rasping, till the commotion behind reminded him of the Retaliator's predicament. Half turning, he saw that a barrier of branches blocked the track, the boxseat passenger was holding a pistol to the coachman's head and

146

the guard had his blunderbuss at the ready but was unable to use it with the boys blocking his line of fire. A cart had pulled out of the woods and stopped behind the coach – too late he realized that the driver of the cart was nearly upon him and spun round to find himself looking down the mouths of two horse pistols.

'Very clever,' growled the third member of the gang, 'but not clever enough.' He motioned with one of the guns. 'Get over there by the coach, and don't try any more tricks.'

'Hey, you there!' A head leaned out of the Retaliator's window. 'What the devil's going on?'

The man's attention was momentarily distracted. Over his shoulder, Simon saw the guard taking aim and dived for cover. There was an explosion of sound as the blunderbuss fired, the girl on the coach screamed, the thief bellowed and cursed with pain. Pellets splattered into the ground about Simon, grazing his shoulder, scorching his leg. He rose to his feet once more and caught the peppered thief, still twitching and swearing, in an armlock.

'Call off your watchdog,' he ordered, but the man only groaned. 'You!' he shouted up to the boxseat passenger, 'throw that gun down while you've got the chance. You're outnumbered.' He jerked his prisoner's arm further up his back. 'Tell him, before I pull your arm out of joint.'

The man squealed with pain. 'All right, all right,' he gasped. 'Just lay off, for Christ's sake. Smithy! Leave it.'

But the man Smith was not giving up his advantage.

'Shut your row, Bennet, I ain't finished yet. And all the rest of you, one foot out of line and the coachy's brains get blown to kingdom come. Get it?'

He looked round to see if everyone was sufficiently cowed, and as he did so the coachman slashed his whip across his face. Smith's hand jerked, the pistol fired and the coachman's hat spun into the air. The guard scrambled across the roof to the front of the coach and between them, he and the coachman subdued the struggling Smith, assisted by the eager schoolboys.

'Well done!' Simon shouted. 'Have you any rope on board to tie 'em up?'

He tightened his grip on Bennet once more.

'Now you, tell me who gave you the tip-off. Don't tell me you went to all this trouble just to play at highwaymen. How did you find out?'

'Don't know, master, honest,' the man protested, then gave a yelp of pain as his arm was forced a further inch up his back. 'For Christ's sake! All right – it was Clayton, he told us.'

Clayton again. So the cut rein had not been just an isolated incident.

'Where can I find him?' Simon demanded.

'Don't know – you just get a message – and go and meet him where he says—'

Nothing Simon could say or do could prise any more information out of the would-be thieves. Whoever the mysterious Clayton was, they were far too frightened of the consequences to give even the sketchiest of clues.

By the time the thieves were securely bound, the cart moved and the Retaliator turned round and driven back onto the turnpike, they were over an hour behind their timetable. Lengthy statements to the nearest constable took an interminable time. So when they finally rolled into the yard of the Crown, it was mid-afternoon and Barty was beginning to get worried. One look at the condition of his employees told him that Simon's premonition had proved correct.

'Can't you keep your nose out of a fight, bor?' he asked Simon as he climbed painfully down and limped over to join him.

'It must be something about this place. I no sooner recover from one set of bruises than I collect another. This time I've picked up a couple of pellets from one of your own blunderbusses.'

Apologies were made to the delayed passengers, and a

message sent by Hendry's porters that Mr Brown would be coming to see Mr John Hendry within the hour.

In the office, Barty listened to the story, commended the parts played by the coachman and guard, and promised to get them a reward from Hendry's. After they had gone, Simon told him about Clayton. Barty looked grave.

'I hoped we'd had the last of him,' he said. 'Everyone's heard of him, but no-one knows just who he is or where to find him. Up till now he's mostly been mixed up with gaming clubs and suchlike. Respectable businesses like ours didn't interest him. How the devil did he get to hear of this?'

'It can't have been from our end,' Simon insisted. 'There was nobody in the office and hardly anyone in the yard at the time.'

Barty agreed.

'Must have been spilt at Hendry's. I'll have a word or two to say to them about this. Putting my company's reputation at risk. It's the last time I do his dirty work for him, I can tell you.'

For Simon, limping off to find a surgeon, it seemed poor consolation. Clayton replaced Job Watkins, Will Page and Henshaw as the man he would most like to get his hands on. He did not notice Amos Burgess's expression as he made his way out of the office.

The three floors of Mrs Letitia Mullins's dressmaking establishment each had an entirely different function, and were furnished accordingly. The ground floor was the public area. Letting onto the street was the shop itself, prettily decorated in pink and white with stiff little gilt chairs and framed fashion plates. Displays of scarves, ribbons and artificial flowers were dotted tastefully about to tempt extra shillings out of the purses of waiting customers. Behind the shop were the fitting rooms, also in pink and white with pier glasses, imitation French sofas, screens and tables scattered with the latest periodi-

149

cals. Here ladies with nothing better to do with their time might while away a pleasant hour or two, or even a whole morning, discussing fashions, having their gowns fitted, gossiping with friends and sipping cups of tea or coffee that Mrs Mullins thoughtfully provided. Few of her clients ever saw beyond these rooms.

Certainly none of them ever penetrated the top floor, where the seamstresses and apprentices laboured all the hours of daylight and often far into the night, stitching and restitching the hems and seams, tucks and flounces, until their fingers and backs and eyes ached. The workrooms were stark and comfortless, the walls whitewashed and windows uncurtained to let in the maximum amount of light, the floors bare for easy sweeping. In the winter the rooms were cold and in the summer, despite open casements, stuffy and stinking of the street.

But some respectable ladies who patronized the establishmant did get as far as the first floor. This was where Deborah Pymer was waiting. She fidgeted about the red and gold room, fiddling with candlesticks and brushes, twitching aside the curtains to peep out, peering at herself in the ornate gilt-framed looking-glasses. Was it something about her face, she wondered. Did he not find her pretty any more? Was it something she had said? Why, why had he not appeared last week? The past seven days had been the longest in her life. The creeping horror of last Wednesday's wait in this room remained with her, the gradual changing of joyful anticipation through impatience and anxiety to dismay, despair, self-doubt. In the intervening days, she looked in vain for a message from him, wrote and tore up a dozen letters, told herself there must have been some pressing reason, vowed she would not go back to be humiliated again. But come back she did, for she was unable to keep away. And already he was ten minutes late.

Footsteps on the stairs, his footsteps. Heart racing, Deborah whirled round to face the door. He stepped inside, slender, strong, smiling. Deborah flung herself into his arms.

'You've come! Oh my darling, I thought – after last week – it was dreadful—'

Seven days' accumulated agonies broke into a storm of tears, punctuated with questions and reproaches. He waited till she had subsided into sobs and sniffs.

'There's a fine welcome for me. All this fuss over one lost afternoon. You must learn to trust me, my love. Did you really think I would leave you without a word?'

His persuasive voice, gentle, cultured. It sent shivers of delight through her.

'No, no, course not, it's just that I love you so—' She believed what she wanted to believe.

'How much?'

'More than anything in the world, more than my life!'

'I wonder—' he mused, hands feeding fires hungry from a fortnight's fasting, 'just how much that is worth?'

She did not even begin to understand him. All she knew was that she burned for him with a need that blotted all thought. With only Seth's lovemaking to compare with, rough and selfish and swiftly over, that first afternoon in the close-shuttered room had been a revelation to her. Simon could take her soaring to peaks of delight she had never known existed, catch her as she drifted downward and show her another way, more tantalizing still . . . and now she had tasted such joy it was like a drug, she could not exist without it.

'I wonder—?' he said again later, half to himself, looking at the lax curves of her satiated body.

She stirred and the pale blue eyes opened, cloudy with love.

'That makes up for everything,' she whispered, certain of him once more. 'What was it that kept you last week?'

'Playing dangerous games, sweetheart, on the Cromer road. Surely you heard about it?'

'Oh – yes—' she cast about in her mind for what Seth had been so cross-grained over. 'There was a robbery, was that it?' She gasped as sudden fear caught her. 'Were

151

you there? Oh my darling, what happened? Were you hurt?'

'Nothing to signify.'

'Thank heaven for that. And to think that I believed you had forgotten me, when all the time you were in danger of your life! Can you ever forgive me? All I thought about it was that it put Seth in a foul temper.'

'It did? And why was that?'

'Oh, I don't know – ' She loved this time afterwards, when they lay talking about themselves. 'He thought it might harm Brown's. He said Hendry would come down on Barty Brown like a ton of bricks. But when the thieves were caught, he was put about something terrible. Been snapping at me all week, he has.'

He ladled out the sympathy she was expecting, then just as an afterthought asked, 'So he knew about it beforehand, did he?'

'No – I mean, how could he?'

'That's just what I'd like to know. When did he first mention it?'

'Lord, I don't know – the days get all muddled – I don't listen to half he says anyway.' Her face took on a peculiarly blank look.

'Try to think,' Simon coaxed. The fact that Hendry's were accusing Brown's of the slip in security was no news to him. Barty had found that out on the day of the robbery. But he could not see where Pymer came into it.

'Wednesday,' Deborah said suddenly. 'I remember Wednesday because – well, you know, I was going to see you in the afternoon. And he was in a very good mood in the morning.'

He fell to caressing her pale body, praising her till she purred like a contented cat. Absently, he asked, 'Has he been holding secret meetings with anyone lately? Or mentioned any names you haven't heard before?'

'No – oh, I don't know. I don't remember.' Deborah was tiring of the subject. She only liked discussing Seth if she was complaining and Simon sympathizing.

'Perhaps in future you could try to listen. Find out, ask

152

questions.'

She felt the first stirrings of unease.

'I couldn't do that.'

Simon raised himself up on one elbow and lay looking down at her.

'It must have been a very long two hours, waiting here last week.'

She went cold as she found herself looking into eyes steel-hard and unyielding,

'It – it was – very—' she faltered, not taking his meaning.

He spelt it out for her.

'You wouldn't like it to happen again, would you?'

Dry-mouthed, she managed to whisper, 'No.'

'Good.' Smiling now, he kissed her fear-filled face. 'Then you'll find out what I want to know.'

Chapter Nine

For weeks, Arthur Harris dithered over the question of his future. The extra mortgage that had been raised on an already overburdened estate to pay off his debts hung heavily on his conscience, but a survey of all the marriageable girls of his acquaintance resulted in only one who seemed to fit his father's description: Stacey Brown. He had not forgotten her kindness and ready sympathy on that black day of his return home, but somehow she just did not conform to his vague idea of a perfect wife. Though he did not admit it even to himself, the turmoil of the summer had left him drained, wanting only to lead a quiet life, which would be unlikely with Stacey. He persuaded himself that it was her large and vulgar family that daunted him, together with an uncertainty as to the extent of her fortune, and it was on these points that he finally got round to consulting Simon Keating.

Simon found himself in the unusual position of being able to influence events, but unsure which way he wanted them to fall.

'Sorry, old fellow,' he said, 'matchmaking's not my line of country. But Miss Stacey would straighten out your finances even if she came to you without a penny.'

Which left Arthur in just as much of a quandary as before.

Stacey was also in a painful state of indecision, though not over Arthur Harris. Despite her aunt's transports of delight, she saw right through his frequent visits to the Red House. She had never admired Arthur, and since hearing a rather garbled version of his disastrous affair, her opinion dropped still further. She felt sorry for him, but with the blindness of ignorance, failed to comprehend how anyone could behave so foolishly. Aunt Eustacia's

154

most strenuous attempts to persuade her of her luck failed utterly. Stacey replied that the Browns were anyone's equals, and continued to worry in private about her cousin Oliver and to work on her plans to halt the company's downward slide into bankruptcy. The two problems came to a head on the same day, for on the Saturday that they were due to map out the company's future, it was Oliver who came to collect her.

All ready and waiting at half-past eight, she came bounding out of the front door as Oliver pulled up by the gate in a neat caned whiskey drawn by a bay mare.

'Why Ollie, you look quite a dandy in this rig!' she exclaimed, climbing nimbly on board.

Oliver took the compliment with a non-committal grunt and set the horse trotting across the green as Stacey turned to wave goodbye to Aunt Eustacia.

'You ain't ashamed to be seen out driving with me, then?' he asked.

'Ollie, how can you ever think such a thing?' Stacey was horrified. She gave his arm an affectionate sqeeze. 'If the day ever dawns when I'm ashamed to be seen with one of my family, I deserve to be hung, drawn and quartered.' But even as she said it, she was aware of a flattening of her usual Saturday euphoria. Oliver always seemed to have a dampening effect on her, as if life was too serious to laugh about, and high spirits obscurely wrong.

'That's all right, then. Just so long as you're not getting too grand to visit us at the Crown.'

'Of course not, silly,' Stacey assured him. 'If I had my way, I'd be there all the time.'

'You could, if we was to get wed.'

It was muttered almost inaudibly, as if he hoped she would not hear, but they both knew she had heard, and the words hung between them in the damp autumn air.

'I - er—' Stacey groped around for the right response. 'You know what Pa's wishes are.'

'Aye, I thought a lot on that.' Oliver was staring

straight ahead at the mare's ears. 'And I wasn't going to speak, like, on account of it, only I do love you, you see—' Hopelessly inarticulate on the subject of his own feelings, he was quite unable to convey the strength of a devotion that had begun when they were children, grown with the years and withstood Stacey's exile at school and at the Red House and the advances of several sets of parents from the chapel in World's End Lane wanting a steady and godfearing husband for their daughters.

Stacey took refuge once more in her father's aspirations.

'But your pa 'ud be glad to have you back with us again, truth to tell, and besides,' sure of his ground now, Oliver burst into a flood of eloquence, 'you're needed, it's your duty. You and me together, Stacey, we could stand up against this evil that's spreading over the company. You might not see it, living out here most of the time, but I do. It's that Keating fellow, he's a bad influence. Ever since he arrived, everyone thinks it's clever to be like him, drinking and playing sly tricks and—' he took a swift sideways look at her '—womanizing. He has your father's confidence, and the company servants see that. And he draws attention to himself, like that business over Pymer's coachmen, and then that robbery. They admire him, they don't see him for what he is. But you and me together, we could fight it, we could be an example, and then your father would come to see what that Keating is doing to the company, and he'd get rid of him. Your father thinks the world of you, Stacey. If you were home, he'd soon listen to you instead of Keating.'

He had caught her on both her weak points, her wish to be back in the centre of things at the Crown, and her jealousy of Simon Keating's standing. The thought of remedying these was tempting, but the price was too high. She did not want to be squashed into the mould of Oliver's preconceptions.

She took a steadying breath.

'I'm sorry, Ollie,' she began, 'but—'

Finally they drove into the yard after what felt like an interminable journey. The unhappy atmosphere between them was obvious to Aunt Peg, watching from an upper window, and Barty waiting at the door of the office, and also to Simon Keating, coming through from the stables with a handful of chandlers' bills. It was the start of a difficult day for Stacey, for though her father backed her, she knew that the rest of the family took Oliver's side. She tried to avoid Aunt Peg and Harriet, going off instead to visit a second cousin who had just produced her first baby, and an ancient great-aunt who had to be spoken to very clearly and slowly. And all the time she was trying to make bright and cheerful conversation with these people, Oliver's words were going round and round her head. It was a relief, when she got back to All Saints Green in the late afternoon, to know that the evening would be spent in grappling with profit and loss, rather than people. Numbers had a comforting reliability. You had only to marshal them correctly and they fell neatly into place. With this thought, she scampered upstairs to change for dinner.

'There you are, chicken.'

She had just reached the landing when Barty emerged from his room looking squarer then ever in a waistcoat of startling red and white horizontal stripes.

'I was just wondering where you had got to,' he said. 'Don't forget we've a guest this evening.'

'A guest?' Stacey stopped short, staring at him. 'You didn't tell me that before. How can we hold a council of war with somebody else here?'

'It ain't any owd somebody else, chicken. If we're going to plan a campaign we must have all the senior officers present. That means Simon as well.'

'Him!' Stacey exploded. 'Hell fire! I meet with that man everywhere I go. I thought I might get away from him in my own home!'

She slammed into her room and began venting her unreasoning anger on her clothes, tearing them off and

157

flinging them on the floor.

'Men!' she growled, throwing down her dress, kicking off her shoes. Oliver, Arthur Harris, Simon Keating, she was sick of all of them. She plumped down on the bed and surveyed the mess, decided she could do without any of them, and began to change into a gown that was definitely not the provincial matron's idea of what a young girl should wear. Though hot irons would not have induced her to admit to being influenced by Simon Keating's words at the Upthorpe ball, she looked with some satisfaction at the reflection of the spring green dress with its low, square neck and trimming of narrow ribbon of a darker green. Nodding to herself, she skipped downstairs.

On the threshold of the parlour, she paused, puzzled by the silence. She had heard Simon Keating arrive, but it seemed that her father was not down yet. She would have to entertain their guest by herself until he made an appearance. And as she hesitated, she spied Simon through the open doorway. With his back to her, he was turning over the music on top of the piano. Then he opened the lid and stood for some moments looking at the keys before striking a tentative middle C. The single note sounded loud in the quiet room, and stirred Stacey into action.

'Good evening, Mr Keating,' she said, walking in as if she had just come down. 'I cannot think what is keeping my father. Do you play?'

Just for a second, she could have sworn he looked slightly embarrassed. And then it was gone, and instead there was the easy smile, the swift appraising glance, approving this time.

'Good evening to you, Miss Stacey. The fault is mine, I arrived rather early, so I deserve to have to amuse myself for a while. The instrument must be yours. You play, of course, being an accomplished young lady.'

'A little.'

He tutted in mock disapproval.

'The reticent maiden's stock reply. I expected better of you, Miss Stacey. Just for that I shall make the stock response, and ask you to be so kind as to perform.'

Unable to think of a way out, Stacey sat down on the piano stool, annoyed at being put at a disadvantage again. Aunt Eustacia insisted that she spent at least half an hour a day at the keyboard, but no amount of practice would ever turn her into a good musician. She forced a light-hearted smile.

'You choose,' she invited recklessly. 'I am entirely at your command.'

He chose, not one of the popular songs that her father enjoyed, but a piece of Mozart that was only just within her powers. Spurred on by his critical presence, she gave the best rendition she had ever managed, until she came to the place where her fingers always contrived to get muddled up.

'You might find it easier if you use a different fingering,' Simon said, leaning over her shoulder to demonstrate. 'Like this, and then you can place your thumb there, and reach for that chord, so.'

Stacey half turned to look at him.

'You can play!'

'I used to,' he admitted, 'but I'm lamentably out of practice.'

'That's a stock reply,' Stacey accused, leaping to the attack. She got up and leaned an elbow on the top of the piano, waiting for him to take her place.

'A point to you,' he conceded, smiling, and sat down.

She found that he had spoken no more than the truth. He stumbled frequently at first, often going back to repeat phrases that displeased him, but gradually he began to gain fluency. Stacey soon recognized a talent far superior to hers. He achieved what her music master was always trying to instil into her playing, without success; he put expression into the music.

'For somebody who is lamentably out of practice,' she said at last, 'that was quite beautiful.'

159

Simon ran over a few notes again.

'I was well taught,' he said, 'and I used to play a great deal at one time. It was a means of escape.'

'Escape? From what?'

Once again, Stacey caught that fleeting look of embarrassment, as if he had let fall something he had not meant to talk about.

'Oh – school, family, whatever happened to be plaguing me at the time.' He raced through a set of scales. 'Did you never want to get away?'

'Well, yes,' Stacey admitted. 'I always hid in the stables. Horses are not so demanding as people.'

'Quite,' Simon agreed. He reached up and shuffled through the heap of sheet music. 'Shall we try this?'

And when Barty finally came in, he found them performing a duet rather badly, wrangling over each other's mistakes.

During dinner, Stacey was unusually silent, trying to come to some conclusion about the man who had dropped so easily into the post of general manager. A bad influence, according to Ollie, a jumped-up horsetrader with a gift for play-acting in Aunt Peg's estimation. This, she decided, could not be true. The well-bred manner could have been learnt from careful observation, but not that standard of playing. Bad influence or not, he had revealed an unexpected facet to his character, and Stacey was interested in spite of herself.

Simon, aware of the curiosity in her veiled observation, wondered what it was about her that had twice now almost inveigled him into dropping his guard.

With the parlourmaid in and out of the room serving, conversation was general, but once she had removed the tablecloth and placed the decanters of port and brandy, the real business of the evening could begin. Stacey produced a notebook and pencil from her reticule and laid them neatly before her on the table. Barty took a swig of port and undid the bottom buttons of his flamboyant waistcoat.

'Now then,' he began, 'we all know why we're here tonight. There's only room in this city for one coaching company of any size, and that one has got to be Brown's. If we go on the way we been doing the last few months, we'll end up running a charity service, and I ain't working myself into an early grave for that. So far we been playing a waiting game to see if Pymer's'd collapse, but they ain't. Lord knows why not, they can't be making much profit, cutting fares like they're doing, so mebbe they're playing a waiting game too, to see if they can steal enough of our custom to run us off the road. ''Course—' he broke off with a chuckle '—I know why owd Seth Pymer's doing this. I cut him out once on a wench he fancied, years ago this was Stacey, before I met your ma, and he ain't never forgotten it. He's had it in for me ever since. Anyhow,' he resumed his chairman's stance, 'it seems to me we got two possibilities: we play it their way and undercut them until one of us goes under, or think up some other way of getting rid of 'em.' He thrust his hands into his coat pockets and looked from his daughter to his general manager and back again. 'Well?' he demanded. 'What d'ye think? Stacey – how d'ye see our financial state?'

Until then, Simon had considered Stacey's inclusion in the conference a mere formality, a sentimental move on Barty's part to have the company talisman present and to let her think she was being consulted. But as Stacey launched into her report, he realized that this was far from being the case. Her facility with figures ranged beyond the ability to add up a few columns of numbers. Neatly worked out in the blue-bound notebook were estimates of the profit or loss margins on every one of the routes at three possible levels of fares. Even though she was cut off from the company out at Raston, she managed to keep in touch with all that was going on and think ahead to what might happen in the next six months. The spoilt girl in the preposterous pink and white frock, inwardly glowering behind a fixed smile, was not the real Stacey at all. She belonged here, with Brown's. Not only belonged, but was very useful. Simon had to admit that neither he nor the Gaffer could have worked out all the projections with the same degree of accuracy. The only other person who could have done it was Amos Burgess, and he could not have worked unsupervised, for he did not have Stacey's imagination.

'. . . for the very lowest fares, we'd have to raise loans to support the loss,' Stacey said. 'It might well be worth it. Hendry's—'

'Hendry's won't advance us a penny,' Barty told her. 'They still think it was our fault the Retaliator was attacked. They insist that absolute secrecy was observed at their end, and that if it wasn't an accidental slip on our part it must have been deliberate. As if we'd put our coaches at risk!'

'Damned insult,' said Simon, 'especially considering it took the sawbones twenty minutes to pick the bits of lead out of me.'

'Nobody on this side of the fence is saying that you were double-dealing,' Barty told him. 'Hendry's can think what they like. But the upshot of it is, they won't be loaning us aught to keep our heads above water.'

'There are other banks,' Stacey pointed out.

'I don't want to run on borrowed money at this stage,' Barty insisted. 'Pymer's will fold before we do or I'm a Dutchman. Then we'll have the field to ourselves and no repayments and no interest charges round our necks.'

'If only we knew for certain,' Stacey said. 'If we could but recruit a spy, someone to take a look at their books.'

Barty gave her a knowing grin.

'Just you leave that one to us, chicken.'

'There is a point I want to raise on that subject,' Simon said. He looked thoughtfully from Stacey to Barty, not liking what he was about to reveal, and not knowing how they would take it. 'My informant,' he said slowly, 'tells me that there might well be a spy in *our* camp. Pymer seems to be working on more than just guesswork.'

162

'Impossible!' Stacey declared. 'Nobody at Brown's would betray us.'

But Barty's face was troubled.

'Has your informant any definite proof?'

'No names or figures, just an increase of confidence on Pymer's part.'

Barty frowned unseeing at his glass, mentally surveying his office staff.

'I picked both those lads myself,' he mused, 'and I'd've been ready to trust 'em with my life. But I might've been wrong. I'll have a word with Amos.'

'There is also the disturbing fact that Pymer seems to have known about the robbery beforehand,' Simon reminded him. 'He keeps some unsavoury company, and he probably heard about it from this Clayton character, who in turn got it from someone at Hendry's. But there is always the possibility that Hendry's were right and somebody here overheard us and passed on the information.'

'Coming from one who just said it was a damned insult, that sounds very odd,' Stacey commented.

Simon could see suspicion flickering in her eyes.

'I know,' he admitted. 'The whole business is beginning to take on a nasty smell.'

Stacey said nothing, but it occurred to her that no whiff of this gathering atmosphere of distrust was ever smelt about Brown's before he arrived.

'We'll get to the bottom of it soon enough, never fret,' Barty assured them. He refilled all three glasses and put the matter behind him. 'We got off the point. Let's have a close look at those fares of yours, Stacey.'

For the next half-hour they wrangled over which prices were best for each route and suggested ways of cutting costs. Barty let Stacey and Simon do most of the talking, merely putting in a word here and there when they could not agree, and in the end they worked out a strategy that pleased all three of them. They sat back, looking at the final schedule as it lay on the table between them, united by a sense of achievement.

'Right,' Barty said, 'that's the fares. Now for any other suggestions. Simon?'

Simon's first thoughts on dealing with the rival company had been coloured by his connections with the racing world. He recalled the time when he attempted to break up Henshaw's insidious organization, which was spreading corruption through the training stables at Newmarket. He had done it by employing the same tactics as the other side, but nearly six months with Brown's had shown him that sabotage and intimidation did not figure amongst Barty's methods. A more subtle approach was needed. Brown's was built on confidence, every employee from swaggering coachman to newly-joined stableboy being proud of belonging to the best coach company in the three counties. The aim, therefore, must be to convey this to their potential customers.

'What we have to do,' he said, 'is to convince people that Brown's is the only company they want to patronize. When they think of travel, they think of Brown's, the two being synonymous. We must convey our pride in the company to them, so they feel it is a privilege to ride with us, that to take a seat on Pymer's or anyone else's stages is only to be resorted to if there is no room left in one of ours. And not only here in Norwich. We must consider the towns we run to – Lynn, Cambridge, Yarmouth – they all have their local concerns, and they're all more than ready to compete with us, but not on the same scale. The further we spread, the better known our name will be.'

Stacey stopped doodling on the back of her notebook and attended with wide-eyed concentration, her imagination fired by the idea of a Brown's monopoly spreading outwards from Norwich. Now the idea had been planted, she saw that they might do more even than cover East Anglia. They could set up a base in London, and from there link with practically every city in the country. She listened to Simon's suggestions for improving their performance and undermining public confidence in Pymer's:

better and more convenient time-tables, informers to report on Pymer's transgressions of the laws governing stages, advertising.

'We could place an announcement in the *Mercury*,' she broke in. 'We could have a little picture of a coach and horses, and the times of all our services, then "Travel with Brown's for a safe and swift journey" or something to that effect.'

'Or, Brown's for speed and efficiency,' Simon suggested.

'Brown's is best.'

'Brown's first – the others nowhere.'

'A rhyme! We could have a rhyme. Something running like – er—

When you want to get from town to town,
Remember . . . .'

'Remember to travel with Barty Brown,' Simon laughed. 'That's capital, that's exactly what I was trying to think of. Something that will lodge in people's minds.'

They looked at Barty for approval. He shook his head, smothering a twinkle of amusement.

'No, no, it won't do. Makes us sound like a sideshow at a travelling fair. Might just as well shout "Roll up, roll up" in the streets. What folks want to see in the newspaper is a dignified and respectful announcement. You go putting something like "Brown's is best" and they'll smell a rat. Folks ain't that hulver-headed.'

Simon and Stacey exchanged looks of annoyance at having their scheme crushed.

'Very well,' Simon agreed, with reluctance. 'But you do approve of the other points I made?'

'The timetables and the informers? Aye, I got 'em written down. We'll set to work on them.' Barty linked his hands in front of him on the table. 'So far, so good. Anyone got aught else to add?'

Stacey drew breath to announce her pet idea, but Simon got in first.

'I suggest we start a new London service, via Ipswich.

There must be enough trade to warrant it. At present, people have to take the Herald to Ipswich and wait overnight to catch Shannon's or the Blue. The only direct way is by the Mail, which we all know is horsed this end by Pymer's. If we ran a really crack stage, we could beat the Mail and be cheaper into the bargain, and we would be offering three different ways of reaching London: the Telegraph through Newmarket and Bishop's Stortford, the Albion through Bury and Chelmsford, and the new one through Ipswich and Colchester.'

'Yes! That's exactly what I was going to say!' Stacey cried. 'A new fast day coach to rival the Mail, with the best teams and the best coachmen.'

'Stops limited to the larger towns, and a maximum of eight miles to every stage. A guaranteed rate of ten miles covered in every hour,' Simon elaborated.

Stacey leaned forward, alight with enthusiasm.

'Norwich to London in twelve and a half hours, cheaper than the Mail, and with more room for outsiders—'

'One coach down and one up every day, six days a week,' Simon took her up. 'Starting at a fairly civilized time of the morning—'

'Seven.'

'Yes, seven, and arriving at Ludgate Hill at half-past seven in the evening, just in time for dinner.'

'And it must have a really appropriate name, something that conjures up an impression of effortless speed—'

'The Expedition?' Simon offered. 'The Rapid?'

'The Highflyer!' Stacey cried.

'Yes, perfect. Brown's Highflyer, the fastest coach in the three counties.'

Barty looked from one animated face to the other with the distinct feeling that his gamble was beginning to pay off. He refilled his glass, shifted in his chair, made a play of not quite knowing where to start.

'Well now,' he began at last, 'it all sounds very fine—'

Stacey and Simon exchanged a glance confirming

unity in defence of their brainchild.

'Point is, though, are folks likely to use this grand new Highflyer? Like you said, they've already got two other stages to London, not counting what Pymer's run, and if they want to go to Ipswich, they've got the Herald, or Pymer's Comet. And don't go telling me we'd pick up more on the way, 'cause like you also already said, there's two running from Ipswich to London, and there's the Eclipse, the New and the Times from Colchester, not to speak of a couple from Chelmsford and our own Albion going through there. All good services.'

'But there's still only one direct way via Ipswich, and that's the Mail,' Simon pointed out. 'Horsed by Pymer's. If people are willing to take the Mail down by that route, they'll be willing to take the Highflyer. More so, in fact, since the Highflyer will be faster, have more outside accommodation *and* be cheaper.'

'Exactly,' Stacey corroborated.

Unconsciously, she and Simon both shifted so that they were facing Barty, presenting a united front. Barty changed his area of attack.

'Have you thought how much it would cost to set up this new service of yours? You've been talking of loans and the possibility of going bankrupt through price cutting, and yet now you suggest we set up a crack run. We'd need four new coaches, close on a couple of hundred horses, two, maybe three new coachmen and two guards.'

'We would contract out the horses,' Simon pointed out. 'Nelson will be more than willing to take up the London end of the run, or Horne, or Chaplin.'

'I'll not share any stage with Horne,' Barty stated. 'Right-on sly customer he is. Will Chaplin's all right. But we've always dealt with Bob Nelson or his ma.'

'Very well, we approach him.'

'And as for the coaches, we build them ourselves,' Stacey said, eager to present one of the strong points of her case. 'Ollie was telling me only last week that they're a mite slack at the works at the moment. Start on the new coaches now and we'll not have to turn off any craftsmen. If they give it top priority, we could have the Highflyer running by Christmas, and get it off to a good start with the seasonal trade.'

'Aye, and have it running empty in the dead period in the first quarter,' Barty objected.

Stacey was unable to come up with an adequate answer for that one. She looked hopefully at Simon.

'So we build a reputation for speed and reliability through the worst part of the winter, ready for when trade picks up in the spring,' he offered.

Barty looked at them both, considering. He played at being reluctantly won over. 'Well—' he cocked a bushy eyebrow at his daughter. 'I suppose you've worked out the possible income from this venture of yours?'

'Six hundred and forty-five pounds, sixteen shillings per month, fully laden,' Stacey told him, without even glancing at her notebook.

'But we can't count on being fully laden every day of the month.'

'Oh, but that's winter rates, with only four insiders. In summer, with six, it would be much better—'

'Besides,' Simon took her up, 'it's not merely a question of profit, but of prestige. The short-haul coaches will always make up the greater part of our income, but the Highflyer will take the glory, which is what I was speaking of earlier. A service like this will create public interest, make us a talking-point. People will come to think of us as the crack company, because we run the best London service.'

'Yes, that's it exactly,' Stacey cried. He put into words what she instinctively felt. 'Like – like one of those things on the front of a ship. What are they called?'

'A figurehead,' said Simon.

'That's it. A figurehead.'

They both looked at Barty, the innovators in league against his conservative caution.

Barty got up, strolled over to the mantelpiece and filled his pipe from the tobacco jar, taking great care to tamp it down thoroughly. Simon waited with apparent unconcern, but Stacey could scarcely contain her impatience.

'Come on, Pa,' she begged. 'What do you think? It is a good idea, is it not? Shall we go ahead with it?'

Barty frowned down the stem of his pipe, concentrating on getting it to draw properly.

'Well—' he said finally, 'sounds a totty-headed scheme to me. You two—' he glared at them from under his eyebrows '—are like a couple of foxy advocates when you get going. Figureheads. Talking-points. Still, seeing as you're so keen on it, we'll give it a try.'

Stacey gave a cry of delight and ran to hug him.

'Pa! I knew you'd see it was a good proposition.'

'I don't see naught of the sort,' Barty retorted. 'And what's more, I'm taking no part in setting it up. You and Simon here can take responsibility for that. It's your pigeon, you can see it pays its way in the world.'

Stacey could hardly have been more ecstatic if she had been handed the Crown Jewels. Even the prospect of having to share the treat with Simon Keating scarcely dimmed her pleasure.

'Pa, you're a darling!' she declared, kissing his rough cheek.

Simon's reaction was more restrained. He refilled the glasses and handed them round.

'A toast,' he said, 'to Stacey's Flyer.'

Chapter Ten

By the end of November, the Highflyer was almost ready to roll. Three of the coaches stood ready, the fourth needed only the signwriting on its panels and the final coats of varnish. The standard of workmanship at Brown's Coachworks, always high, was pushed to new limits under Stacey's exacting requirements. The Flyers had to be the lightest, strongest and safest coaches on the road. For Oliver, supervising every process of the work and doing many of the skilled jobs himself, it was a labour of love. Had Stacey been solely in charge of the new project, or planning it with her father, he would have rejoiced in the opportunity of showing her what he could do, of discussing every small detail with her. But the partnership with Simon Keating ruined any hope of that.

With each passing week, Oliver saw her falling ever more deeply under his evil influence. When she came to the coachworks, it was always with Keating, the two of them caught up in their enthusiasm for their brainchild. And not only during the day, it seemed. To Oliver's horror, he learnt that Keating was to be found at All Saints Green on Saturday evenings as well. According to his sister Harriet, who could never keep any piece of gossip to herself, Keating not only taught Stacey a number of shameful card games involving gambling, but also turned out to be an accomplished musician. Oliver found it increasingly difficult to maintain even a show of civility. He had to keep his clenched fists deep in his pockets, so strong was the desire to smash that handsome, smiling face to a bloody, unrecognizable pulp.

Taken up as he was with the details of the launching of the Flyer, Simon had no idea that dislike and disapproval on Oliver's part had turned to a smouldering hatred. Saturday afternoons spent discussing the week's problems and planning the next step of the enterprise and the congenial evenings at All Saints Green became something to be looked forward to. Though there were myriad minor hitches, the Highflyer progressed apace.

After a trial run to Stacey's timetables, she and Simon were confident enough of the efficiency of their organization to have the times of each arrival and departure along the route carved in ivory and mounted inside the coaches, a refinement that Barty thought was a mite overdone. New sets of harness were ordered from Brown relatives in the trade, at the usual family discount of ten per cent. Stacey had some ideas of silver mountings, like a nobleman's carriage, but was practical enough to see that it was out of the question.

While she was concerned with fares, timetables and finance, Simon was busy with the task of finding horses to pull the Flyer. No coaching company owned all the horses needed for each journey, but contracted out the right to supply them to small innkeepers every eight to ten miles along the road. This arrangement benefited both sides, as it brought custom to the inns and freed the proprietor from the trouble of caring for animals over a distance of a hundred miles or more. Robert Nelson, of the Belle Sauvage, Ludgate Hill, was responsible for the last stage into London, and the route down to Ipswich was already covered by the innkeepers who horsed the Herald. That left Simon with the stretch between Ipswich and the London suburbs to negotiate, and new teams to buy for the first three stages out of Norwich.

The horses which were to pull the Flyer out of the Crown and over the first eight miles were of prime importance, and it was for this stretch that he acquired a team of match bays. The day he brought them home to the Crown, Stacey begged permission from her aunt to be there when they arrived.

In company with practically everyone from Brown's

who could think of an excuse to do so, she was ready and waiting in the yard in the early afternoon, sharing in the sense of anticipation. A cheer went up as they came in under the archway, ears pricked, necks arched, coats shining in the weak winter sunlight. Simon saluted with his whip and pulled them up in the middle of the yard where they could be admired by everyone. The horse-keepers to whose care they had been assigned ran forward with blue and brown cloths to throw over their backs and held their heads as Simon jumped down from the box. Stacey was unstinting in her praise.

'Beautiful, beautiful,' she crooned, stroking the aristo-cratic noses, patting the slim, muscled necks. 'How I wish I could drive them. I'm sure they would fly to the sun.'

Simon was checking that the new collars had not rubbed their shoulders.

'Don't start getting that idea into your head. Look what happened to Phaeton,' he said. 'Oh, and mind the near wheeler, he may look handsome, but he's an incu-rable kicker.'

Stacey avoided the horse in question.

'They'd be even better in a phaeton,' she maintained. 'They really would fly then. One of those lovely crane-necked affairs with the big wheels.'

'Not *a* phaeton, ignoramus, *the* Phaeton. The driver of the sun chariot.'

Stacey frowned, perplexed.

'The Rising Sun in Pottergate?' she asked. 'I thought their name was Armstrong. Has it changed hands?'

Simon convulsed with laughter, startling the horse nearest to him and setting the whole team sidling and snorting.

'Will you kindly tell me what's so funny?' Stacey demanded.

Much to her annoyance, Simon refused to explain.

'This much I'll say for you, Miss Stacey,' he remarked, 'you're no bluestocking. The Rising Sun, indeed!'

He sent the team off to the stables to be bedded down,

and the crowd of admiring spectators began to disperse. Stacey lingered in the yard, asking Simon about the details of the sale, putting off the moment when she would have to go in, meet her Aunt Eustacia and set off back to Raston. She was just remarking on the interest in the Flyer that was already being shown about the city, when she realized that Simon's attention was no longer with her. He was staring over her shoulder at a carriage that had just come into the yard, and he had gone several shades paler.

'Here's a surprise,' he said, with his customary understatement, 'I've a visitor. Perhaps you would care to be introduced.'

Stacey looked at the new arrival and saw nothing remarkable, just a chaise and four, a rather elegant private one with a coat of arms emblazoned on the door and two ladies seated inside. She glanced up at Simon's face and to her amazement found that he had lost his air of easy confidence. Just for a moment. He caught her eye and gave a taut smile. 'Come along,' he said, and took her arm with a hand that shook slightly.

As they approached, one of the ladies stepped down from the chaise, a dark woman in her twenties in an azure cloak. She stretched out both hands to Simon, her lovely face breaking into a smile of delighted recognition.

'Simon! My dear, what an astounding coincidence! After all this time!'

'Coincidence indeed. Almost too much to be believed,' Simon agreed, taking her hand for the briefest moment before turning to Stacey. 'Stacey, allow me to present my cousin to you, Miss Georgiana Christy. Georgiana, Miss Stacey Brown.'

Cousin! Stacey smothered a squeak of surprise as she dropped her best Miss Haveringshaw curtsey. A fact that she had always known but never really taken stock of presented itself. Alone of practically all the people she knew, Simon Keating had no family connections, no background against which he could be set, nothing but a web of conflicting rumours. Until now.

'And what brings you to this part of the world, Georgiana?' Simon asked, a slight edge of provocation in his voice. 'Looking for me?'

'Vain creature!' Miss Christy gave a brittle laugh. 'I've better things to do with my time than round up black sheep. But since we have met, so fortuitously—' she paused, looking at Stacey, clearly disliking her presence.

'You must both have a great deal to say to each other—' Stacey began, trying to get away. But Simon kept hold of her arm.

'Nothing of any importance, I assure you,' he insisted. 'Is there, Georgiana?'

They were interrupted by Uncle Noll, come to see if the travellers cared to step inside and take some refreshment. Simon sent him away, saying that the lady was not staying. An expression of frustration crossed Miss Christy's face, swiftly controlled. She turned her winning smile on Simon again, and Stacey for the first time saw a resemblance between them, an ability to bend people with charm and carefully concealed determination.

'Simon, my dear, I don't know what you've been doing all these years—'

'Enjoying myself, Georgiana, and not missing the family in the least, if that was what you were about to suggest.'

'But it's no kind of life, is it, drifting around from place to place?' She fixed her dark eyes on him, coaxing. 'You must have thought about coming back, surely?'

'Not once. The idea never crossed my mind.'

Georgiana changed tactics, becoming practical.

'Then perhaps you might apply your mind to it now. Things have changed a great deal, you know.' She glanced at Stacey, who was both fascinated and embarrassed at being an unwilling witness, and evidently decided to ignore her presence. 'Ann and Maria have both gone, and Caro's been told that another child will kill her. And as for poor Tim, he's virtually an invalid

174

now.' She gave him a level look. 'That just leaves you and me.'

'So.' Simon turned to Stacey. 'Just think, Georgiana has come all the way from Cheshire just to seek me out and say that. Why do you suppose she should want to go to all that trouble?'

Stacey flushed, not knowing what to say, wishing herself out of it.

'She's up to something, depend upon it,' he said, conversationally.

'Really, my dear, you put far too high a value on your own worth,' his cousin declared. 'I had no more idea of finding you here than on the moon.'

'No? I wonder, then, why you are travelling with only your maid, and just overnight baggage? But I shan't press you on the matter. Don't let me detain you from getting on to wherever you just happened to be going.'

But Miss Christy was not to be so easily dismissed. She smoothed out an imaginary wrinkle in her glove.

'You are being quite remarkably obtuse,' she said, with an air of strained patience. 'I never would have thought you could be so dull, but perhaps that is the effect of spending your time playing at coachmen. Consider. The old man's becoming obsessed with carrying on the line, and Tim's never shown the least inclination to oblige. I would have thought it was obvious where your best interests lay.'

'And where do yours lie, I wonder? In pleasing the old man? Sorry to disappoint you, dear coz, but you should know me better than that. Whatever plot you have in mind, I'm not falling in with it, and I'll thank you not to air it in front of Stacey. Notions such as love and loyalty are more than mere words to her family. You'll shock her.' He raised his hat and bowed with frigid politeness. 'So kind of you to suffer so much inconvenience on my behalf. Good day.'

Stacey found herself propelled towards the office, with hardly time for the briefest of nods to Miss Christy by way of farewell. They sailed past the clerks and into the inner sanctum, Simon closing the door firmly behind him.

'Talbot,' he muttered, taking a bottle of brandy and a glass out of a drawer in his desk. 'It must have been Talbot. I'll break his neck.'

Stacey stood at the window, watching the chaise as it rolled out of the yard.

'You ought to be ashamed!' she declared hotly. 'Behaving like that!'

'Yes,' he admitted, 'you're right. I apologize. I should not have brought you into it.'

'I don't mean that.' She turned her back on the view of the yard and glared at him as he swallowed a generous measure of brandy. 'I mean the way you treated her – Miss Christy. If she's really come all this distance just to talk to you, you should at least be civil to her. And if your father needs you at home, you should go. It's your duty.'

'Duty! I owe no duty to him. For twenty-seven years he's refused to acknowledge me. He can't suddenly change his mind and expect me to come running to fall on his neck with gratitude. Oh no. He can sit there and worry himself into the grave over what I'm doing to carry on his precious line.'

He could see that he had alienated her. How could she, loved and cherished from the day of her birth, secure within the Brown's fold, possibly understand the entrenched bitterness of which he and Georgiana were products? He poured himself another drink and wished his cousin to the devil. Stacey was regarding him with troubled eyes. She came over to his desk and started shifting papers around.

'What do you mean?' she asked. 'About not acknowledging you?'

Simon hesitated, torn between a lifetime's habit of concealment and a new need to explain himself. Looking inward, he walked again through the simmering hush of those graceful Palladian rooms, tasting the embattled atmosphere. And the ghosts walked with him, divided

176

into their opposing camps. The old man, the girls and that bitch of a governess on one side, himself and his mother on the other, and poor Tim running distractedly between the two, forever trying to reconcile them, forever failing.

'Just that,' he said, matter-of-fact, trying to shrug it off. 'A cousin of my mother's had been staying with them at the time – they were very close, he was the only relation she had left – and when I was born I looked like him. What my father did not take into account was that both the cousin and myself resemble my maternal grandfather. But he was conveniently out of the way by then, along with all the rest of them.'

Stacey perched on the edge of the desk, her eyes forming a silent question. Simon brought the side of his hand down with a thud, making her jump.

'Bonjour, Madame la Guillotine, adieu la vie.'

'No!'

She stared at him, trying to take in this revelation. The horrific events of the revolution in France, before she was born and safely distanced across the English Channel, hardly seemed to have any connection with reality. It was difficult to relate the mindless bloodletting to the life she knew. And yet here was someone who was very much part of her life telling her that his kin had perished in the reign of terror.

'All of them?'

'Except for Cousin Eugene. He saw trouble coming and got out. The rest of them were too noble or too damn pig-headed to leave the sinking ship.'

'So your mother was alone, and unhappy?'

'Yes.'

Simon sat turning his empty glass in his fingers.

'I remember my eleventh birthday,' he said slowly. 'There had been a particularly bad quarrel, he had beaten her. She was crying. I begged her to admit that Eugene was my father. The thought of having the old man's blood in my veins revolted me. But she insisted that she had never been unfaithful. She would not give him the satisfaction of having a means of divorce.'

Stacey remembered her eleventh birthday. Her father had given her a new pony, a pretty chestnut gelding, and they all played hide-and-seek round the yard and Oliver found her in the stables and kissed her.

'If – if things are so bad, does your mother not need you there?'she asked hesitantly.

'Not any more. She died a long time ago.'

'Oh – I—' She stopped, not sure how he would react to yet another question, looking at him covertly from under her lashes. 'So there aren't many of you left now?' she ventured.

'Only me on my side of the conflict,' Simon said, still avoiding her eyes. Almost to himself, he went on, 'Perhaps it's getting too dull, perhaps that's why they want me back. There were plenty of us in the old days. I don't know what went wrong between them, my parents, in the first place, but by the time I was old enough to know what was going on around me the entire household was divided into two camps. Very unevenly divided.' He put down the glass, staring through it at the scenes of twenty years before. Stacey found she was holding her breath. 'The governess my father employed managed to turn my sisters against my mother, and of course nearly all the servants took his side, if only to keep in employment. Tim, my brother, tried to keep in with both of them, but he was often too sick to be effective. Which left me. I'm very proficient at spying and eavesdropping and prying into what others do not want to reveal.' He glanced at her and away again. 'Not a very pleasant atmosphere to live in,' he said, with masterly understatement. 'It was a relief to be sent away to school, except that I was always worried about what might be happening at home. Groups of boys when left unsupervised are merely brutal savages. I could cope with them.'

Stacey was appalled at the picture he revealed, unable to understand how such a situation could have come about. There were a dozen questions she wanted to ask, but she did not care to tread on what was obviously painful ground. She came back to the one other member of the family that she had met.

'Where did Miss Christy fit in?'

'Georgiana?' His deliberately bland tone took on an edge of dislike. 'She's something of a poor relation, though you'd never think so to look at her. She came to live with us when her mother ran off with a footman, and joined in the game with alacrity. You never knew which side she was on, it depended upon what she stood to gain. And she hasn't changed much, from today's evidence.'

Stacey bit her lip, trying to think of something constructive to say.

'Couldn't – couldn't you even try to make it up?' she asked tentatively. 'It was all so long ago. I mean – if your father really does want you back, perhaps he's sorry.'

'No, too much has happened, on both sides. You don't know a fraction of it.' He reached out and closed a hand round hers. 'But even that's a good deal more than I've told anyone else, my dear. You understand?'

She nodded. 'I won't tattle.'

'I know. You're a good friend, Stacey.'

He watched her as she slid off the desk and made her way out. A friend to be trusted. There weren't too many of them about.

Stacey was unusually silent during the journey back to Raston. She was trying to imagine having no family, no permanent home. Fitting in everywhere, belonging nowhere, as he had once let slip. It was no life, Miss Christy had said, drifting around from place to place, and she was right. The thought of such loneliness filled her with an ache that kept her sleepless long into the night.

Oliver was not the only one to regard the setting up of the Highflyer with serious misgivings. Amos Burgess was concerned for the company and for his own position. All the expense involved made him sweat with fear each time he looked at the balance sheet. It was eating into reserves already dangerously low from the prolonged price war over the fares. Coupled to this was his complete exclusion from the partnership between Miss Stacey and Mr Keating They did not once consult him on any aspect of the project. He was superfluous. The conviction kept him from confessing the traitor's part he was playing.

It had been a very nasty moment, when Mr Brown asked him whether the clerks were to be trusted.

'First there was that business about the robbery,' he said, 'and now we think someone might be telling Pymer what's going on here. What d'ye think, Amos? Would either of those lads be bribed into giving away our secrets, eh?'

Amos dithered, his frightened brain wavering between possible answers. He longed to admit that it was he who was passing on information, but that the figures he gave were false, so serving to confuse Pymer's. Mr Brown would appreciate that, he knew. He delighted in a clever trick. But to do so would mean confessing to engineering the robbery, and explaining his motives, and that he could not do. Mr Brown was generosity itself, but he would not easily forgive such an act.

'I don't know, I'm sure, Mr Brown sir,' he said, wondering whether to throw suspicion onto one of the young men. He decided that it might not be advisable. 'I would have thought they were both trustworthy. They work quite diligently, as far as any of the younger generation know how to work.'

'Neither of 'em is in any sort of fix over money, are they? In need of a quick penny?'

'I wouldn't know, Mr Brown sir. They are not in the habit of confiding in me.'

'Pity.' Mr Brown's eyes ran round the office, considering. Amos trembled inside, convinced that his guilt was written on his face. 'Ah well—' to Amos's intense relief, he gave up the interrogation, clapping a friendly hand on his shoulder. 'Keep your ears and eyes open, will you? I don't have to tell you that we're running close to the rocks at the moment. Spies! I don't know what it's all coming to.'

He stumped into the inner office, leaving Amos wishing he had the courage to point out that nothing like this had ever happened before Mr Keating arrived on the scene.

It was on the evening after the new and very expensive team of blood bays arrived that his arrangement with the man he knew simply as Will took a new and sinister turn. He was becoming almost used to the clandestine meetings in the taproom of a tavern – a different one each time – to the exchanging of a summary of each week's figures for a little heap of guineas. He no longer looked constantly over his shoulder or started at shadows, expecting every minute to be recognized. And hidden in a tin box at the back of an outhouse behind the haberdasher's was a growing pile of money, frail but welcome security against his eventual losing of the battle with old age. The thought of that hoard of gold buoyed him up that particular day. What with the cost of the new team and the odd behaviour of Miss Stacey and Mr Keating, closeting themselves in the inner office for what sounded like a very serious conversation, he was feeling threatened on all sides.

He made his way through the dark streets to the designated meeting-place, brooding over the pitfalls of his situation. If only he could tell Mr Brown. If only he could shut Martha's mouth as he had done over the parlour curtains. But he dared not give her any more of the money. Her suspicious mind would soon get to work on that. If only he could bank the money, instead of leaving it where it might be discovered. Terrified of exposure, he could not risk some bank official questioning how a humble cashier came by such an amount. The problems were legion. Pushing open the door of the alehouse, he scanned the smoky room for Will's undernourished figure, and found him sitting at a corner table. But he was not alone. A man with a broken nose and the build of a prizefighter was with him.

'Come along, my little friend. Sit down,' Will said, baring his blackened teeth in a predatory smile of welcome. He snapped his fingers at a passing serving wench. 'Get the gentleman a brandy and water, mauther.'

Amos sat, eyeing Will's silent companion.

'Well now, and where's our little proof of friendship?' Will asked.

Fumbling, Amos took the paper out of his pocket and passed it under the table.

Will's smile became a shade more pleasant. 'Drink up,' he invited, as the girl thumped down a glass of spirit. Amos sipped warily, waiting for his reward. Will sat looking idly about the taproom. His henchman gazed at his empty tankard. Amos glanced from one to the other. He cleared his throat.

'Ah – you seem to have forgotten – the matter of—' he trailed to a halt as two pairs of eyes suddenly bored into him.

'You're mistaken, my little friend,' Will told him. 'I ain't forgotten nothing.'

'But—' Amos licked his dry lips. 'The – the money—'

'Money? What money's that? Friends like us don't need to deal in cash. It's just a matter of favours. You do a little something for me, I do the same for you. Nice and easy. See?'

'But I – I do not see – what favour?'

Will jerked his head in the direction of his companion. 'You give me a few little figures. I keep him off you.'

The silent man picked up his pewter tankard in one huge red hand. He held it at arm's length under Amos's nose and slowly, without a word, almost without effort it seemed, crushed it. The crumpled misshapen metal was dropped on the table with a thud.

Amos felt the blood drain from his face as the meaning

of the display took effect. His body trembled uncontrollably.

'See?' Will asked.

Amos nodded.

'Good.' Will seemed to lose interest. He looked about for the serving-girl and ordered another drink for himself and his henchman. Then, affecting to notice Amos, said, 'The Maybush next week. Same time. Right?'

Sick and shaking, Amos stumbled into the street. Fear surrounded him. At work the guilt of betrayal and dread of discovery, at home Martha waiting to torment him and now the threat of physical violence. There was no escape.

Chapter Eleven

On the morning of the third of December, her birthday, Stacey awoke at the first rumble of wheels on the cobbles, starting out of a confused dream of empty stagecoaches and dark ladies in azure cloaks. She lay on her back in the darkness, tense with nervous excitement, waiting for the day to begin. Today she was eighteen years old, and home at All Saints Green for the occasion, but it was not this that kept her sleepless with expectation. Far more important than any birthday, it was the date set for the maiden run of the Highflyer. At seven o'clock sharp, the stage would roll out of the yard of the Crown to become the figurehead of a new era of Brown prosperity. She shifted position, trying to rid herself of the persistent fear that the whole project was going to be a failure. The Flyer was booked solid right up till Christmas, it was going to be the most successful run ever undertaken by the company. It had to be. A great deal of money and all her faith was invested in it.

By a quarter-past six, Stacey and Bart were making their way across All Saints Green, she wearing a new cherry red pelisse and turban trimmed with fur, he muffled in a thick coachman's benjamin. They walked arm in arm, briskly against the early morning cold, Stacey's long strides easily keeping step with her father's. She chattered incessantly, covering up her foreboding.

They arrived at the Crown just as the Albion was due to depart. Caught up in the air of celebration, ostlers and horsekeepers raised a cheer that was taken up all round the yard, the guard blew a fanfare on his bugle, the coachman saluted with his whip. Laughing, Stacey waved her acknowledgement, her fears dissolving as she realized all these people were wishing her new enterprise well. The coach moved forward, gaslight from the inn catching on harness and paintwork, the fresh horses eager to start. Stacey gazed with pride tight within her. The Albion was a fine coach, but the Highflyer was going to be even finer.

Out of the crowd, Simon Keating appeared.

'It's all running smoothly so far,' he told them. 'No last-minute hitches. I had a dreadful premonition last night that the entire team was going to go lame, or a wheel drop off, but all appears to be well.'

Stacey looked at him in some surprise. She would not have thought that he would harbour any irrational fears, let alone admit to them.

'I dreamt it was running empty,' she confessed.

'No danger of that,' Simon assured her. 'Amos tells me the booking clerks are in a fair way of being corrupted by the bribes they've been offered by people wanting a seat on the inaugural run.'

'Really?' Stacey was delighted. 'And what about the other London coaches? The Albion looked well patronized. Are there plenty for the Telegraph?'

She peeped in at the window of the waiting-room, where a mixed collection of people were gathered in dour silence. As usual, the inside passengers had claimed the fire, the outsiders being consigned to the chillier regions of the room. But perhaps it was just as well, for they needed to be inured to cold. They had a bone-freezing journey of over thirteen hours ahead of them.

'Ten,' she said, counting heads. 'That's not bad.'

'We've certainly aroused a great deal of interest in the Flyer,' Simon said. 'Just look at the extra sightseers about the place today. It's bringing additional custom to the Crown, if nothing else.'

Barty chuckled.

'We'll ask Noll for a percentage of all takings above the ordinary. But it had better pay its way after the first excitement's worn off. Whatever you two say about prestige and talking-points, I'm not in the business of providing free sideshows for folks with naught better to do with their time than watch a stage leave town.'

'The Flyer will pay its way all right,' Simon asserted.

Unable to keep still, Stacey paced about the yard speaking to porters and waiters and horsekeepers, looked in at the office to exchange a greeting with Amos Burgess, waved to Harriet and Aunt Peg. The Telegraph set off promptly at a quarter to seven, and the passengers for the Flyer began to gather, eager to be away. Unlike the earlier travellers, they disdained to huddle round the fire in the waiting-room. Young men for the most part, with aspirations to being considered good whips, they swaggered about the yard dressed like so many coachmen, speaking in knowing tones of roads and horses and the finer points of driving. Few of the onlookers were deceived, for the real coachmen were comfortably lounging in their own cosy den, waiting till the last minute before coming out into the cold of the morning. Arthur Harris arrived and found Simon in the crowd. He was halfway through a sentence when Stacey joined them and startled him into forgetting what he was saying.

'Miss Brown!' Somewhat tardily, he snatched off his hat and bowed. 'I didn't think – I did not expect to see you here.'

'But of course I'm here!' Stacey laughed. 'The Flyer is my brainchild. I wouldn't miss this for the world.'

'Oh—' Arthur looked from Stacey to Simon, a worried frown creasing his forehead. 'I thought – but no matter.'

Due to Aunt Eustacia's careful propaganda, he had been under the impression that Stacey had nothing whatsoever to do with the company, and was just interested in the Flyer because it was her father's new project. Simon had seen no reason to enlighten him, but now he threw over all Aunt Eustacia's work with cheerful abandon.

'Oh yes,' he said, with a swift smile at Stacey, 'we would never have got the Flyer going without Miss Stacey's help. She'd be driving it, given half a chance.'

Authur looked doubtful, then decided it must be a

rather poor joke. He could not imagine they were serious. He laughed uncertainly, then changed the subject, asking when the Flyer was due to appear.

'Dead on time, of course,' Stacey told him.

And dead on time it was. The yard of the Crown, seldom empty, was thronged with people wanting to see the show, and by five to seven the windows and galleries were lined with guests and inn servants eager for a good viewpoint. Stacey, tense with nervous anticipation, clung to her father's arm with both hands as the crowd pressed forward. To a renewed round of cheering, the Highflyer was led through from the back stables and brought to a halt in the middle of the yard. Radiant with the pride of ownership, Stacey was struck speechless. The Flyer was the very pinnacle of human achievement in transport, and she had been its creator.

White gaslight gleamed fitfully through the shifting tide of admirers to fall on the shining blue and brown paintwork of the panels, the glossy hides of the thorough-bred horses, the mirror-bright brass fittings. Blue ribbons fluttered from bridles and manes, and in the moving shadows the legendary racehorse on the doors seemed almost to snort and paw the ground.

Horsekeepers held the heads of their restless charges, an ostler placed a ladder for the outside passengers and the guard hurried forward with a great air of importance, supervising the stowing of luggage and checking the tickets of the travellers. At one minute to seven, Harry Cox, newly promoted to the company's prime job, appeared from the coachmen's parlour, massive in his royal blue benjamin, a huge nosegay of winter greenery thrust into his buttonhole. Another cheer went up, led by the exuberant band of outsiders, and Harry saluted his whip in acknowledgement. Two waiters materialized at Simon's side, bearing bottles and a tray of glasses.

'A toast to the Highflyer!' he declared, popping champagne corks with a flourish.

Stacey's cry of delight was echoed by a dozen others

187

and the toast was repeated as glasses were handed round to everyone who had anything to do with the Flyer. Then Harry Cox took up the reins and climbed aboard, and the guard looked around for any stray passengers who just might have forgotten to find their seats.

'Take off the cloths, boys,' Harry told the horsekeepers, and the thoroughbreds were seen in all their glory. 'All right behind?'

'All right, Mr Cox!'

'Give 'em their heads, boys, and look to yourselves!'

Harry eased his hand down a fraction, the bays sprang forward, and the Highflyer rolled out of the yard to the accompaniment of cheers and waves and shouts and a brassy blast of the Huntsman's Chorus on the bugle.

Dancing with excitement, Stacey found the first available member of the family, which happened to be Oliver, and caught his hands in hers.

'Wasn't it magnificent? I've never seen anything to touch it! The Flyer's going to be such a success, I just know it is! Such a crowd – it will be talked about all over town. And champagne!' She let go of Oliver and whirled round to find Simon. 'Champagne, what a marvellous idea! Why didn't you tell me? It added a special touch to the occasion. I don't think I've ever drunk champagne at seven in the morning before!'

'My dear Miss Stacey, you've hardly begun to live,' he replied, his face betraying a sense of triumph almost the equal of hers. 'Have another glass, we'll both have another glass, we deserve it.' He snatched up a half-empty bottle, spilling some of it as someone clapped him on the shoulder and congratulated him on the successful launching.

'I'm only a small part of the show,' he disclaimed. 'This young lady is the moving force – Miss Stacey Brown, the sharpest coaching proprietor in the three counties.'

Stacey laughed with delight and raised her glass.

'To all who have worked to make the Flyer possible!'
she cried.

Barty came up behind her and wound an affectionate
arm around her waist.

'I'll drink to that,' he said. 'But not in this Froggy
dishwater. How about a bite of breakfast? Simon?
You've an hour yet before the Eclipse goes out.'

'Splendid idea. Make it a party, there's nothing I like
better than a party for breakfast. Miss Stacey shall have
another bottle of champagne and drive the Eclipse.'

'Oh yes!' Stacey cried. 'I'll be coachman and you can
be guard, and we'll race the Commodore all the way to
Cambridge!'

Laughing, they began to make their way across the
yard, dogged by a disgusted Oliver. Simon tried to dislodge a street urchin who had wriggled his way through
the cheerful throng and was hanging on his arm, but the
lad refused to be shaken off. Waving a piece of paper and
tugging at Simon's sleeve, he demanded to be heard.
When Simon at last gave him his attention, he thrust the
paper into his hand and made off into the crowd. Simon
glanced at what proved to be a letter, recognized the
handwriting and with a brief apology to Bart and Stacey,
moved into the light to read it.

Stacey watched him as her father talked to one of the
coachmen. The laughter drained from his face as he
read, and he stood for fully half a minute frowning,
oblivious of the people pushing past him into the inn.
Then he thrust the letter into his pocket and looked
about, searching for a face in the crowd, and set off
towards the stables. Seized by a sudden nameless fear,
Stacey darted after him.

'What is it?' she demanded, trotting to keep up with
him. 'Is it bad news?'

'We have a slight problem with the Flyer,' Simon told
her.

'The Flyer? Whatever can be wrong with the Flyer?

189

It's only just gone.'

'True, but it won't get any further than South Stonham. Where's that man gone to? Tom!' he yelled, still looking for the head ostler. 'Tom! There you are. Bring out the fastest pair of horses we've got and put them to Mr Talbot's curricle.'

'Simon!' Shrill with impatience, Stacey caught hold of his arm. 'What do you mean? Where are you going in Mr Talbot's curricle?'

'He won't have to mind my borrowing it, he owes me a favour. And he's booked right through to London on the Flyer, so he won't be back till tomorrow,' Simon said, as if in explanation, and made for the booking office.

'Don't be so tiresome! Why—?'

But Simon was already through the office door. Feeling a fool, Stacey let go of him and stood fuming with frustration while he spoke to Amos Burgess.

''Morning, Burgess. How much have we taken so far today?'

Amos looked at him with thinly disguised distaste, suspecting a test designed to give yet another blow to his authority.

'Twenty-seven pounds, sixteen shillings and sixpence, Mr Keating.'

'Not quite enough, I fear. I need at least fifty guineas at once. Possibly more. We don't just happen to have that much in the petty cash, I suppose?'

Amos pursed his lips.

'I would not describe such an amount as petty, Mr Keating,' he said primly.

'Quite. No matter, I'll find it myself and settle up later.'

And with Stacey in his wake, he marched out.

'Simon!' She dodged in front of him, finally succeeding in bringing him to a halt. He looked down at her, pretending surprise.

'Are you still there?'

'For heaven's sake, Simon, tell me what's going on.

Why do you need fifty guineas?'

'Because, Miss Stacey, our friend Pymer has bought up all the horses at the posting-house at South Stonham. If I don't act very quickly, that is going to be as far as the Flyer is going to run today.'

'*No!*' Stacey stared at him in horrified disbelief. 'He hasn't? Why, the rotten—'

'Careful.' Simon was laughing at her. 'Your Select Academy mask is slipping. Now will you be so good as to explain to your father what is happening while I unearth some cash? I haven't a moment to lose.'

Stacey opened her mouth to protest, then changed her mind.

'Of course,' she agreed, stepping out of his way. But the minute he started running across to the outer steps leading up to the galleries and on to his rooms at the top of the inn, she turned back and charged a waiter with the task of delivering the message to Barty. Then she found the head ostler, supervising the harnessing of two chestnut horses to a low-built bright green curricle.

'Hurry it up, Tom,' she begged. 'This is an emergency.'

When Simon arrived back in the yard, he found the curricle all ready with Stacey in the driver's seat, whip and reins in hand, a scarcely-suppressed grin on her face.

'Thank you, Miss Stacey,' he said, holding out a hand to her. 'You can get down now.'

Stacey merely shook her head.

'Hurry up,' she said. 'We haven't a moment to lose.'

'Come on, stop playing games and get down.'

'No, I'm coming too. The Flyer's equally my concern,' Stacey dropped her left hand a fraction and the horses started forward. 'I'll go without you,' she threatened, laughing, knowing that the need for haste was on her side. Simon capitulated and climbed up beside her.

'God knows what your father will say,' he remarked.

'He won't mind. He'll laugh,' Stacey told him, scattering gaping bystanders as she set the horses trotting under the archway and into Crown Street.

'Not if you break your neck driving recklessly.'

'I am not driving recklessly. Pa taught me far too well for that. I can handle this thing much better than its proper owner, I can tell you.'

By the time they had negotiated the difficult hills and corners and emerged unscathed into Saint Stephen's Street, Simon was convinced that she was speaking no more than the truth. The Gaffer's daughter could probably have taken a stage safely through the same streets, and certainly found no difficulty in driving the light and manoeuvrable curricle. Once out of the city and through the first tollgate, Stacey whipped the horses into a canter.

'How far ahead do you think the Flyer is?' she asked, gazing anxiously down the turnpike, grey in the first light of dawn.

'At least a couple of miles, probably three. They had twenty minutes' start on us, and Harry will be out for a record run today.'

'And what do we do when we catch them up?'

'Overtake, of course. The whole point of this race is keep the Flyer running. We have to get down to Stonham well before the Flyer and find a team of horses to take it into Ipswich, and that isn't going to be easy. There's only one posting-house there and two or three small alehouses. We'll chose whichever seems the most likely and offer the landlord the chance to make his fortune horsing our stage.'

'But what about the landlord of the posting-house?' Stacey asked. 'Hasn't he broken a contract, selling all his horses to Pymer?'

'We'll see to him afterwards,' Simon promised, 'and let him know just how displeased Brown's are with his bad faith.'

In the first grey of the false dawn, cottages and farms were stirring with life, cows being brought in, fires kindled. But with the exception of the occasional farm cart, the turnpike was empty, snaking ahead of them in a pearly ribbon.

192

'Go on,' Simon urged, 'spring 'em, you know you're dying to.'

Stacey needed no further encouragement. Flicking the horses with the whip, she urged them into a gallop. The December air stung her face, bringing tears to her eyes and making her teeth ache, inserting icy fingers down the neck and sleeves and buttonholes of the pelisse, but she scarcely noticed. The race was all that mattered, the heady thrill of speed. At Newton Flotman they changed horses and learnt that the Flyer was now less than ten minutes in front of them. With fresh hope they set off again and as they trotted up onto the level ground above the village, the newly risen sun climbed cold and yellow in the eastern sky, tingeing the trailing edges of the clouds with rose. Simon waved an expressive arm at the landscape.

'Magnificent,' he declared. 'Sunrise, a fast team and a pretty girl. Who could ask for more?'

'I could. We still haven't caught up with the Flyer,' Stacey said, her voice gruff.

They flew along the straight level road, the horses straining with necks outstretched and ears laid back. Stacey whipped them into still greater efforts. They were nearly a quarter of the way to Stonham, and still they had not even seen the Flyer. But at Upper Tasburgh, the Flyer's first staging-post, they gained a couple of minutes, and three miles further on they at last spied the coach ahead of them, rolling along at a hand canter. Stacey let out a yell of triumph. Yard by yard, the lighter vehicle gained ground, and in the growing daylight the faces of the travellers could be made out as they turned in their seats to see the challengers behind them. The outsiders cheered and waved as the identity of the curricle and its occupants became known, and as she drew level with the Flyer, Stacey caught sight of Arthur Harris's face and felt a childish burst of hilarity. If Aunt Eustacia could see her now! She'd have the vapours!

'Hey, Keating!' Talbot leaned precariously over the

side of his perch. 'What the devil are you doing with my rig?'

'Emergency measures, dear fellow. Explain later,' Simon shouted back. 'Harry! Watch out for us at Stonham, you'll be changing at a different inn.'

Inured to the hazards of the road, Harry Cox took the switch of plan in his stride.

'Right you are, Mr Keating.'

With a farewell flourish of the whip, Stacey drew ahead, whilst Simon smiled to himself as he went over one or two alternative rejoinders to Talbot's protest. 'I'm just borrowing your rig to elope with Miss Brown,' or better still, 'Miss Brown is abducting me. Raise a five thousand guineas ransom by Saturday.' But that was too far-fetched even for Harris to swallow, though it would have been worth it just to see his expression.

'What's so funny?' Stacey demanded.

'I was just thinking that you'd be wasted on the likes of Harris.'

The miles sped by as the morning progressed, the low weak winter sun shining fitfully as they clattered through Scole and over the Waveney bridge into Suffolk, the houses changing from flintstone to timber and daub. Racing with other sporting vehicles and overtaking the mail, they galloped across the wide East Anglian heartland, anxiously counting the milestones, calculating their rate of progress. They were still only seven miles ahead of the Flyer when they finally reached South Stonham.

The village was a small one, owing its existence to its position as a staging-post on the Ipswich–Norwich turnpike. It was dominated by the posting-house, an imposing brick-built inn whose sign, the Prince of Wales, straddled the road. On either side of it was a cluster of cottages, a farrier's and a wheelwright's, a small chandler's and a couple of alehouses. Simon looked at them doubtfully.

'They neither of them look quite the place for a

Brown's stopping place. However, we'll take a look and see what they have to offer.'

Stacey held the reins while Simon investigated the first place. He returned shaking his head.

'That won't do. They've no stabling at all and it isn't fit to feed pigs in, let alone our passengers.'

The second one, the Dun Cow, was more promising. In the yard at the rear was a barn that had been partially made into stalls and actually housed a couple of dispirited-looking horses. The landlady who came out to see what Simon wanted was fairly clean and certainly anxious to welcome a new class of customer to her house. After a preliminary glance, Simon went out to consult with Stacey.

'It's going to have to suffice, though I think we're going to be playing at horsekeepers for the day. We only have one small problem: there are just two horses here and neither of them are the sort of cattle we expect for the Flyer. Have you any ideas as to where we can find at least two more within—' he consulted his watch '—forty minutes at the outside?'

Stacey could hardly keep a grave face. She had anticipated this and thought of an answer on the way down. Not for nothing had she travelled the roads of the three counties with her father.

'That is no easy task,' she said, wrinkling her brow. 'But if you would care to give me that fifty guineas, I'll see what I can do.'

Simon handed her the money, not without misgivings.

'What are you up to, Stacey Brown?'

Eyes brimming with mischief, she turned the curricle round and started back up the road.

'Don't fret yourself over me,' she called back over her shoulder. 'You've enough to do getting this place ready in time.'

Ten minutes later she was lurching up a muddy track between straggling hawthorn hedgerows. At the end of it, a five-barred gate stood drunkenly half-open, peeling letters on the top rail declaring the place to be Edgett's Farm. For a moment, Stacey was disconcerted. What had happened to Edgett's? It had always been such a prosperous-looking place. But a quick glance into the fields beyond stilled the worst of her fears, for upwards of forty horses were grazing on the sparse winter pasture. However run-down the place had become, it was still a dealer's. Securing the reins, she jumped down in the mire to heave open the gate, then drove on into the farmyard.

It was unnaturally quiet. Stacey looked about anxiously. Had time not been so precious, it would have been a perfect chance to see what Joby Edgett had standing in his stables without him breathing down her neck, but as it was she had barely twenty minutes to complete a sale. Putting two fingers in her mouth, she let out a piercing whistle. And out from the harness-room limped a scrawny little man in a brown jacket, yellow waistcoat and moleskins. About his neck was a grubby muffler and a beaver hat, almost bald in places, perched on the back of his head. He paused for a moment to weigh up the expensive curricle and its driver, then suddenly his sad monkey's face creased into a gap-toothed grin of welcome.

'Well hang me if it ain't Miss Stacey Brown! How be you, Miss Stacey, and your pa? I ain't seen you these two year nor more.'

Stacey raced through preliminary exchanges as quickly as was decently possible. It was essential, she knew, to be swift without letting Joby Edgett realize what a trump card he held in her pressing need. Accordingly, she made polite enquiries after his health and fortune, remarking on the deserted air about the place.

'Ah, 'tis all changed for the worse, Miss Stacey, and no mistake. There's my son Dick gone off to Americy, and Ben lit off I don't know where, and both my girls got wed and moved out. There's only Sammy here now and he's got no more sense nor a babby since they damned Froggies shot away half his face.'

196

Stacey made suitably sympathetic noises, her mind racing. She discarded the tale she had been going to tell and struck out on a new line.

'I only called in to see how you were faring, Mr Edgett, while our general manager is busy in Stonham. But seeing as things are going so badly for you at the moment, perhaps I could put a little trade in your way. We can always find work for one or two good strong coach horses, if you happen to have any about the place.'

And to her inexpressible relief, he did happen to have not two but three, two bays and a dun, fit young beasts with no visible defects. Still acting as if it was she who was conferring the favour, Stacey managed to cut the usual lengthy negotiations short, labouring the two points that she trusted Edgett as an old friend to sell her reliable animals, and that her general manager was waiting for her even now in Stonham. She could hardly conceal her delight when the dealer let her have them at fifteen guineas a head. Bidding Edgett a friendly farewell, she tied the three horses to the back of the curricle and set off for the village. Once out of the farm and onto a decent stretch of road, she whipped up the team with a yell of triumph. They bounded down the turnpike to Stonham, Stacey singing raucously at the top of her voice, the new animals jostling behind, and pulled into the yard of the Dun Cow just as the Huntsman's Chorus could be heard floating faintly over the still countryside.

Simon's anxious expression changed to one of unbounded admiration.

'Stacey, you're a genius! Three horses! You must be a witch. Wherever did you conjure them from?'

Stacey jumped down, stiff with cold, but glowing in the warmth of his praise.

'From under my broomstick,' she said. 'How did you fare here?'

'I think we may have fallen on our feet. The landlady seems to be at daggers drawn with the landlady of the Prince of Wales, and would do anything to take some of

197

their custom. A contract from Brown's is a gift from the gods. There's one old man here who looks after the horses, and she can find some more beasts and horse-keepers later today, but we're going to have to manage this change ourselves. I suppose it's unnecessary to ask if you know how to harness a team?'

'I can practically do it in my sleep.'

'Spoken like a true Brown. But don't go to sleep now, for the Flyer's nearly upon us.'

Together with the ancient ostler-cum-yardman from the Dun Cow, they stepped out into the street to watch the coach's arrival. The outsiders, merry at the start of the journey and now topped up with brandy and hot water from each of the three staging-posts, whistled and shouted as Harry Cox pulled up. Their chilled fingers clumsy, Stacey and Simon struggled with the clips and buckles as the landlady and her daughters brought out the best the house could offer. Harry, seeing their difficulty, climbed down to help, and Simon explained briefly what had happened. He swore colourfully, then saw the comic side of it and winked at Simon.

'Reckon Pymer's getting his own back for that time you stopped his coaches.'

'He damn near succeeded, too.'

They backed the fresh horses into place and began to clip them into the traces.

'Owd Pymer'll never stop a Brown's coach,' Harry asserted.

With all four horses put to, he walked round checking that everything was securely fastened, took up the reins and made sure each one was running freely, then climbed up onto the box.

'Not bad,' he commented, 'for rank amateurs. Carry on like that and there'll be a shilling apiece for you at the end of the week. All right behind?'

'All right, Mr Cox!'

And with a renewed burst of waving and shouting from the young sportsmen on the outside, the Highflyer set off once more, a triumph to the Brown organization. Standing in the middle of the road to watch it go, Simon threw an arm round Stacey's shoulders in an expansive Brown-like gesture.

'You're the best business partner I've ever had the pleasure of working with,' he declared. 'Come and have a delayed celebration breakfast.'

Chapter Twelve

'You stupid cow, you're as much use as a stuffed doll. Can't you do anything right? Dear God! Why did I marry you? All you've got to do is see it's done, you don't have to think. We got a housekeeper to do the difficult work. Housekeeper! At an inn! My Jenny used to run this place with ten fewer servants than we got now, and it always looked clean, there was always food enough, everyone knew their jobs. Look at it now!'

Seth Pymer took Deborah by the arm and marched her into the principal parlour. Fingers biting into her soft flesh, he pointed out dirty tablecloths, spilt drink, customers waiting while slatternly maids gossiped in the kitchen passage.

'What d'ye say to that, eh? Eh? No wonder folks are going elsewhere. Place is no better nor a common tavern. And that's not all—'

Scared, resentful, Deborah was forced upstairs to the private rooms. Swine! she thought, brute! I hate you, I hate this place.

'See—' Seth flung open a door, revealing a messy, disordered sitting-room with a tray of unwashed glasses left on the floor. Dragging her to the bedchamber beyond, he displayed an unmade bed, grey scummed water still in the washstand bowl.

'Would you want to be shown to a room like this, eh? You know what's happening, don't you? Folks don't come here any more. They go to the Maid's Head, or the Bell, or the Crown. And what happens when they go to the Crown? They travel on Brown's coaches, so we lose both ways. I picked you out of that hovel and saved your pa from debtors' gaol and your folks from the poorhouse, and what do you do in return? Bloody ruin me!'

Deborah thought, I didn't ask to come here. I didn't want to. I hate it. But she said nothing. She knew better than to fan Seth's anger.

Infuriated by her lack of response, he shook her till her eyes felt loose in her head.

'You could do it if you tried, you're just too damn lazy to care. My Jenny knew no more nor you when she first came, but she did it, aye and my Hannah before her and she was only nineteen when we was wed. And they were a damn sight better in bed, too. You – it's like lying with a warm corpse.'

That's because you make me feel sick, Deborah silently told him. I never did like it much with you, and now I can't bear it. It's you that don't know a thing in bed. You're like an animal.

She yelped as he struck her sullen face with the back of his hand.

'There's going to be changes, see?' He hit her on the other cheek. 'I been too soft with you. From now on you're going to bloody earn your keep. Come the new year, I'm going to be buying up Brown's stages, and you're not going to let all that new trade go, see? Learn to manage this place or I'll see – you – regret – it!'

She squealed at each blow, ducking, trying in vain to escape his heavy hand.

'I'll try! I'll try!' she promised.

'You better,' Seth told her, and he flung her down and marched out of the room.

Sobbing, she pounded the unmade bed with her clenched fists.

'I hate you, I hate you!' she cried into the mattress. 'I'll get my own back, you'll be the one to regret it. I'll—'

She had it in her power to injure him, and now at last she found the courage to do it. And it would please Simon. She wanted desperately to please him, for she knew she had very little hold on him. For the last few weeks he had been arriving late, leaving early, so that she never knew if he was going to let her wait in vain again.

201

Often he was abstracted, once he called her by another woman's name. That really frightened her, spurring her to send the note warning about the plan to stop the Highflyer. Each week she kept his interest by promising to bring the figures he wanted, but when it came to the point she was always too fearful of being caught to do it. But now – now she would. She would steal down to the booking office this very evening and copy down everything she could lay her hands on.

By nine o'clock, her resolution was wavering, but a chance glimpse of her bruised, swollen face in a looking-glass reminded her of the pleasure of revenge. First she had to get away from Seth, who had been breathing down her neck all day, and to her satisfaction found that for once a plausible story sprang to her lips.

'I'll go and make sure all the bedchambers are ready,' she told him. 'See them maids is doing their work right.'

Seth, busy supervising the flow of customers downstairs, grunted in agreement.

I'll show you, she vowed, and made for the main stairs. Here she hesitated, and again her new-found resourcefulness came to her aid. She would go upstairs, just as she had said, so that if he checked on what she was doing, he would find nothing to arouse his suspicions. Accordingly, she spent ten minutes looking into rooms and giving contradictory orders to indifferent maids. She knew only too well that they just shrugged the moment her back was turned and did exactly as much as they pleased, but at least she had put in an appearance. Buoyed up by thoughts of revenge, she padded down the back stairs, and stood at last in the yard.

Here her courage began to ooze away. The booking office was dark and shuttered, the clerks having locked up and gone home half an hour ago. Locked up! It was only then that the significance of the words sank in. She would have to go and take the keys. She cringed at the thought. Supposing somebody saw her? Perhaps she would leave it, try again another night. There was plenty of time. But then one of the porters passed by, touching his cap as he did so, and she realized that she was, after all, mistress of this place. Who had the right to question her if she fetched a key?

With an unusual degree of confidence, she marched along the tortuous passages of the inn to the board behind the main entrance where the keys hung on a row of hooks. But here she met with another setback: the one from the booking office was not there. For a minute she was confused, not knowing what to do next, for the chief clerk must have given it to Seth, and so it must still be in his pocket. Frustrated, she stepped into the entrance hall and looked through the open doors into the best parlour, where Seth was talking to a group of prosperous-looking farmers. It was warm in there tonight, and Seth's heavy face was flushed and sweating. He was in his shirtsleeves. Her heart leaping in triumph, Deborah slipped in and searched through the crowd of coats hanging just inside the door, all the time keeping an eye on Seth. She came at last to his familiar snuff-coloured one and went through the pockets, her fingers closing round the cold metal she sought. She was just about to go out again when Seth caught sight of her and came over. In her panic, the only thing she could think of doing with the key was to keep her hand hidden in the folds of her dress.

'You been a nationly long time up there,' he said. 'Everything all right?'

'Oh – yes, quite all right,' she fluttered. Try as she might, she could not think of a single excuse for getting away.

'You made sure the front rooms are all ready?'

'I – I—' She could not remember whether she had looked at them or not.

'You forgot,' he accused, scowling. 'Go and make sure, you stupid cow. We got Lord and Lady Engrave staying there tonight, and they'll be here before the hour's out. Make sure all the little things are right – flowers, writing-paper. The quality might not notice they're there, but they'll soon see if they're not. And they pay well, so see to it.'

Deborah nodded, weak with relief, amazed that he had not noticed the wild pounding of her heart. She flew upstairs again, found that the best set of rooms at the front of the house were mercifully in apple-pie order, and trotted – the nearest she ever came to running – along the passages and back down to the yard once more. This time she did not wait to let her trepidation get hold of her, but hurried heavy-footed round the edge of the yard, keeping to the shadows. At the door of the booking office, she fumbled with the lock, glancing over her shoulder all the while to see if anyone was watching her. Once inside, she felt for the lamp and lit it with trembling fingers. The low light seemed as bright as a beacon and she hastily checked that all the shutters were tight.

Now what? she wondered. Frantically, she tried to recall just what it was that Simon had asked her to do. She could remember every endearment, every avowal he had ever made, but talk of business just slid from her mind. Figures, she thought. Accounts. Sheets? Yes, that was it. Balance sheets, whatever they might be. She scanned the leather-bound ledgers ranged on shelves round the room, and took down the newest one. Was this what he wanted, she puzzled, flicking over the pages. There were the names of the various coaches, and columns of figures, and at the bottom of each page a total. She decided that it would have to do. She would give him this, and listen very carefully to what he said. At least she would have something to show him, and a small voice of cunning told her that she would keep his interest longer that way.

Finding ink and pen, she copied out the last page of the book onto a spare piece of paper, her untidy handwriting sprawling along the lines. Unused to writing, she worked slowly, the pen often scratching and throwing off unruly blots. Outside in the yard voices called, carriages rumbled, hooves clattered on the cobbles. Footsteps rang right outside the office, making her jump with fright. At last it was done. Heady with success, she bundled the ledger and writing implements away, folded the precious paper and slipped it inside her dress, and turned out the lamp.

Out in the yard again, she almost skipped with malicious glee. Let Seth beat her and bully her! She would get her own back now. The brute, he deserved it. And as she crowed, a shining chariot and four came trotting into the yard and pulled up by the main entrance. Lord and Lady Engrave! Deborah froze. Seth would expect her there with him to greet them, but there was no time to get through the inn. And just as she was wondering if she dare risk boldly crossing the yard to the carriage, Seth appeared at the door. She shrank into the shadows, praying that he would not look up and see her. Radiating false geniality, he stood bowing and smiling, welcoming the noble guests to the Three Tuns. The travellers swept haughtily inside, Seth in their wake, the carriage was taken into the stables. Deborah breathed freely again. She rushed inside, hoping to get up to the Engraves' rooms by the back stairs before they arrived there. It was not until gone midnight that she remembered she had left the key in the office door.

'Thass a funny thing,' Seth remarked, emptying his coat pockets. 'Could've sworn Johnson give me the booking office key, but it ain't here, and it ain't on the hook, neither. Bloody clerks! Worse'n bloody useless.'

Exhausted by the hardest day's work she had done in six years, Deborah's sluggish brain refused to come up with an adequate answer. But some sort of reply was expected from her, so she made a noise of agreement.

'Prob'ly gone and taken it home with him,' Seth decided. 'He just better be in early tomorrow, that's all.'

Deborah threw her clothes onto a chair, pulled on her nightgown and dropped into bed, not bothering to so much as run a comb through her hair. All she wanted was to sleep. She closed her eyes to the sight of Seth's corpulent body, but there was no escaping from the sound of him grumbling over the day's numerous problems, nor from the rough demand of his heavy hands as he rolled into bed beside her.

'You done passing well today,' he conceded. 'So now you get your reward.'

Repelled by him, Deborah tried to pretend it was Simon she was lying with, but the gulf was too wide for imagination to leap. Silently she endured, thinking all the while of the paper hidden at the bottom of the closet, and of the reward she might receive for that. It would be worth all the heart-stopping frights of the evening to have him look on her with favour again.

Chapter Thirteen

Christmas at the Crown began in September with the making of the puddings, and then was virtually ignored until the beginning of December, when a flurry of extra ordering and preparation began in the kitchen and gifts were gradually bought or made and secreted about the place. The twentieth and twenty-first saw the beginning of the real celebrations, for then the coachmen's dinners were held, necessarily in two halves so as to keep the service going. This year Barty shared the pleasure of presiding with Simon and Stacey, eating their way through a gargantuan spread of solid food and drinking increasingly incoherent toasts. Stacey, to her annoyance, was made to withdraw with the wives after each meal for decorous tea and gossip, leaving the men to what sounded like a far more lively evening, judging by the gales of ribald laughter. But she was, she told herself, lucky to be there at all. She had feared that her Aunt Eustacia's wish for her to stay at the Red House for Christmas might prevail, and was overjoyed when her pa would not hear of it.

From then on it was non-stop activity at the inn, with an extra flow of travellers on their way to join relatives, spare coaches on every route, a vast amount of cooking to be done and greenery to be nailed up in every available corner. Stacey was busy from morning till night, too busy to sort out the state of her feelings, as she frequently tried to do at the Red House, and all to no effect. It was a state made worse by there being nobody she could talk to. Her family were all far too close to be able to offer unbiased advice. She looked forward to January, when her old friend Annabel Harthwaite was due to visit the same distant relations to whom she had been going when she took Stacey to Dereham all those months ago. Annabel, she thought, was close enough to be confided in, detached enough to see matters in a clear light. But before then was Christmas, always an occasion for riotous celebration amongst the Browns, and she threw herself into the preparations with all her usual enthusiasm.

At four o'clock on Christmas Eve, the spare Eclipse was led into the yard and loading started on a huge pile of luggage ready for the last extra run to Cambridge. Simon, after seeing his own bags safely stowed, looked about the yard for Stacey, and caught sight of her disappearing indoors with an armful of ivy. He followed, reaching the foot of the staircase just as she arrived on the landing outside the family parlour.

'Stacey!'

She turned, her face still glowing from the cold outside, rebellious locks of hair tangled in the trailing strands of ivy.

'Hello, I thought you were taking the Eclipse out.'

'I am, but it's not ready yet. I came to say goodbye.'

He ran up the stairs two at a time, and as he did so, he noticed the great branch of mistletoe nailed over the door.

'What further invitation do I need?' he laughed, taking the greenery out of her hands and dropping it on the floor.

He meant just to kiss her briefly, but her lips were soft and responsive, their winter chill melting instantly. He drew her into his arms, filled with a curious sense of homecoming, and caressed the lithe curves of her body, tantalizingly muffled in layers of clothing. He felt her tremble as he pressed her to him, tasting her sweet mouth.

'Stacia,' he murmured, releasing her with reluctance, uneasily aware of treading on forbidden territory.

Her sherry-coloured eyes gazed back at him, trusting, bright.

My God, he thought, what have you done now?

Forcing a careless laugh, he pinched her chin, turning the moment into a brief meaningless incident.

'That's for tomorrow,' he said.

'Tomorrow?' Her face puckered with perplexity, as if it

208

were too difficult to understand. 'Won't you be here?'

'No.'

'But – where else will you go? Not home to your family?'

'In a way.' He drew a flat package out of his capacious coat pocket and put it into her hands. 'That's why I wanted to give you this now.'

'Oh!' She turned the parcel over, trying to guess its contents, flushed with delight. 'May I open it now?'

'Please do.'

She undid the narrow red ribbon and slid off the paper revealing a framed aquatint of Phaeton driving the sun chariot.

'I saw it in a print shop window and couldn't resist it,' Simon explained. 'You're not still cross with me over that, I hope?'

'Oh – oh no! Of course not. It – it's charming, really, I – thank you so much.' She looked up at him with unaccustomed shyness. 'I do have one for you, but it's at home.'

'I shall look forward to opening it when I return.' He gave her arm a swift parting squeeze. 'I must go, the Eclipse is waiting for me. Have a merry Christmas.'

'A merry Christmas,' she repeated mechanically.

He could feel her eyes on him as he ran down the stairs and into the yard.

'Keating!'

Simon turned, fast enough to see the fist aimed at his face, but not quite in time to take avoiding action. He caught the blow square between the eyes and staggered backwards, crashing onto the cobbles. For a moment he was dazed, his head ringing, then through the clearing haze he saw legs crowding round, forming a circle, and someone standing over him.

'Get up and fight, you lousy rat!'

It was Oliver.

Cautiously, Simon stood up, shaking his head to clear his vision. At once Oliver attacked, aiming a rain of blows at him, but this time he was on his guard and

209

dodged the worst of them. He tried to fight back, but was defeated by Oliver's longer reach. The few times he did hit him, his fists glanced harmlessly off Oliver's massive body. His only advantages seemed to be speed and a cool head.

'What's annoying you?' he goaded. 'Been excluded from the Kingdom of Heaven?'

With a roar, Oliver came at him with the light of murder in his eyes, pounding Simon on both sides of the head before he managed to get under Oliver's guard and jab viciously upwards at his jaw. Through the yells of encouragement from the spectators, he half-heard Stacey's voice begging them to stop. He pressed forward to follow up his advantage, but then strong hands clamped onto his arms and dragged him back. Feet away, Oliver was struggling between two beefy porters, and the Gaffer was looking from one combatant to the other, arms akimbo, scowling.

'What the hell d'ye think you're doing?' he demanded. 'This is a respectable posting-house, not a common tavern.'

'He was—' Oliver began.

'Hold your tongue!' the Gaffer ordered. He swung round to glare at Simon. 'You – there's a coach and fifteen passengers waiting for you to stop fooling around. I'll talk to you when you get back. Now move!'

Simon held his eyes for a moment, unused to taking orders issued in that fashion. Then realizing he was on shaky ground, he retrieved his hat and made his way through the fascinated circle of onlookers to the Eclipse. He had no wish to have his actions examined in public, and by the time he returned, everyone's tempers would have cooled. He took a perfunctory walk round the horses, mopping the warm trickle of blood from his nose, silently cursing Oliver. Thanks to the crack on his old wound, his skull was already throbbing with the beginnings of one of his blinding headaches, and he had sixty miles to drive through fading light to Cambridge. He was going to be in no fit state to enjoy Perdita's company.

Taking up the whip and reins, he climbed up onto the box and searched over the heads of the crowd for Stacey.

'All right behind?'

'All right, Mr Keating.'

She was standing by the kitchen entrance, white-faced, the print still clutched to her breast. With a resilient grin, he raised his whip in farewell, and received a tremulous smile in reply.

'Give 'em their heads, boys!'

The horsekeepers snatched off the cloths and let go of their charges, the guard blew a line of The Holly and the Ivy and the Christmas Eve Eclipse moved off.

By the time the apple-bobbing started on the afternoon of Christmas Day, Stacey had had enough. She stood against the wall in the long room of the Crown, empty glass in hand, and watched thirty-five assorted Browns, Jupps and Maddoxes making fools of themselves in the cause of celebration. All day long she had been trying to enter the spirit of the occasion, through the service at All Saints, the exchanging of gifts, the dinner and now the fun and games. But the false smile finally drooped and she was left gazing wretchedly at the red-faced, laughing crowd. All those months at Raston, she had been looking forward to a family party after the insipid affairs her Aunt Eustacia made her attend, but now she was here all she wanted was to be alone.

Glancing round to see that no-one was watching, she slipped out and made her way down to the yard. The winter air struck cold after the heat inside, but the quiet was like a blessing. Hugging herself to keep warm, Stacey walked through into the back yard, making for her refuge in time of stress. She dragged open the heavy doors of the first block of stables, and once inside the noise of revelry died away and only the soft sounds of the horses filled the silence, the clop and whisper of hooves shifting in the straw, the lazy swish of a tail. She wandered down the line of stalls, dim in the half-light, stroking a nose here, patting a neck there. The near wheeler of the Flyer, nicknamed

'The Killer' by the horsekeepers, laid back his ears and picked up a hind leg ready to lash out, so she avoided him, stopping instead at the stall of one of his team-mates and leaning against his sturdy shoulder, grateful for his undemanding warmth.

'What's to be done?' she asked, but the horse only rubbed his nose on her arm, expecting a titbit.

Now at last she understood what had driven Arthur Harris to bankrupt himself last summer. And Oliver – did he live with this ache of longing? It was all so wretchedly hopeless. What possible chance was there that a man like Simon would ever give more than a passing careless kiss to plain Stacey Brown? He regarded her as a business partner, and possibly as a friend. She clung to the fact that he once had confided in her. But beyond that there was nothing but a few brief moments of magic yesterday, and even they were tarnished by Oliver.

'If only he were here today,' she sighed, twisting a coarse strand of mane in her fingers. 'Where can he have gone?'

It was Oliver who first noticed she had gone. He only relaxed his watch on her a moment, and she disappeared. He could guess where. He shouldered his way through the crowd and traced her footsteps through the yard. Yesterday's encounter had left him almost without a scratch physically, but emotionally he was torn apart. The scene he had stumbled upon had shattered the idealized image he had of Stacey as innocent and untouched. He never even allowed himself to imagine the pleasures of enjoying her, but now he was racked with visions of what Keating might have done. His own inept part did not help. He had been so shocked at the time that his first reaction was to back away. What he should have done, he realized now, was to run up those stairs and throw Keating over the rail and onto the stone floor below. Not even his charmed life would have survived that unless, as his obsession was beginning to whisper, he really was the Devil incarnate.

One thing was clear: he must save Stacey from his evil influence.

'Stacey?' He paused in the doorway of the stable, looking along the rows of stalls. 'Stacey, I've got to talk to you.'

He began to search for her, suspecting her of trying to hide as she used to when they were children. Then silently she stepped out in front of him, her face and the white lace on her dress glimmering ghostly in the twilight.

'Go away, Oliver. I don't want to talk to anyone. I've got a headache.'

'Stacey, you must. I have to make you see—' he reached out to her, but she sidestepped nervously and backed away.

'Not now, Oliver. Please.'

'Yes, now.' He caught her by the arms and stared into her eyes, pools of darkness, unreadable. 'You must tell me, how long has it been going on between you and that man?'

'Nothing's going on.' She twisted, trying to free herself. 'Let me go! You're hurting!'

'But I saw you,' he insisted.

'That was nothing, it didn't mean a thing. Please, Oliver!'

'Listen, do you know what sort of a man he is? Do you know where he is now?'

She did not answer, but she stopped struggling and stood still, shaking.

'I'll tell you where he is, he's at Newmarket with his mistress. He's spending the day of the Lord's Nativity with his fancy woman—'

'No!' Her voice rang shrill. 'No, it's not true.'

'It is true. That's where he goes every Sunday, too. When decent folk are going to chapel, he's over there with her. Fornicating.'

'Lies!'

'And that's not all,' Oliver went on inexorably. 'Do you know where he is Wednesday afternoons? He goes to

Mullins dressmaking shop and meets some other woman there. One of the girls at the chapel is skivvy there, and she's seen him come in the back way.'

'Gossip, nothing but gossip!' she cried, tears thickening her voice. She fought to get away, but he held her hard. 'Let me go, I don't want to hear any more, it's all lies!'

The dreadful truth of the matter was beginning to reveal itself.

'Are you in love with him?' Oiver demanded.

'Yes,' she declared passionately. 'Yes, yes, yes. There! And he's not as bad as you think. You don't know the half of it. You don't know anything. He's—'

The last vestige of control snapped inside Oliver, leaving only a blind rage against Keating, a desire for Stacey, a craving for revenge.

'He shan't have you,' he growled, fastening his mouth on hers, stifling her scream of terror.

Stacey fought and kicked but made no more impression than a shadow against his massive strength. His huge hand ripped at the neck of her dress and kneaded her breasts. She was suffocating, choked, powerless. And then she was being forced back, down, her legs buckling under his weight until she was lying in the dirty straw with him on top of her, his knee parting her legs, his hand tearing at her drawers. She screamed, begged, pleaded, but he only repeated, 'He shan't have you.' And high above, totally unconnected with the horror of reality, there was a dark movement, a dull shine, a double thud. Oliver cried out and his hands clamped vice-like on her flesh. The thud came again, jerking Oliver's body, and with it the wheezing squeal of an angry horse. Dimly, Stacey's numbed brain realized that they had fallen behind The Killer's heels. The deadly hooves landed again, this time striking Oliver's skull. He grunted and went limp. Stacey edged out from under his inert form, rolled clear of the flailing hooves and staggered for the door, crying with terror and relief. Panting, clutching the torn remains of her dress about her, she stumbled into the main yard, conscious

214

only of the need to get as far away as possible from Oliver.
A male figure loomed in front of her and she gasped in
fear, tripping as she tried to avoid him. Strong arms
caught her as she fell.

'Stacey! What is it? Whatever's happened, chicken?'

'Pa!' Sobbing, she clung to his secure bulk. 'Pa - oh
thank God - he tried - he's in there—'

Barty began to lead her towards the nearest entrance.

'It's all right, chicken,' he soothed. 'Come on in, you're
safe now.'

'But Oliver - he - he—'

'I'll break his neck,' Barty promised. 'Now come inside,
pet, we'll see to you first.'

Chapter Fourteen

The Maybush tavern was recovering from the midday rush as Simon made his way through the taproom and out to the untidy yard at the back. He threaded round a couple of rotting benches, an old table and filthy heaps of sacks, ropes and garbage to the sagging back gate. Here he paused, strongly tempted to go back. On the other side was the neat, paved patch belonging to Letty Mullins's establishment. He looked up at the first floor window, where the red curtains hid the room beyond, and was disgusted by the whole situation, and particularly his part in it. It seemed that wherever he went, he became involved in deceit and double dealing, presenting half a dozen different faces to the world at once. He found himself wishing for someone from whom he kept no secrets.

The curtain twitched and he stepped back behind a derelict outhouse. The thought of another two hours of Deborah's stupidity and complaints was uninviting in the extreme. He loathed having to listen to the continuing tale of her hardships. She had very little to whine about, when compared to the ordeal Stacey had suffered, and yet Stacey kept up an appearance of normality, even though she was troubled with recurring nightmares. But then Stacey was altogether different from Deborah. Simon was disturbed to an unprecedented degree over the Christmas crisis. If he had been there, he felt, he could have done something to avert it. Oliver would have taken it out on him, Stacey would have been protected and even Oliver himself still in one piece, and not lying helpless and semi-paralysed, refusing to speak.

Pushing the gate open, he came to a decision. This part of his life at least was going to be cleared up. Whatever the advantages to the company, they were not enough to justify going on. He would tell her, for he owed her that, and no doubt there would be a scene, but after that – freedom. He gave his usual jaunty greeting to the scullerymaid toiling in the kitchen, and ran up the stairs two at a time.

'Darling!' Deborah flung herself into his arms and raised her face to be kissed.

Simon said, 'Hello, Debbie,' and disengaged her clinging body.

She was disconcerted by this for a moment, but soon overcame her misgivings. She turned away, sending him a coquettish glance over her shoulder, and began taking the pins out of her hair.

'I've got something to tell you,' she said.

She was already half undressed, her over-generous curves threatening to burst out of her soiled corset. Simon wondered at his ever having found her desirable. He could look at her now quite unmoved.

'Have you?'

'Yes, but I shan't tell you unless you're nice to me.'

Her voice was seething with suppressed excitement. Whatever it was she had to impart, she evidently thought it was of great importance to him. Simon considered the shaky state of Brown's finances, but was not swayed.

'Very well,' he said, 'keep it to yourself.'

She put on a little-girl pout.

'Darling, don't be so horrid. Come and unlace me.'

Simon stayed standing just inside the door.

'I think you had better sit down, Deborah. I only came here today to tell you something.'

Alerted by the finality in his voice, Deborah came over to him, eyes wide with alarm.

'No, no—' she could not quite keep up the note of gaiety. 'You must have my news first. You'll be so pleased! I could hardly believe it at first.' She wound her arms round him once more and rubbed her head against his shoulder. 'I'm expecting a baby.'

Simon went cold, seeing first the jaws of the trap, then, mercifully, a way of escape.

'Are you indeed?' he responded, with polite calm. 'Pymer must be pleased.'

'But it's not his!' she declared, gazing up at him. 'It's yours! I thought you'd be thrilled. Our baby!'

'I doubt it,' Simon said. 'It's a fairly long chance.'

'But it is. I know it is!'

'You do? Has Pymer not touched you these last few weeks, then?'

'Well – yes – but it must be yours. We've been married six years and nothing's happened, and neither of his other two wives bore him any children—'

'Then you had better take great care of this one, had you not?' Simon freed himself of her embrace once more and made her sit down on the bed. 'No more fun and games for you if you're going to produce the heir to the Three Tuns. You're a responsible matron now, Debbie. That means behaving yourself and acting like a good wife and mother. You don't want to risk losing the child, do you?'

Deborah's face crumpled as the meaning of his words sank in.

'You mean you're not—? But I can't—'

Simon picked up her frock and handed it to her.

'Get yourself dressed, there's a good girl. I'll tell Letty we won't be needing the room any longer and you wait for ten minutes or so before leaving. We don't want to risk being seen together at this late stage, do we? Pymer might get the wrong idea.'

'No! Oh no, no, you can't leave me!' Deborah flung herself at him, tears welling in her eyes. 'I can't live without you, I'll die! I'll do anything you want. I'll leave Seth, leave everything, I'll run away with you, anywhere at all—'

It was some time before he could prise off her desperate, clinging fingers, still more before he calmed her hysterical pleading.

'Listen,' he said, holding her by the shoulders at arms' length. 'You must know this would have ended sooner or later. If you use this pregnancy with even the barest amount of intelligence, you can make life very comfortable for yourself. Pymer's not going to do anything to jeopardize the child's health, so make the best of it. Understand?'

Sobbing uncontrollably, she showed no sign of having taken in a word.

Simon made his escape. 'I hope the child brings you great happiness,' he said. 'Goodbye, Debbie.'

He ran down the stairs, shutting his ears to her cry of despair. Once through the back yards and into the street, he was filled with a sense of release. One dark corner gone, one less secret. He hired a horse from the first inn he came to and set off for the country, resolutely unaware of having left Deborah with her world lying shivered around her.

While Simon's life shed one of its entanglements, Amos's gained a further sinister twist.

It was quite a shock for him to come in from his midday break to find Miss Stacey looking over the day's accounts. His immediate assumption was that she had found out something to his detriment, and his entrails quaked as he tried to check in his mind all the figures he had entered since arriving at the booking office that morning.

Her curving smile put some of his fears to rest.

'Hello, Mr Burgess,' she said, friendly, a shade anxious. 'I hope you don't mind my usurping your seat for ten minutes.'

'It's not my place to mind,' he replied, acutely aware of the junior clerks' covert watch on him.

She sat staring at the page in front of her, her brow creased.

'Mr Burgess—' she began, then stopped and sent the two clerks off for their break. The moment the door had closed behind them, she tapped the ledger with her finger.

'What do *you* think, Mr Burgess? We've been holding on and holding on ever since the autumn, cutting fares as much as we dare, and still Pymer's haven't given up. How much longer can we go on like this?'

Amos felt quite giddy at the sudden turn in his fortunes. One moment he thought he was about to be found wanting, the next he was being consulted about the company's future.

'Now Mr Brown's raised this loan, we should get through the winter, barring accidents,' he said. 'But you never know what might happen, this time of the year.'

'That's just it. You know as well as I do that we only ever break even during the first quarter, what with the high costs and few people travelling. This year we seem set for making a loss, and the loan's hardly going to cover it.'

It was just like old times, being included in earnest discussions over possible disasters.

'Mr Brown would hardly have taken out the loan if he were not confident of winning through,' he pointed out. 'And neither would the bank have lent it to him.'

'No – quite—' Miss Stacey leaned her chin in her hand and sighed.

Even Amos, the least observant of men, had noticed that of late she had lost her sunny sparkle. She was pale and there were dark shadows under her eyes. Not for the first time, he wished for a daughter of his own. Children he had never cared for, noisy, demanding creatures. But a grown-up daughter to care for him in his old age, that would be a comfort and a blessing.

'I've never yet known the Gaffer to fail, and I've been with the company from the beginning,' he said.

'Yes, I know, you're quite right.' She summoned up a cheerful smile. 'Silly of me to doubt for a moment. But I do wish we could get on and win this battle. A loan to buy up Pymer's bankrupt stock, now that would be worth taking out!'

It was on the tip of Amos's tongue to tell her that the

figures he would be passing on to Pymer's tonight might well tempt them into taking the sort of financial risk that would topple them. For a heady moment he imagined her admiration, her gratitude. But just as he was on the point of spilling his secret, a customer came into the office.

Miss Stacey slid out of his chair and bade him a friendly farewell.

Amos dealt with the booking in his usual precise manner, but his mind stayed on his visitor. There was a disturbing tale going about the yard concerning Mr Oliver's accident in the stables on Christmas Day. It seemed Miss Stacey was somehow involved in that. And at the bottom of it, inevitably, was Mr Keating. There appeared to be no hope now of Miss Stacey's marrying Mr Oliver, but if he could prove himself to be instrumental to Pymer's defeat, Amos thought, at least he would not be in danger of being completely usurped by Mr Keating. It was a prospect worth all the terrifying risks he was taking.

He hobbled through the bitter winter streets late that evening on the way to the appointed meeting-place, the incriminating slip of false figures thrust deep into his inside pocket, trying to ignore the ache in his old bones, the grating of his swollen joints. If only he had a daughter waiting at home for him, instead of Martha. A daughter who would make up the fire for him and warm him some soup, and listen with interest to his recital of the day's events. He was elaborating on this pleasant daydream when a hulking figure emerged from the shadows just behind him, clamped a brawny arm round him and silenced his cry of terror with a huge hand over his mouth.

'One squeak out of you, and I knock your nasty little head off,' a voice threatened, bringing with it a sickening stench of onions and ale. 'Mr Clayton wants to speak to you.'

Effectively dumbfounded, Amos was hustled through a darkened doorway and up a flight of stairs to emerge, blinking, in a room of startling splendour. An oriental carpet spread before his feet, a huge bank of seacoals crackled in a marble fireplace, light from a crystal chandelier sparkled on displays of porcelain and silverware. Amos was pushed towards the hearth, where a figure was half-hidden in a large wingbacked chair. A large, impassive man of indeterminate years sat there, dressed in a claret-coloured coat and dove-grey pantaloons of finest cut, immaculate linen at his neck, gold fobs dangling from his watch-chain. Eyes as hard and implacable as granite regarded him from a craggy face.

'Let him go, Joby.' Clayton's voice was soft and expressionless.

Amos stood by the marble hearth, scorched on one side by the blazing fire, acutely aware of Joby's hovering presence.

Clayton held up a small sheaf of papers.

'Do you recognize these?'

Amos nodded. They were the slips of paper he had passed. He swallowed.

'You are certain of that?'

Amos nodded again.

'And are you certain that the figures are accurate?'

In spite of the heat, Amos shivered in icy apprehension. His mouth opened, but no words came out.

'I am disappointed in you. Very disappointed.' Clayton appeared to speak more in sorrow than anger. 'I took you to be a man of sense, one who understood the nature of the little arrangement Will made with you. He kept his side of the bargain, but you – you have been passing rubbish.' The stone-grey eyes swept over Amos. 'You are shaking,' he remarked. 'Are you cold? We will have to warm you up. Joby!'

Obedient as a well-trained mastiff, the man stepped forward and picked Amos up by the scruff of the neck until he was dangling like a rag doll. Effortlessly, he swung Amos round until his feet were inches above the dancing flames. The heat seared his boots, licked round his ankles.

'Rubbish belongs in the fire,' Clayton said, dropping

the papers on the coals. 'Does it not?'

Paralysed with terror, Amos could only pray for a miracle. There was a smell of burning as the worn leather of his soles began to scorch. He tried to lift his feet but his legs had no strength.

'I trust your feet are warm now?' Clayton enquired. 'Good. We will now make sure your hands are all right.'

Abruptly, Amos was dropped on the carpet. His knees gave way and he collapsed in a limp, aching huddle. Job stooped and grasped his wrists and, helpless against his strength, Amos found his hands extended towards the fire. Instinctively, he tried to clench his fists to protect his palms, but the great hands that had once crushed a pewter tankard clamped on his brittle bones. Nearer and nearer to the flames his hands were forced.

'No!' he begged, 'No, please!' His thin voice cracked in terror.

'So you do have a tongue,' Clayton remarked. 'That's enough for now. Joby. Stand him up.'

Amos was jerked upright, facing Clayton once more.

'I think you understand that I mean what I say now,' Clayton said. 'So we shall talk business.' He leaned back in the deep chair, elbows on the upholstered arms, finger-tips together. His stony eyes bored into Amos. 'You are a married man, I believe? And of course you would not like to have anything – unpleasant happen to your wife?'

Through the nightmare a wild possibility flickered, enticing Amos as he had been tempted that evening he first saw John Hendry in the office.

'You – you wouldn't—' he croaked, playing for time. 'Just try me.'

He knew he had to appear to be horrified by the threat. Fear was easy to show with Clayton's merciless stare fixed on him.

'But – an old woman—'

Clayton gave his predator's smile.

'Her safety lies in your hands, Mr Burgess. You do understand that, I trust?'

Amos nodded.

'Good.'

Tired of the game, Clayton picked up a glass of Madeira. 'Take him away, Joby. He no longer interests me.'

Amos was propelled out of the room, through a bewildering maze of darkened corridors and out into a quite different street from the one in which he had been captured. Dazed, weak, aching in every bone, he slumped against a wall, trying to take his bearings. The walk home seemed an endurance test immeasurably beyond his strength, but home he must go, or spend the night in a back alley like a drunken vagabond. He hobbled painfully onward, moving his feet with the dogged ability for survival that had kept him going through thirty-five years of marriage to Martha.

Martha. At the bottom of the stairs to his rooms he paused, gathering himself for the last climb. He was no longer afraid of Martha. He began to haul himself up.

'Burgiss! Burgiss, is that you?'

Her safety was in his hands.

'Yes, it is I.'

For the first time in his existence, the power of life or death was his.

For Stacey, the New Year brought the long-awaited visit from her friend Annabel Harthwaite. Now, more than ever she needed someone to confide in, and Annabel seemed the ideal person to turn to. A shy, gentle girl whom Stacey had defended from the potential tyrants at Miss Haveringshaw's, she had listened for hours in the past to Stacey's stories of her family, helping her over her bouts of homesickness, but the present situation perplexed her.

'I don't understand it,' she said, her soft blue eyes anxious, 'You always seemed so close to your family. I used to envy you. You received all those long, chatty letters from your cousins and aunts and your father, and all I ever got was one thin little note once a fortnight. And you were always so eager to be home. Whatever has happened?'

Stacey wandered over to the window of the Red House morning-room and gazed out at the green, dismal in a shroud of grey January rain. Now that Annabel was here, she was not sure whether she could bear to relate everything that had happened. Up till Christmas Eve, yes, or maybe that as well, but not the rest. The terror was still too close.

'Nothing,' she said, defensively. 'At least – oh, everything. It's all gone wrong. Nothing is at all how I thought it would be. It's all changed.'

Annabel regarded her shrewdly.

'You're different,' she said.

'I'm not,' Stacey responded automatically. But staring unseeing at the sodden world outside, she knew she was not quite the same carefree, confident person who had waved goodbye to her friend at the Rose.

'Then perhaps it's me,' Annabel said. 'I know I've changed. You remember what a coward I used to be? I would never have thought, six months ago, that I would dare defy my father, but I did.'

'Oh, Annabel!' Ashamed at her own selfishness, Stacey flew across the room and perched on the sofa beside her friend, taking her hands. She had been so immersed in her own problems that she had forgotten Annabel's, told in letters over the last few months. 'Do you mean that dreadful man, the one your father wanted you to marry?'

'Yes I—' Annabel paused, struck anew with the enormity of what she had done, 'I said I wouldn't and nobody was going to make me. Stacey, he was *fat* and he had grown-up children older than me. My father was furious. He said that had nothing to do with it, that what mattered was that he, this man, was gentry and his family had lived on their own land for hundreds of years.' She bit her lip and looked down. 'It was a victory for him, you see,' she explained, seeing both sides of the situation. 'My

225

grandfather used to work for this man's family, and it proves just how far my father has risen. He's worked hard all his life, Stacey, since he was four or five years old, and now he owns two mills and we live in a great new house, and this is like a – a prize for all he's done.'

'But you're not a prize,' Stacey objected. 'You're a person.'

'My father doesn't seem to think so. I'm in disgrace. The relatives I'm staying with now are all trying to make me see how undutiful I am. I was very lucky to be allowed out to see you today.'

A new and revolutionary thought was beginning to take shape in Stacey's mind.

'You know,' she said slowly, 'it's not right, the way we're used. Just because someone's your parent, they should not be able to dictate your whole life. Why shouldn't we be able to choose what *we* want?' She thought back over the past half-year and came to a startling conclusion. 'My pa's up to something. He sends me out here because he says we need new blood in the family, and yet he treats Arthur Harris as a joke. He says it's not proper for me to have anything to do with the running of the company, and yet he lets me set up the Flyer. And now he's fallen out with nearly all the rest of the family over this – this – what happened with Oliver – he's the only one who believes me –' Before she realized what she was saying, she found the story was beginning to come out. 'They all think we left together, but it's not true, he followed me. They say it was my fault, that I should have agreed to marry him when he asked, and I was – was leading him on, but I didn't do anything of the sort, I told him to go away, but he wouldn't, he kept on and on about Si – about Mr Keating – '

She faltered to a halt, and Annabel, dimly comprehending what it was all about, picked up the name that had featured so often in Stacey's letters.

'And where does this Mr Keating come into all this?'

'I – I don't know – I mean – ' The words jerked

raggedly from her aching throat. 'At first, I thought he was to blame for everything going wrong, for the company being in trouble and me being sent out here, and I couldn't wait to be rid of him. But now I know he'll never stay here with us and I've hardly seen him since Christmas. He's always out of town seeing to something on Saturdays and he doesn't come to dinner with us any more and – oh, I wish we could go back to when we were planning the Flyer. It seemed as if he really belonged to Brown's then. The Flyer was our project, something we built together, but now it's all changed. I want so much just to see him again, and every time I go home, I'm afraid that he might have left.'

'But – 'Annabel could not follow her reasoning, 'why should he leave? What makes you so sure?'

Stacey found that she could not possibly explain. To do so would somehow make his going inevitable.

'I just know,' she said, her face set in a stubborn mask. 'It just isn't possible that he would stay here as Brown's general manager for the rest of his life.'

The summons from his father finally came three weeks after Christmas. Arthur had been expecting it for some time, and hoping against hope that it would be later rather than sooner. Reluctantly, he presented himself as requested in the library, where he found his father seated behind the huge carved desk with estate papers spread out in front of him.

'Ah,' he said, as Arthur came in, 'come here, my boy, and take a look at these.'

Arthur did as he was bid, and found as he expected the accounts for the past year.

'I have seen them already,' he said. 'It's – er – not a very promising picture, is it? I did think that if we made some economies in – '

'No amount of minor economies are going to solve this,' his father interrupted, jabbing a finger at the massive debit figure at the bottom of the page. 'If we do not have a drastic improvement in our fortunes within the next quarter, we're going to have to let Upthorpe and go and live extremely quietly somewhere like Tunbridge Wells. I'm not saying that this is all your fault, because it's not. All landowners are in a sorry way these days. But paying your debts off last summer was the last straw. Without that, I could have managed to hold on providing we made some retrenchments.' He sat back and looked levelly at his son. 'You have not forgotten, I hope, what I asked you to do when you came home after that escapade of yours?'

Arthur had not. He felt his responsibilities to his family acutely, but he had been putting off making a positive move in the vain hope that something else might turn up.

'No, sir,' he said. 'Of course not.'

'And – ?'

'Well – er – as I think I said at the time, I don't happen to be acquainted with any – er – heiresses,' Arthur stalled.

'Stop beating about the bush,' his father told him. 'You've had five months now to get something settled. How much progress have you made with the Brown girl?'

Finally cornered, Arthur had to admit that he was not altogether sure.

'I'm always made very welcome at the Red House,' he said.

'Yes, I can imagine you are. The question is, how much longer are you going to dither about? If you're not careful, someone else will come along and snatch the girl from under your nose.'

'You see, sir,' Arthur cast about for an adequate excuse, 'I wasn't quite clear how you would feel about the Browns. I mean – innkeepers and such like – '

'Good God!' Mr Harris's patience ran out. 'Use your sense, boy, if you've got any. You don't have to associate with 'em. You have a quiet wedding, you invite them all to a supper party or something once a year, and you let the girl go and visit them every couple of weeks. You don't have them all running in and out of Upthorpe.

228

Your mother tells me there are no objections to Miss Brown herself, and from what I've seen of her she seems a pleasant enough girl, so what are you waiting for?'

Put like that, Arthur could find no answer.

'That's settled, then,' his father said. 'I've made a few enquiries as to the extent of her fortune, and all I can find is that she does have some money in trust, but Brown must be a pretty warm man and he'll be pleased as Punch to have his daughter marry into our family. He's no fool, he'll know that privileges like this have to be paid for. So – when are you going to ask her?'

Arthur shifted uneasily in his seat.

'I – er – '

'No time like the present.' Mr Harris looked out of the window across the parkland. 'Rain's clearing. Why don't you ride over to the village now?'

There was nothing to do but comply.

Trotting along the dripping lanes towards Raston, Arthur weighed up his prospects of happiness. In spite of his parents' approval, he had a sneaking suspicion that Stacey Brown was not quite what she appeared to be. His mother had only seen her at genteel parties and morning calls and not, as he had, bargaining for horses or driving Talbot's curricle down the Ipswich turnpike with all the assurance of one of Brown's coachmen. His mother would certainly not approve of a girl who went racing about the countryside with someone like Keating, on whatever pretext. And there was another thing. Keating had once said that she would sort out his fortunes even if she came to him without a penny. Arthur found the thought of his wife organizing his finances alarming in the extreme. On the other hand, she was a nice girl, kind, and entertaining company when out of earshot of her elders. If only, he thought, he found her more physically attractive.

He was still hoping for a reprieve when he arrived at the Red House. Perhaps she would be out. But no, the mistress was not at home, the maid informed him, but Miss Brown was in the drawing-room. An all-too-perfect opportunity to propose.

But she was not alone. There was another girl with her, 'My schoolfriend, Miss Harthwaite,' as she was introduced to him. Arthur hardly heard Miss Brown's polite enquiries after his family's health. He was entranced by her friend's shy smile, drowning willingly in her gently blue eyes. Her name, he soon discovered, was Annabel. It was the most beautiful name in the world and suited her entirely, matching her pretty round face, her quiet voice, her soft figure. Scarcely aware of Miss Brown's presence, he sat and talked to her, oblivious to time. They found shared preferences, held identical opinions. It was only when Miss Brown's aunt came in that he recalled the original purpose of his visit, but by then it was far too late. His father could say what he liked, but it was absolutely unthinkable that her should even consider marrying Stacey Brown.

Through the first weeks of the New Year, Simon fetched up against the full force of the Brown's solidarity. At the Crown, they put about a fiction of an accident at Christmas, and with the exception of Barty, closed ranks against him. Just as he thought he was accepted by practically everyone except Oliver, they put him firmly back where he belonged – on the outside. Even Harriet was distantly polite, and Aunt Peg, whom he had charmed out of her original suspicion by asking her advice on Perdita, no longer made him welcome in the family parlour. Though Oliver was slowly recovering from the trampling he had received from The Killer, the Browns were unforgiving.

On Stacey's visiting days, Simon made a particular point of being absent, and found that being free to travel to Newmarket the night before instead of waiting till Sunday norning was no compensation for the loss of the Saturday evenings at All Saints Green. He made a few half-hearted attempts to find a successor to Deborah, but found the memory of Stacey's pliant warmth and curving smile came between him and anything but the most usual course and move on, abandoning it as an impossible situation, as he always avoided at all costs examining his motives. The only way open seemed to lie in giving the Browns time to simmer down and mend the rifts behind their united front, and in making himself indispensable.

To this end, he worked consistently harder than he had done for years. He travelled the length of the Brown network in wind, rain and snow, sorting out crises caused by minor accidents and bad conditions, standing in for sick or injured coachmen and guards, keeping up the supply of horses as the heavy work took its toll of older and weaker animals, and when nothing else was pressing, making spot checks on unsuspecting innkeepers to ensure that Brown's standards were being kept up.

And then came the letter from Cheshire. It was waiting for him when he came in soaked and weary from a journey down to Yarmouth and back on an almost empty coach. He scanned through it quickly then sat down and read it more thoroughly, looking for hidden implications. His first impulse was to tear it up and forget about it, but instead he sat for a long while with the sheet of paper in his hand, looking about the room that had been home to him for the past nine months. He had stayed here longer than anywhere since leaving Oxford, and the small sitting-room and the bedchamber beyond bore the marks of his occupation. He had rearranged all the furniture to his satisfaction, put up bookshelves and a couple of prints. His eyes came to rest on a small wooden plaque propped up on the mantelpiece. On it was painted a galloping racehorse, and round the edge in the neat signwriting of Brown's coach finisher, 'The Highflyer, 3rd December 1820'. Stacey's Christmas gift, belatedly passed on to him by Barty. He had seen her once since to thank her, and she had flushed and looked embarrassed and muttered something about having meant to have given it to him on Christmas Day. Stacey would expect him to obey the summons, he realized. She would insist that it was his duty. He walked over to All Saints Green for a brief interview with Barty, packed, and left early the next morning.

Chapter Fifteen

It was on the Saturday after Simon's departure that Stacey arrived at the Crown to find herself pressed into Peg's efforts to settle the family difficulties.

'I got Oliver talking at last,' she said, sinking wearily into a fireside chair. 'Been up half the night I have, and I'm fair jowered-out, but it was worth it.' She stretched out a hand towards Stacey in apology. 'I was wrong about you, my love, and I'm sorry. Truth is, I didn't want to believe you.'

Stacey smiled wanly and said that it was all right, and after a while discovered that Aunt Peg had a favour to ask of her.

'If you would just talk to him,' she begged, 'and make him see he ain't damned to hellfire forever. I can tell him a hundred times and it won't make any difference, but if you say you forgive him, he'll be able to live with himself again.'

Stacey promised to try, but it was no easy task. She was torn between compassion as Oliver hobbled in as painfully as an old man, and a sick fear at the memory of the last time they were alone together. She managed to assure him that all was forgiven and forgotten, for which Oliver was pitifully grateful, but the spectre of Simon stood unacknowledged between them. Neither was able to take back a word they had said about him. Stacey finally felt she could not endure another moment of the strained silences and outbursts of soul-searching without screaming or doing something violent.

'Now hurry up and get completely better,' she said in the cheerful voice of the professional nurse. She forced herself to go up to him and lay a fleeting hand on his shoulder. 'Pa misses you terribly at the coachworks. He says the whole place is falling to pieces without you.'

Just how true this was she did not find out until that evening. Barty came in late for dinner and slumped down at the table, rubbing his hands over his tired face.

'I'm getting old, and that's a fact,' he admitted. 'I can't run round doing three people's jobs any more. It was bad enough having Oliver off sick, but now with Simon gone as well, I don't know whether I'm coming or going. Tell you the truth, I didn't realize just how much work he'd taken off my shoulders.'

Stacey stared at him, cold with foreboding.

'Gone?' she repeated. 'Gone where? What do you mean?'

Barty started carving generous slices off the saddle of mutton.

'Cheshire, I think he said – how much do you want, chicken? That enough? – yes, Cheshire. Got a letter from his folks about three days ago and said he had to go back straight away. Urgent family business.'

'Oh *no!*'

Alerted by the break in her voice, Barty shot a speculative look at her from under his eyebrows.

'It ain't so very far up there,' he pointed out. 'I expect he'll be back in a week or so. Are you going to help me to some of that pie, or have I got to do everything round here?'

Stacey gazed unseeing at the spread of food before her. How could her father talk about pies when the world had just come to an end?

'He won't be coming back,' she muttered, so low that Barty could hardly catch her words.

He snorted in mock impatience.

'That's foolish talk, for a start.'

'No it's true. I'll show you.'

Stacey stood up and walked over to the bookshelves in the alcove, aware of a vague surprise that everything was just as it always was. When all she hoped for had just crumbled, it seemed odd that the rest of creation had not changed in the least. She took down an old copy of the Peerage and dropped it on the table by Barty's plate, where it fell open at 'Lathenbridge'.

'Read that,' she said, pointing.

Her father leaned forward, peering at the small print.

'Lathenbridge, Baron (Wynwood) UK. Baron 1601,' he read.

'Charles Timothy Henry Wynwood, 4th Baron. b.1762 ed. Harrow and Oxford. m. 1787 Anne-Marie Celine, d. of the late Comte Etienne Essagné d'Argenville. Seat: Lathenbridge Hall, Cheshire.'

He skipped over the detailed description of the coat of arms and arrived at the section headed 'Sons Living'.

'Hon Timothy Charles Vernay b. 1789

Hon Simon Henry Eugene b.1793'

He looked up at his daughter's stricken face.

'That's never our Simon.'

'It is.' Stacey's finger stabbed further down the page at Georgiana Christy's name. '*She* came to see him before Christmas. They wanted him back home then. This is an old book. They're not all here now. These two,' she pointed to the list of three daughters, 'are dead, and this one, Caroline, is married but can't have any children.' In a flat, expressionless voice, she asked, 'What is the most likely form of urgent family business, the sort that would send him posting up there without delay?'

Barty considered.

'Funeral?'

'Exactly. Either his father or his brother. More likely his brother, because he was ailing when Miss Christy came here. But whichever it is, that makes Simon next in line.' Stacey took a deep breath and spelt it out. 'The future Fifth Baron Lathenbridge is hardly likely to return to Brown's Coaches.'

Barty ran over the entry again, and had to agree.

'I mind a time,' he said slowly, 'when you would have been very pleased to learn that. Very keen to be rid of our general manager, you were.'

Stacey dropped into her chair and buried her head in her arms, scattering glasses and cutlery.

'Not any more,' she sobbed. 'Not any more.'

Putting an arm round her, Barty drew her onto his knee.

'There, there, chicken,' he soothed. 'Don't cry. Plenty more fish.'

'I d-don't want anyone else.'

Awkwardly, Barty stroked her hair. It had occurred to him very soon after Simon appeared at the Crown that here was just the man he would like to leave the business to, just the man likely to make his daughter happy. An ideal arrangement. And with the hatching of the Flyer, he thought that things might well be working out just as he hoped. Now it seemed that all his careful manoeuvring had gone awry. It was years since Stacey had last wept broken-hearted on his shoulder, and then it only needed a kiss and a few words of sympathy to make it better. Now he felt helpless, seeing no way to console her.

Across the stark fenland, the glinting waters of the cuts reflected the sullen grey of heavy clouds, and shivered with the threat of snow. The two postboys hunched against the biting cold, urging their horses to greater speed the sooner to gain the comfort of the next inn, whilst inside the chaise, protected from the worst of the elements, Simon stared at the bleak landscape. With five thousand pounds in his pocket, he could afford to travel in style, afford to go anywhere and do anything he wanted. Of course, he knew what he was supposed to do with the money: find himself an impeccably bred female and settle down for long enough to produce a few pure-blooded Wynwoods. But if his father thought he could be bought at that price, he was soon to find that he was much mistaken. As it was, he was now able to do whatever he pleased.

'Freedom,' he mouthed, but the word rang hollow. Freedom merely meant having nothing to lose.

Try as he might, he could not recapture the sense of adventure he had felt last April when he set off with four horses and no fixed plans. Then he was leaving the corruption of the racing world behind and heading, though he did not know it at the time, for the loyalty and friendship of the Crown. Now – now he could travel the world. Even after settling half of his newly-gained wealth on Perdita, it would still leave enough to wander round Europe and into the orient. Italy, Albania, the Isles of Greece. He repeated their names like a charm, but they held no magic. There was only one place that called him, and he was unsure of his welcome there. He could even admire the Browns for the way they closed up against him. The various members of his own family would have seized on such a disruptive element and used it in the continuing strife.

West Walton, Walpole, St John's, the miles passed under the horses' hooves. Across the empty, open land and into King's Lynn as the sleet began to fall, driven by an evil wind all the way from Norway. At the Mitre, Simon looked for familiar faces, but the cobbled yard was almost deserted. Still undecided, he followed the landlord into the blessed warmth of the inn. The heat and good cheer enveloped him, the smell of ale and spirits and roasting meat, the drift of tobacco smoke, the genial faces flushed from the seacoal fire banked in the huge open hearth. And above the buzz of voices came a shout of recognition.

'Mr Keating! Good to see you back, sir! Will you join us in a drink?'

Sam Fletcher, the Tantivy's new coachman, was stoking up prior to the bone-freezing journey back to Norwich. With new purpose in his step, Simon went over to his table.

'Good day to you, Sam. You're a welcome sight. I was hoping to get here in time for the Tantivy.' He sat down opposite the coachman, ordered a meat pie and a tankard of mulled ale and steeled himself to shed a layer of protection. 'The name's Wynwood,' he said, 'from now on.'

Sam took it with hardly a flicker of surprise and proceeded to bring Simon up to date with all that had been going on in the company during the fortnight he had been away.

'Business is bad, even for February,' he remarked. 'Been running mad women some days, we have. Plenty of room for you inside, sir, on the way home.'

'If it's all the same to you, Sam, I'd rather be up on the box.'

The coachman snorted his disgust at such folly.

'Must be off your head, turning down an inside seat on a day like this. Be coming on to snow soon, if I'm not mistaken.'

Simon grinned and ordered another round.

'You don't know how good it is to be back,' he said.

The five-hour journey to Norwich was as bitter an endurance test as Sam had predicted, but for Simon the coachman's company was a tonic after two weeks of reading double meanings into even the smallest remark. Even surviving the piercing wind was a pleasure of sorts contrasted with the unceasing battle of wits at his home. They were late pulling into Dereham, unlike the warm midsummer's day when they had arrived at the Rose to meet an excited and palpably hostile Stacey waiting for a lift home. Simon was irrationally disappointed to find only the landlord, grumbling about the weather like every other person they met along the route. Even at the Crown, Simon reflected, he would not receive the welcome Stacey had been given on her return. Sam's reaction proved that the company servants were moderately pleased to see him but what of the Browns?

They trotted into Norwich with wet flakes of snow accumulating in the folds of their clothes, the guard's fingers almost too cold to hold the bugle for their final fanfare. Their passing caused no stir of excitement in the streets today. Everyone was too concerned with staying out of the weather to spare any attention for a homecoming stagecoach. Under the archway and into the Crown, solid and comfortable as the Browns themselves, looking in on itself and minding its own business. Even Barty did no more than watch their arrival from the office window. Frozen passengers disappeared into the early twilight or hurried to thaw themselves before the crackling fires of the inn, and the horsekeepers led the Tantivy into the stables. Simon and the guard made for the office. At the inner door Simon hesitated, knocked, and waited for the Gaffer's gruff 'Come!' before entering.

Barty was sitting behind a littered desk, frowning over a chandler's bill, his round face shining from the suffocating heat thrown out by the stove in the corner. When he looked up, he was wearing his bland, horsedealer's expression, hiding all emotion.

'Well,' he said, 'if it ain't the Honourable Simon Wynwood. You back to stay, bor, or just passing through?'

'That depends.'

Simon draped his sodden greatcoat over the back of a chair and let the blaze of the red-hot stove seep into him. He was thankful to find that one stage of explaining had already been done for him, but it was impossible to guess just what the Gaffer's reaction was going to be to his proposals. He briefly touched his waistcoat pocket, needing the reassurance of the banker's draft to support his flagging confidence. The most important deal in his life lay ahead of him and all his experience in driving a bargain counted as nothing if he did not have Barty's good opinion. Without that, he was sunk.

'I've a couple of propositions I'd like to put to you,' he began.

For fully a minute Barty regarded him from under his bushy eyebrows, giving away nothing. Simon suppressed a juvenile urge to fidget or make a facetious remark. In the nerve-cracking silence he could not think of one good reason why the Gaffer should be the least interested in anything he had to offer.

At length, Barty reached for the horse's hoof paperweight and thumped it down on the pile of bills and demands.

'You eaten properly today?' he asked. 'No, I thought not. Never talk business on an empty stomach, that's what I say. Come on over to the inn and we'll find a quiet corner, then you can have your say.'

The light had completely gone and snow was falling thickly by the time Simon set out again. Barty, coming out into the yard with him, looked up at the dizzying fall of flakes and shivered.

'Rather you than me, bor, it's starting to lay. You sure you hadn't better wait till morning?'

Simon wound a borrowed muffler more securely round his face and swung up onto the horse that an ostler led out for him.

'I've waited long enough,' he said. 'I'm taking no more chances.'

'Thass the spirit.' Barty gave him an approving slap on the knee. 'Good luck to you, bor.'

'Thank you.' Simon gathered up the reins, turned the unwilling horse's head to the archway and trotted off with a hand raised in farewell.

Once out of the sheltering streets of the city, the full force of the storm hit him, the snow turned to hard granules now, lancing his face with needles of ice, freezing his hands and feet, knifing his lungs with each breath. The high wind sculpted the snow into drifts, obliterated the familiar landscape, turned the short journey out to Raston into a nightmare battle with the white darkness. The whirling confusion reflected his inner uncertainty. 'If that's the way it is, that's fine by me,' Barty had said, 'but it's Stacey as has the final word, remember. I can't speak for her.' And when pressed for an opinion, he would only suck in his breath and shake his head and deny any special knowledge of his daughter's thoughts. 'I couldn't say, lad, and that's a fact. Been passing quiet these last few weeks, she has, what with one thing and another.'

Brooding on this, Simon twice missed his way and had to retrace his steps, the horse's hoofprints blotted out almost immediately by the fresh fall. It was with vast relief that he at last found the bare, stone-towered church and set the weary horse trotting the last stretch over Raston green towards the chink of light showing between the shutters of the Red House.

A maid peeped warily round the door in answer to his knock, squeaked in surprise and sent a resentful Hopkins out into the night to stable the horse.

'Mr Keating! Fancy you coming out here on a night like this! You must be frozen to—'

'Wynwood, the name's Wynwood,' he corrected wearily. 'Miss Brown is at home, I trust?'

'Oh yes, sir, and the mistress too, sir,' the maid chattered as her arms were loaded with the outer layers of Simon's clothes, 'wouldn't nobody—'

'Simon!'

Stacey stood in the drawing-room doorway, cinnamon eyes huge in disbelief, lips parted.

'I thought you had left us.'

'It's not as easy as that to be rid of me, you'll find. Are you sorry?'

'Oh *no*, it's just—'

She was still staring at him, unable to take in the fact that he was actually here, standing in the cramped hallway of the Red House.

'Stacey!' From inside the drawing-room, her aunt's voice sounded, sharp with disapproval. 'Will you kindly remember your manners and not stand whispering in the hall?'

Simon closed a chilled, stiff hand round her warm one.

'Come on,' he said. 'I'm going to follow correct form for once in my life.'

And summoning up his most disarming smile, he went in to face Aunt Eustacia as she sat, ramrod straight in her chair, pinched with indignation at this invasion of her territory.

'Pray forgive my intruding at such a late hour, ma'am. I know you were not expecting visitors, but I do come on rather a special mission.'

Aunt Eustacia's stony eyes glared at him, unimpressed.

'Indeed, sir, we were not expecting callers, but considering the weather outside, I suppose you had better stay a while.'

'You are most kind, ma'am, so much so that I am emboldened to ask another favour: might I be allowed a few minutes' private conversation with your niece?' He took in her unmelted hostility and produced his trump card. 'I do have her father's permission.'

Long practice in wrangling with Barty over Stacey's upbringing had taught Eustacia when a tactical retreat was necessary. She stood up, her gaze shifting from the young man who was threatening to overthrow all her years of dutiful care to her niece's flushed, expectant face.

'Stacey, will you be so good as to entertain your visitor for a while? I have to see what that fool of a girl is doing in the kitchen.'

As the door closed behind her, Simon found himself floundering once more in a sea of uncertainty. Disapproving old ladies he could handle with ease, but Stacey . . . Stacey was a different matter. All the conventional words withered in his mouth, worn out and meaningless with repetition and insincerity. Stacey filled the uneasy silence with the first thing that came into her head.

'You should be in mourning.'

He could not follow her at all. 'Mourning?' he repeated.

'Yes, it's only right. I know you don't like your family, but when somebody dies, you ought to wear black.'

The truth dawned on him.

'Nobody's died, my dear,' he explained. 'They're all in remarkably good health, or enjoying bad health, according to temperament. No, I went not to bury Caesar, but to marry him.'

'Marry?'

This time it was Stacey's turn to be perplexed.

'Timothy and Georgiana. I told you she was up to something, didn't I? I always knew she was devious, but I

241

never realized quite how far she was prepared to lie herself out of a corner until I found myself at the centre of her deceptions. Tim, poor devil, has made himself the martyr to family honour.'

He drew her into his arms, the one point of stability he had held on to through the shifting sands he had been treading the last two weeks. 'Stacey, I tried, I did try. When Tim invited me up there, I thought maybe I'd been making them all into monsters over the years, that my – my father was just a disillusioned old man who would be willing to make at least some gesture of conciliation if I made the first move. But they haven't changed, Stacey, except to get worse. I ended up playing the game by their rules, making such a damned nuisance of myself setting one against the other that in the end they had to buy me off.'

Stacey clung to him, as though if she held him tightly enough, their two bodies might blend together and he would never go away again. All through the endless march of empty days and lonely nights since Christmas, she had fed on a dream of this happening, and now that it was, she could hardly believe it. She dared not listen to the small voice that had begun to whisper he needed her as much as she needed him.

'And so – you came back?'

'I was coming back anyway, darling. I only went to lay the ghosts.'

He moved his hands over her young, supple curves, and found her every bit as warm and responsive as he had remembered, her lips as soft and yielding. More than that, she was loyal and dependable and loving. She was everything his own family were not. 'Stacey, I'm lost,' he admitted. 'I've been running away from them for so long I'd no sense of direction left when I met you. Marry me, and come back to the Crown where we both belong.'

Stacey was possessed of an odd sensation of being outside herself, of watching a character in a play. Soon the play would end and dull reality would assert itself. She looked up at the face she carried constantly in her mind's eye, the broad forehead and the thin, aristocratic nose, the cerulean eyes, not sapphire-hard now but anxious.

'You – you want me to marry you?'

Misinterpreting her hesitation, his mouth twisted into a defensive smile.

'That was the idea, yes,' he agreed. 'Does it not appeal to you?'

'Oh yes, yes, more than anything in the world.' The impossible had happened, making her practically incoherent in her haste to explain. 'It's just that I couldn't believe – you seemed to be avoiding me, and I thought – and when Pa said you'd gone away I thought you were never coming back – I missed you so terribly – I never imagined you might return for – for me.'

He held her face in his hands.

'My darling, the only place I want to be is here. You're the truest friend I ever found, I want to keep you by me for ever.'

She waited breathlessly for the next line, but it did not come, so that even as he kissed her there was a slight sick feeling of disappointment dragging at her joy.

'Oh Simon, I love you so much. I could hardly bear it when you went away,' she whispered, and hoped again for the right response.

'You don't know how good it is to be back, sweetheart.'

And as she wanted him whatever the terms, with that she had to be content. She had infinitely more than she had dared dream would be hers.

Chapter Sixteen

The news received a mixed reception. At the Three Tuns, Deborah fervently hoped that Seth's forecast of Brown's imminent downfall was correct, though even that would be insufficient revenge. She invented frightful accidents that might befall Stacey and send Simon back into her arms. Amongst the company servants at the Crown the match generally met with approval, for both Simon and Stacey were popular figures. A few cynical souls voiced the opinion that Mr Keating, or Wynwood as he now inexplicably wished to be called, had done very nicely for himself, but Barty soon squashed that by letting it be known that the junior partnership Mr Wynwood had bought in the firm had saved it from bankruptcy. Amos Burgess knew this to be true, but it only underlined his conviction that his last hope of security was done away with.

For Oliver, the intended marriage was a uniquely excruciating punishment, for which his new position as foreman of the coachworks was no compensation at all, though it did give him a reason for keeping away from the Crown for all of every working day. Sundays he devoted entirely to attending chapel.

Amongst the rest of the family, Aunt Eustacia was soon won over with the revealing of Simon's ancestry.

'Far better,' as Stacey slyly pointed out, 'than any of your paltry squires and curates.'

Barty accurately guessed that Aunt Peg was the key to the Browns' blessing. To her he imparted how worried he had been about Stacey, and the future of the company, and what a miracle it was that Simon had reappeared to solve both problems for him. Aunt Peg had to agree that it did seem to be an ideal arrangement, and Stacey's transparent happiness was almost irresistible. Simon finally won her over by appealing to her for motherly advice. What, he asked her, should he say about Perdita?

'Tell her,' Aunt Peg decided. 'Skeletons in cupboards always get found out in the end. Besides, Stacey's a sensible girl, she knows how the world wags. If she does make a fuss, send her to me and I'll soon talk some sense into her, but I don't think it'll be needed.'

It was fortunate that this concurred with Simon's new and often difficult policy of openness.

'How would you like to travel out to Newmarket on the Eclipse with me tomorrow?' he asked. 'There's someone I'd like you to meet.'

'I'd be delighted,' Stacey replied rather too brightly, covering the twist of foreboding. 'Who is it?'

They both knew perfectly well that she had heard the gossip currently going about the yard. Everyone's private business was public property at the Crown and only those like Amos Burgess who kept entirely to themselves escaped the inn's grapevine system.

'Wait and see,' he told her. 'I rather think you are going to take to each other.'

Stacey was quite sure she was not, but bit back a sharp query as to whether they would be welcomed on a Friday, seeing as he usually went there on Sundays.

She was learning, by degrees, that there was no point in pressing Simon for explanations. She was bursting with curiosity about just what had happened during his visit to Lathenbridge, but in spite of her careful probes and clever guesses, he refused to expand on the cryptic remarks he had made about Timothy and Georgiana. She wanted to know everything about him, to share in his past as well as his future, but instead was forced into being patient and waiting till he was ready. Patience was not one of her strongest virtues, but for Simon she was willing to try to cultivate it.

She arrived in the yard the next day dressed in the cherry red pelisse she had worn for the launching of the

Flyer – a deliberate reminder – and a heavy travelling cloak. The February snows had melted, but March was coming in with leonine ferocity, the high winds bringing rain and flooding.

'Inside for you,' Simon insisted, 'there's room enough.'

Stacey was about to point out that she hated travelling inside when she remembered that her nose was likely to go as bright as her turban, and she needed to look her best today. Never very confident about her appearance, she had spent an uncomfortable night with her hair in curl-papers worrying about how she compared to this unknown rival. So she climbed in obediently with two corpulent tradesmen and a nursemaid with a squalling child, and prepared herself for an uncomfortable and boring journey, laced with a growing anxiety about whom she would meet at the end of it. The long five hours brought home to her just how important this person must be to Simon, if he travelled so far to see her every week, summer and winter. By the time they were within a couple of miles of New-market she was convinced that she was going to have to share him with this woman for the rest of her life, if she did not think very quickly of some way to get rid of her. She was mentally checking her assets and possible weapons when the coach stopped at a small village and Simon climbed down to open the door.

'Time to step down, sweetheart,' he said. 'This is where we leave the Eclipse.'

Mystified, Stacey joined him in front of the small country inn and stood stamping the circulation back into her frozen feet while he hired a rather dilapidated whiskey to take them the rest of the way.

'It's not much further now,' he promised, and set the horse trotting briskly out of the village and along a muddy track. Stacey answered his remarks about the journey and how they would make their fortune if they could only invent a way of heating coaches with only half her atten-tion. She grew more and more puzzled as they drove into the countryside. This was not her idea of the sort of surroundings in which fancy women were found. They came at length upon a labourer clearing a choked ditch.

''Afternoon, Zacchy,' Simon called.

The man straightened up and raised a hand to his battered hat.

'Good day to you, Mr Fane sir,' he responded, and stared at Stacey.

Stacey just managed to contain herself until they were out of earshot.

'Fane?' she cried. 'Just how many names do you have?'

'No more in current use,' he assured her. He pointed with the whip to the farmhouse whose smoking chimneys showed beyond a tree-lined hedge. 'We're nearly there. That's Bridge Farm.'

As they turned into the muddy farmyard, scattering foraging hens, a pair of sturdy children appeared at the doorway of one of the barns and let out yells of excitement.

'Mr Fane! 'Tis Mr Fane!'

They bolted back inside, and their shrill voices could be heard calling, 'Perdy! Perdy! Look who's come!'

Smiling broadly, Simon jumped down, just as the two returned with four others, ranging in age from eight to a chubby toddler, all of them brown-haired and ruddy-cheeked except for one mite of about four years old, with a mop of black curls escaping from under her grubby bonnet and a pair of cornflower eyes bright in a face disfigured by a strawberry mark spreading across the left side. Frisking with delight, she bounded across the yard.

'Pa! 'Tis my Papa!' she cried, and flung herself into Simon's outstretched arms.

Stacey stared at the pair of them, open-mouthed with astonishment. And as she grew used to the idea, so it struck her how ridiculous all her fears had been. How utterly stupid to be jealous of an adorable little scrap like this. She stepped down from the whiskey and found herself being studied over Simon's shoulder by curious black-fringed eyes. For a long moment, the child summed her up, and Stacey smiled encouragement and waited for her to make the first remark. What she finally said brought a look of alarm from Simon.

'Are you my mama?'

'No, pet, but I wish I was.' Stacey reached out to hold a dirty little paw. 'Simon, why didn't you tell me? She's so pretty! And so like you it's almost uncanny.' She smiled at the little girl again. 'What's your name, pet?'

The solemn stare held for a few moments more, then melted into a giggle. She half hid her face, looked sideways at Stacey, gave a shy smile.

'Perdy.'

'Perdita,' Simon enlarged. 'My little lost princess. She was christened Prudence, but that's an ugly name. Perdita is far more appropriate.'

Stacey was bursting with questions, but managed to contain them. One of Aunt Peg's firm rules was that children should not be discussed over their heads, and this child obviously had an unconventional past. Quite probably she had not been told everything herself.

Simon, in the meantime, was trying to ask what his daughter had been doing during the past few days, but Perdita was not listening.

'What's your name?' she asked Stacey.

Simon feigned shock.

'For shame! Where are your manners?'

He set the child down and, unabashed, she bobbed a curtsey and gabbled, 'Please'm, would you be so kind as to tell me your name'm?'

Disregarding the clinging sea of mud, Stacey squatted beside her, so that they were of a height.

'That was very nicely asked, Perdy. You can call me Aunt Stacey, though I'm not exactly a proper aunt. Your papa and I are going to married, so I shall be your stepmama.'

'Oh.'

Perdita considered this, whilst Stacey held her breath, waiting for comment.

'Tab's had kittens,' the child confided. 'In the barn. Come and see.'

Delighted, Stacey took the proffered hand and trailed across the yard to where the other children were standing silently watching them. She shot a mischievous smile at Simon, following behind.

'I take it these are not yours as well?'

'Not guilty,' he said. 'These are blessed with steady, respectable parents. I'll introduce you in a minute.'

It was rather more than twenty minutes later that Stacey was met at the kitchen door by a round-faced, homely woman who went by the name of Mrs Hankin. Slightly flustered by the unexpected visit, she insisted on showing them into the best parlour, a room stiff and chilly from lack of use. She offered them tea and slabs of fruit-cake and answered enquiries after Perdita's welfare, then disappeared into the kitchen on the pretext of having to supervise the brewing. The afternoon passed quickly in entertaining Perdita and being taken by her on a con-ducted tour of the nearer fields and her favourite animals. By the time they left, Stacey was quite sure that her very first reaction had been correct, and told Simon so as soon as they had driven out of the farm.

'She must come and live with us at All Saints Green.'

Simon put an arm round her and kissed her.

'Sweetheart, you never cease to surprise me. I wasn't expecting that, it was enough that you accepted the child. But do you think it would be for the best? She's had such an unsettled life, and she's happy with the Hankins.'

'It all depends on what you want for her,' Stacey said slowly, thinking as she went along. 'Mrs Hankin seems a very pleasant, motherly woman, but if she stays there, Perdita will grow up a farmer's child.'

'There are worse fates. She nearly grew up in a poorhouse.'

'No!' Stacey was appalled. 'How dreadful! However did that come about?'

'She was abandoned, in best melodramatic tradition,

in a church porch.'

'How dreadful! The poor little scrap. But what about her mother, did she not tell you?'

The question came out before she could stop it, and she sat biting her lip, furious with herself, as Simon hesitated over a reply.

'Yes, she wrote to me, informing me what she had done but—' he flicked at the horse with the whip, stirring it into greater efforts, 'I didn't believe her when she insisted the child was mine. Truly, Stacey, it could have been anyone's. She was an actress with a touring company, she was only in the town three weeks, I never saw her again after that. I – tore the letter up, I regret to say, and forgot all about it. I shall never forgive myself for that. For two whole years that child was treated like a pauper, farmed out to an old crone who was generally dead drunk on gin by mid-afternoon. It was only by chance that I happened to pass through the place and the name jogged my memory, and of course once I saw her, it was obvious she was mine. The poorhouse staff were glad enough to let me take her, it was one less mouth to feed, but it was only when I drove off with a bewildered child and her pitiful little bundle of belongings that I realized just how ill-fitted I was to care for her. So I brought her to the Hankins, where she's had a proper family life, and I try to see her as often as possible. But I'll never be able to make up for those two lost years.'

Stacey pounced on this as supporting evidence for her case.

'All the more reason for her coming to live with us. She'll be with you, and a stepmother is better than no mother at all, and soon she'll have half-brothers and sisters as well.'

A thoughtful frown creased Simon's face as he pondered this. Stacey shivered in the raw wind and drew her heavy black cloak more firmly around her. At length the silence was broken.

'Why are you doing this, Stacey? To please me?'

'Partly, but mostly because it's obviously the best course.'

'A great many girls would not think it obvious at all. They'd rather the child was kept where she is, hidden from public comment.'

'Then they would be very foolish, in my opinion,' Stacey declared.

'And what about the family? How is your father going to react to having a child about the place?'

'Oh, you don't have to worry about Pa. He likes children, he's always saying the house is too quiet. And as for the others,' she took a sideways look at him, 'I shouldn't think they'll be the least bit surprised. Oliver will be disgusted, of course, but he disapproves of you so entirely that this won't really make any difference.'

The horse was allowed to amble along at its own pace as Simon laughed and held her close to him.

'You know, my love, I much prefer you when you're not trying to be tactful.'

Stacey nestled against him and rested her head on his shoulder, a glow of delight starting within her.

'That's the very first time you've called me that,' she sighed.

'Listen, Stacey,' Simon spoke slowly, choosing his words. 'Love is easily come by, and just as easily fades. Witness Perdita's mother: three weeks and then disappeared into oblivion. I cannot for the life of me recall her name or how she looked. But friendship is rare and precious, and it endures.'

Part of her acknowledged that he was right, the part that had seen love matches crumble into resentful bickering, that knew the family would approve of a marriage between Barty's daughter and the company's general manager as a splendidly practical arrangement. But it did nothing to alleviate the hurt of knowing that she was not touched with the same entrancing magic that made him so special to her. She thought again of his travelling all the way down here every Sunday without fail, of the very evident bond between him and his small daughter, and had to smother an unbidden regret at having insisted on taking the child in. She knew she had done the right thing, but could not quite quell the thought that there was more than mere friendship in his relationship with Perdita.

While Perdita's future was being settled, that of Amos Burgess was becoming more and more uncertain. Each week he weighed company loyalty against the threat to his wife, and slowly his reasoning began to change. It would make no difference, he decided, whether Clayton and therefore Pymer's knew the correct figures or not. Somehow or other, Mr Brown would pull the company through the difficult winter months, and then all would be well again. Mr Brown had got them out of worse situations in the past. And in the meantime, the knowledge of his power brought a new dimension into his home life. He developed a habit of sitting or standing perfectly still whilst Martha was in the midst of one of her tirades and staring at her, imagining the huge bruiser Job beating the daylights out of her. This uncanny stare was beginning to unnerve Martha, accustomed as she was to his fidgeting around trying to avoid her eye and creep into the nearest hiding-place.

'And another thing, Burgiss,' she would screech at him, 'you can just stop looking at me like that. It ain't right. Other men don't do it, proper husbands . . .' And so on in her usual vein until Amos found a space to enquire mildly just what sort of a look she was objecting to.

'*That* sort!' Martha declared, waving a beefy arm at him. 'Like – like I was dead. Fair gives me the creeps, it does.'

And Amos gave a small smile and continued to think on her coming doom.

When Mr Keating disappeared so suddenly on the excuse of 'urgent family business', Amos prayed that he might not come back, and for two whole weeks it seemed as if his prayer had been answered. Mr Brown, harried with having to be in the yard, at the coachworks and out on the road, unloaded all the routine decisions on to Amos, hardly glancing at letters and receipts that his chief clerk put in front of him before scrawling his signature at the bottom. Amos was back in his old position again, trusted and indispensable. The extra workload did not trouble him. He thrived on work, and expected the junior clerks to do the same. But then Mr Keating returned, bought a partnership in the company and was promised Miss Stacey's hand in marriage, and shattered all Amos's hopes of security. When the news broke, Amos left the office with the sound of revelry in his ears and picked his lonely way through heaps of dirty snow to Vulgate Street, in need of a reassurance he knew he would not receive.

Martha took one look at him as he crept up the stairs and sensed that she had back all her mastery over him.

'And what's brought you home at this hour?' she demanded. 'How can I be expected to make decent dinners when I never know what time you're going to be in? And all with no help at all but for that slut of a girl, and she's worse than useless which is what you are as well . . .'

Too dispirited to look her in the eye, Amos slumped into a chair. Briefly, for speaking of it pained him, he outlined the change of events at Brown's.

'Ha! So that's the way of it!' Martha commented. 'Well, *she's* got herself a decent husband, for all she's so plain. Fancy him falling for her. A real man, he is, not like some I could name. But it was the money, I suppose. Now *he* knows how to get on in the world. You don't see him tied to a desk for a pittance and never know what time he's going to be home. Oh no! But I wonder at him marrying her, all the same. Great gawk of a girl . . .'

With a new target for her vitriolic tongue, Martha was in fine form. Amos's depression turned slowly back to thoughts of revenge, and hardened. Criticism of himself he was accustomed to, had come to expect, but he could not sit by and have Miss Stacey reviled, Miss Stacey, who was the nearest he ever had to a daughter of his own. Tomorrow he was due to see the weasel-faced Will and his henchman again. Tomorrow he would take a set of figures quite obviously incorrect.

It took two glasses of gin to steel himself to passing the sheet of paper over without betraying his churning fear, another to get him home to face Martha, knowing what was in store for her. But a flow of invective from her on the subject of his drunkenness dulled the worst of his guilt. He spent a restless night beside her, his few moments of sleep troubled with confused dreams. The raw cold morning inflamed his rheumatic joints to a point where getting to work required an effort of dogged endurance that would have taken a fit man to the top of a mountain, but the office spelt a warm stove and his own corner, it meant getting away from Martha. The junior clerks, seeing his bent figure and drawn features, made expressive faces at each other and knew that any errors or lapses of concentration would bring the rough edge of his tongue.

The day dragged by on leaden feet, whilst the yard and the office buzzed with gossip. Miss Stacey was to come home from her aunt's and take up the running of her father's house, one report went. Mr Wynwood was the son of a belted earl and meant to carry her back to his family's vast estates in the North. Mr Wynwood was an escaped felon who changed his name to slip the law and was relying on the Browns to protect him. Amos desperately hoped this one was true. The couple were to be married in the cathedral by the bishop. They were to be married at All Saints. There was to be a roasted ox and twelve barrels of ale for company servants to drink their health. And in the midst of it all, Mr Wynwood kept his usual calm but wore the look of the farmyard cock who knows he is king of the midden, whilst Miss Stacey appeared in the office around mid-morning, glowing from the cold outside and joy within, having ridden in alone from Raston. She could not, she declared, endure sitting around at the Red House any longer, so here she was, and here she intended to stay.

'Oh Mr Burgess, is it not a beautiful day!' she cried, regardless of the sombre grey of the sky outside. She peeped over his shoulder at the pile of the day's takings so far. 'No need to worry about the company going under now. We'll be able to keep our heads nicely above water.'

But that was little consolation for Amos, when he could not see himself being part of it for much longer.

In the office, there was enough demanding his attention to keep his mind off what might be going on outside for sometimes half an hour together, but once the day was over he was struck by the full force of the events he had set in motion. Even now, as he made his painful way along the dark streets, Martha might be lying dead. The thought no longer filled him with relief, but with apprehension. What now? What was he to say? How was he to behave? He opened the door to the rooms above the haberdasher's, and at once knew something had changed. There was an unnatural quiet. He lingered at the threshold, afraid to go in, afraid of what he might find. Something brushed past his legs, making him start. Yellow eyes glimmered in the dark. The cat. Amos pulled himself together and stumbled up the stairs. Feeling his way, he crept into the cramped kitchen and lit the candle that stood on the table. There was no smell of fish today, no drying dinner waiting on the range, just a faint mustiness, a whiff of rancid fat, as if the place had been empty for a week.

Trembling, Amos took up the candle and went into the parlour with the cat, traitor that it was, curling round his calves. There was nothing lurking in the shadows of the parlour, nothing in the little bedchamber at the back. Even the fire had died in the hearth. For a long while Amos stood, candlestick in hand, not knowing what to do next, until the cold stirred him to practical matters. He remade the fire and left the poker in it to make it draw while he foraged in the kitchen. The larder yielded bread, some rather old cheese and the dried remains of the seed cake that had been offered to Mrs Vennor on her last visit. Amos carried them back to his seat by the hearth, and waited.

It was in the early hours of the morning that he was woken out of a fitful doze by hammering on the outside door. Stiff and aching from having slept in the chair, he relit the candle from the now glowing fire and scuttled crablike down the stairs, his heart hammering in alarm. The narrow alleyway seemed crowded with people, and standing in the doorway was a man he vaguely recognized as one of the horsekeepers from the Crown.

'Mr Burgess? We brought your old woman home. Someone give her a rare owd jammocking, they have.'

Amos stood with mouth agape, unable to say a word. The horsekeeper took charge, telling him to go ahead with the light, directing the two other men who carried the inert body up the stairs and into the bedchamber. Martha was laid on the sagging bed they had shared for thirty-five years.

'Shall I send for the sawbones, Mr Burgess?'

'S – sawbones?'

'Surgeon,' the horsekeeper elaborated. 'Got to get her patched up, Mr Burgess, or she ain't going to last the night.'

Dumbly, Amos nodded, as the meaning of the question sank in. She was not dead. She lived still to plague him. As one of the men set off in search of a doctor, he raised the candle and looked at her. Her face was a disfigured mess of bleeding bruises, her clothes dishevelled and muddy, her sparse grey hair matted with blood from a dark, ugly wound on top of her head.

'Wouldn't be surprised if she ain't broke her brainpan,' the lugubrious horsekeeper informed him. 'Found her down an alleyway behind the market, we did, and a fine old job we had bringing her back here. Wouldn't have known who she was, but Jemmy here, he can read, and he found her card in her bag.'

Martha's precious calling-cards. Cheap, printed affairs she had ordered years ago and very rarely used but liked to refer to as one of her claims to gentility. Amos had always resented them.

'We got an early start at the Crown,' the horsekeeper went on, heavily meaningful. 'Come out of our way, we have, bringing her here. Reckon we saved her life. Wouldn't have lasted the night in that alleyway, she wouldn't.'

Amos realized what was expected of him.

'Oh – I – I am prodigious grateful to you,' he faltered. 'Grateful. Yes.'

He fumbled in his breeches pocket but could find only a shilling and a few coppers. That was not enough for the service rendered. He must remember to act the part of a man shocked at the dreadful treatment of his wife. He took a precious guinea out of the old tobacco jar on the mantelpiece.

Satisfied, the men expressed perfunctory sympathy, bade him goodnight and clumped out of the house. On the bed, Martha moaned faintly. Amos fled into the parlour to await the surgeon.

By the time he got to the Crown later that morning, the tale was all round the yard. For the first time in twenty-seven years, his affairs were the subject of gossip. He slunk into his fortress in the corner of the office and tried to study the job in hand, but his new set of worries kept breaking his concentration. There would be the doctor's fees to pay now, extra laundry, a woman to come in and attend to Martha. The surgeon had not held out much hope of her living beyond a week, but Amos knew otherwise. Martha would hold on, just to spite him.

'Now look here, Amos,' Mr Brown said when he heard what had happened. 'There's no need for you to be here today. Just you get off home again, we can manage without you. Take as much time as you need.'

Amos looked at him in alarm. The last thing he wanted was for Mr Brown to find he could manage without him.

He mumbled a confused excuse, saying that his wife had been ordered complete rest and that there was someone sitting with her. But not only did Mr Brown insist, but Mrs Noll Brown appeared from the inn, pressed him to accept a large basin of broth for the patient and sent a maid with him to carry it and do any other tasks he might ask. Amos could only give in and look suitably grateful.

The sympathy and practical help continued throughout the week. One day Miss Stacey appeared at his door with a basket over her arm, the next it was Miss Harriet. When he made up the wages on Saturday evening, Mr Brown slipped an extra two guineas onto his pile.

'Expensive business, illness,' he remarked, and waved away Amos's stuttered thanks.

By then he knew the extent of Martha's revenge. The blow to her head had left the entire right-hand side of her body paralysed, the right side of her face nerveless, so that she had the lopsided look of a stroke victim. She was unable to speak, which unnerved Amos more than he would have thought possible, but her left eye followed him with undimmed hatred. She was bedridden, and needed to be spoon-fed, slowly, to be washed, to have her bodily functions attended to. She was going to be a liability for the rest of her days. Amos felt as if the dark waters were closing over his head.

Chapter Seventeen

Through the first week of March, there was news enough about the Crown to keep everyone's tongues wagging. Close on the heels of Amos Burgess's domestic tragedy came the astonishing announcement that the coach services were to be suspended on the day of the wedding. Such an unprecedented step had the whole yard buzzing for days, and raised hopes of a really splendid celebration.

'You've not seen a Brown wedding,' Stacey laughed, when Simon asked if this was really necessary. 'Just you wait!'

She was floating on a rose-coloured cloud, having been recalled from exile at Raston. Barty placated Aunt Eustacia by asking her to supervise the bride's clothes, and soothed Aunt Peg in turn by putting the entire organization of the wedding breakfast in her hands. Simon, on hearing of this arrangement, spoke a discreet word in the ear of his old conspirator, Letty Mullins. She and Stacey between them would have quite enough guile to outmanoeuvre Aunt Eustacia. In the meantime, he was beginning to see what Stacey meant by a Brown wedding. There was to be a breakfast in the Long Room of the inn for family and friends, and the main coach house was to be cleared out for a second feast for company servants. The lists of guests, food and drink soon grew to monumental proportions. There was to be a band, garlands, baskets of wedding favours, and of course a cake, which had already been baked in the Crown kitchens. Nothing could be more different from the quiet, private ceremony that had joined Timothy and Georgiana. And that was one point on which he was adamant. Nobody from his family was to be invited.

There were days when the prospect of being drawn into

the close-woven web of the Browns appalled him. Used to living alone, moving on when he pleased, keeping his own secrets, the demands of living within the confines of family life were oppressive. But he had only to witness the way in which they rallied round any member of the clan in difficulties, or their whole-hearted enthusiasm for the coming wedding, to decide that the good points far outweighed the disadvantages. And clear in his mind still was the day on which he had been free to go where he wished, yet wanted only to be part of the tribe. A test of his new attitude came quite early.

'No point in taking a house,' Barty said one evening, seeing Simon reading the advertisements in the *Mercury*. 'Where's the sense in paying for two lots of expenses when there's room enough for all three – four – of us here? This place is far too big for me to live in alone, but I certainly don't want to leave it.'

Simon protested that he could not possibly impose himself, his daughter and his future family on Barty. Barty replied that it was not imposing, just sense. And he disliked living alone. After several minutes' wrangling Stacey, who had been clenching her jaw in an effort not to influence events one way or the other, was applied to for an opinion.

'Well,' she said slowly, 'it does seem like a sound idea.'

Which was what the rest of the family thought as well. And with a certain amount of rearrangement, the right mixture of privacy and company could be achieved at All Saints Green.

Less easily settled was the question of Amos Burgess.

'Poor old fellow, he looks so ill and worn,' Stacey said. 'It must be very hard for him, coming in and working at the office all day then going home to a sick wife.'

'Do you know, in all the years he's worked for me, I never even knew he was a married man,' Barty mused. 'He never acted like one, somehow. I always got the feeling the company was his life.'

'He ought to be retired,' Simon said. 'He's slowed up a

260

lot even since I've been here, and what with this trouble with his wife, it won't be long before he starts making serious mistakes. His eyes have been getting weak as well. He's simply getting too old for the job.'

He could not have said anything more likely to rouse Barty's opposition.

'Age is no reason for throwing a man off when he's been a faithful company servant for twenty-six, no twenty-seven years,' he declared. 'Old Amos has been with me ever since I took over the company. There's nothing he doesn't know about running the finances. He's irreplaceable.'

Simon shifted his ground slightly.

'I'm not suggesting we throw him off, merely that we at least think about retiring him. I should imagine the company can afford something in the way of a pension for someone who's been with us for so long. But as to his being irreplaceable, that's nonsense. Stacey has a far better head for figures than Amos in his prime—'

Stacey started to exclaim, 'Oh I'd—' as the prospect of having a real position in the firm opened out, but her father cut her off.

'I'm not having Stacey sitting behind a desk all day counting out shillings and scratching in ledgers,' he stated.

'But I would enjoy that,' Stacey protested.

'Nonsense, you'd be bored senseless within a week,' Simon told her. 'That's not what I'm thinking of. When it comes to counting up coins and scratching in ledgers, young Bates in the outer office is actually several years older than me, has been with us for ten years and is perfectly capable of handling the routine work. We promote him to cashier and take on a new lad to help Simpkin with the dogsbody work, the bookings and the general penpushing. What we need Stacey for is to oversee the situation, make sure we've enough for purchasing, plan the future policy and so on. She's more than capable of doing it, she's proved that already with the Flyer and the rescue plans last autumn.'

Barty looked unconvinced, Stacey was pink with pleasure at having her talents recognized.

'The rescue plan didn't work, though,' she pointed out with meticulous honesty. 'We'd be in serious trouble by now if it wasn't for your money.'

'It should have worked,' Simon insisted, 'and it would have done if Pymer wasn't hand in glove with this Clayton character. I keep trying to find out about him, but he's as elusive as a fox. Plenty of people have heard of him, but nobody seems to know who he really is. Most of all I'd like to know just why he's concerning himself with us at all. I've met his sort before, in racing and gaming, but they don't usually bother with respectable businesses like ours.'

'We got off the point,' Barty broke in. 'We was talking about Amos, and as long as he's able to do the job he's hired for, then he stays. I couldn't have succeeded the way I did without him in the early days, and I ain't kicking him out now, and that's final.'

Simon began, 'There is no question of kicking him out—' but Barty cut him off.

'I said that's final,' he growled. 'I'm still the senior partner here, and don't you forget it.'

With which he got up and stumped out of the room in the direction of his den at the back of the house.

Stacey exchanged a look of astonishment with Simon and made to go after him, but Simon laid a restraining hand on her arm.

'No, wait,' he said, as the door swung to. 'Was that genuine or is he playing some game of his own? I can never quite tell with your father.'

Worried, Stacey frowned at the space Barty had left in the room.

'I think he meant it. We've upset him. Best not to mention Amos again, though I'm afraid the poor old thing's going to die quietly behind his desk one of these days. He ought to be pensioned off. I expect he's dreadfully worried about his wife.'

'There are too many old dodderers about the company to my mind, men who've been in it from the beginning. We cannot afford to keep them on just for sentiment's sake. But evidently I'm being far too heavy-handed.' He smiled. 'Patience and cunning. I'm still the junior partner here.'

Stacey put her arms round him, anxious now to smooth over any resentment on his side.

'He's been in sole charge of the company for nearly twenty-seven years. It's difficult for him to get used to your sharing it with him. You're not really offended, are you?'

'I am deeply and irreparably humiliated,' Simon assured her soulfully. 'Only you can alleviate the horror of it.'

Stacey chuckled and pressed closer to him. 'Fraud,' she whispered, and responded eagerly to his kisses.

As always, he found her warm and inviting until he inadvertently touched on the fear that lay just beneath the surface. This time it was when he drew her down onto the sofa. He heard her sudden intake of breath and felt her stiffen, and knew that once again Oliver had come between them. Cursing inwardly at having so much promise stunted by a few minutes' madness, he held back, taking her face in his hands and kissing her forehead, asking about some detail of the wedding plans until she relaxed again. Gradually he was repairing the damage done that Christmas afternoon, and he was helped by the conviction that in the end his patience was going to be well rewarded.

While Stacey and Simon's affairs were prospering, the course of Arthur and Annabel's true love was running anything but smoothly. Annabel's rambling, ecstatic letters to Stacey ceased suddenly about two weeks after her return to her father's mansion in Yorkshire, and instead there arrived a short, stilted note giving news of her continuing good health and the revealing information that she now had a lady living with her as companion and chaperon. A few days later, Arthur turned up at All Saints Green, pale with anxiety.

'I keep writing her letters and they're returned to me unopened,' he explained to Stacey. 'I don't know what to think. Is it something I've said? Has she mentioned anything to you?'

'It's my guess her father's appointed a wardress,' Stacey said, watching him with sympathy as he paced about the room. 'I think her correspondence is being interfered with. Look at what I received from her, it hardly sounds like Annabel writing at all.'

Arthur ran over the note, lingering at the signature.

'What can I do?' he asked. 'Companion! You are right, I do believe you are right. He – her father – is holding out for a match with this – this elderly widower. It's disgusting! He cannot be allowed to compel her – but what can I do? There must be some way—'

He ran his fingers through his hair with that distracted air that Stacey had seen before, his thin face drawn. Stacey wondered why it was that the most obvious course never seemed to occur to him. It was quite clear to her what should be done.

'Why, you must travel up to Yorkshire straight away and carry her off,' she declared.

'Oh!' Arthur looked startled. 'Do you really think so?'

'But of course. Think how romantic! You bribe some maid to take a message, you have a chaise and four waiting at the end of the drive at midnight, Annabel lets herself out of a side door and off you gallop to Gretna. And once you're married, nobody can do a thing about it.'

'Yes – no—' Far from being fired by her enthusiasm, Arthur looked doubtful.

Tired of his spineless reaction, Stacey began to lose patience.

'You do *want* to marry Annabel, I take it?'

'Oh yes!' He looked down at the note he still held in his hands. 'More than anything in the world. It's just – well – it's the question of money.'

'Money! Good heavens, who thinks of money at a time like this?'

Arthur gave a despairing sigh.

'I have to,' he said.

Simon, regaled with a lively account of the conversation, found it all highly amusing.

'Poor old Harris, still being made to pay for his mistakes. Did you suggest to him that her father would probably come round with the appearance of the first grandchild?'

'Yes, but he said *his* father couldn't wait that long. The situation at Upthorpe is as shaky as we were, it seems. An impossible problem.' Stacey could not suppress a triumphant smile.

'But you have solved it, have you not? Poor Harris! Always at the mercy of some scheming woman.'

Stacey laughed. 'I've simply invited them all to the wedding – Annabel, her father, the companion. And if Harris cannot think of some way of presenting himself to the old man and getting them all out to Upthorpe to be impressed with his inheritance, I wash my hands of him.'

Simon was not as admiring as she had hoped.

'What makes you think they'll come?'

'They'll come,' Stacey said, with airy conviction. 'I've let your full name drop. Her father will think it's a grand occasion packed with titled heads. He won't be able to resist it.'

'Stacey! Such deviousness! How would Harris manage without you to direct his affairs for him? He should have married you while he had the chance, he would never have had to take another difficult decision in his life.' Simon's smile took on a more predatory quality as another aspect of the situation occurred to him. 'If this goes the way you've planned, Harris will have cause to be very grateful to you. That could prove useful.'

265

But Stacey was struck by the first part of what he had said.

'He really was going to ask for me, then?'

'Oh yes, last October or November. He spoke to me about it.'

'He did? And what did you say?'

Simon looked at her breathless, uncertain expression and saw no harm in feeding the hope he read there.

'I put him off,' he lied cheerfully. 'Didn't want him poaching on my territory.'

It was enough to set Stacey singing for the rest of the day.

Throughout the busy time leading up to the wedding, Stacey was dogged by a nagging conviction that the Wynwoods ought to be informed. Simon had steadfastly refused to invite any of them, even his brother, whom Stacey thought he at least tolerated. She accepted this, though reluctantly, but it did not change her belief that they should at least be told, and not hear of it by chance through the likes of Mr Talbot. So after a great deal of thought and many false starts, she drafted a brief note to Timothy, took it personally to the post office, and almost immediately regretted it.

For four days she was kept in painful suspense waiting for an answer, wondering if she ought to tell Simon, hoping for a friendly reply that might please him. And then came a letter, not from Timothy, but from Georgiana.

'My dear Miss Brown,

I was not altogether surprised to receive the news of your forthcoming marriage to my misguided cousin and brother-in-law. I do most sincerely wish you joy, but fear it may be shortlived. You, my dear child, are young and inexperienced and are no doubt dazzled by Simon's charm and rank. He knows very well how to please when he wishes, but do, I beg of you, be on your guard. Forgive me – it pains me to have to say this – but I cannot help suspecting that he is entering this match merely to harry his father with the prospect of a low-born heir to the title. A vain hope, as I am happy to be able to tell you that a new branch is already expected to the ancient Wynwood tree.

I think I must, for kindness' sake, tell you that you can expect no recognition from the family. Simon may not have told you, but he was given the most generous sum of £5,000 in February in lieu of any further expectations. This match will now, I am sorry to say, sink him completely in his father's eyes.

Let me conclude, however, on a hopeful note. Love can work strange wonders, and I can only wish Simon and yourself the same happiness in the married state that I have been fortunate enough to find,

Your sincere well-wisher and friend,
Georgiana Wynwood.'

Stacey skimmed rapidly through it with growing anger and dismay, exclaiming aloud at the more pointed insults. Barty looked at her across the breakfast table.

'Bad news?'

'No – no – it's nothing.'

Stacey pushed the offending thing aside and opened a note from Annabel that had arrived with the same post. But her friend's writing blurred before her eyes, making no sense. All she could see was Georgiana's lovely dark face, framed in an azure hood against a dull November afternoon. Georgiana travelling all that distance just to try to persuade Simon to return home. Georgiana up to some devious plot of her own. And Simon, the foiler of bullion robbers, the bane of Pymer's coachmen, was afraid of her. She read through the letter again, more slowly, telling herself all the while that Simon was right about her, she was a troublemaker and not to be heeded. But the traitorous doubts remained.

'Pa,' she said, with overplayed unconcern, 'it was two

and a half thousand that Simon invested in the firm, was it not?'

'That's right. Why do you ask?'

'Oh – I just wondered, that's all.'

It was a lie, she decided, especially designed to arouse suspicion between them. She would think no more about it. But she found her usual hearty appetite had deserted her.

Barty drained his coffee cup and stood up.

'I'm off to the yard, chicken. What is it you're doing this morning? Dress fitting?'

'Mm.' With difficulty, Stacey brought her attention to bear on what he was saying. 'Harriet's coming round and we're both going to Mrs Mullins with Aunt Eustacia when she arrives.'

She lingered at the table, crumbling pieces of toast on her plate, brooding over what she should say to Simon, if anything, and coming to no firm conclusion except that she should never have sent that letter to Timothy. She was startled out of her fog of indecision by a hammering at the front door. Jumping up, she ran through to the front parlour and looked out. It was Simon.

Heart thumping with a premonition of coming disaster, she dashed back into the dining-room, grabbed the letter and thrust it into the fire. The sheets curled and browned as the maid opened the door, and finally burst into flames as footsteps sounded on the stairs and Simon marched into the room. Stacey spun guiltily round to face him, and the small part of her mind that still remained detached noted that she had never seen him angry before.

'Just what have you been doing behind my back?' he demanded.

Acutely conscious of the still-glowing ashes in the grate, Stacey assumed a look of wide-eyed innocence.

'Doing?' she echoed, playing for time.

But Simon was not to be deflected by such an amateur effort.

'I told you I did not want my family involved in any

way. That was my decision, and no concern whatsoever of yours. I don't care what reason you think you had, you should not have acted without saying a word to me.'

All her own misgivings about the rights and wrongs of her action melted away in front of this withering blast. Never one to give way under pressure, Stacey sprang to the attack.

'If I'd have told you, you would have stopped me.'

'So you say nothing and do the very thing you know I object to, you write to Georgiana.'

'I did not write to Georgiana,' Stacey protested, standing on what little ground she had. 'I wrote to Timothy. I thought you quite liked him or at least weren't at loggerheads with him.'

Simon slammed the flat of his hand on the table in a gesture of frustration, making the chinaware rattle.

'But that is tantamount to writing to her, you silly little girl. You have absolutely no idea how that woman's mind works. You think that just because you can meddle with the life of a saphead like Harris, you're strong enough to take on Georgiana. You are nothing of the kind, she would eat you for breakfast. And you played right into her hands.'

In Stacey's mind suddenly the vision of Oliver in a towering rage arose, starting a tremor of fear. She edged round, putting the table between Simon and herself, until reason told her that the circumstances were not the same, and though Simon might be angry, he never lost control.

'You make her out to be a monster,' she flung at him. 'You're afraid of her, I do believe! Well, I'm not.'

'That's because you don't know her.'

'How can I, when you're just about as informative as a doorpost when it comes to your family? At least from Georgiana I learnt—'

She broke off, furious with herself, while Simon held her hot defiant gaze.

'So,' he said at last, almost conversationally, 'she did write to you as well? I rather thought she would have.

269

Might I be permitted to see the letter?'

Stacey's glance flickered to the fireplace and back. She licked her dry lips.

'I burnt it.'

'That's the first sensible thing I've heard today. And what did it contain?'

'A – a lot of veiled insults and – and wishes for our future happiness. And that there was no hope of your getting the title because the succession was already taken care of.' With forced frivolity, she tried to make a joke of it. 'That was quick work, was it not? They've hardly been married six weeks.'

With a wry smile of resignation, Simon pulled out a chair and motioned for her to do the same. The rancour drained from him, leaving him looking tired. When he spoke again, it was with a defensive touch of irony.

'Sit down, Stacey, and I'll tell you a happy little story of Wynwood family life. For a start, that child Georgiana so carefully mentioned is not Timothy's.' He met her startled look and went on, 'Yes, history repeating itself, but this time there's no mistake. Timothy is impotent – you understand me? – and believe me, that's not something a man will admit till he's driven to it. He's terrified lest the old man finds out, and was persuaded to cover up for Georgiana because of the story she fed to him.' He paused and went off at a tangent. 'It's a risk she's been taking for years. I wonder she's never been caught before. Perhaps she became careless.'

Stacey waited for him to go on, but he appeared to be pursuing some thought of his own.

'What – story?' she prompted.

Simon focused his attention on her once more.

'You remember the time she came to the Crown? How long would you say she stayed?'

'Oh – about ten minutes, perhaps a quarter of an hour. Not much longer.'

'And you were with me the entire time?'

'You know I was.'

270

Stacey could not imagine where this was leading.

'And you were still with me when she left?'

'Yes, and afterwards. We went into the office. I remember that very clearly. But why—?'

'The reason Timothy was willing, even quite pleased to accept that child is that she claimed it was mine. It's clever, you have to admit it. Tim knew he would never get a son, and so I and my children, if I married, would be his legal heirs. To pass off one of my children as his own made the best of the problem. It saved his face, and it kept the old man happy. It also got Georgiana out of a difficult corner. Of course, when she came here it was with the intention of staying the night, so there would be no proving her wrong. She was holding out a chance for me to get back into, if not family favour, at least recognition and a cut of the income. But whether I was her principal object or just the second string, I don't know. Whichever, she was forced to work on Tim when I refused to play. It would still have succeeded if I had not turned up just before the wedding. It must have been a very nasty moment for her when I arrived. She took fully half a minute to force a smile.'

Stacey sat riveted throughout this recital, unable to take her eyes off him. She could understand now why he had been reluctant to say anything about his visit to Lathenbridge. Rushed weddings and so-called premature births were one thing, this tangle of deliberate deceit was quite another. In the same position, she would have been desperately ashamed of having to relate such a tale.

'But I—' her voice came out as a croak, and she cleared her throat and started again. 'What I don't understand is, why was all this necessary. What about the real father?'

Simon gave a slight shrug.

'Evidently out of the running as far as Georgiana was concerned. A footman or stableboy perhaps, or a married man. No use to her when it came to marriage.'

'I see.' Stacey could think of nothing constructive to add. She said lamely, 'What a mess.'

'Mess!' Simon jerked back into animation again, 'It's a farce, a sordid, degrading farce and I want nothing more to do with it. I took what I could from them all and I left them to it. I just wanted to come back here to sanity and – and decency and forget they ever existed, but you would insist on stirring it all up again.'

Remorseful now, Stacey swallowed back the rising tears.

'I'm sorry,' she whispered. 'I just thought, at the time, that I was doing the right thing, but I see now that I wasn't.'

Simon reached across the table and gripped her fingers.

'You were doing the right thing, by ordinary standards. But Georgiana uses a different set of rules.' He released her hand and gave a grim smile. 'I'll show her once and for all that she'd do better to keep out of my affairs. I think I ought, as a dutiful son, let the old man know he's got a cuckoo in the nest.'

'Oh no!' Stacey jumped up and hurried round to lay a pleading hand on his arm. 'No, don't do that. You said you wanted nothing more to do with them, can't you just ignore this?'

Simon looked up at her anxious face, considering the alternatives.

'No, I can't,' he told her.

'But what good will it do? Your – your father might not even believe you.'

'Probably not, though he has his suspicions already. But Georgiana has to be stopped, and this will keep her so busy proving her innocence that she will think several times before meddling with me again.' He held her troubled gaze with steady eyes. 'I don't want her touching you, darling. She's still smarting from the last upset to her plans, and she'll use you to strike at me, if she can.'

The unaccounted-for two and a half thousand pounds rose in Stacey's mind and was dismissed. Another deliberate lie.

'She cannot do anything to us so long as we trust each other,' she said.

'Maybe, but I'm not taking any chances. Let me handle this my own way, Stacey. I know them, and you don't.'

Stacey sighed.

'Of course I don't. You never tell me anything about them.'

'They're not worth discussing,' Simon stated, with a note of finality in his voice that she was forced to recognize. Stacey wondered if she would ever find out exactly what had happened in his past.

Chapter Eighteen

Barty drew out his watch for the third time and checked it against the clock on the mantelpiece. For the third time, they agreed. A quarter to ten. He took a last look at himself in the glass and grunted in approval at his reflection, satisfied that he looked the part. His new bottle green coat fitted to perfection, and so did the new cream and gold striped waistcoat and new buff breeches – he could not bring himself to follow the fashion for trousers. His boots were polished to mirror brightness and his linen was snowy white. Capital. He turned away and picked up the framed pencil sketch of his late wife from the bedside table. It was not a very good likeness, but it was the only one he had of her, and it was precious to him. He was in the habit of talking out loud to it at time of family crisis or triumph.

'Well, Eliza, and what d'ye think, eh?' he asked now. 'I got our Stacey well matched in the end, didn't I? Mind, I thought a while back the whole thing was going to fall through, but it came right in the end.' He chuckled at the thought of the manoeuvring he had carried out, sending Stacey off to Eustacia's, persuading Simon into the affair with Pymer's wife and letting him think he was the last person he'd allow his daughter to marry, throwing them together to set up the Flyer. 'Forbidden fruit,' he said. 'Never fails.' And suspecting disapproval on Elizabeth's pencilled features, he went on, 'Maybe he's a mite wild, but he'll settle to harness, you'll see. And our Stacey's a lively one, she needs something to keep her occupied. He'll let her take a hand in the company. Aye – they'll do well together, you'll see.'

He stumped out of his room and across the landing to

knock on the door of the large bedchamber at the front of the house.

'Ten to,' he warned.

From inside came a flurry of female voices, dominated by his sister-in-law's, reminding him that it was the bride's privilege to be late. Barty left them to it and went down to wait in the parlour. His patience was well rewarded, he was the first to admit. When Stacey finally appeared, anxiously attended by her aunt and three of her cousins, Barty found it difficult to speak through the rush of sentiment and pride.

'Well,' he said, surveying his daughter, 'is this really my little girl?'

Stacey suppressed a smile of delight and turned round to show him the full effect. The dress that had cost many hours of consultations and fittings and alterations was one of Letty Mullins's masterpieces. Of white silk, with a foot-wide band of light quilting round the hem to make it stand out slightly, it had long tight sleeves, puffed at the top of the arms and finished at the cuffs with quilting. A similar band of decoration bordered the v-shaped neckline, which was filled in with a fine lawn chemisette and double-ruffled collar. A garland of primroses and myrtle encircled Stacey's upswept hair, and to this was fixed the silk gauze veil that had been her mother's.

'Pretty as a picture,' Barty approved. 'Worth every penny and more.' He looked more closely and reached out a hand to touch the double row of pearls round her neck. 'Where are these from, then? I don't recognize them.'

'They're from Simon, they arrived this morning, aren't they quite, quite beautiful?' Stacey, pink with nervous excitement, rustled over to the glass to take another peep at them. 'It was such a surprise, I never expected – I think they must have been his mother's, the case had a French name on it. Oh, I'm so lucky, I can't believe it's all happening.'

Her aunt gave a small cry of overstrained patience.

'Stacey! A bride is supposed to be demure and modest, and give a becoming show of reluctance.'

'Fiddlesticks! I might have been reluctant to marry Arthur Harris, but this is quite different. Why should I pretend to be something I'm not?' Stacey went to peer out of the window across the green to the church. 'They've all gone in. Hadn't you better go over, aunt? Pa and I are ready.'

With a sigh of resignation and a last peck on her niece's cheek, Eustacia went. The bridesmaids, dressed alike in white muslin with flounces and high collars, watched her safely into the porch then lined up behind Stacey. Harriet handed her the posy of primroses and made a last-minute adjustment to her veil. Barty turned to his daughter and offered his arm.

'Ready, chicken?'

Strangely silent for once, Stacey nodded, and the little group paraded downstairs and processed across the green to All Saints.

For Annabel, the service was one protracted daydream of longing. She was vaguely aware of her father looking about and grumbling at the lack of persons of rank in the congregation, mechanically she obeyed her companion, Mrs Winter's, instructions to sit up straight. But all her attention was focused on Arthur, sitting in the front pew in his role of groomsman. Simon she hardly noticed, though she freely admitted he was a handsome man and especially so today in his royal blue coat and tightly-fitting grey trousers. It was Arthur she gazed at, imagining his position reversed with that of his friend, waiting there for her to arrive.

Mrs Winter nudged her impatiently, wanting to know who everyone was. Annabel did the best she could, pointing out Stacey's nearer relatives, but the more distant ramifications of the Brown family were beyond her.

'Yes, yes, never mind them. Where are the Wynwoods?'

her companion demanded. 'Where is Lord Lathenbridge?'

Annabel had to confess that she did not know. The only complete strangers in the gathering were a yeoman farmer and his wife and their string of children. Annabel could not place them at all, but they quite clearly were not Wynwoods. It was with relief that she heard a stir behind her and turned along with the rest of the congregation to see the bride and her father enter and begin to process up the aisle. She stepped back into her happy fantasy, walking beside her own father to join Arthur at the chancel steps. Deaf to the muttered comments beside her, she drank in the familiar, ever-new lines of the service, echoing the responses and exchange of vows in her heart until even the voices seemed to change and instead of Stacey's clear tone and Simon's firm, confident one, she heard her own shy murmur and Arthur, hesitant but fervent.

The ceremony was over only too soon, the ring put on, the register signed, the blessing pronounced, and Stacey was stepping down the aisle again on the arm of her new husband, fairly glowing with happiness and possessive pride. The bridesmaids followed on, smiling now that the solemn part of their duty was done, and the family fell in behind, Barty openly wiping away sentimental tears, even Aunt Eustacia moved by the occasion. Arthur passed by Annabel's pew, so close that she could have reached out and touched him. Their eyes met for a brief, speaking moment before the press of people swept him on towards the door. Recklessly, Annabel joined the slow-moving throng, tantalizingly parted from him by two bulky Brown uncles.

They emerged, blinking, into the April sunshine where bride and groom stood relaxed now and laughing, receiving congratulations and good wishes. Annabel wriggled her way through chattering aunts and cousins and arrived, breathless, at Arthur's side as he stood surrounded by giggling bridesmaids.

'Annabel!' Stacey claimed her attention. 'I'm so glad

you're here. Is your father with you?'

'Yes,' Annabel looked about anxiously but could not see him in the crowd. 'Oh Stacey, I'm so grateful to you, I don't know what—' she broke off, remembering that this was her friend's day, and hastened to kiss her cheek. 'Stacey, you look so pretty, I'm sure you'll be very happy. Both of you,' she added, with a shy smile at Simon, who scared her. She could no more consider marrying him than riding a tiger. But Stacey was never frightened of anything.

'Your turn next,' she was saying now, 'you'll find your Arthur is placed next to you at the breakfast, so make the most of it.'

Annabel had just time to gabble her breathless thanks before another group of relations came up to add their congratulations.

Simon looked at her as she rejoined Arthur.

'Babes in the wood, the pair of them,' he commented to Stacey. 'What would they have done without you?' And softly, in her ear, 'What would I have done without you?'

Flushing with delight, Stacey was prevented from replying as a knot of second cousins descended upon her, all claiming kisses. And then the carriage arrived, a gleaming landau with the hoods down, drawn by the bays from the Flyer with white ribbons fluttering from their bridles. Simon steered her through the parting throng and handed her up into the vehicle, laughing as a gust of wind blew her veil in his face.

'How fortunate we have Harry on the box,' he said as he climbed in after her. 'His weight should prevent us from flying to the sun.'

Though later, he thought, when Harry and everyone else was left behind, they might well reach the stars.

'The Crown will do for now,' Stacey said, as if reading his mind, and waved as they set off for the short trip round the streets to the inn. She was still possessed by a strong feeling of unreality, as if this was not actually happening to her. She was just part of a ritual that had been set in motion, immaculately stage-managed by the Brown organization. And then she remembered the day's unexpected incident.

'The pearls!' she exclaimed. 'Your present. Thank you so much, they're beautiful, I've never worn anything so lovely before.'

'On you they look beautiful,' Simon responded, and brushed aside the shadow cast by the memory of how he had contrived to wrest them away from Georgiana. That was all part of the past.

They swept under the archway and into the yard of the Crown, where all the inn and coach company servants who had not been able to get to the church were assembled to greet them. Hard on their heels came the near relations, then a flood of guests joined the cheerful confusion. With the ease of long practice, Uncle Noll and Aunt Peg sorted them all out, directed them upstairs to the Long Room and with only a few minor hitches the whole crowd sat down to a meal in the very best tradition of Brown hospitality. Spring flowers decorated tables laden with cold meats and raised pies, flans and trifles, syllabubs and pastries, and a procession of maids trooped in with steaming joints and fowls, vegetables and sauces. Glasses were filled with the best the extensive cellars of the Crown could furnish. Toasts were called, unashamedly fulsome and dripping with sentiment, and responded to with wholehearted thanks. Faces became red and the noise grew steadily louder.

Simon took advantage of a chance break in the merriment around him to sit back and survey the scene and was aware of the great store of goodwill readily extended to him by the assembled clan. Laughing, gossiping, sweating now in the rising heat, their wedding favours wilting a little, the Browns, Jupps and Madoxes gathered here to celebrate would be just as eager to rally round in times of trouble. The freedom he had held on to for so many years was gone, but he felt few regrets. It had taken the Browns to show him that he was not so much a lone wolf as a stray dog. It was good to be part of the pack.

Further along the table, Tom Harthwaite ran his calculating eyes over the crowd with very different feelings.

'Nowt but a pack of tradesmen,' he summed up, disgust plain in his hoarse voice. 'Look at 'em, there's neither blood nor money here. I could buy up half a dozen of 'em in an afternoon and not feel the difference.' He turned his accusing stare on his daughter, who had been the cause of this wasted journey. 'This young man Wynwood, why ain't he asked any of his folks to his wedding? I suppose they wouldn't come, what with him being an hon'rable and this lot smelling of the shop. I wouldn't have come neither, if I'd known.'

Annabel flushed, biting her lip. It was all going wrong. It was all very well for Stacey to say 'Make the most of it,' but how was she to do so? Half a dozen times she had tried to introduce Arthur to her father, but on each occasion he had either not heard her or brushed her hesitant request aside before she was able even to mention his name.

'Well?' Tom demanded. 'What's become of the rest of the Wynwoods, eh?'

'I – I'm not sure,' Annabel faltered, and finding that her father was for once waiting for a reply instead of answering his own question, was suddenly visited with inspiration. 'But there is somebody here who might be able to tell you,' she said, hurrying the words out before her courage failed. 'Papa, I'd like you to meet Mr Harris – of Upthorpe Hall.'

Alerted by the telltale 'of', the millowner's shrewd glance took in Arthur's well-bred manner, his accent, the hands that had never known a day's serious work. He gave Arthur a curt nod, attempting both to deny his lowly origins and treat this young sprig of the gentry as if he were one of his clerks.

'Harris, eh? Groomsman, weren't you? You related to the Wynwoods?'

'No, sir. I'm – ah – merely a friend.'

'Aye? And would you know why Lord Lathenbridge has stayed away?'

'I – ah – believe there is something of a breach between his lordship and his son. I hardly know the details. A delicate matter, you understand.' To Annabel's delight, Arthur launched out on just the right course, almost losing the habitual hesitation in his speech as he did so. 'A mistake on my friend's part, in my opinion. After all, there's nothing to replace family connections. Family and land, that's what holds society together. Without it, what are we?'

'Aye, you've the right of it there, young man,' Tom agreed, new interest in his expression. 'Add money to that and you've power.' He addressed himself to his plate again, shovelling in a vast forkful of roast beef. 'I'll say summat,' he remarked, swallowing, 'they do know how to feed a man in this place.'

Annabel and Arthur exchanged a glance of despair, seeing the chance to steer the conversation into the right channels slipping from them. They both hastened to speak at once, stopped, waited for each other to go on. Tom Harthwaite cut through their confusion.

'I'm a stranger hereabouts, don't know this part o' the world at all,' he said. 'Your folks been settled here long?'

'Five generations,' Arthur told him, personal diffidence mixing oddly with family pride.

'Upthorpe's such a fine place, Papa,' Annabel put in breathlessly. 'It has a lake and – and a very pretty park—'

Arthur grabbed at the chance before it slipped through his fingers again.

'Perhaps you would care to visit us, sir?' he suggested. 'If you are in no hurry to return tomorrow, that is?'

Tom looked from one to the other, nodding slowly.

'Happen I will,' he said.

Under the table, Arthur's hand closed round Annabel's and squeezed it in delight.

By the time the bridecake was carried in, Oliver was

reaching the limits of his endurance. With the free flow of alcohol, talk around him was becoming lavishly laced with double meanings and gusts of bawdy laughter, and the cake heralded a new burst of backchat. After the first cut, the top layer was whisked away to be saved for the christening of the first child, then tiny fingers were sliced and wrapped in twists of paper. Stacey drew off her brand-new wedding ring and the pieces were passed through and distributed to the guests. The only sober person in the room, Oliver sat stony-faced as the cheerful remarks washed round him.

'Put that under your pillow tonight, Dinah, and dream of that tongue-tied beau of yours.'

'Oo, look at the way Jenny's hiding hers away so slyly! Have you a lover, Jenny? Who is he? Oo, she's blushing!'

'Aye, I'll take a piece, though much good it may do me. At my age, dreams are all I'm likely to have.'

'I know someone who'll not be needing dreams tonight.'

Involuntarily, Oliver's eyes sought out Stacey once more as she sat at the head of the table in her bridal white, still holding up her ring for the slivers of cake. As he watched, Simon said something in her ear and they both smiled, excluding the entire noisy crowd for a moment with a private joke.

'Ah, did you see that?' an elderly great-aunt asked him, with a sentimental sigh. 'Does your heart good, it does, to see them together. Puts me in mind of my Henry . . .'

Oliver stuck it out until the feast came to an end and the guests strolled downstairs to sit about and recover while the Long Room was cleared for dancing. He went out into the yard to try to get away, but the whole building was pervaded by the sounds of celebration. The back yard, usually a scene of bustling industry, was just as bad. Here the space was crowded with coaches that had been turned out of the main coach house to make room for the company servants' party. The eating was finished there, it seemed, for the scrape of the fiddle could be heard above the shouts and laughter, the shrill warbling of a flute, the insistent beat of a tambour. As Oliver leaned, hands in pockets, against a coach, a small detachment from the bridal party came through, led by Stacey and Simon. A roar of welcome went up to greet them, cheers and applause.

Through the now open doorway, Oliver heard the slightly incoherent speech made by Harry Cox in his capacity as senior coachman, and Simon's reply, perfectly pitched at the level of his audience, with frequent references to 'my wife', each one of which produced an enthusiastic response. A cold stone of misery heavy within him, Oliver watched as Stacey was whisked off to join in the dancing, and Simon turned to Harry's portly wife and led her onto the floor. Nobody, but nobody shared his sense of disaster.

And then out of the coach house reeled a small, bent figure clutching an earthenware jug too heavy for his feeble arms. He staggered as he reached the spring after- noon air of the yard and collapsed against the heavy door. It was Amos Burgess. Startled out of his stupor, Oliver strode over to help.

'Mr Burgess! Are you not well? Come and sit down, I'll carry that for you.'

He put an arm round the chief clerk's bony frame and tried to take the jug from him, but Amos held on to it with surprising strength, protesting that it was his. He was not ill, Oliver realized, but practically falling-down drunk. Oliver sat him down on an upturned bucket and Amos began to weep maudlin tears into the jug on his knees.

''Tis a tra – tragedy,' he confided brokenly. ''S the end. Nothing left now. Always wanted – a daughter. Daughter of my own. Gone now, gone with – that man . . .'

He meandered on for some while before Oliver fully comprehended that here was a fellow sufferer.

'Aren't you pleased about this wedding, Mr Burgess?' he asked.

''S a tragedy,' Amos repeated. 'Have a drink.'

'Drink won't make it any better,' Oliver told him.

''S a lie – 's the only way – only way – to forget—' Amos insisted, and became offended, thinking Oliver too proud to drink with him.

Through the door of the coach house, Oliver caught a glimpse of Stacey as she danced down to the bottom of a set. He grabbed the heavy jug and took a long pull, and then another, not stopping till he was out of breath. The ale, strong nag for which Norwich was famous, slid down easily but kicked him as it settled.

'Hellfire!' he gasped, choking. 'What has this got in it?'

''S only a drop of Blue Ruin,' Amos told him. ''S no good without.'

The world swayed as the combination of gin and strong ale began to take effect on a body that had not tasted alcohol for nearly four years. The noise of the dancing faded and he slid down beside Amos, his back against the sun-warmed brick of the stables. He stared at the blurred outline of the coach nearest to him and tried to focus on its lettering. With a great effort, he managed to read its name – The Highflyer. Oliver raised the jug again and took another drink.

Nobody noticed the missing faces when the entire concourse of family, friends and company servants gathered in the main yard in the mid-afternoon to see the happy couple off. They stepped out onto the first floor gallery to cheers from the assembled crowd, Stacey dressed now in a spring green pelisse and matching bonnet trimmed in brown velvet, Simon enveloped in a dark blue benjamin. Farewell kisses were showered on Stacey from her cousins, from Aunt Peg and Aunt Eustacia and finally from Barty, who squeezed Simon's arm and muttered something about taking good care of her. And then they were sitting in the curricle that stood waiting with their luggage strapped on the back, Simon took the reins of the pair of chestnut horses and, waving and ducking to avoid the rain of old shoes hurled after them, they bowled under the archway and out of the yard.

Noll clapped a heavy hand on his brother's shoulder.

'That's them well started,' he said. 'Wish I could've got my daughters settled half so easily. Come on in, I've got a bottle of fine old brandy I've been saving for a special occasion.'

It was only when they were alone together, not on show to dozens of curious eyes, that the feeling of unreality faded. Trotting along the turnpike towards the coast, they laughed over the easy way in which Arthur and Annabel's problems had so swiftly been overcome, passed the place where the Retaliator had been ambushed and vowed revenge on Pymer, Clayton and anyone else who tried to stand in the way of Brown prosperity. It was all utterly delightful for Stacey, the drive through the late afternoon, the charming flintstone and pantile cottage that Simon had borrowed from one of his myriad acquaintances, the supper that awaited them, the evening walk along the clifftops. And every time she looked at him, Stacey was struck anew with the wonderful truth that the impossible had actually happened, that this handsome, charming, clever man was hers to hold.

But as the light faded and the candles were lit, she found herself chattering nervously, spinning out the time, saying anything to delay the moment she was afraid to face. She was in no doubt as to what was expected of her. A childhood spent running about an inn had early made her aware of what went on between men and women, a knowledge absorbed as naturally as that of the inevitable sequence of birth and death. If it had not been for her narrow escape from Oliver at Christmas, she would have felt nothing more than a slight apprehension, but as it was she was caught in the jaws of an unreasoning fear. She had to force herself not to shake when Simon drew her into his arms and silenced her flow of words with a kiss.

'There's no need to be frightened of me, sweetheart,' he assured her. 'I won't harm you. Just trust me.'

'Oh I do, I do, but – it's just—'

285

Simon held her close, gently stroking her tense back and shoulders.

'I know, I understand. But this will be quite different, I promise you.'

He was as good as his word, infinitely patient, leading her until she found that he was right, that what was given in love was as far removed as could be from what was taken in anger: not a painful trial, but an expression of all that she felt for him.

Simon awoke the next morning to birdsong outside and light seeping through the yellow curtains to fill the small, low-ceilinged room with sunshine. He watched Stacey sleeping, her tousled brown hair spread across the pillow, her head turned trustingly towards him, and was awed by the extent of his good fortune. All his own misgivings about taking this step, tying himself to one place, one person, had flown, leaving him with a sense of contentment entirely new to him. Studying his new wife's strong-boned face, he decided she would grow handsome with age, where a superficially pretty woman would fade, and smiled at himself that he should be thinking ahead with complacency instead of refusing to look beyond the next six months at the most. He would grow prosperous and cultivate a paunch, he decided, and take his wife visiting on a Sunday afternoon, and teach his children to drive four-in-hand, and he laughed silently that he should find the prospect so very appealing.

Stacey stirred and opened her eyes, puzzled at first then smiling softly as she remembered where she was. Simon rolled nearer and kissed her.

'Good morning, Mrs Wynwood. Sleep well?'

'Mm – very well.' She gazed at him, drowsy still. 'It all seems such a long time since yesterday. Like another world.'

'Yesterday belonged to the family, today is all our own.' He slid a hand along the smooth curve of her waist. 'No coaches, no accounts, no organization of any kind.

286

We don't even have to get up if we don't wish to.'

Chuckling, Stacey wound her arms round his neck.

'Sounds a very lazy way to start a marriage.'

'It's the only way to start a marriage.'

Chapter Nineteen

Bright early morning sunshine slanted into the main yard of the Crown, glancing off shining panels and brightly polished harness, adding an extra gaiety to the already animated scene. Always bustling and busy with the pressure of getting the long-distance coaches out on time, the yard today took on an air of festivity. From the first floor gallery, Perdita looked down on the Telegraph as it stood ready to leave, her small face pink with pleasure. The coaches were a continual source of excitement to her, part of the colourful, important world her father inhabited, and today they were looking especially splendid. Bunches of coloured ribbons fluttered from the horses' bridles and sprigs of greenery peeped jauntily from behind their ears.

'They've got new bonnets on!' she exclaimed to Aunt Peg, who was watching the spectacle.

Aunt Peg chuckled and gave her an affectionate squeeze.

'Mayday bonnets, just like yours,' she agreed.

Perdita's sunny smile disappeared and she tugged at the strings under her chin with irritation. The little straw hat in question, with its gaily coloured flowers, had been a present from her Aunt Stacey. If anyone else had bought it for her, she would have been charmed, for it was quite the prettiest she had ever owned, but she had set herself against anything to do with her new stepmama. Aunt Stacey had taken her papa away from her. Aunt Stacey had made her leave Bridge Farm and the Hankins. Aunt Stacey could buy her a whole shopful of Mayday bonnets, but Perdita would not forgive her for turning her entire existence upside-down.

'Look at Smiler Perks!' Aunt Peg was saying. 'He must have a whole garden in his buttonhole.'

Perdita gazed at the coachman as he sauntered over to the Telegraph, exchanging a barrage of cheerful banter with his colleagues waiting for the other two London coaches.

'You watch it, Smiler bor. Get that stage o' yours going more'n a trot and the passengers'll drop dead o' surprise!'

'The day your little owd Albion goes faster'n a trot, *I'll* drop dead o' surprise.'

'Tell you summat, Telegraph'll clip the wings off that there Flyer o' yours today. Twelve hours dead to London, that's what we're doing.'

Smiler strolled round his team, checking their harness, while his guard settled the passengers. Rivalries might run high in the yard for record times on Mayday, but friendships were rarely broken over them. The real sport began out on the road, when Pymer's or one of the other competing stages appeared. Company rules on racing were thrown to the winds on this traditional day of celebration. The easy summer months lay ahead, with the prospect of warm weather, long light days, full coaches and plenty of tips. Smiler flourished his beribboned whip and down in the yard Perdita's Uncle Barty raised a hand in reply. As the coach moved off to a cheerful fanfare on the bugle, her father came into view.

'There's my pa!' she shrilled, bouncing up and down and waving, and glowing with pleasure as he looked up and smiled, calling a greeting to her. 'I've got the best papa in the world,' she told Aunt Peg, with total, unshakable conviction.

Her papa was her own special property, her one advantage at Bridge Farm over the Hankin children, who had so much. They might have a mother and father, the farm, the animals and each other, but when they taunted her, she could say, 'You haven't got my papa, so there!' and know that they couldn't answer that. For her papa was a marvellous person, quite different from the ordinary run of men, from the farm labourers, from the fathers of children in the village, even from Uncle Hankin. He was more like the squire, whom she saw in church, but better. He came to see her riding beautiful glossy horses or driving carriages. He brought her presents and told her about the exciting things he had been doing in the great strange world beyond the farm, and when he came Aunt Hankin bustled around getting out the nice things as she did when the squire or the parson called, and both she and Uncle Hankin called him 'sir'.

Once he arrived looking strange, with his head and arm all bandaged, and stayed for a long time, for weeks and weeks, until she thought he might live with them for ever. She cried herself to sleep the day he went away again, but after that he came every Saturday night to see her, and stayed until Sunday afternoon. She did not like it so much when this was reduced to just Sundays, and was disturbed at Christmas when he was ill again. It was after that that everything started to go wrong. Her papa seemed always to be tired and sad, and for two dreadful weeks in the dead of winter did not appear at all, but sent a letter explaining that he had to go away and would be back soon. It was after he did arrive back that he brought Her with him.

Perdita gripped the gallery rail as Aunt Stacey walked across the yard to her papa's side, sliding a possessive arm through his. She glanced up briefly at Perdita and smiled, then said something to her papa. He switched his whole attention to her and after a moment they both turned and went off towards the back yard together. Perdita glared after them. It was always the same now. *She* was always taking her papa away.

At first she had liked Aunt Stacey. She was funny, and laughed a lot, and wore pretty clothes, so that the Hankin children wanted to know who the beautiful lady was. Perdita told them proudly that she was going to be her stepmama, and to her consternation Tommy Hankin said that stepmamas were always wicked. Perdita flew at him, shrieking that it was not true, that she had the best papa in the world *and* the best stepmama.

290

'But you ain't got a proper ma,' Tommy jeered. 'Your ma gave you away.'

She remembered very little of her life before her papa appeared in it. There were a few isolated incidents of fear or pain, but mostly a blur of hunger and cold from which her papa had rescued her. When she asked why she did not have a mother, he said she was too poor to keep her. This puzzled Perdita.

'You're not poor, are you?'

'I'm not rich.'

'But – why was she poor? Why didn't you give her some money?'

And Papa silenced her in the way grown-ups do when they do not want to answer questions.

'Because I didn't know where she was. That's enough now, Perdy. Why don't you show me these new hens you were telling me about?'

It was not long before she realized that her papa did not belong to her exclusively any more. She had to share him with Aunt Stacey. Even on the Sundays she did not come to Bridge Farm with him, he talked a lot about her, about the wedding, about a whole new family of people she had never met. Perdita decided she did not like them, these Browns. Neither did she like the house they were to live in, or the town. And when she finally came to All Saints Green, she found it was just as she had expected. There were no fields, just a garden at the back and a bit of grass at the front, the hordes of new 'cousins' she was introduced to were horrid and stared at the mark on her face, and worst of all she hardly saw more of Papa than when she was at Bridge Farm, for he was up before her and often not home till after her bedtime and when he was there, Aunt Stacey was as well.

The only nice things about her new life were Uncle Bart, who looked frightening but was really very kind, and Aunt Peg, who reminded her of Aunt Hankin. These two she liked, but not Aunt Stacey. So she hid from Aunt Stacey and refused to do anything she told her. Once she ran away, but she was seen by one of the horrid Browns and brought back again. This made Papa very cross, and he talked to her a long time about how kind Aunt Stacey was to let her live with them, and how she ought to be grateful. Perdita did not run away again, but neither was she grateful to Aunt Stacey.

'She's horrid,' she growled, glowering at her stepmother's retreating back. All her pleasure in the day's treat dimmed. She did not want to be stuck here on the gallery while Papa was down there with Aunt Stacey holding on to him. She darted off towards the steps, intent on reaching him, catching his arm, pulling him away from Her, but Aunt Peg saw her and moved with astonishing speed, gathering her up and hustling her through the door into the family parlour.

'Now then, Perdy, don't you go running off like that. You might get trampled under the horses,' she said, with a mixture of authority and concern that Perdita found impossible to disregard. Against her will, she found herself distracted from her resentful mood and caught up in 'helping' supervise the breakfasts until it was time for the Telegraph to leave.

Outside in the yard, Stacey deliberately shut all thought of her troublesome stepdaughter out of her mind as she stood with Simon surveying the colourful Mayday scene. The spring sunshine was warm on her back, Brown's coaches had never looked better as each team of horsekeepers vied to produce the best turn-out, and the man she loved belonged to her. She was still not quite used to this, needing to touch him sometimes just to assure herself that it really was true. She looked up at his clear-cut profile now as he spoke to the men harnessing the Telegraph's team, congratulating them on the horses' condition. At times he still seemed like a stranger to her, keeping great areas of himself aloof, foiling all her efforts to come close, but gradually he was opening out, giving her glimpses of his inner thoughts, and of his wild and colourful past. She had not been surprised to discover that he was an Oxford graduate.

'I only scraped a third,' he said, dismissing her admiration.

'What does that mean?'

He grinned. 'It means I didn't work very hard.'

'What did you study – when you were working?'

'How to fix a game of Rouge-et-Noir.'

She sighed, foreseeing another conversation that was going nowhere.

'No, seriously,' she persisted.

'Yes, seriously,' he mimicked her gently. 'I had a very profitable partnership in a gaming club. When I wasn't engaged there, I read Classics.'

'Oh,' Stacey said, considering this. As so often happened when she did get underneath Simon's guard, she found herself in very debatable territory, her love of and belief in him warring with the standards of her upbringing. She remembered Arthur Harris on the morning of his return home. In his case all had turned out well in the end, but his brief plunge into the turbulent waters of gambling could easily have ruined his life and drastically affected his family. She shied away from the thought of Simon being involved in anything so cruelly dishonest, and cast about for some exonerating circumstances. 'Were you very pressed for money yourself, at the time?' she hazarded.

He was wearing that brazen look that she knew from past experience did not bode well for her peace of mind.

'Not at all,' he said. 'The old man had to keep me in a manner as befitted a Wynwood, whatever he thought about me in private. No – the opportunity arose and it was irresistible. All those young innocents practically begging to have their fingers burnt.' He looked at her disturbed face and his expression softened. 'But you are perfectly right, as usual. It was not a particularly honourable occupation. I didn't have you to act as my conscience then, you see. Even so, when I saw what the consequences were for some of our patrons I backed out,

293

and made sure my ex-partner could not start up again in the town.'

And Stacey relaxed, her faith in him justified. He could not have been any older than the undergraduates who patronized his club, and yet she wondered if he had ever been a 'young innocent'. Always it came back to that appalling family of his. The more she learnt about them, the more unspeakable they became.

Now, however, on a bright May morning with the festive air about the yard and trade likely to pick up in the summer months ahead, Stacey's natural optimism asserted itself. The Wynwoods could not touch them now. Simon had left them behind for ever. The future was with Brown's.

'Splendid, is it not?' she said, nodding at the Telegraph as it was led through to the main yard. 'The King himself would be proud to ride in it.'

'If he could get through the door,' Simon agreed. 'But the Flyer's looking even better. I know one shouldn't have favourites, but Harry Cox and the Flyer will always take precedence over the others for me. We'll wait to see them leave, then join the family breakfast.'

Breakfast was not usually an occasion for a gathering, but today the inn and the coaches were given the minimum attention needed to keep them running and the coachworks were closed, so that everyone had a chance to enjoy their own brand of fun, be it a rowdy and uncontrolled game of camp-ball, dancing or a well-earned doze over a tankard of ale. By the time Stacey and Simon joined the crowd in the family parlour, there was only just room for them to squeeze in at the long polished oak table and the babble of cheerful voices almost drowned the clatter of plates.

Stacey looked around at all the people she loved best in the world; her father, discussing some point with Uncle Noll, Aunt Peg, admiring the new dress of one of her young nieces, Harriet, pink with anticipation of a whole day with the young apothecary who was 'keeping com-

'pany' with her, as the local term had it, Oliver – here she paused, a slight frown creasing her forehead. Her feelings were still very ambivalent about Oliver. She wished him well, but kept out of his way as much as possible. Today he was his usual repressive self, a small cloud of disapproval gathered about him. He considered Mayday a pagan rite, and likely to lead to sinful excesses. Stacey had no patience with him. People who had laboured hard through the cold, dark winter and the sparse days of early spring had cause to rejoice at the coming of summer. She leaned across the table to speak to Harriet, raising her voice against the general noise.

'You're in the best of looks today, Harriet. I do like your hair pinned that way. When is your beau calling for you?'

Her cousin blushed and giggled.

'Do you? Oh thank you – it took me over an hour to get it right – does it really look nice? He'll be here at eleven. Oh, Stacey, is this dress all right? Ma said yes, but you know what she's like, so old-fashioned. I'm not at all sure about these ruffles.'

Stacey assured her that she looked ravishing, calling on Simon to second her. This finally assuaged Harriet's doubts, for even though her heart was now given to another, she still could not resist a compliment from Simon. Stacey smiled, glowing with an inner superiority. She wished Harriet every joy of her apothecary, shared in her hopes for the future, but was convinced that Simon was better in every conceivable way.

Her satisfaction was broken by Perdita's appearing at Simon's side, worming her way between them and climbing up onto his lap, effectively claiming his attention. Stacey fought to suppress a familiar stab of jealousy. Try as she might to reason herself out of it, she could not help resenting Perdita's monopolizing even five minutes of Simon's time when it could have been devoted to herself. She knew very well that it was unworthy or her, and felt guilty every time, trying to make up for it by attempting

295

to win the child's confidence and affection. But whatever she tried, presents, bedtime stories, tea parties with other young members of the family, all she got from Perdita was a sullen silence broken by the briefest of monosyllabic replies. And when she was roused to anger by the little girl's running away and hiding from her, she had only to see the ugly mark on her face and remember the insecure life she had led to feel guilty again that she had not more patience in dealing with her. All in all, Perdita was a problem she could well do without, but she had a sneaking suspicion that if the child were not living with them, their Sundays would be spent in visiting her, and Sundays were infinitely precious.

Perdita was not the only cloud on Stacey's horizon. She had fondly expected that all troubles would just fade away once she was married to Simon, but instead discovered that though living with him was every bit as wonderful as she had imagined, it brought its own difficulties. She found she was having to act as a buffer between Simon's ideas for expansion, and her father's conviction that the company was in far too shaky a state to go making plans for any wild new enterprises. With both men busy during the day, it was over the dinner table that differences were aired. Only yesterday evening, Simon had brought up a scheme he was particularly keen on.

'With the coachworks proving so useful, we ought to extend the idea and provide our own horses,' he said. 'It's the next logical step.'

'Expensive step,' Barty objected. 'And just how do you see us doing it?'

'By breeding our own. It would be a long-term project, of course. Even if we started right now, it would be five years before we began to reap the benefits, but it's worth considering.'

Stacey had already heard of this idea, for Simon had talked it over with her at some length, but she did not want her father to have the impression that they were

296

combining against him. She started to cut up the rhubarb pie.

'Five years is a long time to wait for a return on investment,' she said. 'And in the meantime the mares and foals would need feeding and caring for and the young stock would have to be broken. It means employing at least two skilled men, surely, and perhaps a couple of boys as well.'

She passed a plate to Simon, who caught her eye for a brief moment to let her know he understood what she was at. He continued a show of convincing her as well as Barty.

'I'm not suggesting going straight into running a full-scale stud farm,' he explained. 'We would start small, with half a dozen mares, and gradually expand. Eventually we would have a good supply of horses for the prestige ends of the runs.'

'Hardly seems worth the effort when we can buy all we want from the dealers and the fairs,' Barty commented, and applied himself to the pie with the air of one who has said the last word.

Simon exchanged another look with Stacey, who took up the argument.

'I don't know,' she said, sounding undecided. 'Matched teams are a terrible price. Look at what we had to pay for the Flyer's set for the home ground. If we bred all bays, say, or chestnuts, we'd only have to match them up for strength and stride. There's always a market for a good matched team, so we could sell the surplus.'

Barty merely made a grunt of disagreement. Simon appeared to give up the fight. He leaned towards Stacey, sitting opposite him.

'You know that flash set of piebalds Pymer puts to the Magnet? One of them is really a grey. He has it dyed to match the others.'

As he had expected, this caught Barty's interest.

'So where do you intend keeping these horses of yours?' he asked. 'Breeding stock needs good pasture and it has to be near enough for you to keep an eye on things.'

Stacey suppressed a gleeful grin and waited for Simon to produce his trump card.

'There's plenty of room at Upthorpe,' he said, refilling the glasses. 'We could come to some agreement with Harris that would suit all concerned.'

'Oh yes!' Stacey chimed in. 'That is a good . . .' She trailed off as an ominous look of obstinacy settled over her father's face.

'That's fine for now, but I doubt if they'd want upwards of thirty youngsters taking up room in their paddocks in five years' time. What then?'

'By then we shall be in a position to take over a place of our own,' Simon said. 'We could grow some of our own feed as well, and cut down our costs in that direction.'

Barty held his eye, seemingly interested.

'Rent or buy?'

'Buy, preferably. It would be a good investment.'

'Ha, I thought as much. I thought that was what you was leading to.' Gesturing with a fork, Barty spoke to the table at large, as if addressing a meeting. 'The trouble with connecting yourself with the landed classes is, they always want to get back where they came from. Not happy without a little owd piece of farm they can call an estate.' He raised a tufted eyebrow at Simon, taking the sting out of his words. 'That so, eh? Sorry, bor, but we can't go setting up expensive schemes like that till we get rid of Pymer, and God knows how long that'll take. He seems to have a bottomless chest of gold to keep him going.'

It was not until later that Stacey realized that Simon had by no means been talked out of the idea.

'I still think it would be a profitable undertaking,' he insisted, pushing up one of the sash windows of the bedchamber they occupied across the front of the house. He leaned on the sill, breathing the cool night air, idly watching a couple of revellers weaving their way homewards across the green. 'Landed classes,' he muttered. 'There are times when I wonder whether it was wise to move in here. Perhaps we should have found a place of our own.'

'Oh but—' Stacey came up behind him, winding her arms round his waist and resting her head on his back. She could feel the heat of him through his fine shirt, and the tenseness of his body betrayed the frustration he managed to hide. Tempers had been short that day at the yard. Simon had been called upon to sort out any number of irritating muddles and delays, and now his latest brainchild had been dismissed out of hand. Stacey nestled against him, trying to distract his attention. 'Pa would be terribly hurt if we moved out now,' she pointed out. 'I expect he's just tired. When he's thought it over, he's sure to see what a good idea it is.'

'Whether he does or not, I intend going ahead with it. I'll raise my own money if he won't back it with the company's.' He straightened up and Stacey let go of him, feeling rather foolish. It was as a business partner that he was talking to her now. 'Would it be possible to work out the comparative costs of breeding our own and buying as we do now, on the open market?' he asked.

Stacey frowned, thinking of the calculations involved. 'I should think so, but it would only be an estimate. There are so many changeable factors.'

'Would you do it for me, then?'

'Of course.' Stacey was always delighted to prove useful to him.

'Capital. I wonder how I ever used to embark on a project without you to do the difficult parts for me?' Closing the window, he put the matter behind him. 'How are your other plots maturing? Is all well out at Upthorpe? I've not seen hide nor hair of Harris these past two weeks.'

'Oh, couldn't be better,' Stacey replied, fighting to keep the slight edge of envy out of her voice. 'The Harrises have the money they need, the Harthwaites have the connection they want, Arthur and Annabel have each other. Everybody's happy.'

Yes, I am happy, Stacey thought, basking in the family

warmth at the Mayday breakfast. She had everything she wanted, she told herself. Everything, that was, except the same consuming love from Simon that Annabel received from Arthur. She gave herself a mental shake. Simon's trust and friendship was worth a thousand times more than Arthur's doglike devotion. She touched his arm to attract his attention.

'I could start working out those figures for you today, if you like.'

'Figures?'

'Yes, for the horsebreeding scheme.'

'Oh, those.' He covered her hand with his, smiling. 'You don't have to do it straight away, sweetheart, it's not that urgent. I was hoping we could take some time off today.'

And as if he had heard, Barty leaned back in his seat several places along the table and called behind a row of backs to them.

'I'll look after things here. You two go off and enjoy yourselves while you're still young enough.'

It took very little extra persuasion to make them comply.

The long summer days brought their usual increase of business at the Crown, with people taking advantage of the good weather to make long-delayed journeys. Coaches rolled out fully-laden and the company began to show a reasonable profit again. To Amos Burgess, hunched over each day's crop of bills and receipts, it was poor consolation. Ever since the wedding, he had daily expected some move to be made to dismiss him, and trembled every time Mr and Mrs Wynwood came into the office together and took ledgers with them into the inner office, watching them covertly with sunken eyes in a defeated face. Just as long as Mr Brown had overall control of the company, he was safe. Safe, that was, if nobody found out about his dealings with Mr Clayton. But if ever Mr Brown should meet with an accident – perish the thought – Amos did not give a farthing for his chances of staying in employment. With every new morning, he wondered if it was worth the effort of going on. If he lost his position, there would be nothing to live for at all.

Unaware of Amos's silent despair, Simon would look round the yard and imagine how it could be without Pymer's taking their trade, with extra coaches running and maybe a parcels service, whilst Stacey frowned over the weekly accounts and said that they were not making enough to carry them through another winter. She was further disturbed by an odd change in herself. She found she was snapping at people for no good reason, and crying over trivial incidents, she who had never been one to weep.

'What a little shrew I married,' Simon remarked when she railed at him for moving a book she wanted.

Instantly remorseful, Stacey fought a losing battle with the rising tears.

'I'm sorry, I didn't mean it,' she sobbed. 'I don't know what came over me. I n-never used to be like this.'

Simon held her until she was calm again.

'There's an indictment,' he teased. 'I shall begin to think you're regretting it if that's what marriage does to you.'

'Oh no!' she declared vehemently, taking him seriously. 'Not for a moment!'

For the troubles faded to the merest pinpricks the minute she heard his footstep in the hall of an evening, or when he looked up from something he was doing to smile at her, and disappeared altogether each night when they closed the door on the rest of the world.

Towards the end of July, they took four days off to travel up to Yorkshire for Arthur and Annabel's wedding.

'Nothing like ours,' Stacey reported to Barty when they arrived back. 'That dreadful companion person has absolutely no idea how to organize a good party. Everyone so stiff and formal! The Harrises hardly spoke to anyone other than themselves and the Harthwaites' guests were either on their best behaviour or being deliberately vulgar to show they weren't impressed by the Harrises. I don't think anyone would have mixed at all if Simon had not been there bridging the two camps.'

'Romeo and Juliet were nothing to it,' Simon corroborated, 'Though it was not so much enmity as disparagement on either side. What they needed was one of Aunt Peg's magnificent feasts to thaw them out.'

'Aye, there's no-one does a party like Peg and Noll,' Barty agreed. He lit his pipe with an air of satisfaction. 'It's been passing quiet here with you two away. I been thinking over that plan of yours for breeding some of our own horses. If the figures are as good as you make them out to be, it might be worth considering.'

'Pa! I knew you would see it was a good proposition. I wasn't sure at first, but once I started working out the costs, I was quite convinced.' Alight with enthusiasm, Stacey went over to the writing-desk to find the sheet she had spent so much time preparing. 'As you saw, it won't take too much to set the scheme up,' she said, shuffling papers around. 'Ah, here it is. And if you take into account the factors you can't put a price on, like the prestige of driving our own top quality cattle, I'm sure it will be an asset. It's the sort of thing that gets us talked about, like running the Flyer or having better-built coaches than Pymer's or anyone else in the three counties. Look, even if we just start with four mares . . .'

'We're not starting anything this late in the day,' Simon interrupted her. 'Once you begin juggling numbers about you go on all night, and you've been yawning this past hour. We were on the road at six this morning, remember.'

'I'm not tired!' Stacey protested, though she knew very well she was. She sat on the arm of Barty's chair and laid the neatly-written columns of figures on his knee. 'It takes more than a paltry journey from Yorkshire to wear me out. We used to do more than that when I was little, did we not, Pa?'

But her father told her to do as she was bid and kissed her goodnight with the promise of discussing it fully the next day. More glad than she would admit at the thought of a night's sleep in her own bed, Stacey plodded upstairs, the plans for the horses forgotten as a suspicion that had been lurking in her mind for the past month again rose to the surface. With a bubble of excitement gathering inside, she hurried out of her clothes and examined herself critically in the glass, turning this way and that to get a better view. She didn't look any different, she decided, though maybe some of her dresses were a little on the tight side. She certainly did not feel any different, and yet . . . pulling on a dressing-gown, she ran over dates in her head, making sure.

When Simon came in she cut through his remarks with impatience.

'It is the twenty-fifth today, isn't it?'

'Yes, why?'

'That's it, then. It must be, that's two I've missed. And the other things too, being tired and snapping at people.' She hugged herself, glowing with the thrill of achievement. 'I think, I'm nearly certain, that I'm pregnant.'

Unwanted, a vision of Deborah making the same announcement flashed before Simon. He had seen her about the town a few times in the past seven months, growing steadily bigger, but had always managed to avoid running into her. Her child must be due any day now, he realized.

Stacey looked at him anxiously.

'Are you not pleased?'

'Sweetheart, I'm delighted. Absolutely delighted.'

He hurried across the room to catch her in his arms and swing her round.

'My darling, it's wonderful news,' he said as she clung to him, dizzy and laughing. 'When is it to be?'

'Sometime in February. Not the best time for a baby, right in the middle of winter.'

'Don't worry, our child shall want for nothing, whatever the season. And you must look after yourself from now on. I wouldn't have let you go gallivanting all the way up to Yorkshire if I had known.' He pulled back the covers for her to climb into bed, then sat down beside her, holding her hands and dragging out his scant knowledge of how her condition should be affecting her. 'Nobody would guess yet, looking at you,' he said. 'Shouldn't you be feeling sick, or having fainting fits?'

'Not everybody does,' Stacey told him. 'I feel as fit as a flea. I just seem to tire more quickly than usual, that's all.' She was about to tell him not to start fussing round her as if she were made of glass when it occurred to her that to do so would be throwing away a golden opportunity. If it meant giving up a degree of freedom in order to gain Simon's solicitude, she was more than glad to make the exchange. 'Of course,' she added, 'it's early days yet. Things may change as I get bigger.'

'You'll have the best attention money can buy,' Simon promised. 'I'll call the doctor in first thing tomorrow to see you. Or better still, go and talk to Aunt Peg. I should imagine she knows more about babies than any physician.' He smiled at her bright, happy face. 'No need to ask you if you're glad.'

'I'm glad because it's yours,' Stacey said simply. 'I wanted to bear your child.'

'Your father will be beside himself. An heir to the Brown empire,' Simon said, thinking of the implications to those beyond the two of them. And quite probably an heir to the Lathenbridge title, he reflected, for rumour had it that Georgiana's child was sickly and not likely to live. But he pushed that possibility aside. 'We'll tell him in the morning.'

With a sigh of contentment, Stacey lay back on the pillows.

'Why am I singled out to be so fortunate?' she asked.

'Because life is gloriously unfair,' Simon told her. 'That's why I enjoy it so much.'

They were asleep, folded together in sweet oblivion,

when a figure came racing across the green, stumbling in the darkness, and pounded on the door of the Browns' house. Simon awoke with a start, quelling a panicky spurt of foreboding, picked his way across the room and threw up the sash window.

'What the devil's the matter?' he demanded. 'You'll wake the neighbourhood.'

'Mr Wynwood, sir—' Below, a man's pale face was dimly discernible, his breath could be heard rasping in his chest. 'There's a fire, sir, in the coach house—'

'Fire? Oh my God!' Unconsciously, Simon's fingers gripped the window-frame as if his very life depended upon it. 'Has the engine been sent for?'

'Yes, sir.'

'Good. Go and rouse every company servant you can get hold of. I'm coming directly.'

His mind already formulating a plan of action, he groped for his clothes in the gloom, and was momentarily dazzled by the flare of a candle being lighted.

'Simon, what is it? Did you say "Fire"?'

Stacey was half out of bed, staring at him with eyes wide in horrified disbelief.

'Yes, in the coach house. Let's pray it's not too serious.'

'I'll wake Pa.'

Snatching up the first garment that came to hand, his dressing-gown, she pulled it on and lunged out of the room, clutching it about her. Simon, thrusting his feet into his boots, heard her calling urgently to her father, and a minute or so later met her on the landing.

'He's coming,' she said. 'You go on, I'll met you there.'

'No!' Simon stopped short in his dash for the stairs. 'You'll do nothing of the kind. You stay right here.'

'But—'

'No buts. You do not fight fires, especially in your condition. I promise I'll send you word as soon as it's under control.'

Stacey bit back a retort and leaned over the banister as he ran down. 'Take care, oh do take care!' she called.

There was a clatter of bolts being drawn back, a whistle of a draught, then the door slammed shut behind him. Stacey darted back into her room and began scrambling into her clothes. She did not care what he said, it was absolutely inconceivable that she should wait at home chewing her fingernails down to the bone whilst the entire business went up in flames. She listened for her father's departure, then slipped out after him, closing the front door carefully and silently dogging his hurrying footsteps.

The silence of the streets snapped at her heels as she hastened, imagining horrors ahead of her. The timber coaches and the straw-filled stables would flare up like a torch, and at this time of night there would not have been enough people in the yard to stop the fire before it took hold. If it had not been discovered early, the whole coach house might now be ablaze, and the stables threatened. As they drew nearer the Crown, she could smell smoke in the still air, overpowering the summer stench of the streets. Flakes of ash floated down around her, and crackling and shouts could be heard. In front of her, Barty broke into a trot, and in her desperation to find out the worst, Stacey had to stop herself from picking up her skirts and overtaking him as they covered the last stretch along Crown Lane and under the archway of the inn.

Here lights glowed in the windows and the air was acrid with the smell of burning, catching at her throat. Three of the coaches, she was relieved to see, had been dragged through into the main yard, and a fourth was at that moment being manhandled through from the stables. A chain of inn servants stretched from the kitchen, passing buckets with frantic haste, and from the galleries inn guests in their nightclothes leaned over the balustrades to watch the drama.

Dodging past the coaches, Stacey darted into the back stables and stopped short, momentarily dazed by the heat, the noise, the frenzied activity, her eyes watering and lungs rasping from the smoke. At first sight it was total chaos, a vision of hell. Against the lurid, leaping light from the blazing coach house, dirty, dishevelled figures scurried to and fro, bearing sacks and buckets and brooms, two men swung at the yard pump handle with demonic energy, orders were yelled, terrified horses screamed, another coach, its rear end already alight, was pulled out of the inferno. But as Stacey watched, some kind of order began to emerge. The flames on the coach were beaten out by the sacks and brooms, water from the bucket chains was used to damp down the threatened stables and the part of the coach house nearest to them, whilst the rest of it had evidently been abandoned as past control. Directing operations, the still eye of this hurricane, Simon stood apprising Barty of the situation whilst sending a newly-arrived party of men to help with the saving of the burning coach. Stacey had just decided that she would be most use on a bucket chain when she saw him turn and wave a group away from the entrance of the coach house.

'Get back, get back!' he yelled. 'Leave it! Get those horses out before the stables catch. Take sacks and blindfold them.'

Merging with the crowd, Stacey ran across to the stables, gasping as the furnace heat struck her. The soaking door timbers were steaming and men with brooms were sweeping away straw and beating out sparks as they landed. She picked up a damp sack from the pile by the entrance and plunged inside, where the air was thick with a pungent mix of sweating, panic-stricken horses and smoke. The first half-dozen were being untied and led out, and beyond them someone yelled with pain as with an infuriated snort, a beast lashed out with its hindlegs.

'Damn you, you devil! Stay there and burn!' the injured man cursed, and went on to the next animal.

It was Stacey's old friend, The Killer. Snorting and sidling, throwing his weight against the restraining halter rope, he was difficult enough to handle when the stables were quiet. Now, frightened and angered by the noise and the smell of fire, he was a menace. But Stacey could not leave him there. Swiftly, she sized up the problem. It was no use approaching him from behind, as his deadly hooves would soon stop her. The only way was to climb over from the next stall and blindfold him.

Hitching up her hampering skirts and tying the sack round her waist, Stacey scrambled onto the wooden manger and stood up, feeling for foot and handholds on the dividing wall. Many a time as a child she had done this, but then she had been in short dresses and tackling it in daylight. She settled her feet on the strut that ran the length of the partition, pushed up and leaned forward, swinging a leg over the top. For a moment she balanced precariously astride, then changed her handhold and slid down into The Killer's stall, dropping lightly on the straw beside his neck. The surge of triumph was abruptly checked as the horse, eyes rolling white in the gloom, butted her in the stomach and pushed her back against the manger. Biting back a curse, she reached out and caught his halter, speaking gently to him. At the touch of her hand The Killer flung up his head, nearly jerking her arms out of their sockets, but Stacey hung on. Having got so far, she was not going to give up now.

'Steady now,' she soothed, stroking his nose, sliding an arm over his neck. 'Good boy. Stand still. That's the way.'

Moving cautiously, she undid the sack and manoeuvred it over the horse's eyes, knotting it before he had time to shake it off. Still talking to him, she unclipped the halter rope and began to back him out of the stall. At first he went obediently, quietened by not being able to see, bunched muscles trembling. But as soon as he sensed they were headed for the stable door, he sprang forward, squealing and kicking, trying to escape Stacey's restraining hold. They erupted into the yard, scattering men, smashing an abandoned bucket, while Stacey hung on with all her strength, throwing her weight against the horse's mad flight. Just as she thought she was about to lose the battle, another pair of hands snatched at the rope and The Killer was brought to a halt. It was Simon.

'I thought I told you to stay at home.'

The quiet force of the statement cowed her as anger would never have done.

'I – I had to save him,' she stammered, avoiding the central issue. 'He saved me.'

'Granted. I haven't the time to argue with you, and I have too much to see to without looking out for your safety. Daniel!' Simon called to a passing horsekeeper and consigned The Killer to his care. 'Now you can take two of the quieter horses and go with the others down to the Cups, or failing that, the Running Hare, and then you come back here, find Aunt Peg and stay with her. Do you understand?'

'Yes.'

She wanted to apologize, to explain why she had come, but already he was striding off to deal with the next problem. Stacey threaded her way to the bunch of horses by the entrance and obediently helped lead them to their temporary refuge.

The coach house was now an inferno, the vehicles still inside so many bonfires. Flames reached up to the ceiling, ate through and into the horsekeepers' quarters above. Smoke poured out from under the eaves, a shower of sparks flew up as a coach, the one in which the fire had started, collapsed in on itself with a crash. The heat was intense, and in spite of the valiant efforts of the water chains, the stables nearest to the burning building were beginning to smoulder. Now that all the horses were evacuated, the heavy doors were dragged shut and soaked, Simon taking his turn at the end of the line where the heat was only bearable for minutes at a time. Burning debris fell around him, each piece a new threat to the stables, to be kicked clear before it could ignite the door. He worked till his face and eyes and hands were seared, until his head began to swim, and at last relinquished his place to the next man and reeled away to where Barty was standing watching the conflagration with a look of dazed despair.

'Where the devil's that damned engine got to?' he demanded, gasping and choking as he dragged down the relatively cooler air. 'What's the point of paying for the insurance if they can't get here to save the place before it's ruined? Buckets are useless against this.'

Barty seemed not to hear him.

'Twenty-seven years,' he said dully. 'Twenty-seven years I been building this business. All up in flames.'

'Not all.' Simon threw an arm round the older man's shoulders. 'We'll salvage enough to go on, or perish in the attempt.'

But Barty only shook his head.

'Pymer'll sweep the floor with us,' he predicted.

Caught up with the immediate practical problem, Simon had not given a thought to the future. But now he did, and one thing was certain: Seth Pymer was not going to gain any advantage from the catastrophe, even if it meant resorting to the lowest trick in the book.

'Not if I have anything to do with it,' he vowed.

But even as he said it, the battle for the stables was lost. The heat from the coach house beat back the desperate attempt to keep the doors wet, flames from the roof licked across the short gap and took hold on the stable eaves. Simon raced over and sent men up onto the roof with axes to try to hack away the burning sections, but then had to bring them down again as they were in danger of being injured. Just as it seemed that the fire would eat its way relentlessly round the entire yard, stables, smithy, feed-store and harness-room, a new sound was heard beyond the shouts and the roar of the flames, a sound of pounding hooves and rumbling iron-bound wheels.

A hoarse cheer was torn from parched throats as through the entranceway came the fire brigade and their unwieldy, horse-drawn pumping engine. The crowd parted for them and cleared a space for the engine to be manoeuvred into position. The foreman checked with Simon that nobody was trapped by the flames, the leather hoses were attached and a dozen volunteers leaped forward to man the parallel handles of the pump. The firemen, protected by their helmets and leather gauntlets and jackboots, climbed up on the roof and began to chop at the lighted timbers, and the hose was trained on the doors. Gradually, the stable fire was brought under control.

'We're winning! By God, we're winning!' Simon shouted. 'You see,' he said to Barty, 'we'll save the place yet. It takes more than a paltry fire to finish Brown's!'

Infected by his elation, Barty regained some of his customary optimism.

'Aye, we're maybe not done for yet,' he agreed.

But even the water gushing from the hose could do nothing to save the coach house. The whole building was ablaze now, flames leaping from the rafters and lighting the yard with a lurid glare. With an accelerating roar, the roof dipped, sagged, then collapsed. Most of it fell inwards, but the projecting end gable leaned perilously out and a corner of it dropped across the entrance, one jagged, flaring end crashing through the harness-room window. Seeing yet another building threatened, Barty started forward, yelling at nearby men to help rescue the valuable gear inside. Too late Simon saw him go.

'No!' he bawled. 'No, come back, we've already got it!'

But his voice was lost in the cacophony. Pushing people aside, he pounded through the milling crowd, still yelling to Barty to stop. As they neared the harness-room, the two men with him heard the warning and paused, looking up, and as they did so another part of the gable gave way and toppled to the ground, pinning Barty beneath it. With a cry of anguish, Simon shot through the horrified spectators, every sense centred on saving Barty as he lay helpless and ominously still under the flaming beam.

Heedless of the warning shouts behind him, he was feet away from his goal when someone cannoned into him from the side, felling him and heaving him back out of danger just as another rafter landed, scattering lethal broken tiles. For several moments he was stunned, and by the time he struggled to his feet, a dozen men were straining to lift the heavy timbers clear. He staggered forward and found himself alongside Oliver, neither of them even noticing that their hands were getting burnt as they worked. In desperate haste, they freed the Gaffer's broken body and carried him to a safer spot, but even as they laid him down they knew they had tried in vain. One side of his head was crushed and sagged grotesquely, the neck broken.

Simon sank down onto the cobbles beside him, his mind rejecting the proof of his eyes.

'No, no,' he groaned. 'Not dead, he can't be dead . . .'

He tore at the filthy, bloodstained shirt, searching for the faintest flutter of a heartbeat, but found none. Somewhere above his head in the shocked silence, Oliver was muttering a halting prayer, commending Barty's soul to his Maker, and the stunned circle of porters, ostlers and horsekeepers, men who did not see the inside of a church from one year's end to the next, repeated a fervent 'Amen'. Simon looked up at Oliver who seemed shaken but not overcome by the awful finality of death.

'Why him?' he demanded. 'He didn't deserve to die now. He was a good man, the best – he had years of active life ahead of him.'

'It ain't for us to question,' Oliver said. 'He's in a better place now.'

Simon could only envy him his faith. As far as he was concerned, the essential Barty Brown, the man he had loved and respected, existed only in this form and on this earth. Beyond that he could see no further existence.

Someone produced a royal blue and brown horse cloth to cover the body.

'Where shall we take him, sir?' one of the porters asked Simon. 'Can't leave him here.'

'No, of course not—' Simon ran a hand over his head, trying to think through the paralysis of shock. He was dimly aware of the engine being moved over to put out the harness-room fire. 'We'll carry him through to the inn,' he decided, and then remembered the task that awaited him there. 'Stacey! Oh my God, how am I going to tell her?'

Stacey was spending the night hours prowling up and down the family parlour, unable to rest while she could see the flames, desperate to know what was going on but not daring to risk Simon's anger by finding out for herself. Most of the inn guests had returned to their beds now, having decided that the whole place was not about to be burnt to the ground, and Aunt Peg and Uncle Noll were dozing fitfully in chairs ready to give help if needed, but not sharing in Stacey's vigil. She set herself to pace three circuits of the room each time before peering once more from the window, but even so the time dragged by on leaden feet and still she did not know if the firefighters were winning or losing. She was gazing for what seemed like the five hundredth time at the sinister glow above the stableyard when she caught sight of the sombre little procession coming through the entranceway. Gripped with a cold sense of foreboding, she ran out of the room and down the stairs, meeting Simon as he hurried ahead.

'What is it?' she demanded. 'What's happened?'

She strained to look over his shoulder at the drooping figure carried by Oliver and one of the porters. Simon took her in his arms.

'Stacey, there's been an accident,' he began.

She heard the break in his voice and knew with chilling certainty what he was about to tell her.

'Pa?' she whispered.

'It was a falling timber, when the roof gave way. He must have been killed instantly, sweetheart, he can't have felt any pain.'

With a tearing cry, Stacey struggled to get to the sagging burden that was all that was left of her father, but Simon held her back.

'Don't, my darling. Don't look,' he said gently. 'Remember him as he was.'

By the time the fires were finally damped down, light was growing in the sky and the full extent of the destruction could be seen. The coach house was gutted, along with twenty-one of the coaches. Part of the largest stable was damaged, and so was the woodwork of the harness-room. The normally bright and tidy yard was filthy with smoke and ashes and there was a choking smell of wet charred wood in the air.

When the last spark was extinguished, Simon climbed wearily onto the fire engine to speak. There was no need to ask for quiet, for an unnatural hush hung over the place like a thick grey blanket. Along with all the others, Oliver slumped against the nearest support, the smithy wall, to hear what was to be said. He looked critically at the man who was now their sole overlord. Grimy and dishevelled, his face cut by the falling tiles, his shirt torn and tangled curls singed at the front, still he carried his air of authority. Oliver could not help imagining what might have been if he had not acted on impulse at the fatal moment of the roof fall. If he had not been there at that precise time, if he had not seen the danger, if he had not rushed forward to stop him, then Simon Wynwood might now be lying as dead as Uncle Bart. And Stacey might now be a widow. It did not bear thinking about.

'My friends,' Simon began, looking slowly round the silent, deflated gathering so that every man there felt he had been noticed, 'I have no words to thank you sufficiently for your herculean efforts tonight. Without your untiring help, all this would now be so many smouldering heaps of ashes, and Brown's Coaches entirely destroyed. As it is, we have saved the company but are bereft of the man who made it. We all, every one of us, have lost not only the best Gaffer, but the finest friend any man could hope to have.' Around the drooping, dog-tired crowd, there was a rumble of agreement. Even Oliver found himself nodding assent.

'I know that some of you here have been with Brown's since the first days. Some of you have grown up with the company. I can claim only a short acquaintance with Barty Brown, but during that time he became more than a friend, he became – a father – to me—' he faltered to a halt, and Oliver, against his will, found himself almost believing his grief was genuine. Simon recovered himself and picked up the thread of what he was saying. Every eye was now riveted on him. 'This much I know,' he went on, 'the Gaffer would not let one setback such as this ruin the company. He spent twenty-seven years building the finest coach service in the three counties. The only fitting memorial we can make to him is to keep that service going. If we fail now, we will fail a man who would never have let us down.'

His audience was with him to a man, not one wishing to be found wanting. Oliver was put in mind of a good preacher carrying his congregation along, though his style was very different. He spoke with quiet force, under-stated, and but for the one lapse, controlled.

'To do this, I have to ask a great deal of you. I know that none of you have had more than a couple of hours' sleep tonight, but if you wish to keep this company alive, you will have to set to and work twice as hard through the coming day. We shall all take one hour's rest, in which time there will be breakfast provided for everyone at the inn and a chance to clean up. After that, we start clearing the mess and sending out the coaches. Not one service is going to be put off the road. The whole of Norwich will see just what Brown's Coaches is made of.'

On a happier occasion, there would have been shouts and cheers and applause. As it was, the subdued rumble of assent growled again and the crowd began to shuffle in the direction of the inn, weary but resolute, ready to pick up the pieces.

When Amos Burgess arrived at the yard, it was to an atmosphere of sombre activity. The horses from the burnt stable had already been retrieved from their temporary homes, Simon had decided which of the remaining coaches should be used for which service, Oliver was in the process of bringing in from the coachworks every vehicle remotely suitable for conveying passengers, and as Amos walked towards the office, bewildered by the scene, an errand boy came in with a bundle of black ribands for the horses' bridles.

It was Simon who broke the news. Cleaned up now and dressed in a sober black coat, he told the chief clerk briefly what had happened during the night.

'I know I can rely on you to help us pull through, Mr Burgess,' he said. 'If we can survive today, we have a good chance of saving the business you and Mr Brown built up.'

Dazed, Amos replied, 'Yes, Mr Wynwood,' mechanically, and finding no adequate words in the face of such total disaster, shuffled off into the office. He went through the familiar routine of unlocking, getting out the books for the day's work and doling out change from the petty cash for the booking clerks. Nobody said more than was absolutely necessary. Over the office, as over the rest of the yard, the sense of loss hung heavily in the air.

As the day progressed, Amos became aware that though Mr Brown was dead, Brown's was far from being leaderless. Always where he was most needed, directing the company's depleted resources, placating and reassuring passengers, arguing with the insurance company's assessor, Simon Wynwood had the reins firmly in hand. Whatever the problem or difficulty, Mr Wynwood dealt with it with calm and efficiency. Even when a message arrived from Yarmouth that the reserve Trafalgar was out of action, he remained unruffled. As far as Amos was concerned, the very worst had happened. Mr Wynwood was in complete control.

But by degrees, he found it was a strange release from the gathering anxiety of the past months. His mind cleared dramatically as the solution that had been lurking for some time became the logical, the wished-for way out. Nobody noticed his silence during the day as he dealt with

316

the paperwork with his usual skill. In the evening he made doubly sure that everything was seen to, cleared the top of his desk and checked that all the drawers were impeccably tidy, then saw the juniors out and locked the office door. Everything was as it should be. He hobbled home through the summer twilight, ways and means already worked out, free for the first time in months from all worry and doubt.

Even Martha could not deflect him from his course now. As was his usual habit, he went directly in to see her in the small, poky bedroom that smelt of illness. A shapeless, stranded wreck of the tyrant who once ruled his life, still demanding his all by her sheer helplessness, she greeted him with an unintelligible sound, a mangled travesty of speech, and her cold eyes reproached him as surely as her tongue had once done. Amos was seized with a thrill of sadistic pleasure. She had brought him to this. If she had been a proper wife, he could have survived events at Brown's. But she was a shrew, a hag, a virago. And now she could lie there and watch the inevitable result of her persecution.

'Just you wait,' he told her. 'I've a shock in store for you.'

After Amos had departed, when the final coach was unhitched and the passengers dispersed, Simon thanked the men who had worked beside him to keep the services running and was at last free to make his way home. Now that the exhausting day was over, he was seized with doubt as to whether he had made the right decision. Perhaps he should have left the company to its own devices and stayed with Stacey. He should not have left her side at a time like this, when she so desperately needed his support. And with a rush of alarm, he remembered the child she carried, and the possible effect of the shock. Stumbling with fatigue, he began to run through the streets and across All Saints Green to where the house stood sightless, its blinds drawn in mourning.

317

In the half-light of the dining-room, three silent figures sat on the hard-backed chairs round the draped body on the table. Simon stopped in the doorway, immediately thinking the worst.

'Stacey? Where is she?' he demanded.

The largest of the figures heaved herself up and became recognizable as Aunt Peg. She plodded wearily over to him and laid a reassuring hand on his arm.

'It's all right,' she murmured, propelling him into the parlour, 'she's just gone outside, she'll be back in a moment.'

'Thank God for that.' Simon dropped into a chair and held his head in his hands. 'I was afraid the shock – she was so pleased about the baby – if she miscarried—' He could hear his speech becoming slurred but was no longer able to control it.

'She's had no pains so far, so let us pray she'll keep it.' Aunt Peg sounded hopeful. 'If she does, it will be a great comfort to her, bearing her father's grandchild.'

Simon considered this, and found that there was some consolation in the sense of continuity. He asked about the funeral.

'All arranged,' Aunt Peg told him. 'Eleven o'clock Monday morning.'

'I should have been here,' Simon said. 'I shouldn't have left all this to you. But it was the only thing I could do for him, you see, keep his company together.'

'Of course, I understand, and so does Stacey. But now that you're home you must help her to let go. She hasn't been able to shed a tear yet, poor lamb. I don't—' She broke off as footsteps could be heard on the stairs.

Simon stood up, held out his arms as Stacey came into the room and rocked her gently as she clung to him.

'Go to bed, both of you,' Aunt Peg commanded. 'You can hardly see straight, you're that tired. You'll be in no fit state to face tomorrow.'

'But I can't, how can I when – there must be someone to keep watch.' Stacey protested.

'That's all taken care of, don't fret,' Aunt Peg told her. 'Now off you go.'

They did as they were bid, dragging their feet up the stairs and shedding their clothes in disordered heaps before falling into bed. They took what comfort they could of each other, a release that undamned the flood of tears neither had been able to let fall before. Simon was on the point of slipping into the sleep of exhaustion when a small, hoarse voice beside him said,

'He never knew about the baby.'

With a last effort at clear thought, he dismissed any number of platitudes and settled for the only possible answer.

'He did, I told him. I know you wanted to, but I couldn't wait.'

In the confusion of events since the fire, he could hardly tell whether it was a lie or not, but in any case it had served the purpose. Stacey took a long, uneven breath and laid a hand on her still flat stomach.

'Ah,' she whispered. 'I'm glad you did.'

Chapter Twenty

The next day, Sunday, was a black one. The coach services did not run on the Sabbath, which meant a much-needed rest could be taken by all those who had worked right through Saturday from the time the fire broke out in the early hours till nine or ten o'clock in the evening when the last horse was bedded down. But for Simon it also meant there was nothing to distract him from the contemplation of what he had lost. He would have preferred to have been left alone with Stacey to mourn in private, but as with the wedding, they were drawn into the ritual, only this time it was the ritual of death. A steady trickle of Browns, Jupps and Maddoxes trooped in and out of the house to pay their last respects and condole with each other. The smell of cooking drifted up from the kitchen as food was prepared for the funeral breakfast the next day. Letty Mullins called to fit the black dress Stacey was to wear.

It was almost a relief when the parlourmaid told him there was 'a person' waiting at the back door, insisting on seeing him in spite of the maid's most strenuous efforts to be rid of her. Simon told her to show this importunate person up to the study. He did not like to invade what had been Barty's own territory so soon, but it was the only room in the house where he could be sure of getting away from the family.

His visitor was a plain, freckled girl in a maidservant's apron, strands of mousy hair escaping from under her mob cap. For a moment Simon suspected she might be a messenger from Deborah.

'And what brings you here on such urgent business?' he asked.

'Oh sir, I'm sorry sir, Missus didn't know as there was someone died here as well, or she might not have – only she didn't know as there was anyone else to send for,' the girl began, shifting nervously from foot to foot. 'And we was all in such a taking, like, finding him there like that.'

Simon had the distinct feeling that another blow was about to fall.

'Finding whom?'

'Why, Mr Burgess, sir. Him as lives above the shop. Terrible, it was. Missus says she don't think she'll ever sleep easy in the place again, for thinking on it. It was her as found him, you see, sir. Not that she goes up there usually, on account of she don't get on with her, with Mrs Burgess, but she wanted to get back a plate what'd been borrowed, and when he didn't answer the door she got the spare key and went in and there he was, hanging from a beam in the ceiling with his eyes all bulging and her, Mrs Burgess, lying there in bed all helpless and just staring and staring at him—'

'God Almighty!' Simon gazed at her in horror. 'Amos Burgess hanged himself?'

'Yes sir, he—'

'All right, all right, spare me the details.'

He frowned down at the worn carpet, trying to make some kind of sense out of it, and failing. He turned instead to the immediate practical problems. As far as he knew, Amos had no relatives. Even Barty had only discovered he was married when his wife was assaulted. There was therefore nobody to be informed, and equally nobody to take responsibility for burying him. Amos being what he was, there were probably some savings to cover funeral expenses, but finding a parson willing to lay a suicide in his churchyard was going to be difficult. He looked at the maid again as she stood twisting the end of an apron-string in her fingers.

'Tell your mistress,' he began 'No, wait—'

He sat down at the desk and wrote a quick letter informing Amos's landlady that it was impossible for him to come at the present time, and asking her to make all the necessary arrangements and refer any costs involved to him. He dismissed the maid, uneasy at having shuffled off the task. Barty would not have done so. But it was because of Barty that he could not see to it personally.

As he came out of the study, he met with Oliver walking up the stairs and on impulse told him of Amos's tragedy. Oliver listened in grim-faced silence, nodding slowly as Simon pointed out that it was unthinkable that he should leave home today on any pretext.

'Aye, but we can't leave the poor unhappy soul to strangers. And there's his wife to be looked after.' Oliver came to a decision. 'I'll see to it,' he offered. He brushed aside Simon's thanks with an ungracious grunt and set off downstairs again.

Simon went into the parlour, where Stacey asked anxiously what had called him away.

'Nothing of importance, just a misunderstanding,' he lied, not knowing whether she could take any more bad news at the moment. 'How are you feeling? No pains?'

Stacey laid a possessive hand on her stomach.

'No, still all right.'

He sat down beside her, still thinking of Amos. In the shadow of the far greater tragedy of Barty's death, he could feel nothing for the chief clerk's passing. And it occurred to him that it opened a way to a task that would keep Stacey busily employed in something she enjoyed doing. Tomorrow, when the funeral was over and she was able to look ahead a little, he would tell her what had happened and ask for her help. Help he was certainly going to need if he was to pull the company through. He corrected himself. If they were to pull the company through. He said once before that she was the best business partner he had ever worked with, and now they would both prove how right he was.

The house that used to be so full of cheerful voices raised in laughter and argument was strangely quiet, shrouded and hushed in sorrow. Perdita, sensing the atmosphere, crept about trying to avoid being seen. Uncle Bart had died, they told her, he had had an accident and gone to heaven. She thought about Uncle Bart, who played with her and had pockets that often hid toffees or small presents. She had seen dead animals at Bridge Farm, rabbits that had been shot, stillborn calves, chickens ready for the pot, pigs slaughtered and cured for the winter. They were still and cold and dull-eyed, and it distressed her to think of Uncle Bart looking like that. He was always so jolly and loud, teasing her and making her smile when she most wanted to go back to Bridge Farm.

Thinking of him, she padded along the passage to his study at the back of the house and pushed open the door. The little cluttered room was not empty. Aunt Stacey was there, sitting at the desk with her head in her arms, and as Perdita looked, she realized she was crying. She hovered in the doorway, not knowing what to do. The sight of a grown-up weeping disturbed her. And then she walked hesitantly forward, and touched Aunt Stacey's arm. She started and sat up, brushing away her tears with her fingers.

'Oh – Perdy – I didn't hear you come in.'

Perdita stared at her. Her face and eyes were all red and puffy.

'Why are you crying?' she asked.

Aunt Stacey put an arm round her.

'Because of Uncle Barty,' she said. 'He w-was my papa.'

Perdita felt a new fear. She allowed herself to be lifted onto Aunt Stacey's lap and sat stiffly as she held her, rocking to and fro.

'Why did he die?' she wanted to know.

'Be-because he had an accident.'

Clutching her arm with small strong fingers, Perdita asked, 'My papa is not going to die, is he?'

'Oh darling, no! Your papa will be with us for a long, long time. He will always look after us.'

Relieved, Perdita nestled against her. She was not as

soft as Aunt Hankin, but she was comforting.

'My papa's the best papa in the world,' she said.

'Yes, darling, he is,' Aunt Stacey agreed. Perdita felt her chest move as she took a shuddering breath. 'We're both very, very lucky to have him.'

Perdita closed her eyes. Somehow she did not mind quite so much now having to share her papa.

'Is he coming home soon?' she asked.

'Quite soon. In a minute, we'll go and make ourselves ready for him, shall we?'

'Yes,' Perdita said. 'In a minute.'

During the weeks that followed his death, the close bonds of loyalty forged by Barty wavered and shook alarmingly. Popular though Simon Wynwood had been as junior partner and general manager, not everyone was overjoyed to find him suddenly the sole head of the company. It was not forgotten, particularly by men who had been with the firm from the beginning, that Mr Wynwood had only arrived just over a year ago. Over saddlesoap and leatherwork in the harness-room, between games of nine men's morris or over tankards of strong nag, it was muttered darkly that he had done very well for himself, that he had coolly walked in, carved a comfortable place for himself, married Miss Stacey then stepped into the Gaffer's shoes. The fact of his having invested enough money in the company to save it from the rocks that winter was at times conveniently forgotten, as was his attempt to rescue Barty from the fire and his evident shock and grief afterwards. When all was said and done, he was a newcomer and a sprig of the nobility to boot. Whoever heard of a lord's son running a coaching company?

Then gradually confidence returned. It helped that Mr Wynwood was seen to be working all hours, and that he followed Barty's tradition of knowing each man and his background personally. It helped that Miss Stacey was about the place each morning and evening supervising the office and keeping in touch with what was going on at the yard. But it was the news of the expected child that finally brought all but a few extremists behind the new regime. An heir to the company seemed to be a sure pledge for its future.

Just how ill-founded was this confidence, only Simon and Stacey knew. Their commitment to the company's success was total, but their ability to secure it was very much in doubt.

'I don't know,' Stacey would sigh, chewing the end of her pen and frowning at the depressing total at the foot of a column of figures, 'it seems to get worse. Perhaps if we put off paying these people for a little longer, and make a better deal with these others—'

But play with the numbers as she might, there was no getting away from the fact that they needed more income. The reserve coaches at the end of each route had been used to replace those destroyed by the fire, but whenever something happened to one of them, the service went awry. There was nothing in the insurance policy to cover the loss of business this entailed. Oliver and his team were working full stretch to build new coaches, but this in turn meant they had to cut back on the regular work of building and repairing private carriages.

'Just look at how much we pay out on tolls every week,' Stacey said, searching for ways to economize. 'Even though we've come to an arrangement with most of the turnpike trusts to pay for three horses instead of four because of our regular custom, it's still an exorbitant amount going out. Would it be worth our while to try toll-farming, do you think? If we bid for some of the most-used gates, we could not only let our own coaches through free, but make a profit collecting from the rest of the traffic.' She gave a crafty smile. 'We could charge Pymer double.'

'It's a good idea on the face of it,' Simon agreed. 'Some people make their entire living out of toll-farming, after all. But I'm not sure whether it would answer for us right now. In the long term, maybe, but before we could start collecting we would have to bid for the gates in question which means using up more precious capital—'

'Which we have very little of,' Stacey finished for him. 'Very well, what else is there that we can economize on without reducing the quality of the services?'

Simon looked at the neatly-written accounts, and could see very little room for manoeuvre.

'We could try to stop swallowing,' he suggested, referring to one of the unofficial perquisites of the job. The fares of short-distance passengers who had not booked seats in advance and were therefore not down on the waybill were generally 'swallowed' by the guard and shared, or 'shadowed' with the coachman. But even as he said it, he knew what Stacey's answer would be. 'However, it would be next to impossible to enforce and it would cause a good deal of bad feeling.' He hesitated before making the next proposal. 'Of course, we could start running on Sundays. I'm perfectly willing to work seven days a week if it would pay off. What do you think?'

Stacey rolled her pen between her fingers, imagining the upset this would cause. Many coach companies did function on Sundays now, but Brown's had always avoided this in the past, not only on religious grounds, but because everyone worked more efficiently for having one day a week off. It could be arranged for free days to be taken in rotation, as already happened with the ostlers and horsekeepers, but that would mean taking on extra men to cover those who were absent. And as Simon had implied, nobody was going to give him a day's rest. He would have to be there as long as there were coaches running.

'It could be done,' she said slowly, 'but I don't know whether it would be worth it. There are only a certain number of people wanting to travel, surely, and if they cannot go on Sunday, they'll go on Saturday or Monday instead. We could even lose money, with extra expenses and no extra custom.' She heaved a sigh. What had seemed more like a game back in the autumn when they were setting up the Flyer, spending with cheerful abandon in the blithe hope that it would all pay off in terms of prestige, had now turned into a deadly battle for survival. 'I just don't know what else to suggest,' she admitted.

'The only things I can think of are long-term projects, like breeding our own horses or growing our own feed and bedding,' Simon said.

Stacey remembered the last time the horsebreeding scheme had been discussed, just two or three hours before the fire. She threw the pen down and jumped up.

'Why did it have to happen?' she demanded, pacing the tiny study in frustrated rage. 'Why did Pa have to be killed? Why him?'

'I don't know,' Simon admitted. 'I don't think there are reasons for these things. We shouldn't look for them.'

'But of course there are reasons! There have to be. I just don't see *why*. It's so unfair! Pa should have lived for another ten, fifteen years, and instead the gable falls on him and he's dead. Why did it have to be him?'

Simon took her by the shoulders.

'I can't tell you the answers, because I don't know them myself. But I think maybe you'll find them one day, and then you can tell me. In the meantime, go and do something violent. Break the greenhouse windows. Go down to the yard and borrow a horse and ride it into the ground.'

Stacey stared at him in astonishment, and saw that he meant it. Without stopping to think, she asked, 'How old were you when your mother died?'

'Fifteen.'

'And you were at school at the time, and had no-one to turn to.' Her anger collapsed into remorse. 'Oh, I'm so selfish! I've got all the family round me, I've got the baby, and most of all I've got you, and still I want more. Why do you put up with me when I'm so horrid all the time?'

He rejected a number of flippant answers and settled for the truth.

'It's not a question of putting up with you. I wouldn't

expect you to be cheerful and lively at a time like this. It's all part of you, you've given me so much, I'm happy if I can give something in return.'

'I've brought you nothing but a pack of troubles.'

'None that can't be solved.'

It seemed to Simon that the key to the solution still lay in Seth Pymer, and his connection with the elusive Clayton. The association puzzled him. It was natural enough that the rivalry between Pymer and Barty should have grown up. The coaching business thrived on cut-throat competition, and if Barty was to be believed, there was an old score to be settled over the girl they had both wanted. But Clayton – where did he fit in? If he was as powerful as people appeared to think, he could have finished off Brown's months ago, but instead he just seemed to be playing cat and mouse. Simon wondered if he owed Pymer a favour, and was repaying it by weakening the opposition. He did a round of the gaming clubs, chanced on an old acquaintance and learned the rumour that Clayton had his fingers in the shadier side of horseracing, but found no clues that might explain the link with Pymer.

And then, taking a short cut through a churchyard one day, absorbed in finding possible answers to the problem, he came face to face with Deborah.

'Oh!' she cried, blushing. 'Fancy meeting you! What a surprise!'

Automatically, he raised his hat, bowed.

'Good morning, Mrs Pymer. A surprise indeed. I trust you are well?'

His gaze rested on the baby she carried in her arms.

'I am now, thank you.' She too looked at the tiny creature, swaddled in a long white shawl. 'But I had a dreadful time. It was *terrible*. Eighteen *hours*.' She glanced up at Simon, making sure he was taking this in. 'Would you like to see him?' Without waiting for a reply, she loosened the shawl and revealed a cross, pink little face.

Not without some trepidation, Simon looked, and found that the child had kept its own secret. The soft, unformed features were Deborah's, her nose, her round chin. To be sure, the eyes that gazed unfocussed at him were blue, but so were all babies'. So were Deborah's.

'He's a fine child,' Simon commented. 'What do you call him?'

'Daniel.' A downward twist of her lips showed that the choice had not been hers.

'Very nice,' Simon said, and drew breath to make a few formal excuses and escape.

But Deborah forestalled him.

'I hear your wife is expecting,' she remarked.

'Yes, we're both very pleased.'

'Of course, it must be difficult—' Deborah smiled knowingly, looking at him sideways. 'Being a mother myself now, I know how it is. She probably doesn't always feel quite the thing – and you're such a gentleman. And of course it gets worse as you get bigger—'

Simon held her gaze, tempted by the possibilities she seemed to be holding out.

'—Right round my finger, just like you said,' she was saying. 'Now I tell him I haven't got over the baby yet, and if we – you know – too soon it might do something dreadful to my insides and I'd not be able to have another. But it's all nonsense really. Baby's six weeks old now. It's just that Seth—' she left the sentence unfinished, and gave Simon a look that suggested that with him it would be quite different.

She had put on a great deal of weight, Simon noticed, and had not regained her figure yet. He sickened at the thought of inventing another trail of lies, just when he thought he had put all that behind him.

'I'm glad it all worked out so well for you,' he said. 'And now if you will excuse me—'

Her attempt at cunning crumbled and she clutched at his arm with desperate fingers.

'I could be very useful to you, I could find out things,

lots of things,' she gabbled, her longing plain on her face. 'If it was just like it used to be. I think about those days all the time. I'd give anything to go back to them. I'll do whatever you say, I'm not afraid of Seth any more.'

'Does Seth tell you who he's meeting when he goes out?' Simon asked, and regretted it before he even finished speaking.

Deborah's face lit up.

'Sometimes. Sometimes he does. I could ask him, I could insist he told me. I will if you want me to. I'll ask him where, too. Shall I do that?'

For a moment he wavered, thinking of all that he might be able to get out of her. But the price was too high.

'I would not dream of putting you to so much trouble, Mrs Pymer,' he said, and took his leave before she could make her case any stronger.

Over dinner, he went so far as to mention her to Stacey, saying that he had passed her in the churchyard, and that she had her child with her.

'I heard she had been safely delivered,' Stacey commented. 'A boy, was it not?'

'I believe so.'

'Old Seth Pymer must have been delighted. She's his third wife and neither of the others produced any children.' A slight edge of superiority crept into her voice, to Simon's amusement. 'How was she looking? She used to be rather pretty.'

Simon made a show of trying to remember.

'I wouldn't call her pretty now. She certainly didn't strike me as being so.' He produced a local colloquialism. 'She always was rather nabbity, and now she's belsized too.'

For the first time in days, Stacey gave an unforced smile.

'You're turning into a proper Norwicher,' she said.

Simon felt something like gratitude to Deborah for unwittingly being the source of a glimmer of the old Stacey. A few days later, however, he was not so sure. A

330

note arrived for him, in Deborah's untidy, sprawling hand.

'I asked him, and he told me,' it said cryptically. 'Meet me the same place as the other day, four o'clock.'

Right up till the last minute, Simon determined not to go, but in the end he could not let such an opportunity pass him by. Deborah was waiting for him in the porch, and this time she had left the baby behind.

'I knew you would come,' she said, pressing close to him, gazing up at him with hungry eyes. 'You did love me really, didn't you, last winter? And you still do. I know you do really.'

It did not take Simon long to realize that she had learnt a great deal in the past months. At his suggestion, she had learnt to bargain with Seth, using the child. And now she was using her new power over her husband to attempt to bring back something that had never been there in the first place. He went along with her, listening as he had always done to her rambling complaints, interlaced now with references to her small victories over Seth. Just how much she knew of her husband's business outside the Three Tuns, he could not yet make out. Even if he could establish what the link was between Pymer and Clayton, he was not sure how he could use it, but it would be the first step and the rest would no doubt follow.

At length, she brought out what she was offering as her side of the deal.

'He didn't like it at all when I asked him where he was going,' she said. 'He told me it was none of my business, but I kept on. He shouted at me, but he doesn't frighten me any more when he does that, and in the end, after a long time when I kept him and he wanted to go because he was late, he told me who he was going to see, but not where. I couldn't get him to tell me where, but I might be able to another time.'

Simon maintained a front of mild interest and patience.

'And who was he going to see, Debbie?'

Deborah looked sideways at him and gave a secretive,

irritating smile.

'He said I wasn't to tell a soul, that it was life and death that I didn't let it go any further than the four walls.'

Gathering up his hat and gloves, Simon made to stand up.

'Then you had better not do so, had you?' he said.

And just as he knew she would, Deborah gave way. She had not the guile nor the patience to play a waiting game.

'Clayton. That's what his name was. Mr Clayton.'

Simon looked unimpressed.

'Is that so? I cannot think what all the fuss and secrecy was about, in that case.'

'I'll find out where next time,' she offered eagerly. 'Would you like me to? I'll find out and then we can meet again.' She twined her arms round him and reached up to kiss him. 'You do love me, don't you? I know you do. The others, Seth and – and your wife, they don't matter. I was made to marry Seth, I had to, I didn't want to. It was the same with you, wasn't it? I do understand. But they can't stop us, can they? We can meet again, just like we used to. It will be so wonderful, to be together again. When shall I see you? Wednesday afternoons, like before?'

'I'm a very busy man these days,' Simon stalled. 'Even seeing you is very difficult to arrange. But send me a note when you have something to tell me, and I'll try to get away.'

And as she was willing to snatch at the slightest encouragement, Deborah agreed.

For more than a week, Oliver turned over and over what he had learnt, wondering whether to say anything about it. During the two months since Barty's death, his opinion of Simon Wynwood had changed very slightly for the better. Against his will, he had to acknowledge that Simon had proved an able leader of the company. That his motives were entirely selfish, Oliver did not doubt, but the fact remained the the livelihoods of dozens of men and their families depended upon the prosperity of Brown's.

Oliver was honest enough to know that he could not have done so well had he found himself in the same place. He was finding command of the coachworks beyond him at times. There was nothing he did not know about coach-building, but it was plain that a different kind of skill was needed to handle the men who did his bidding. He knew that he was lacking in some quality of leadership, some-thing he could not even put a name to, a lightness of touch combined with authority that Simon Wynwood appeared to achieve without even trying. When seeing him solely as head of Brown's, Oliver could almost begin to admire him, but towards Simon as a man, and most of all as Stacey's husband his hostility was as strong as ever.

Even so, it took him several days to decide whether Stacey should be told this latest piece of information. Working patiently at the many processes involved in building each replacement for the coaches lost in the fire, from the sawing and joining of the ashwood frames to the application of the last of the eleven coats of paint and three of varnish, he had plenty of time to think. He knew that he ought to speak to her, but the memory of the last time he tried to open her eyes was burnt deep into him. He did consider, briefly, consulting his mother, but knew that she would try to protect Simon. To Oliver's utter incomprehension, she seemed to regard Simon as one more lost chick that needed to be taken under her wing. Oliver could not think of anyone less in need of sheltering. It was other people who needed to be guarded from him, principally Stacey. And in the end he decided that whatever the consequences, she ought to be told the truth.

His chance came when she called in at the coachworks, coming quietly up beside him as he supervised the two apprentices who were laying hessian into the thick coats of white lead paint on the insides of the mahogany panels. As always, his heart twisted painfully at the sight of her and today as if to reinforce his resolve she had the child, Simon Wynwood's bastard, with her.

'She always loves coming here,' Stacey remarked,

watching Perdita anxiously as she clambered into the half-finished coach and peered at what was being done. 'Perdy, you can look around as long as you don't get in the way. Be a good girl, now, and don't touch any wet paint.' To Oliver she added, 'It's a pity she's not a boy, you could have made a coachbuilder of her.'

Oliver gave a non-committal grunt and showed her how the work on the new vehicles was progressing. The Lord Nelson was practically ready for service, needing only the portrait of the Admiral on the doors and the final varnishing before it could go on the road. In spite of the need for the replacements, it had been decided not to sacrifice Brown's high standards in order to finish them more quickly.

'That's splendid,' Stacey commented, stopping to give a word of praise to the signwriter, painstakingly completing the last of the lettering. But clearly her mind was not on the stages. After a cursory inspection, she led the way over to a large shed at the end of the complex of buildings that made up the works, where the motley collection of second-hand stock was kept. Oliver followed, trying to think of some way to broach the subject that had caused him so much anxiety.

'We must sell some of these, Oliver,' she said, producing a notebook and writing each one down with a possible price. 'How much would this whiskey fetch if you repaired the canework? It's not a very long job, is it? And this gig? There's always a demand for a strong gig, and this one's on its first wheels, surely? It only needs a new coat of paint.'

Oliver reminded her that all his men were still working on the new stages.

'Yes, yes, I know,' she said, tapping her pencil impatiently on her notebook. 'But once the first four are finished, I think you should take at least half of them off company coaches and put them back on private work. I'm sure I could persuade the Harrises that they need, say, a new landau. And Simon meets so many people, he's

334

always hearing of potential sales.'

Almost before he knew he was saying it, Oliver heard himself muttering, 'He certainly meets a lot of people, but he don't always discuss sales with them.'

Stacey looked at him sharply.

'And just what do you mean by that?'

Avoiding her eyes, Oliver examined the lamps on a worn-out travelling chariot, automatically noticing that the catches needed seeing to.

'I know you'll say it ain't none of my business,' he began. 'But I don't like seeing you deceived. It ain't right.'

'What ain't – isn't?'

'The way he – your – I heard about it the other day. You know that dressmaker you go to?'

'Letty Mullins?'

'That's the one. There's a girl at our chapel as works as skivvy there. What she sees going on there, you'd never believe. Wicked. While there's respectable ladies like your Aunt Eustacia and you having dresses fitted, there's some as go to this room upstairs, and then their men – lovers—' he stumbled over the word 'come in at the back. She sees them go past when she's in the kitchen, this girl, and last week she saw – she saw your Simon.'

He caught his breath as Stacey's notebook slapped into his face, stinging his cheek.

'Lies!' she shrilled. 'It's all wicked lies! I won't listen to a word of it, do you understand? You make it up, because you're jealous of him!'

He looked at her, pale and stiff with fury, daring him to say more, and was miserably aware that once again he had done the wrong thing. But having started, he had to go on.

'I don't make it up,' he insisted. 'He did go there, last Wednesday, the same day as he used to before – in the winter. She didn't know who it was he was – seeing then, but this time she found out, this girl, she saw – her – the woman as she came down. It was Deborah Pymer.'

'*Deborah Pymer*!' Stacey gave a harsh, incredulous

laugh. 'Oliver, you must be insane. You're insane with jealousy. You must stop it, Oliver, you must get over it. You think Simon took me and the company away from you, but it's not so. Pa would not have left the company to you, he said as much the first evening I came home from Miss Haveringshaw's. I don't know what would have happened if Simon had not come along, but you certainly wouldn't have been made the heir. And you certainly wouldn't have married me, either. Don't you see, Oliver, we're not *right* for each other. Simon and I, we're the same in all the right ways, and different in all the right ways, but you and I are different in all the wrong ways. Deborah Pymer! It's ridiculous!'

Oliver shook his hed slowly, trying to ward off the truth of what she was saying.

'I didn't want to upset you, Stacey,' he muttered. 'That's the last thing I want to do.'

'Then stop—' she paused, rested a hand briefly on the swelling that hardly showed yet beneath the black muslin dress, made a palpable effort to control her voice and went on, 'stop trying to come between us, Oliver. I'm married to Simon now and nothing you can say is going to change it. I hope, I really do hope you find someone who's suited to you as well as I'm suited to him.'

He answered mechanically as she hastily took her leave, listened as she crossed to the other shed, calling to Perdita to come, heard her and the child bidding goodbye to the craftsmen and apprentices. For a long time he stood thinking of what she had said, knowing it was impossible. There would never be anyone else. If he could not have Stacey, he would rather be alone.

Chapter Twenty-One

When Simon suggested to Arthur Harris that he might consider investing some of his new wealth in Brown's Coaches, it was put with such an air of conferring a favour that it did not even cross Arthur's mind that it might actually be a desperate last resort to raise some cash.

'It's a shame everything's so tied up in trusts,' he lamented to Annabel. 'That would have been a very profitable venture. Anything that Wynwood puts his hand to is worth trying, he always seems to know what he's doing.'

But Annabel was not so sure. She had seen Stacey push sheets of figures out of sight and try to erase the anxious expression from her eyes when she called at All Saints Green.

'Yes—' she said uncertainly, for she always agreed with Arthur, 'he does appear to. And yet Stacey has been looking very worried lately, and she never talks about their future plans. She always used to be full of some scheme or other.'

'Stacey's lost her father, remember,' Arthur pointed out.

'Of course, yes, you're right. I expect that's why she's so subdued. She was very close to her father,' Annabel agreed. 'But all the same, I do wonder whether all is quite as it should be with their company.'

The doubt nagged at the back of Arthur's mind on and off all the next day, when he was in Norwich to have a new coat fitted. He was aware of a sense of obligation to both the Wynwoods. Practically every difficulty he had encountered during the past year, either one or other of them had helped him over. Sitting in a coffee house looking idly at the passers-by outside, it occurred to him that the only time Wynwood asked a favour of him, he not only failed but completely forgot about it. He had been so preoccupied with his own affairs that his promise to look out for those two men had gone right out of his head. Now, thinking about it, he could not even remember what their names were or how Wynwood had described them. He gazed absently across the street, to where a small, foxy-looking man in clothes that had once been a gentleman's stood looking impatiently up and down. Presently he was joined by a shambling great hulk of a man, heavy with the fat of a bruiser gone to seed, and the pair of them walked off together, igniting Arthur's sluggish memory. Will Page and Job Watkins. An ex-jockey and a failed prizefighter. On impulse, Arthur jumped up and ran into the street.

They were almost at the corner by the time he reached the doorway. Trotting in an effort to catch up, Arthur set off, dodging past fat housewives and gossiping tradesmen. He turned the corner and spied the ill-assorted pair disappearing down a side alley, and as he did so more of what Wynwood had said came back to him. 'If you do see them, stay clear of them, they're not to be trusted an inch, and Watkins can still pack a punch like a steam hammer.' He hesitated. It seemed highly unlikely that these were the same two men, but if they were, it might be better to heed Wynwood's warning. And then he felt ashamed of his cowardice and plunged down the alleyway after them. But it was too late, they were gone. He searched through the maze of winding, filthy passages to no avail. They must have gone into one of the blank-faced, anonymous doorways. Annoyed at himself for having failed once more, he made his way back to the street and consulted his watch. He was due to meet Annabel at All Saints Green in half an hour, which gave him just enough time to walk over to the Crown and see Wynwood.

Simon made little of the information, thanking him but saying that it was very improbable that the men Arthur had seen were the same two that he was seeking. He kept

338

up his usual front of calm confidence for the remainder of Arthur's brief visit, but once he had gone off to join his wife Simon dropped into the swivel chair that had once been Barty's with a weary sigh of disappointment. For a glorious moment he had thought that Harris was about to say that he had, after all, some spare capital to invest, enough to keep them limping along for another few weeks. Already he had tried to raise another loan, but received nothing but polite expressions of regret from the banks. Word had gone round, it seemed, that Brown's was running on borrowed money and he had not yet had time to establish any personal credit. Barty they might have taken a chance on, Simon was a new man and Hendry's had put it about that he was not altogether reliable. The days when he had nothing more pressing to worry about than wreaking revenge on Page and Watkins seemed incredibly far away. If Arthur had heard something about Clayton, it might have been worth listening to, but as it was he had himself caught sight of the two characters Arthur had seen maybe half a dozen times during the last few months and not bothered to take any action. Once he had found himself properly part of the company, during last autumn when the Flyer was first planned, the likes of Page and Watkins had faded into insignificance.

Now he wondered what they were doing in the city. Perhaps they had become too well-known in their old haunts round the racetracks. Perhaps, like him, they had turned their hands to a respectable occupation, but he doubted it. They were probably either engaged in some criminal activity of their own, or else working for a wider concern. When first Simon had come into contact with them, they had been on the fringes of the illegal organization run by Henshaw that he had managed partially to break up. He stared out of the window, to where one of the two-horse slow coaches had just pulled into the yard. Emblazoned still on its doors were the words 'Prop B. Brown'. He jerked upright as it occurred to him that Page

339

and Watkins might be very useful to him if they were now part of the Norwich underworld. His fingers crept to the thin ridge of the scar at the side of his head as he worked out possible ways of prising information out of them. It was definitely worth trying.

On his way through the outer office, he stopped to speak to the newly promoted senior clerk.

'If anything occurs that you can't handle, Bates, make a note of it and tell me first thing tomorrow, or if it's really urgent consult Mrs Wynwood. I shall probably be out for the rest of the day.'

Guessing that the Harrises were still drinking tea and chatting in the front parlour of All Saints Green he went in through the kitchen, changed, and left a message to Stacey that he might not be back till late. When he emerged again from the back entrance, it was not as the elegant proprietor of Brown's Coaches, but as the disreputable horsekeeper who had started the fight with Pymer's coachmen. He had a long task ahead of him, for the city was crowded with inns and taverns, and the men he sought might be in any or none of them. But he knew from Harris whereabouts to start, and they were distinctive enough for somebody to have noticed them. Glad to be taking some positive action, he set off whistling cheerfully.

It was gone eight o'clock when he walked into the coachworks and found Oliver on the point of telling his underlings to pack up for the night.

'Carry on,' he said to the astonished foreman, 'I'm not here to spy on you. I'll wait for you in the office.'

He lounged against the untidy desk, resisting the temptation to go through the paperwork. It was essential that he did not antagonize Oliver just when he needed his help. The horsekeeper who had joined in his last adventure was no use this time, when secrecy was of prime importance. He knew he could rely on Oliver to keep his mouth shut, so long as he could be persuaded to assist in the first place. The problem lay in convincing him that the end justified the means.

Oliver came in, eyeing Simon's working garb with undisguised suspicion.

'We finished the new Retaliator today,' he stated. 'It'll be up at the Crown as soon as you send some horses for it.'

'That's the first good news I've heard for days, Oliver. You've worked miracles down here since the fire. Will you pass on my thanks to your craftsmen? I'll see if we can manage something in the way of a bonus for them.' He looked thoughtfully at Oliver. 'Has it ever occurred to you,' he asked, 'that there was anything odd about that fire?'

Oliver admitted that it had not.

'Must've been one of the lamps left burning.'

'That was what I thought, at first. But think, Oliver. We got the long-distance coaches out, they were nearest the doors. The ones that burnt out were the short-haul ones and the reserves. The reserves had not been out at all that day, and the others were back before it was dark. Their lamps had not been lit. It might have been a cigar butt left smouldering that was missed when they were cleaned, but I doubt it. I have a suspicion that it was started deliberately.'

Oliver stared at him.

'Who would do a thing like that?'

'The same person who had the Eclipse's rein cut. The same person who found out about the bullion and nearly had the Retaliator robbed. Probably the same person who suggested to Pymer that he should buy up all the horses at South Stonham and stop the Flyer. We already know that someone called Clayton was behind the first two, and we know there is a connection between him and Pymer. I've now tracked down a man who may know something about this Clayton, but persuading him to talk may be difficult.' He regarded Oliver's stiff, hostile expression, and decided that it must be presented to him in stark black and white, as a fight against evil. Shades of grey did not exist for Oliver. 'Clayton is responsible for

Ned Shears's and the Gaffer's deaths, and he also has his fingers in a number of questionable enterprises about this town. Gaming clubs and similar dens of corruption.'

He wondered if he was sounding too melodramatic, but Oliver was looking interested. Evidently he was swayed.

'Bringing him to justice is not going to be easy,' Simon went on. 'It will entail using his own methods against him, and the man I'm going to start with might not know anything of use, but I cannot stand by and let him ruin the company.'

'No—' Oliver said slowly. 'No. Clayton. I've heard that name somewhere before.'

'Any number of people have heard of him, but nobody seems to know where to find him.'

But Oliver was not listening. He was still trying to remember.

'It was somebody in the company,' he muttered. 'Somebody – Amos Burgess!'

'Amos Burgess?' Simon repeated, disbelieving. 'What the devil did he know, and why did he talk to you? He never spoke to anyone unless it was on company business.'

'It was at the – the wedding,' Oliver explained, wooden-faced. 'He was upset and he had too much to drink and we – he talked, rambled on. He mentioned Clayton several times. He seemed to be afraid of him.'

'Afraid? Are you sure?'

Oliver looked uncomfortable.

'Not completely. He was very drunk at the time and so—'

And so was Oliver, Simon remembered. He had been told about it on his return.

'Yes,' he cut in. 'Do you realize what this could mean? If Clayton had some kind of hold over Burgess, that could be one more death at his door.' And, he thought, it could be the clue to the spy in Brown's camp, but he did not want to confuse the issue. 'I need someone to help me,' he said. 'Someone I can trust, and you are the obvious choice. Are you willing to take the risk?'

He waited with carefully concealed impatience for Oliver to weigh up the rights and wrongs of the situation, and was finally rewarded.

'Yes,' he agreed, 'I'll come.'

Their first task was to dispose of Page. A false message flushed him from the tavern, a quick crack on the head knocked him unconscious.

'He probably knows more, but he's sharp enough to evade questions and to guess who we are,' Simon said, looking at the man's crumpled, inert form with distaste. 'Leave him behind the wall there. He can find his own way home when he wakes up.'

Oliver looked doubtful but did as he was bid. He was still not entirely sure that Simon's methods were justified.

'Now for Watkins,' Simon went on. 'Remember, when we come out, follow at a safe distance and only step in if he tries to make off.'

And leaving Oliver lurking in an alleyway, he pulled his shabby hat down over his eyes and went into the smoke-filled taproom. Watkins was easily found, sitting by himself at a greasy table, nursing a pot of ale in one meaty paw. Simon slid onto the bench opposite him.

'Something's going on,' he said. 'Important like. Will said as you was to come and meet him.'

Watkins looked at him with vague puzzlement on his bovine face.

'I don't know you,' he objected.

'New round here, ain't I?' Simon said by way of explanation. 'I knows you though, Joby, from the old days. Come on, Will said you was to hurry. I'll show you where.'

But Watkins was not convinced.

'Will only just left.'

'It's urgent, ain't it? Move along, he's waiting for us.'

Watkins at last got to his feet and shambled into the street in Simon's wake. Unseen, Oliver tagged after them. They threaded through the back lanes, Simon warding

343

off Watkins's occasional query as to where they were going and why, and finally came to a small back-entry to the coachworks that led into a store shed.

'In here,' Simon said, and hustled him into the dimly lamplit interior.

By the time Watkins had looked round the clutter of old tools and discarded paintpots and realized that his partner was not there, Oliver slipped in and locked the door. Watkins looked from him to Simon and back again, suspicion dawning.

'Who's he?' he demanded. 'And where's Will?'

'This is Jack, he's in on this as well,' Simon explained. 'And Will should be along in a minute. Why don't you sit down while we're waiting? Take the weight off your feet.' He nodded at a broken-backed chair set against a post that supported a heavy shelf, and set an example by lounging against the door. Reluctantly, Watkins followed his suggestion.

'You been with this lot for long?' Simon asked conversationally.

'Fair while.'

'Decent to work for, is he? Him what gives all the orders?'

'Aye.'

Watkins refused to be drawn. He looked uneasily at the door.

'You have much to do with him?' Simon persisted.

'More'n you'll have if you ask too many questions. He don't like questions.'

'Just passing the time,' Simon placated. 'Can't all sit here numb as posts, can we? It ain't friendly. You ain't been in Norwich that long, have you? I used to see you round the racecourses. Newmarket. What made you come here?'

'I was sent, wasn't I?' Watkins growled. 'Look, I thought you said this was urgent. Where's Will?'

'He should be here by now. Can't think what's keeping him, can you, Jack?'

344

Oliver shook his head.

'You must know one or two folks about the town now, I reckon,' Simon went on. 'You heard anything about Clayton?'

'I told you, he don't like questions.'

Simon suppressed a surge of excitement as he realized he had hit a run of luck.

'All right, all right,' he placated. 'I just like to know who I'm working for, see? I ain't never met him. If you been with him a fair while, you might have seen him, like, if he trusts you.'

'Aye, he trusts me because I keeps my mouth shut. And if you wants to keep a whole skin, yours'll stay shut too.' The prizefighter's bloodshot eyes kept returning to the locked door. Without Page to think and talk for him, he was at a loss.

''Course. I know what's good for me,' Simon told him. 'But this is just amongst friends, ain't it? You was working for Clayton back in the old days, was you?'

Watkins finally decided there was something wrong about this meeting. He stood up. 'I ain't sitting around here any more listening to you clacking,' he said. 'Open that door.'

Simon was ahead of Oliver in leaping to hold him prisoner, and made no impression at all on his massive bulk. Watkins shook him off and sent him sprawling amongst a stack of carriage fitments. But then Oliver jerked into action and Simon picked himself up and rejoined the fray, and the three of them lurched and struggled in the restricted space, knocking into the lantern and setting it swinging, throwing crazy splashes of light in black corners. It was Oliver who, with a well-aimed stomach punch, winded their captive and held him down on the chair whilst Simon tied him to the post. Simon looked down at him, breathing heavily.

'Now then, Joby, I thought you was going to be sensible and talk to us nice and friendly like. But since you're not being helpful, we'll have to persuade you.'

'I ain't saying nothing,' Watkins wheezed.

'I think you will, my friend, if you want to keep a whole skin. Certain folks is very put out by what you done to Mr Gregory Ward last year. Very upset they are. After your blood.'

Watkins looked blank.

'Never heard of him.'

'I think you have. Last February? Over Wretham way?'

Remembrance dawned in Watkins's eyes, but he tried to maintain a fiction of ignorance.

'Dunno what you're talking about.'

Simon was not deceived.

'Yes you do. But you were only obeying orders, weren't you, Joby? Whose orders? Clayton's?'

'Dunno what you're talking about.'

Simon fetched a theatrical sigh of regret.

'You leave us with no choice. Such a pity.'

He nodded at Oliver, and was surprised at his brutal thoroughness. Briefly, between spells of forcing answers from their victim, Simon wondered if it was him and not Watkins that Oliver was beating. Piece by piece, the facts emerged. Page and Watkins had been working for Clayton for nearly three years. It had been Clayton who was behind the Newmarket racket that Simon had partially broken up. Clayton who had decided he should be robbed and left for dead, Clayton, through Page, who had corrupted Amos Burgess. As to the connection between Clayton and Pymer, Watkins was unclear, but Simon had a sick conviction that it was not particularly important. Clayton's Norwich address Watkins absolutely refused to divulge.

Simon regarded the battered, ugly hulk of a man in front of him, and regretted ever having started. But it was too late now for squeamishness, and he had yet to make sure Watkins did not repeat anything of the interrogation to his master.

'How much of Mr Ward's money did you and Page

keep for yourselves?' he asked, feeling for a hold over the man. 'I know how much he had on him, remember.' A wary look on Watkins's fleshy face told him he was on the right track. He pressed the point home. 'He wouldn't be very pleased if he found out you cheated him, would he? And he'll be told if you squeal a word of what's been said tonight.'

As a last safeguard, they blindfolded him, drove out of town and set him free on the Ipswich road. Simon scarcely noticed Oliver's silence during the short journey home, for he was still trying to come to terms with his part in bringing tragedy into his adoptive family. For once, he could see no way to escape the blame, or simply shake it off as he usually managed to do, and on top of the guilt was the immediate task of telling Stacey, and the prospect of losing her unquestioning love when she learnt that he had been the indirect cause of her father's death. When he parted from Oliver at All Saints Green with a brief word of thanks, he had no idea how he was going to face her.

Stacey, who had been trying not to watch the hands of the clock as they crawled past midnight, jumped up and flew into the hall the moment she heard the front door open.

'Simon! Where have you been?' she cried, running to fling her arms round him.

He stepped back, catching her wrists, and she knew something was wrong, something so bad that he was not able even to try to cover it up.

'I'm not fit to be touched,' he stated, avoiding her eyes, and letting go of her tramped heavily upstairs.

Stacey stared after him, unsure whether to follow.

'I'll – I'll have some hot water sent up,' she offered, taking what he said literally.

His automatic thanks drifted down to her before the bedroom door closed behind him, just enough encouragement for her to see to it. She had forgotten that she had sent the servants to bed. Simon's taut, closed expression changed to one of concern as she came in lugging a heavy can.

'Sweetheart, you shouldn't be carrying weights around.'

'It's all right, I'm very strong.'

'I've brought enough trouble on you without making you fetch and carry for me.'

Unable to make sense of what he said, she watched him as he turned to the washstand in the corner, kicking aside the discarded heap of horsekeeper's clothes. Even during the dreadful days after the fire, he had not been like this. Then they had shared the sorrow. Now he was shutting her out.

'What is it?' she asked, coming up behind him and putting her arms round his waist. 'What's wrong?'

'You married the wrong man,' he told her, scrubbing away the evening's accumulated dirt with single-minded concentration. 'You should have taken Oliver while you had the chance.'

She gave him a playful squeeze, trying to distract him.

'That's the most hulver-headed thing I've ever heard you say!'

But the use of one of her father's expressions produced not a flicker of response.

'And I should have kept running. Once I stand still, the past catches up with me,' he went on, as if she had not spoken. He reached for a towel, stepping out of her embrace. 'I should have realized back at Christmas that it was time to go.'

Chill fingers of fear clutched at Stacey at the thought of existence without him.

'What have I done?' she whispered. 'What is it? Why do you want to go?'

He stopped in the act of drying his neck to look at her face properly, pale and drawn, trying to divine his mood.

'I don't want to go,' he assured her. 'God knows, that's the last thing I want to do. But you would be better off without me.'

348

She went to him, winding her arms round him and pressing against his damp body, felt him resist at first and then give in and hold her tightly to him, as if she might at any moment be torn away.

'Tell me,' she coaxed.

For a moment longer he hesitated, then finally took a breath and began.

'You remember my talking about a man named Henshaw?'

'The one you thought was behind the attack on you?'

'That's right. This evening, I found out that it *was* him, and also that he and Clayton are one and the same . . .' Baldly, he told her of the information he had gathered, winding up with the inevitable conclusion. 'So you see, everything that has happened, the fire, the robbery, poor Amos Burgess, is because of my being here.'

Her mind still reeling, Stacey could not quite follow his reasoning.

'I'm sorry, but I don't see.'

He sat her on the edge of the bed, pulled on a dressing-gown and began to explain.

'A couple of years ago I was making a tidy living in the racing world, dealing mostly, though I had a share in one or two other enterprises, and I gradually became aware of the influence of a man named Henshaw. Whenever a race went unexpectedly, whenever an outsider won or a favourite failed, he was behind it, though it took me a long time to find out because of the way he covered his tracks. He worked through the weak and the powerless, under-paid stablelads and jockeys on the way down, and they were all too frightened of him to give the game away. Racing's a risky enough business without someone like him systematically trying to change the odds, but more than that, he was ruining the lives of dozens of small people, making them exist under a continual threat. So I set out to break his hold, and to some extent I succeeded, but I never came close to catching the man himself. He got rid of me before I could do so.'

'Or thought he did,' Stacey put in.

'Yes – one of his few mistakes.' He took her hand and studied her face, his eyes deadly serious. 'Stacey, you know me better than anyone. Why do you think I tried to bring him down?'

Just at that moment, Stacey was not certain that she knew him at all, but of one thing she was sure.

'For the reason you said: because he was spreading corruption, and harming people.'

'Not because I wanted to take over his position?'

Her eyes widened in shock.

'Of course not!'

He relaxed slightly.

'There are plenty who believed that that was what I was after. I think Henshaw himself believed it. He must think I'm using Brown's as a respectable cover for a future bid for power. It's the only reason I can discover for his pursuing me like this, for that's what he's been doing. And for some end best known to himself, instead of finishing me off quickly this time he's been using the rivalry between Brown's and Pymer's to play cat and mouse with me.'

Stacey sat frowning at their linked hands. There was a flaw somewhere, and for the moment her tired, battered brain could not grasp it.

'But Seth Pymer,' she said slowly. 'You've hardly mentioned him. Clayton had that rein cut on the Eclipse before you came here. It was that which brought you to the Crown in the first place.'

'Clayton has some sort of a deal with Pymer. I'm not sure quite what, but I should imagine it's a courier service on his coaches. In exchange he undertook to have the opposition slowed a little. Getting that man Platt to do the job was easy enough.'

'Oh.' Stacey passed a protective hand over her growing belly as Clayton's power to harm them was gradually borne upon her. He had already struck at her family, and could well do so again. For the first time in her life she was threatened, and the usual defence of Brown solidarity was useless. 'What are we going to do?' she said.

Simon stared at her.

'Is that all you have to say?'

'Why, yes.' It was quite clear to her. 'Clayton's trying to ruin us, so we have to fight back. How do you fight a man like that? I don't know.'

'But my dear, do you still not see? If it were not for me, Clayton would not have hounded Brown's. None of it would have happened. Your father—'

Stacey realized they had at last arrived at the core of the matter, and that their usual positions were reversed. It was she who must be the wiser, the more experienced, the giver of strength. She pressed closer to him and put an arm around his slumped shoulders.

'Pa's death was an accident. You did your best to save him, I know that. And as for the rest of it, it probably would have happened anyway, if Pymer was already in with Clayton. If he arranged the Eclipse accident, why not all the other things?' Seeing that she was having very little effect, she tried a weak joke. 'And just think, if you had not come along, I might have had to marry Arthur Harris! There's a fate worse than death for you. Fancy having to behave myself in front of that sour-faced mother of his for the next twenty years.'

Simon produced a ghost of a smile.

'It would have been something of an effort for you.'

'Effort! I think I would have exploded within a twelvemonth. So,' she became business like, 'tell me what we're going to do about Clayton. We haven't very much time left.'

Faced with her complete confidence in him, Simon had to produce a plan of action. Thinking as he spoke, he began to outline the first steps. He would start the next morning with a visit to Newmarket to look up some of his old contacts and try and find someone willing to speak out against Clayton. If he could convince people that Clayton's power was on the wane, and that they were not alone in their stand against him, the tide might begin to turn.

351

Chapter Twenty-Two

It was Aunt Peg who first noticed that Stacey appeared to be in a state of shock. She was in the best parlour, supervising the clearing up after the midday rush when Stacey walked in, dragging a reluctant Perdita by the wrist. One look at her niece's white, wild-eyed face brought her bustling over, anxious to help.

'Stacey, whatever's the matter? Are you ailing? You look as if you've seen a ghost.'

'Not a ghost,' Stacey said, and stopped abruptly on the brink of telling it all.

'You come along upstairs, pet, and sit down,' Aunt Peg coaxed. 'You don't look at all the thing.'

But the first paralysing numbness was wearing off, bringing back her ability to think, exposing the raw pain of betrayal and a growing anger.

'No thank you, Aunt Peg,' she said, struggling to keep her voice level. 'I'm really quite all right.'

If she allowed herself to be lulled by Aunt Peg's well-meaning cossetting, Stacey realized, she would be sure to let it all out and she could not bear to admit to anyone the humiliation she had just experienced. Even less could she bear to be told that it was not a humiliation, that it did not matter, when she knew that it mattered more than anything else in the world.

'You don't look all right,' her aunt persisted. 'Where's Simon? Is he in today?'

'No, he's out tracing a man he wants to talk to.'

A lie, the same lie he had told her. She knew just where he was now. Why had she not had the courage, the presence of mind to walk up those stairs and confront him? There was still time to do it now. She weighed the idea, and rejected it. She would wait, let him come home and compound the lie, then face him with it.

'I've some work to do in the office,' she said, 'and then I've to see someone about selling Ballyfein, so would you mind keeping an eye on Perdita for me? If it's not too much trouble.'

'Of course it isn't.' Delighted, Aunt Peg held out a hand to the little girl. 'You're never any trouble, are you, my lamb?'

Stacey thanked her and walked out into the yard, glad to be rid of the child. Perdita had turned into the living proof that her initial distrust of Simon, that very first day at Dereham, had been correct. She would never be able to believe a word he said, ever again. Once seated behind the scarred desk in the inner office, she tried to concentrate on the figures in front of her, but failed. Instead she saw only the interior of Letty Mullins's shop, herself just redressed after a fitting, pleased at the progress of a new pelisse of heavy black wool for the coming winter, Perdita playing with snippets of cloth, Letty twittering about trimmings. And then a new customer entering, a brief, swiftly-controlled look of consternation passing over Letty's face, and the reason for it: Debbie Pymer, open-mouthed at the sight of her, oozing guilt. Like a sledge-hammer between the eyes the realization that Oliver's recital of two weeks ago had not been the fevered production of jealousy, but fact. Rather than attack Deborah in public, she had walked out.

With an almighty effort, she closed at least part of her mind to the scene, made herself study the sheets before her, and as she went through the depressing figures for August, it occurred to her that as one piece of gossip had been correct, perhaps others were as well. Perhaps Georgiana had been telling the truth when she said that Simon had been given five thousand pounds. And if so, what had happened to it? The missing two and a half thousand would have pulled them out of danger for a few months longer.

The arrival of Talbot to look at Ballyfein brought yet

353

another reminder of Simon's ability to lie himself smoothly out of a difficult situation. He had done it with unruffled ease when confronted with Talbot at the Harris ball. Simmering, Stacey had an ostler lead the horse out and subjected her purchaser to a blistering round of bargaining. Unused to making deals with a woman, Talbot was cornered into paying far more than he had intended. Stacey felt she had scored a point against men in general.

The long afternoon dragged by, and still Simon did not appear. Stacey took Perdita home and put her to bed. For once, there were none of the usual tantrums that ensued when Simon was away. With a child's sharp instinct for self-preservation, Perdita knew that any protests would be given very short shrift, and did as she was told. Stacey forbade herself to keep watch at the window, and instead sat down in her father's little study at the back of the house and started the task of writing out their exact financial position. When she had finished, she sat gazing at the figures and knew that this was what was meant when people spoke of staring ruin in the face. It was just as she had come to this conclusion that she heard the front door open and Simon's familiar footsteps in the hall. Resolutely she kept her seat, refusing to answer his call, letting him find her. She listened as he looked into the dining-room and parlour, ran upstairs to their bedchamber, up again to the nursery, and refused to think of the poor deluded creature who only yesterday would have run down to meet him. After a consultation on the stairs with the parlourmaid, he at last ran her to ground.

'Here you are, Stacey. What are you doing hiding away? Good news at last, I've managed to find someone who's not afraid to speak out against Clayton.' He bent to kiss her but met only with an unresponsive cheek. Solicitous, he asked if she was tired, and received a bare negative in reply. 'Downhearted, then?' he went on, unrebuffed. 'There's no need, I believe we may be at the turning-point. Just listen to this.'

He pushed aside Stacey's neat piles of papers and

perched on the edge of the desk, looking down at her. Eager and animated like this, he was at his most attractive, his handsome face alight, his slender frame speaking strength and vigour. Stacey hardened herself to resist. She knew the real reason for his jubilation. She set herself to marvel at his powers of invention.

'That's very good,' she commented woodenly, when he had finished his account.

'Good! It's what I've been seeking, sweetheart, a lever to use against Clayton. I've still got to move very carefully, of course, but once people realize he's not all-powerful more of them will be willing to join me.' Finding he still had no response from her, he took her stiff, tense hands in his. 'What's wrong, Stacey? Has something happened to upset you? What have you been doing today?'

At the last moment, Stacey backed down.

'I sold Ballyfein this afternoon,' she told him.

'Oh Stacey, there was no need for that, we're not that desperate for money.'

Hoping to rouse a spark of interest in their mutual passion for horsedealing, he asked, 'How much did you get?'

'Two hundred and fifty.'

Simon gave a low whistle of admiration.

'A hundred guineas profit! Your father couldn't have done better. But you really don't have to make the sacrifice, I'll buy him back.'

Stacey ignored him, her outrage rekindled. If he thought she could be appeased with a mere horse, he was very much mistaken.

'But before that,' she said, speaking slowly and distinctly to the worn leather desk top in front of her, 'I went for a fitting at Letty Mullins's.'

'Oh yes?'

'Yes. And while I was there, Deborah Pymer came in. And I remembered what day it was.'

'Wednesday,' Simon supplied. 'Is it of prime importance?'

Infuriated by his calm, she snatched her hands out of his grasp and thumped the desk with clenched fists.

'Of *course* it is! How *can* you sit there and pretend you don't know? I'm not stupid, Simon, I know what goes on upstairs at Letty Mullins's! I've known for a long time. But what I refused to believe, what I laughed at the very idea of, was what I heard about you and her. Until this afternoon. I know all about what is – is going on between you and Debbie Pymer.'

Simon shifted position slightly and folded his arms.

'Then you are better informed than I,' he said. 'And what is the source of this knowledge, pray?'

She glared at him sitting there so bland and unruffled.

'It's no use taking that tone with me! You've been seen, Simon. The scullery maid sees you go in at the back.'

'And?' he prompted.

'And she's a member of Oliver's chapel.'

Hot-eyed, she dared him to deny it.

'Now we come to the heart of the matter,' he said. 'Let us consider the personalities involved. Oliver has been hoping for a chance to avenge himself on me for a long time, instead of taking the long-term course and waiting for the Lord to do it for him. I don't blame him, I've taken the position he thought was his by right and I've married the woman he loves. In his place I would have done something drastic long before now. As for the girl, she probably knows this and is telling him what she thinks he wants to hear. Just because you refused the man, it doesn't follow that she would. Our Oliver would make a very good match for any female with a scrap of sense to appreciate him.'

It was exactly Stacey's own reasoning when Oliver had told her, but now it sounded weak and feebly defensive.

'But I saw Deborah Pymer at Letty Mullins's this afternoon. I saw her with my own eyes,' she protested.

356

Simon held her gaze unflinching.

'I'll not argue with that. I imagine Deborah was there for just the same reason as you – a dress fitting. If you had gone upstairs to this trysting-place Oliver has been so kind as to tell you of, however, you would not have found me there.'

Stacey stared at him, poised on a knife-edge between suspicion and belief.

'I was doing precisely what I have just told you,' Simon insisted. 'If you wish, I can refer you to witnesses.'

Stacey leaned back in her chair, limp and hollow inside with relief, her anger turning against herself for being so wicked and disloyal as to have doubted him for a moment.

'And you haven't ever had an affair with her,' she said, more as a statement than a question.

Simon hesitated, and in doing so gave himself away.

'You haven't have you?' Stacey persisted, now wanting desperately for him to deny any relationship with Deborah.

He looked away, and her new-born confidence collapsed.

'I did have,' he admitted, 'but it was all over a long while ago. I ended it at Christmas, and I wanted to get out of it some time before that.'

'Then why did you not? Why start it in the first place? Just think what you might have told her when you – you – Seth Pymer's wife! She could have wrung all sorts of things out of you!'

'There was no danger of that,' Simon told her flatly. 'It was I who wrung information out of her. That was the idea of the exercise.'

'Are you telling me that you – you seduced Deborah Pymer with the sole intention of finding out what was going on at the Three Tuns?' Stacey's voice was shrill with outrage. 'That's horrible!'

'Would you rather it was because I was hopelessly in love with her?'

'No!'

Simon gave a slight shrug.

'Then I'm wrong either way,' he remarked.

Stacey jumped up, pushing the heavy chair away with a grating scrape.

'Yes you are!' she shouted. 'How can you be so – so cold about it? Deliberately planning to – to use her in that way. It's – it's nauseating!'

'No more than any other method of recruiting a spy,' Simon maintained. 'And that was first suggested by you, if my memory serves me correctly.'

'Only you would have thought of that particular method.'

'As a matter of fact, I didn't think of it. Your father did.'

'*Pa?*' Stacey was incredulous. 'Pa would never have suggested such a thing! It's absolutely inconceivable.'

'True, nevertheless. Your pa was a wily old fox, he was very good at guessing how people would behave.'

Stacey was seized with the desire to hurt him, and abandoned Deborah in order to take up the weapon that would do it.

'And he was good at running the company, too. We never had figures like this when he was alive!' She jabbed a finger at the balance she had made out. 'And what's more, he was always ready to put everything he had into the company in times of trouble. You wouldn't have found him keeping back half his personal fortune and not even telling anyone it existed.'

To her satisfaction, she saw that she had succeeded. Simon dropped his pose of judicious patience and stood up abruptly.

'And what precisely do you mean by that?' he demanded.

'You know very well what I mean. The rest of the five thousand pounds your father bought you off with.'

She saw him grow pale and his face set into the lines of sick anger it always took on at the mention of his family.

'Georgiana?' he asked.

'Yes, your lovely cousin was so kind as to inform me.' To smother a qualm of fear, she doubled her attack. 'I can see now why you were so adamant about my not having anything to do with her. You were afraid that I might see how alike you are. You're both cheats and liars!'

There was an omnious silence before he spoke, and when he did so, it was with palpable restraint. 'Stacey, I did not deliberately deceive you over that money. It simply did not seem to me that it was any concern of yours.'

'Of course it was a concern of mine! We need that money. What happened to it?' Stacey demanded, ignoring the instinct that told her she was rushing headlong into disaster.

'I settled it on Perdita.'

'You did *what?* You took money that would have saved the company, and the livelihoods of dozens of men, not to mention the future of our child, and you gave it all to your – your—' Too late she realized she had put herself in the wrong.

'Go on, say it,' Simon taunted. 'My bastard. That is the term, is it not? My God, you're as bad as that sanctimonious cousin of yours, eager enough to mouth speeches of love and charity when it suits you, but once any actual sacrifice is demanded of you, you're a selfish little hypocrite. It's not the child's fault she was cursed with feckless and irresponsible parents, and yet she'll bear the stigma of it all her life. And as if that is not enough, she's marred by that birthmark. What would become of her if anything were to happen to me? She has to have a secure income.'

'Oh splendid, she has a secure income, and what becomes of us?' Stacey retorted, too furious now to care what she said, as long as it scored a point over him. 'What about our child? What's he going to live on when his father's in the debtors' gaol? I suppose I shall have to ask Perdita if she will kindly lend us enough to enable us to eat.'

'I imagine his mother will be well able to provide for him by trading horses round the country. One look at you and the toughest dealer would turn white and agree to whatever you asked just to be rid of you.'

Tears scalded Stacey's eyes and throat, and she fought to suppress them.

'So that's what you think of me!' Her voice rose in an ugly squeak. 'Thank you. I've often wondered. I always knew you only married me to get your hands on the company, and a fine pig's ear you made of that!'

'That's not so, and you know it. I bought the partnership before I asked for you, so stop trying to twist the truth.'

'Truth! You wouldn't know what the truth was if it stood up and hit you in the face!' Stacey flung at him. 'Your whole life is nothing but lies and lies. I knew that, when I first met you, but I let myself be deceived, just like all the rest—' Her breath was coming in tearing sobs now, hot tears spilling down her face. 'I trusted you! I thought – I really thought – these past months, when you were so n-nice to me—' With a last vestige of caution, she stopped on the brink of confessing her cherished dream, of telling him how she had come to hope that he was learning to love her, a small but growing hope that had helped her through the worst of her grief for her father. Now the flame was extinguished, and the darkness was unbearable. 'But it was nothing but an act,' she accused. 'You take and take and give nothing in return!'

'Stacey, dearest—' Simon began, reaching out to take her in his arms. But she twisted away, putting the width of the desk between them.

'Don't you dare! Don't you dare d-dearest me!' she shrilled, and groped blindly for the door, wrenched it open and stumbled up the stairs. She flung herself on the wide four-poster bed, weeping for her lost dream, for the aching sense of betrayal, cursing her own weakness in letting herself be taken in. Then gradually the discomfort of lying face downwards began to obtrude and she rolled onto her side, curling into a defensive ball round the scrap of humanity she carried in her womb. The baby. She still had the baby to care and fight and plan for. She must be strong, for it was utterly dependent upon her. Silently, she told it not to fret, for she would never betray its trust. Its future was safe with her.

Gradually, the storm of weeping subsided to an occasional hoarse sob, but even as she determined that neither she nor the child would ever feel the need of the man who had fathered it, she heard Simon's footfall on the stairs. She held her breath, unable to tell whether the surge of painful longing that possessed her was a hope or a fear that he would come in. The steps slowed and hesitated outside the door and she found herself willing him to open it. An age ticked by with her racing heartbeats, then the handle turned, light spilled into the room and Simon trod softly across the floor to sit down on the bed beside her. The nerves of her spine tingled at his presence, but she remained with her back to him, not daring to make the first move lest she wreck this last chance.

'Stacey, I have been trying to think of some proof I can lay before you, but there is none,' he said, and the lack of the usual confidence in his voice wakened a vivid memory. The night he turned up at the Red House in the snowstorm he had sounded like that. The night he proposed. Half of her dismissed it as a deliberate act, the other half listened, ready to accept anything he told her. 'I know my life was nothing but lies,' he went on, 'it was a habit with me, one that I only began to want to break when I came here. You are the one person I have striven never to deceive. I value your trust more than I can say, if you can only try to believe me, and the only reason I did not tell you about – the money or – or Deborah Pymer was that both were – dealt with before I became engaged to you.'

Stacey turned over and studied his face by the light of the candle he had set by the bedside. He met her eyes with an undisguised look of appeal, and her last resistance dissolved. She reached out and took his hand.

'I'm sorry I said what I did about Perdita,' she whispered huskily. 'I didn't mean it, I spoke without thinking.'

'I know. I know. Nobody could have tried harder to make her feel wanted than you have.' He pushed the damp hair back from her face, a caress that travelled down to linger on her breast, instantly arousing her overwrought senses. Catching a shuddering breath, she pulled him down, trembling inside at the feel of his body against hers. The scorching quarrel faded into insignificance beside the strength of their need for each other.

It was only afterwards, when Simon lay deeply asleep with an arm flung across her, that Stacey realized they had got no further forward, reached no new level of understanding. Gently she eased the blankets over his naked shoulders, careful not to disturb him. He stirred and sighed, and she stroked his springing curls, conscious of a deep ache. She was his, body, mind and heart, but he still kept part of himself aloof. Try as she might to tell herself that she was almost certainly closer to him than any living person, still she longed for more, and could not reconcile herself to the thought that he had given all he was capable of giving. And when she finally fell into an exhausted sleep, she had still not come to terms with it.

For some time, Perdita had been coming to think that Aunt Stacey was not so bad after all. It was gradually borne upon her that it was nice to have a nursery of her own, and toys that did not get broken by heavy-handed older boys or troublesome toddlers, and nicer still not to have to compete with a crowd of other children for notice. Aunt Stacey did quite often tell her to amuse herself or go to the kitchen while she frowned over the piles of books and papers in the study, but when she had finished she gave all her attention to Perdita, inventing games and stories or teaching her her letters and numbers.

'When you can add up and read and write, you will be able to help your papa and me,' Aunt Stacey promised. 'I used to help my pa when I was not much older than you.'

It sounded an exciting prospect, joining the huge colourful world her father inhabited, worth making an effort for. Gradually the odd shapes in the primer began to make sense, forming themselves into recognizable patterns that were the names of familiar objects. Aunt Stacey let her stay up and show Papa the day she read five words without any prompting.

Today Aunt Stacey seemed restless, pacing about the house picking things up and putting them down.

'Let's go out, Perdy,' she said at last. 'It's a sunny day, we'll go for a walk. You can choose. Where would you like to go?'

Perdita thought. She liked going to the stables, but she had been there yesterday. She liked looking at the river, and watching the ships going by and the ducks feeding. She quite liked shopping, particularly if Aunt Stacey bought her toffee, which seemed very probable. What she had not done for a long time, because Aunt Stacey always had some reason not to go, was visit the coachworks.

'To see the coaches being made,' she decided.

Aunt Stacey hesitated a moment, biting her lip.

'Oh well, I don't know—' she began, then changed her mind, smiling again. 'Very well! The coachworks it is. I'll ask Uncle Ollie how the second-hand sales are doing while I'm there.'

But just as they were about to set out, visitors arrived, one of her many new aunts and some of her cousins, two boys and a little girl. The grown-ups went into the front parlour, talking and talking, and Perdita was left staring at the other children.

'Off you go and play now,' Aunt Stacey said. 'Why not go out in the garden? We'll go to the coachworks later, Perdy.'

Perdita glared at the door as it closed behind her. She did not want to go later, she wanted to go now. The boys were already scampering along the passage towards the kitchen, dragging their sister with them, but Perdita refused to follow. She plumped down in the middle of the hall and sulked until the parlourmaid came bustling through with a tray.

'Whatever are you doing there, Miss Perdy?' she asked. 'You run on out in the garden before I trip over you. Worse'n a cat, getting under my feet like that.' Dragging her feet, Perdita went.

The boys were rushing round and round the paths with their arms spread wide, being ships, and the toddler was poking her special flowerpots with a stick. Perdita went up and pushed her away.

'They're mine!' she said. 'They're my tea things and you can't have them.'

The little girl shrieked and the boys came over to see what was wrong.

'You leave her alone, she's younger than you,' one of them shouted.

'She's got my tea things, she'll break them,' Perdita protested.

'We're guests, you've got to let us do what we like,' the other boy stated self-righteously.

Perdita thought longingly of big Tommy Hankin, who could lam them both good and proper. But Tommy was miles away at Bridge Farm, and they were two to her one.

'I hate you, you're horrid!' she cried, and ran off to the bottom of the garden where she had a den behind the greenhouse. She sat there for a long time, thinking of Bridge Farm, and what she would like to do to the two nasty boys, and the spoilt trip to the coachworks. And then it occurred to her that she could go there by herself. She stood up, climbed up the back gate to reach the bolt, lifted the latch and crept out. It was rather gloomy in the alley, but she knew the way to go and trotted off towards the street, only to run slap into a huge, tall man who picked her up and put a hand over her mouth. Terrified, Perdita kicked and struggled, but he only held her tighter. He smelt of beer and onions.

'Hold still, yer nasty little brat,' he growled. 'This the one, Will?'

Another man appeared, smaller but just as frightening.

'Aye, thass the one, with the strawberry mark,' he said. 'Piece of luck. Bring her along, quick and quiet.'

Stacey did not notice Perdita's disappearance until after her visitors had departed. At first she thought the child was just hiding about the house somewhere and in some annoyance sent the maids to look for her, inwardly vowing to complain to Simon about her this time. She was heartily sick of Perdita's escapades. But when a search of the house, the garden and then the surrounding area brought no results, she began to worry. Forcing herself to think calmly, she remembered the promised expedition to the coachworks and set off to find out if Perdita had gone there, asking along the way if anyone had seen her. Nobody had, and neither was she at the coachworks. Really anxious now, Stacey ran all the way to the Crown and found Simon talking to the head yard porter. He took one look at her and led her into the office, then listened grave-faced to her account.

'. . . And I don't even know how long she's been gone, it was only when they left that I realized,' she concluded. 'It's all my fault, I should have watched her more carefully.'

'No, no, it's not your fault, it's mine. I should have foreseen this,' Simon assured her. 'I'll organize a search of the inn and stables, in case she's here somewhere. It may just be that she's playing a trick on us. Sit down and stop blaming yourself, I'll be back.'

Her knees suddenly weak, Stacey dropped into one of the office chairs as the meaning of his words sank in. Until now, it had not occurred to her that this was anything but a trick to gain attention. Perdita's attempts to escape and hide were growing rarer now, but she still resorted to them at times. Unbidden, the picture formed in her mind of Platt's desperate expression, and the admission Simon had forced from him. 'It was Clayton . . . he forced me. He said he'd get at my missus if I didn't.' And Simon had always kept his daughter's very existence secret in the past. Not, he claimed, because he was ashamed of her, but because she could so easily be used as a weapon against him.

Stacey got up and paced about the cramped room, gnawed by guilt. She had never accepted Perdita, she admitted. She always resented the close bond between Simon and his daughter, she who had so much, family, a child of her own, more of Simon than he gave to any other adult. And yet she coveted Perdita's claim on the only person the child had in the world, and let her wander off into dreadful danger. She bit at her tightly-laced knuckles, praying that Perdita would be found safe and well in some corner of the Crown.

Simon's face as he came in some twenty minutes later put paid to that hope. 'She's not here?' she questioned.

'No.'

'You don't think—?' She could not force the entire sentence out. 'Clayton?'

'I don't know yet. I pray not. I'm coming home with you immediately to see if I can find out anything.'

In silence they made their way back to All Saints Green, where questioning of their own and their neighbours' servants revealed very little. Perdita had been seen in the garden, but not outside either in front or creeping round the backs of the other houses.

'She still might just be lost,' Simon argued, but without conviction. He sent down to the inn for a dozen horse-keepers and stableboys, and dispatched them to comb the streets, and further afield to where the orchards and open land started. They straggled back in ones and twos, reluctantly admitting lack of success, and needed no urging to try again. The long day crawled by, each hour deepening the certainty that something serious had befallen Perdita. Either she was trapped in an outhouse or lying unconscious from a fall, or she was being held captive. Stacey prayed it was the former, but each passing minute made it less likely.

Then as the day faded into evening and they sat over an

untouched meal, the parlourmaid brought up an envelope addressed in a neat, educated hand to Stacey. It contained a formal invitation written on a sheet of thick, expensive paper. 'M. Clayton requests the pleasure of the company of Mr and Mrs S. Wynwood at their earliest convenience. He begs to assure them that their daughter is safe.' In silence, she handed it to Simon, who scanned through it.

'So, now we know,' he commented, tossing it aside and standing up. A nerve at the side of his face twitched, betraying his gnawing anxiety. 'Our friend Clayton persists in playing cat and mouse with us, it seems. When will he send us an address, I wonder? Tomorrow? Next week?'

Stacey called back the parlourmaid and enquired whether anyone was waiting to take back a reply, and learnt that not only was there a manservant in the hall, but a carriage standing outside.

'So,' Simon said again, 'transport is provided. How thoughtful. Are any of the stableboys in the kitchen at the moment?'

As it happened, two of them were, and were promptly sent down to the Crown for Oliver.

'Oliver? What do you want him for?' Stacey asked, standing ready with her bonnet tied on. 'Come on, do, we must hurry.'

'And play right into Clayton's hands? Think, Stacey. If we lose our heads at this stage we're sunk. Clayton expects us to leap into that carriage of his and agree to anything so long as we get Perdita back. That is not what we are going to do.'

Stacey stared at him, shocked.

'But you must agree to anything. Nothing is so important as rescuing Perdita.'

'If we do that, Clayton will prove his ascendancy over us. We'll have the threat of his doing the same again forever hanging over our heads. I have some bargaining power, which I shall try to make him believe is greater than it really is, and by making him wait we'll give the impression that we're not frightened of him.'

'But Oliver—' Stacey began.

'Oliver is going to stay here with you. He would guard you with his life, if need be.'

'I'm not staying here,' Stacey declared. 'That horrid note asked for both of us. How can I possibly wait at home when it might mean the difference between success and failure?'

'It's too dangerous,' Simon told her.

'I tell you I'm coming. Simon, if anything happened to Perdita I would feel it was my fault. It's bad enough already, knowing she was in my care when she was abducted. Please, Simon.'

It took until Oliver arrived for her to persuade him that she might actually be an asset. But though he was not now needed as a bodyguard, there was still a task for Oliver. Simon briefly outlined the situation.

'I'd like to find out just where Clayton goes to ground when he's in Norwich,' he explained. 'If we keep within the town, you'll be able to follow us easily on foot. If we go outside, leave off, you won't be able to keep up and you'd be seen on horseback. But whatever you do, be careful. No heroics, this is neither the time nor the place for them.'

Oliver nodded.

'Why are you taking Stacey?' he asked.

'Because she's got a head on her shoulders,' Simon told him, and sent him out by the kitchen entrance again to await their departure. When he had gone, he turned again to Stacey.

'It's my guess that man in the hall will ride inside the carriage with us,' he said, 'so there will be no further chance for us to confer. Don't answer any questions directly, and try to keep outwardly calm, no matter what he says. Once you show you're angry, or shocked, or upset, he'll have the advantage of us. Do you understand?'

Stacey swallowed. 'Yes.'

'Good.' Simon kissed her swiftly on the lips. 'Courage, sweetheart. Whatever happens, we'll get Perdita back, and we might even gain something from this if we tread cleverly.'

As Simon expected, they were not left alone to hatch last-minute plans during the journey. Not only did the man who had delivered the note sit opposite them watching their every small movement, but another henchman was waiting for them as they stepped in. Simon greeted them both cheerfully, enquiring whether they were to have the pleasure of a lengthy trip in their company, and receiving only a curt order to 'shut his row' proceeded to tell Stacey of the rumour he had heard that somebody in the west country was experimenting with propelling coaches by steam power. It was not, he asserted, such a ludicrous idea as it might first appear. Without horses, and all the labour needed to look after them, the cost of running a service would be cut considerably. In spite of herself, Stacey was interested. Though part of her mind still dwelt on the test to come and the terror and bewilderment Perdita must be experiencing, she managed to keep up at least the semblance of a discussion on the possibility of Brown's running steam coaches. And as she did so, the motion of the carriage changed as they rolled off the paved streets of the town and onto the turnpike, and again as they swung into a rutted country lane. When they pulled up, she saw Simon look at his watch, and guessed that he was trying to work out how far they had come. She wondered if Oliver had obeyed instructions and given up at the city boundary, or whether he was still following doggedly behind.

Simon squeezed her hand and gave her an encouraging smile as she stepped down from the carriage.

'Keep it up,' he whispered, as they were hustled into what appeared to be a small country inn.

With one guard in front of them and another behind, they were herded along a passageway and up a narrow stair, stopping on a dark, cramped landing. The leading man opened one of the doors and hustled them into a small ante-room, hardly bigger than a cupboard, furnished only with a couple of stick-back chairs.

'She stays here,' he stated, indicating Stacey. 'He wants to see you first.'

'He can see us both, together,' Simon said. 'I'm not leaving my wife with the likes of you.'

'Listen, you ain't got any choice.' The man's face folded into an unpleasant smile. 'Mr Clayton's word is law round here, see?'

Stacey, seeing that they could waste precious time on a minor point, settled the matter by sitting on one of the chairs.

'You go in,' she said.

The man gave a grunt of approval, knocked on the inner door, waited for a reply and led Simon in.

Simon glanced swiftly round the room, noting possible exits, taking stock of the surroundings. There was a heavy old-fashioned four-poster bed, a table and chairs, bare walls and floor. No sign of lengthy occupation, he decided, so this could not be Clayton's permanent base. And then he turned his attention to the man he had been summoned to meet, and was instantly transported back eight years to a brightly-lit, noisy Oxford basement. It took all of his ingrained self-control to prevent the shock from showing on his face.

From his seat in the only comfortable chair in the room, Clayton regarded him with a slight gleam of malice in his eyes, the only sign of emotion in his still, expressionless features.

'You know me, I perceive,' he said. 'Do sit down, Mr Wynwood. It is Wynwood again now, is it not, rather than Ward, or Keating?'

'Wynwood will serve for now,' Simon returned. 'And which do you prefer – Clayton, or Henshaw, or shall we revert to Anstey?'

He pulled out one of the high-backed chairs and sat with every appearance of ease, crossing his knees and leaning an elbow on the table, whilst his mind raced, taking in this new turn of events, trying to place them in some logical pattern. So Clayton was not only Henshaw, his unseen enemy at Newmarket, that was bad enough, but he had come to terms with it and worked out some sort of strategy to deal with him. Far more difficult to assimilate was his also being Anstey, the man with whom he had collaborated in his undergraduate days, bringing wealthy and impressionable young men along to Anstey's gaming club and assisting in relieving them by degrees of small fortunes.

'Names, what are they but a convenient reference?' Clayton said indifferently. 'Unless, of course, they happen to belong to one of the ancient families of the land. Minor nobility, but all the more to be protected because of that.'

Simon could not immediately see the significance of this, so he ignored it, trying to keep some of the initiative.

'It must have been something of a surprise for you to find that Gregory Ward did not after all die out on the Breckland last year.'

But Clayton was not to be moved by this.

'Not at all, Mr Wynwood. It was not intended that he should die. He merely had to be – discouraged. Indeed, it was most agreeable to have Mr Keating take his place, and in such a convenient situation too, right under my eye. He was something of an amusement. I was highly entertained by his ingenuity in foiling the moves made by our mutual friend Pymer. The staged fight was in the best traditions of epic drama, and the thwarting of the bullion robbers also. Most resourceful. But then you do have a taste for mock heroics, do you not?'

'I certainly do not have your taste for sitting like a spider in the dark corner of a neglected room.' More than ever, he wondered why Clayton was bothering to play this game at all. He could not understand why he had not just had him murdered. It would have been easy enough. Why just 'discourage' him? It seemed to him unlikely that it was a long and subtle revenge for his change of heart over their Oxford enterprise, when Simon had sickened at what they were doing to their hapless victims and warned

371

them off. There must, he thought, be some other reason for letting him live, and if he could but find out what it was, he could use it to his advantage.

Clayton, meanwhile, was continuing to comment on his past record.

'I must confess, however, to being just a little surprised at your latest role. When Mr Keating left to visit his ancestral home, I thought that one of two things might happen. Either he would stay there, or he would cast about for fresh woods to hunt. I did not expect him to take up every appearance of a permanent position in a tribe of tradesmen. Your marriage in particular interests me. It seems out of character. A rich widow or an unprotected heiress would have been more your style, I would have thought. Your alliance with the daughter of a coaching proprietor puzzles me. What can have prompted you, I wonder? The lady in question does not even appear to be blessed with any personal attractions beyond youth and good health.'

Simon studied the ceiling as if trying to alleviate his boredom.

'I really cannot think why you are so interested in my private life,' he remarked, though he guessed Clayton was trying to divine just how useful a weapon Stacey might be in bending him to his will. 'If you have quite finished taking my likeness, perhaps we could come to the real business of the evening?'

'You refer, I take it, to your daughter?' Clayton's unmoving stare waited for a telltale reaction.

'Precisely. Return her to me, and perhaps we could start to discuss matters of interest to us both.'

'Indeed, there are many matters of interest to us both, and to – other parties.' Clayton paused momentarily to make sure this point was taken. 'Your private life, as you put it, is of some importance, whereas your daughter is of minor value. An illegitimate girlchild has no claims beyond those of – affection.'

Looking at that grim, remorseless face, its granite quality

372

emphasized rather than softened by the candlelight, Simon had the distinct feeling that the shadow-boxing was about to end, and that Clayton's next move was going to be a devastating one.

'Claims to what?' he asked.

Clayton, naturally, did not answer directly.

'We were talking of names,' he remarked. 'We neither of us care to keep one for too long. But I have the advantage of you, Simon Wynwood. Any one of mine will serve just as well as another. I can discard them like outworn coats. But you cannot escape from your true identity.'

A new suspicion formed, one that had not even occurred to Simon before: was Clayton thinking of using him to gain a hold over his family? Perhaps he was finding his present field of action too restricting and wanted an entrée to the network of families who held the reins of power in their hands.

'I would have thought it was fairly obvious,' he said, 'that I am not making any attempt to escape from it at the moment.'

'Exactly so, in fact you are flaunting it in order to be a source of embarrassment to the more conventional members of your family, something which you have frequently done in the past. But you should beware of such irresponsible behaviour, Mr Wynwood, for it can be used against you. You must be well aware of your father's wanting an excuse to disown you publicly as he does privately.'

So he was correct, Clayton did intend joining in with the tangle of Wynwood enmities. Simon strove to keep his expression bland as he struggled with a sick loathing at being dragged into it once again, mixed with a predatory exhilaration. He knew how to play this game. He had been in training for it all his life.

'You are well acquainted with my father's wishes, presumably?' he enquired, as if making polite conversation.

'Better than you imagine, and for far longer than you

might suspect,' Clayton told him, watching him with the unwavering intensity of a stoat. 'Had you continued our first association for a little longer, you would have fallen in with them very neatly.'

He stopped again, waiting for some reaction to this statement, and seeing none, went on to explain more fully.

'Lord Lathenbridge and I have long been known to each other,' he said, a glint of malicious enjoyment colouring his voice. 'I have several times been in a position to render him certain – services, for which, naturally, he was grateful. So much so, indeed, that I soon became aware of the, shall we say, irregular state of his lordship's family life. So when the keeping up of appearances necessitated your being given the usual gentleman's education, who more suitable than I to keep a discreet eye on your activities?'

His inquisitor's stare was rewarded at last. Try as he might, Simon could not keep the shock from registering on his face.

'I rather suspected that might surprise you,' Clayton remarked. 'But that is not all. Your father did not trust you to go to the devil in your own way. He wanted to be sure that you would do so in such a way that would be most useful to him. You would be amazed at how many of your past acquaintances have also been very well known to me. Most particularly at Newmarket. You were playing a dangerous game there, and playing it with some degree of skill and subtlety. But I knew what you were up to, Simon Wynwood. I knew all along, and so did Lord Lathenbridge.'

A cold paralysis gripped Simon's powers of reasoning as he realized that all the time he had thought he was acting as a free agent he had in fact been at least partly manipulated by his father. Exposure as a partner in a corrupt gaming club would have been a first-class excuse for cutting him off from all family recognition, and his activities at Newmarket could well have been used to engineer his downfall.

'But unfortunately for both of you, I changed direction,' he said, attempting to gain time as his numb mind tried to grasp the point that was eluding him.

And as he reviewed the exchange so far it came to him: why had he not been either killed or disgraced, if his father wanted him out of the way? It could only be because the situation had changed. He was being kept under observation, as a reserve, in case of Timothy's failure to produce an heir. He had suspected for a long time that his father's convictions about his parentage were wavering. Georgiana must have known this as well, when she came to see him last November. As usual, she was backing both sides in order to stay with the eventual winner.

'No, Mr Wynwood,' Clayton said. 'Not unfortunately, as things have turned out.'

'My father has different plans for me now, I take it?' Simon said. 'And you think you are in a position to make me fall in with them? Or is it the other way round: you will restore me to family favour in exchange for services to be rendered in the future? Either way, Clayton, I'm not playing.'

Clayton's voice dropped almost to a whisper, dry and menacing.

'I think you will, Simon Wynwood. Consider what is at stake: a title, a fine estate, a seat in the Lords. Only one small obstacle stands in the way of your gaining these, an obstacle which I could remove.'

Simon suppressed the desire to tell him just exactly what he thought of such an abhorrent suggestion, and displayed mild interest.

'I think we had better stop this fencing in the dark and speak in plain terms. You are offering to get rid of my sister-in-law's child, and presumably any others she might bear, thus putting me back in the direct line of succession. Is it a scheme entirely of your own making, or are you still working in conjunction with my father?

Either way, there must be some demands you wish to make of me.'

In Clayton's eyes there flickered a passing light of amusement.

'I do appreciate dealing with you,' he remarked. 'I find you most stimulating, you have a splendid grasp of the realities of life. I shall indeed expect some recompense for my trouble, but nothing that will prove beyond the resources of your exalted position. And from now on you will, of course, be required to live in a manner suitable to that position.'

'Give up my coach company and return to Lathenbridge?'

'Precisely. A small sacrifice, surely.'

There was a flaw in it, he was certain. Clayton stood to gain rewards from the present Lord Lathenbridge for persuading the prodigal son to return, something which, Simon realized, he had been trying to do by attempting to ruin the business these last few months. He was also setting up a splendid means of blackmailing the future Lord Lathenbridge with exposure over his complicity in the murder of Georgiana's child. But something did not quite fit. The timing.

Why suddenly force matters now, when both Clayton and his father had been content to drive him inch by inch into bankruptcy, presumably then to bail him out on promise of good behaviour? Something must have happened that he was not aware of, something to do with the succession. And he remembered that Georgiana's son was said to be a weak and sickly infant. What if it had died and Timothy had been driven to confess that any others would not be of his getting? His father would then send to Clayton asking him to force Simon to conform and have his children brought up in a manner befitting their birth, before Simon realized that he could now do whatever he liked and still inherit the title.

The only weak point in this theory was that he would have known about it himself. Timothy, already extremely ill at ease over his mockery of a marriage, would have written at once to tell him of the latest disaster. And with the possible answer to this came the solution to another link that had puzzled him: Clayton's association with Pymer. Pymer horsed the mailcoaches. Between the two of them, they must have devised some way of tampering with the mail.

He became aware that Clayton was waiting for an answer, and decided to test his theory.

'Far too great a sacrifice, Clayton, and particularly when it is not required. Next time you meet with Lord Lathenbridge, you may tell him that he will have to accustom himself to the prospect of a pack of honest, shrewd members of the bourgeoisie taking over the place after he's gone and turning it into a cross between a dealer's yard and a rather superior inn.'

This time there was not even a hint of amusement in Clayton's expression.

'You forget that without my help you will not gain the title.'

'But I shall, Clayton, and without any of your doubtful assistance. And even if some unforeseen event carries me off before my brother, my sons will inherit. I know my family too well, you see. I understand how their minds work. It takes more than a trumped-up plot like this to force me to do his lordship's bidding.'

Clayton changed tactics, and Simon knew that his guess had been right.

'You also forget that I still have your daughter.'

'The illegitimate girlchild of minor value?'

'Please do not pretend that you do not care what becomes of her, Wynwood. You and your servants have been scouring the city for her all day.'

'I have no intention of any such pretence. But I must point out that several people know that you abducted her, and that my wife and I have come to collect her. You cannot dispose of all three of us, or even just of her, and get away with it.'

377

He had not expected that such a threat would have any effect, and nor did it.

'Do not make the mistake of underestimating me, Wynwood. Others stronger than you have done so in the past, and regretted it.' His gaze shifted momentarily to the guard standing silently inside the door. 'Bring in our other guest.' And as the man went out, he remarked to Simon, 'I should imagine your wife might be more than a little annoyed to find you have turned down the chance for her to become a lady.'

That, Simon reflected, was where he was underestimating Stacey. But he could not quell a chill fear of what pressures Clayton might try to bring to bear on her.

As Stacey was ushered into the room, her first thought was for Simon who she could sense was strung tight as piano wire behind his mask of indifference. They exchanged a quick smile of mutual reassurance as he rose and pulled out a chair for her. She sat, trying to emulate his assumed ease, and then turned her attention to the man who had been chipping away at the foundations of her life for the past year. Studying his cold, stony face, she knew that here was a man infinitely more dangerous than any of the petty rogues she had come into contact with. His very stillness disturbed her, his lack of expression. When he greeted her, though his mouth moved, his features remained untouched. His voice had the same quality, flat and implacable.

'Mrs Wynwood. How good of you to come at such short notice. I trust you have been quite comfortable?'

The conventional words sounded sinister in such unconventional circumstances.

'Tolerably so, I thank you,' she replied, and was relieved to find that though her voice sounded unnaturally high, the words came easily enough. She was just congratulating herself on this when she was further disconcerted by one of the silent guards taking the branch of candles that had been standing on the mantelpiece and placing it on the table before herself and Simon, so that they had to look through the light to see Clayton, now an unmoving presence in the dim twilight. Simon reached out and pushed the candles to one side, but Clayton still retained the advantage of seeing far more of them than they could of him.

'Your husband and I have been conducting a most interesting discussion on the subject of his family connections,' Clayton told her. Stacey immediately understood why Simon was so tense. Any reference to the Wynwoods was likely to shatter his composure.

'Indeed?' she said.

'Yes, and I was curious to see what your reaction would be when you learnt that he has refused an opportunity to regain his claim to the title.'

Before she could answer, Simon broke in wearily.

'Once and for all, Clayton, can we clear this point up? I have my own means of collecting information, and I know very well that nature has already removed the child that you were prepared to . . . murder.'

'Really?' Clayton dismissed this and concentrated on Stacey. 'And what are your feelings on the matter, Mrs Wynwood? No doubt you are eager for the day when you will become Lady Lathenbridge.'

Stacey had never in the past given the possibility more than a passing thought, but now that she did, she found it rather daunting. She remembered Simon's instructions about not answering directly.

'I don't see what it has to do with you,' she said, and rather than just sit fending off his questions, added, 'I thought you had us brought here to claim my step-daughter.'

'Ah yes, your stepdaughter.' A faint note of interest crept into Clayton's voice. 'It was most generous of you, Mrs Wynwood, to take in your husband's – byblow. Another woman's child.'

'It was only what any right-minded person would have done,' Stacey said. 'And it was all over years ago.'

'That is what he told you, naturally,' Clayton agreed.

'I wonder if you were equally well-informed about his seduction of Pymer's wife? A particularly neat way of combining business and pleasure, I thought, and so well in keeping with his character.'

Stacey swallowed nervously and sent silent thanks to Oliver for his interference. But for that, she would have been completely thrown.

'Pymer was the only person who did not know, it seems,' she retorted. 'We are obliged to you for forebearing to mention it to him.'

'It would have been a pity to spoil the game, since it was not doing any harm to my concerns.'

Under the table, Stacey's hand found Simon's and was enclosed in his comforting grasp.

'If you are seeking to divide and rule, Clayton, you will find yourself failing miserably,' he stated. 'You won't succeed in driving a wedge between my wife and myself. We understand each other completely.' And with an air of dismissing the subject he went on, 'Personally, I think this interview has gone on quite long enough. As my wife said, we came to fetch my daughter. Restore her to me, and I might be willing to discuss some sort of agreement, as you are quite evidently eager to enjoy the patronage of the Lathenbridges.'

For a moment Stacey's heart beat faster as it sounded as if Simon was about to take the initiative. But Clayton refused to be diverted.

'All in good time, Mr Wynwood. You forget that you are here by my invitation. Let us first examine this good understanding you claim to have established. Is your bride aware of your continuing, shall we say, friendship with Pymer's wife? Hardly proper behaviour, surely, for a man so recently married.'

Stacey felt the sweat break out on the palm of Simon's hand and pressed it to show that even if it were true, it did not matter.

'As my husband said, we have no secrets from each other,' she replied, and gaining confidence went on,

'Deborah Pymer is a useful source of information to us. It was through her, of course, that we learnt of Pymer's association with you. Though what your interest in him can be I really cannot imagine. He is nothing but a crude bully.'

'Oh, I think we have the answer to that little riddle,' Simon told her. 'It concerns the carriage of His Majesty's Mails.'

In the darkness beyond the pool of light cast by the candles, Clayton shifted slightly in his seat, and Stacey wished she could see if their words were having any effect. He ignored Simon's aside and remarked.

'You are quite an unusual young lady.'

'Unique, in my opinion.' Simon allowed an edge of impatience to show in his voice. 'If you have quite finished taking notes to report back to the present Lord Lathenbridge, perhaps you might care to restore my daughter to me and discuss terms with the future one.'

Stacey tried to look as if the references to Simon's inheriting the title were not perplexing her, and waited for Clayton's reply. When it came, his monotone was flatly discouraging.

'Too vague, Mr Wynwood. I do nothing for the prospect of a few possible future favours.'

'Very well, let us take Pymer, since you are so interested in him and his wife. He, as my wife has pointed out, is nothing but a crude bully. I could be far more useful.'

'Ah.' Again a movement from Clayton's chair. Stacey could see he was leaning forward, and she could swear there was interest in his voice. 'An alliance. But you forget, Mr Wynwood, that our last – association ended somewhat abruptly. You do not seem to be able to decide whether you are on the side of the angels.'

'That was eight years ago,' Simon pointed out. 'I am now on whichever side profits me most.'

For a moment, even Stacey wondered if his proposal was genuine or a bluff.

'A sensible position,' Clayton commended. 'And what

exactly do you have to offer that our mutual friend Pymer does not?'

'Hand over my daughter and I shall be more specific.'

In the silence, Stacey felt like a watchspring that was in danger of being overwound. She held her breath, and concentrated on not yelping as Simon's fingers crushed hers.

'You interest me,' Clayton admitted slowly. 'Not a great deal, but enough. Wat! Have the child brought in.'

Stacey went limp with relief. The object of the interview had been achieved and now this nerveracking game of pretence could cease. Doors opened and footsteps sounded, then Perdita was hustled into the room. With a cry, she hurled herself at Simon and clung to him, sobbing. Joy wrestled with a sense of rejection in Stacey as she watched, shut out from the reunion. She reached out to touch Perdita's arm, saying how happy she was to have found her, and to her surprise and delight the little girl clutched her hand and held on to it.

Gradually, Perdita's sobs subsided, though she still clung limpet-like to Simon. Clayton judged it possible for speech once more.

'Now, Mr Wynwood, what exactly are you proposing?'

Simon looked at him steadily over his daughter's tousled head.

'We come back to the question of names once again. Some people keep the same one for generations, and build up a store of goodwill. I am in a position to use the good name of Brown's for any number of purposes.'

There was a pause, and in the silence Perdita begged to be taken home. Simon hushed her and promised they would be leaving any minute now. Stacey only just restrained herself from adding her voice to the plea. She foresaw only constant danger and worry from Simon's bid to gain Clayton's confidence and penetrate his web. She just wanted to get as far away from him as possible, but instead was forced to sit and wait for Clayton's judgement on Simon's offer. Her eyes adjusted now to looking beyond the candlelight, she saw that he was leaning forward, his elbows on the armrests of the chair and his fingertips pressed lightly together. An odd sense of familiarity nagged her, and then she recalled a friend of her father's, a formidable chess player, assuming just such a position when considering a move. Her fingernails bit into the palm of her free hand as she waited.

'And how do you aim to prove that you will be just as useful to me as Pymer in – the other business, always supposing that you can gain the contract to horse the mails?'

'Oh, I can take the mail contract easily enough,' Simon asserted. 'Brown's are, and always have been, a better company than Pymer's, and you know it. It has only been your support, and the money you have poured into them that has kept Pymer's solvent. Remove that – and then, for added measure, deal Pymer's one devastating public blow, some kind of failure on their part – and Brown's will be what they have always been – Norwich's top coaching company . . . and working solely for you.'

'What kind of public blow?' Clayton asked softly.

'A race . . . how about a race?'

Stacey caught her breath, wondering what Clayton would make of such a facetious suggestion. She was certain he would demand something dangerous if not downright criminal from Simon. But she was wrong. From the wing chair came the dry travesty of a chuckle.

'A race, Mr Wynwood? How quick you are to turn matters to your own advantage. And just what kind of a race are you envisaging?'

'Norwich to Ipswich,' Simon elaborated. 'With the usual working coaches and a normal load of passengers. No extra horses or staging-posts to be put in, and two neutral judges to be appointed to ensure fair play.'

'By all means let us ensure fair play.' Clayton's two middle fingers tapped together as he considered. 'When do you propose to run this contest?'

'The sooner the better. How about the day after tomorrow?'

'Very well,' Clayton decided.

Stacey could hardly contain a cheer, so astonished was she at their good luck. They were being handed a chance to save the company from bankruptcy. The amount they would make in bets were enormous, and the public notice would be a tremendous asset. From Norwich to Ipswich, nothing on four wheels could beat the Flyer.

'I leave the rules for you and Pymer to agree between yourselves,' Clayton said. 'I have only one stipulation, concerning the choice of coachman.'

'I'm more than willing to take the ribbons myself, if Pymer is,' Simon told him.

'Pymer, yes. He shall drive his stage, but not you, Mr Wynwood.' He paused before delivering his bombshell. 'I think your wife should be allowed that privilege.'

'No!' Simon was jolted out of his carefully maintained assurance. 'That is completely out of the question.'

Clayton was unruffled.

'Really? How unfortunate. In that case, I do not see that I can sanction the affair.'

Stacey gazed at his dark shape and smiled inwardly. He thought he had the measure of her, but he was greatly mistaken. She was not going to play into his hands by backing down.

'I'll do it,' she said.

'You will not,' Simon told her. 'I absolutely forbid it.'

'Why? I'm quite capable of driving to Ipswich. I've done it before.'

'That was a light curricle, not a stage. And you were not carrying a child. You would kill yourself and the baby.'

Disturbed by their arguing over her head, Perdita began to whimper.

'Nonsense, I'll do nothing of the sort,' Stacey retorted. 'Be quiet, you're upsetting Perdy.'

'You—'

Ignoring him, Stacey looked once again at Clayton.

'I'll do it,' she repeated, 'but you'll have to make it worth my while. Shall we say a prize of a thousand guineas?'

'You're very sure of yourself, young lady.' There was a trace of amusement in Clayton's voice.

Stacey swallowed her annoyance at being patronized. They had his interest, that was the important thing, and they had the prospect of retrieving the company's fortunes. She knew she could rely on the support of every one of Brown's servants right down to the lowest stable-boy.

'I am confident in Brown's, Mr Clayton,' she replied. 'The coachman is only one of a large team.'

When Clayton spoke this time, it was almost with a hint of admiration.

'Your husband was correct, Mrs Wynwood. You are unique. Very well, there shall be a prize of a thousand guineas. I shall await the outcome with interest.'

Chapter Twenty-Three

There was no need on the return journey for an elaborate play of discussing steam coaches, for Perdita took up most of Simon and Stacey's attention. Safely back at All Saints Green, they both suppressed the urgent need to talk over the evening's events whilst they gave her a light supper and put her to bed. Terrified of being left alone, she insisted that they stayed with her, so they sat at her bedside, Simon holding her hand whilst Stacey told a rambling story in a low monotone. Gradually Perdita's tense little body relaxed and her breathing became regular. Stacey allowed her voice to trail off, Simon eased his fingers out of his daughter's grasp, and with infinite stealth they stood up and crept from the room, propping the door open as they left.

Stacey dropped onto the sofa in the front parlour with a sigh of relief.

'I expect she'll wake in the night. I think I'll have Hannah make up a bed in the nursery and sleep with her,' she decided. 'Poor little mite! What she must have suffered. And I cannot even see why Clayton kidnapped her in the first place. He gave her back without a great deal of persuasion.'

'He was just putting us at a disadvantage, making us so sick with worry that we would agree to anything he asked. And of course now he thinks he's got me in his pocket he can use her again as a weapon, knowing that I cannot admit to an association with him.' Simon busied himself pouring drinks. With his back to her, he said, 'I think you ought to know about Deborah Pymer—'

'I'd rather not,' Stacey interrupted. 'You said it was over and I believe you, truly. I wish you'd forget what I said yesterday. I was upset at the time, I spoke without thinking.'

'And I'd rather everything was as open between us as we persuaded Clayton,' Simon insisted. He handed her a glass of Madeira and sat at the other end of the sofa, looking into the dark pool of neat brandy in the goblet he held. 'I did meet her one more time at Letty Mullins's. That must have been when Oliver's informant saw me. I went because she made out that she knew where Pymer met with Clayton. We talked for a while but that was all, Stacey, I swear it. I've not seen her since, and I only went that time because it was the only clue I then had about Clayton.'

'It's of no importance,' Stacey said. 'Clayton and Oliver and anyone else can say what they like.' For a long moment the question of Deborah's baby hovered unspoken in the air, neither of them quite sure whether the bond between them was strong enough to bear any disclosures on that matter. It was Stacey who finally decided that enough had been said. 'Anyway, we've seen Clayton ourselves now. Simon, what was said while I was out of the room? What were those references to your inheriting the title, and to your having worked with Clayton in the past? Was that him trying to make trouble again?'

'No, no, it's all too true.' Simon swallowed half the brandy and swirled the remainder round the glass, reviewing all the revelations that had been made in the course of the evening. 'Do you remember my saying that I had a partnership in a gaming club at one time?' he asked at last.

Stacey nodded. 'I think so. At Oxford?'

'Precisely. My partner was none other than Clayton – under yet another name, of course.' He gave a brief, bleak smile at her astonished expression. 'Yes, I was somewhat taken aback as well. But that's not the worst of it, Stacey. He's in collusion with my – with the old man. Every time I've had dealings with Clayton, he's been there in the background influencing the outcome. God knows what sort of an agreement they've come to over me, but it's sure to be convoluted in the extreme. Neither would trust the other an inch, and rightly. They're two of a kind.'

'Oh.' Stacey considered this, and decided that she really did not want to hear any more about it. One Clayton she found sinister enough, two were appalling. 'And – the inheritance?' she asked hesitantly.

'Yes, the inheritance,' Simon repeated. 'The title, the house, the estate. It's laughable really. They all assume I can't wait to get my hands on it, when nothing could be further from the truth. I shall sell it, what's left after poor Tim's mismanagement and Georgiana's squandering. Unless—' he broke off abruptly and looked at Stacey. 'Would you want to live there?'

'No,' Stacey was emphatic on that point. 'But why—? Has your brother—?'

'Not Tim, he's still with us, poor devil,' Simon assured her. And he explained about Georgiana's baby.

Stacey stared at him.

'That's – that's utterly horrible,' she whispered. 'Did they really think that you would agree? And poor Georgiana, losing her child.'

Simon reached out to take her hand.

'You don't want to waste any sympathy on her, sweetheart. She's sure to have had it put out to nurse. I doubt if she set eyes on it from the moment it was born.' And he turned away from the painful subject of his family to the consideration of the future. 'It's you and our child we should be discussing. Stacey, you cannot go ahead with this race. I was an idiot to suggest it, I set my own trap and walked right into it.'

'But it's not a trap,' Stacey argued. 'It's a gift of a chance to save the company.'

'My dear, you cannot do this,' Simon insisted. 'If it's a choice between the company going under and you harming yourself, then the company will have to go. We'll manage somehow, start a new enterprise.'

'We will do no such thing!' Stacey declared, quite shrill with indignation. 'Do you think I'm such a poor creature as to be afraid of racing against the likes of Pymer? Hellfire! Pa must be turning in his grave. He spent twenty-seven years building the company up and I'm not seeing it collapse for want of a little effort on my part. And besides,' she gave a sudden mischievous grin, 'I want to do it. I'm looking forward to it.'

Simon realized that short of locking her up he was not going to stop her. But he did make one last effort.

'What about the baby?'

'He's a Brown too,' Stacey said, patting her stomach. 'He won't object to his mama taking the ribbons, and he's going to be very disappointed if he does not have a company to inherit. And just think of the odds! Anyone who doesn't know me will offer you fifty to one. We'll make a fortune! If only we had more time, one day is hardly enough to make the most of the chance, but we'll just have to work extremely hard tomorrow. If I tell Aunt Peg first thing, it will be all over the family by midday, and you'll have to contact all the people you know who will be willing to put on a really large amount.'

Eyes dancing and face alight with excitement, she was the old Stacey again, the girl who launched the Flyer, produced coach horses out of nowhere and organized the hapless Harris. Simon allowed his fears to be dulled as he was caught up in her enthusiasm.

'Very well,' he agreed, 'let us start planning the campaign. Before even we think of the money, the race itself must be as near as possible guaranteed. We'll have to switch some of the teams about to give you crack cattle all the way, and the Flyer must be thoroughly greased and checked over when it comes in tomorrow. I think we'll have someone guard it all night, I don't trust either Clayton or Pymer not to attempt sabotage. If only we had more time, there's plenty we could do to slow the opposition down.'

'Simon!' Stacey feigned shock. 'I'm sure that is not a gentlemanly way of carrying on.'

'This is no gentleman's race, sweetheart. Fair play has

389

nothing to do with it.'

Stacey laughed happily. 'How about bribing the pikers?' she suggested.

Twenty-four hours later, after a frenetic day of organization, Stacey was sound asleep whilst Simon, for the first time in years, lay awake checking over all the details in his head. Everything that possibly could be done to smooth the journey had been taken care of and the amount they stood to gain, as Stacey had predicted, was enormous. If only he were driving he would now be as blithely unconscious as Stacey, confident that barring a genuine accident he had the race all sewn up. The prize money he did not believe was to be depended upon any more than his own offer to work with Clayton, but that did not signify, so long as he appeared to be taken in. He must gain Clayton's trust sufficiently to obtain another meeting, and move in to arrest him. Lying staring up at the bedhangings, he went over the intricacies of this, weighing the possibility that some of the city's magistrates might be in Clayton's pocket, but it only briefly distracted him from the real worry that beset him. Inevitably, it had been Oliver who voiced what Simon least wanted to admit.

'Uncle Bart would never have allowed Stacey to do such a foolhardy thing.'

'Nonsense,' Simon had retorted. 'The Gaffer had even less control over her than I have.'

Oliver's heavy face reflected his disgust at such levity. 'If anything happens to her, I'll break your neck.'

Simon held his gaze steadily.

'That I can well believe,' he said. 'But don't worry, I shan't give you the opportunity.'

He only hoped that his assumed confidence was well-founded.

The atmosphere at the Crown the next day was akin to that on the morning of the Flyer's maiden run. The regular passengers, alarmed at the prospect of racing at breakneck speeds, had either transferred to one of the other London coaches or postponed their journeys, but their places had been readily taken up by young men eager for a day of unsurpassed sport. Stacey had won their admiration with her spectacular dash down to Stonham, and the fact that she was now both married and pregnant did very little to dull their appreciation.

When Simon and Stacey made their appearance at the yard at a quarter to seven, a cheer went up and inn guests and servants ran out to join in the welcome. Stacey was at once lifted out of her fit of last-minute nerves and waved gaily to her supporters whilst Simon shouldered a way through the crowd for them. He consigned her to the care of a disapproving Aunt Peg and went to check with his chief henchmen that all was proceeding according to plan, exchanging jokes and good-natured insults with acquaintances who accused him of letting his wife rule him. Nobody watching him would have guessed that he was within an ace of calling the whole thing off. He conferred with the judge whom he and Pymer had agreed upon, a fellow innkeeper called Foxwell and inevitably nicknamed Foxy, then caught sight of the Harrises amongst the crowd.

Arthur spoke for both of them.

'I say Wynwood, do you think this is wise? I mean to say, letting a lady drive four-in-hand all the way to Ipswich . . .'

'My dear Harris, if it were you in the box, I would doubt very much the wisdom of putting my shirt on the outcome, but as it is I have every confidence in the result. The odds are down to thirty-three to one, I believe, how much would you care to lose?'

Arthur flushed.

'I would not dream of betting against Mrs Wynwood,' he replied stiffly.

'Sensible man,' Simon commended, and was about to turn away when Arthur detained him.

'I say, Wynwood, I don't know whether it's of any importance, but we saw that man again, that jockey fellow, Page. He was skulking in a doorway at the corner of Crown Lane, and I just happened to catch sight of him as we passed.'

'When was this? Just now?' To Arthur's surprise, Simon gripped his arm and regarded him with a disturbing intensity.

'Yes,' he said, perplexed. 'Not ten minutes ago, as we drove in.'

'Capital.' Simon released him, smiled, regained his usual composure. 'It's always interesting to know where these odd characters are hiding. If you'll excuse me—'

He bade them both good day, a possible course of action already beginning to form in his mind, and found the guard about to start checking the passengers on board.

'Unruly crowd we've got here, Nat,' he commented, as the exuberant young sportsmen climbed aboard. 'One hint of trouble from any of them and throw them off, no questions asked, understand?'

The guard nodded, marking them against his waybill.

'Right you are, Mr Wynwood sir.'

'And Nat – look after Mrs Wynwood for me.'

'Like she was my own daughter, sir.'

It was five minutes to seven, the passengers were in their places and the luggage – not much of it as this was not a normal run – strapped on. The four matched bays snorted and fidgeted, impatient to be off. Simon went back into the Crown to fetch Stacey.

'All's well outside, we're just waiting for our coachman,' he said, and when they were out of Aunt Peg's hearing, 'Do you mind very much if I'm not in Ipswich to meet you? Something rather important has just arisen, it's a chance I cannot afford to let slip.'

Stacey tried to swallow her disappointment. It had been arranged that Simon and Harry Cox would leave immediately after the Flyer in a fast curricle and post down to the Angel at Ipswich before the stage arrived. Harry would then wait to take the return Flyer back whilst Simon drove Stacey home.

'That's all right,' she said, carefully unconcerned.

'I'll try to follow you down, but I cannot tell what time I'll arrive. If I'm not there by mid-afternoon, take a post chaise.'

'Don't fret yourself,' Stacey told him. 'I can look after myself.'

They arrived in the yard at that point, and there was no time for further explanations as Stacey acknowledged a renewed burst of cheering from her admirers. She was looking her best this morning, a tall and dashing figure in the new pelisse that had been the cause of her meeting with Deborah Pymer. Black suited her, and as Simon insisted that just because she was in mourning she need not look dowdy, the pelisse was cut in the latest style and sewn round the hem and sleeves with a deep pattern of braiding, and set off with a narrow-brimmed bonnet trimmed with sable. With a fine sense of the dramatic, Simon stopped as they reached the coach and pinned a late red rose from the garden to her wide collar before handing her up to the box seat and passing her her whip. The significance of the gesture was not lost on the outside passengers, reminding them that however unconventional the situation, Wynwood's wife was still very much his property.

Stacey settled herself in the seat and shortened in the reins, feeling the horses' mouths. The Killer lifted a threatening hindleg and was growled at by the horse-keeper holding his head. Taking a steadying breath, Stacey looked over the team's ears, anticipating the first and technically most difficult hazard of the journey: manoeuvring four fresh and high-mettled horses and a heavy vehicle through the narrow archway and out into the restricted space of Crown Lane. Even the most skilful coachman occasionally scraped the sides. She remembered the times her father had patiently sat beside her, making her practise until she could do it with a proficiency that Harry Cox would have been proud of.

'All right behind?' she called, her clear voice ringing round a yard now quiet and tense.

Beside her, Foxy Foxwell sat with his pocket watch lying open in his hand.

'All right, Mrs Wynwood,' came Nat's reply.

'Take off the cloths, boys.'

The horses' ears flicked forward and their hooves clattered restlessly on the cobbles. There was a hush as spectators and passengers alike held their breaths.

'Ready . . .' said Foxy, his eyes on the minute hand as it crept up to the hour. 'Go!'

Stacey eased her left hand down, the team surged forward, shouts and cheers and the brassy notes of Nat's bugle echoed round the crowded yard. Her face set in lines of fierce concentration, Stacey had no time to wave farewell. Too fast the horses were trotting under the archway, The Killer prancing and throwing his head up as he felt the unfamiliar hand on the rein. Stacey checked them, hearing as she did so Foxy muttering, 'Steady, steady,' between his teeth. The leaders emerged into the lane, and she 'pointed' them round, 'shooting' the wheelers so that they did not follow directly in the tracks of the horses in front but held the coach straight long enough for the back wheels to clear the inn. At the same time, the offside horses had to be held back and the nearside sent on, ensuring a smooth turn. The team responded, the coach rumbled out, The Killer gave a last defiant kick and settled into the collar, and the Highflyer set off down Crown Lane. Foxy visibly relaxed.

'Very pretty, if I might say so, Mrs Wynwood.'

Relieved herself at having passed the first test, Stacey gave a swift smile.

'You may say so, Mr Foxwell, but we're not off the stones yet.'

She slowed the horses to a walk through the steep slopes and sharp corners down from the hill on which the Crown stood close to the castle ditches, to the comparative safety of St Stephen's Street. Race or no race, she must get the

Flyer clear of the city before thinking about speed. As she rounded the last corner into Red Lion Lane, a couple of artisans leapt suicidally into the road, waving their arms and yelling at her to stop. Stacey hauled at the reins, the wheelers threw their weight against the heavy coach and the Flyer slithered to a halt just in time to avoid running into a dray that was slewed right across the road, completely blocking the way.

'Hellfire!' cursed Stacey. 'That's all we want!'

And then she realized that the name painted on the side of the dray was that of the brewery that supplied the Three Tuns.

'I'll lay you fifty guineas Pymer's behind this,' she said to Foxy, her voice shaking with fury. She twisted in her seat to look back up the street, and sure enough already a couple of carts behind them made it impossible to reverse. But she had reckoned without her band of supporters. Jumping down from the stage, they enlisted the help of the two artisans and other passers-by and proceeded to shift the dray, the two ponderous shires pulling it and the scattered barrels, ignoring the protests of the drayman and offering to knock down anyone foolish enough to stand in their way. Laughing now in triumph over Pymer's failed scheme, Stacey called her thanks, the passengers climbed aboard again and the Flyer started forward. What had set out as a disparate group of wild young men bent on a day's sport had been welded into a team.

The road out of Norwich was thick with incoming traffic, mostly farm carts bringing produce to feed the human and equine population of the city, but the outgoing lane was comparatively clear. Stacey let the horses break into a trot. They rolled past the last straggle of houses and the hospital and turned off the Newmarket road onto the Ipswich turnpike, Nat blowing a snatch of the Huntsman's Chorus to warn the pikeman of their coming. As Stacey pulled up and the piker came shambling out of his house, a shout went up from the

Flyer's outsiders. Ahead of them on the road, half a mile in front, was the garish black and orange bulk of Pymer's Comet. The outsiders yelled at the piker to hurry, Stacey handed over the money and was given a ticket that would open several gates down the road, the white painted barrier with its row of spikes was swung open. Stacey needed no pressing from her eager passengers. Cracking the whip above the horses' heads, she urged them into a trot, a canter, a gallop. The cool early morning air rushed past her, catching her long bonnet-strings and whisking them over her shoulder, the outsiders shouted encouragement, the Flyer rolled and swayed on its newly-overhauled springs. The team surged forward with necks outstretched and powerful muscles rippling. With the exception of The Killer, they were a joy to drive, matched as they were for stride as well as appearance. They were well-fed and well-rested, and they threw themselves into the task of catching up with their rivals as if they knew how much depended upon it.

The turnpike ran straight and level for nearly a mile and a half, and as they gradually gained on the coach in front Stacey's hopes rose high. If they could make up for the time lost moving the dray before even they reached the first stage, they practically had the race in their pocket. She could hardly wait to see Seth Pymer's face as they overtook. They gained ground even faster as the Comet slowed on the slope down into the Yare valley, then Stacey too checked the headlong flight of the horses. Tempting though it was to keep galloping and gather impetus for the upward slope on the far side of the valley, there was the Harford bridge to negotiate at the bottom, and the danger of the heavy coach overrunning the wheelers.

Down they thundered to the valley floor, still at a hand canter, whilst people from the little cluster of houses leaned out of windows and doorways and waved and shouted. The Flyer clattered over the bridge, and as it did so a dog came pelting out of a gateway, barking and snapping at the horses' heels. The Killer shied and kicked out at the animal, sending his team-mate sideways, the coach lurched and the back hub caught on the parapet with a grating scrape, the whole team faltered in their stride. Stacey held them together, lashed The Killer into submission, and sent them on through the little village and up the hill after the Comet. Beside her, Foxy cautiously let go his grip on the seat rail.

'Frightened, Mr Foxwell?' Stacey taunted. 'You cannot get down now, I'm afraid, you'll have to wait till we arrive at Tasburgh.'

'No, no,' Foxy assured her with unconvincing fervour. 'But that's a vicious beast you've got for a near wheeler. I can't think why you keep him.'

'He's a crack horse,' Stacey told him, 'and he's supposed to be vicious. He protects me.'

Foxy gave her an odd look and tried to find out more, but Stacey held her peace and let the bays slow to a trot up the incline.

'Now,' she said, as they gained level ground once more, 'let's give Pymer a run for his money! Hold tight!'

With Nat blowing a challenging chorus and the outsiders yelling hoarsely, Stacey sent the team galloping after the Comet again, shortening the distance between the coaches with every stride. Seth Pymer, warned of their approach, pulled out to the crown of the road, but still Stacey held on, inching up until the leaders' noses were level with the Comet's back wheels, edging over onto the wrong side of the road. The Flyer lurched and swayed as the offside wheels ran over the hard-baked ruts in the grass verge. Stacey trusted in Oliver's sound construction work and urged the bays to greater efforts. In the distance she could see a ponderous stage waggon lumbering towards them, but judged that she would be able to overtake before it came too close. The leaders were gaining the front of the Comet now, their ears laid back and flecks of foam flying from their mouths. Seth Pymer was leaning forward, cursing and lashing at his team of greys. Stacey caught a brief glimpse of his infuriated face as he glanced over his shoulder and realized she was not going to give way and fall back. With a growl, he lifted his whip and cut sideways at the bays' heads, making them falter and swerve almost off the road. A crescendo of sound broke round Stacey as her passengers roared in protest and Pymer's jeered back. She braced her feet against the splashboard as the coach bumped and jarred beneath her.

'Right, Seth Pymer,' she muttered, unheard amongst the clamour, 'now you're really going to see some driving.'

Hauling the horses back onto the road again, she steered them closer and closer to the Comet, until their wheels were within an inch of locking. Ahead of them, the stage waggon had pulled right over to the hedge, but its offside wheels and canvas-covered tilt were still partly on the road, making the passing space perilously narrow. Even if she wanted to, Stacey was now too far over and going too fast to drop behind. There was only one way out of trouble – to pull ahead. The two teams were running neck and neck now, and Pymer was forced off the crown of the road. For what seemed like an age, neither coach was able to gain the lead, until the Comet's near wheels ran onto the verge and jolted over the ruts. Pymer was thrown off-balance and jerked at the reins, upsetting his team's stride. The Flyer surged ahead, cutting in under the Comet's leaders' noses and avoiding the waggon by inches.

The outsiders cheered, the waggoner bawled abuse, the Comet's passengers yelled defiance, but nothing could stop the Flyer's triumphant progress now. They dashed through tollgates with hardly a pause, swept down the street and over the bridge at Newton Flotman, steadily built up a lead over the last mile into Upper Tasburgh. It was not until they pulled in at the Black Bull that Stacey found she was shaking with effort and delayed shock. But there was no time to consider what might have happened if the Flyer had been crushed between the Comet and the waggon. The horsekeepers, alerted the day before, were ready and waiting with the next team, the chestnuts that usually hauled the Albion over its first stage, and the landlord of the Bull had his waiters lined up with trays of drinks.

'To Mrs Wynwood!' one of the young sportsmen declared, snatching up a glass. 'The finest whip in the three counties!'

'Mrs Wynwood!' his enthusiastic cronies responded.

Then one of them spied a late-flowering rose bush in a neighbouring garden.

'Red roses!' he shouted, and of one accord the group leaped down off the roof, decimated the bush and swarmed back on board again just as the last buckle was fastened. With a snatch from the bugle and a cheer from the bystanders, the Flyer set off on its next stage to Dickleburgh, leaving behind a trail of trampled rose petals.

The moment the Flyer disappeared out of the yard of the Crown, Simon shoved his way through the crowd of spectators, cut through the kitchens and along a service passage and eventually out into the street by a little-used side door. Here he paused, looking down the narrow lane to where Stacey had just rounded the corner, and there, just as Harris had said, the small figure of Will Page could be seen leaning in a doorway watching the main entrance of the inn. Waiting, Simon guessed, to see him safely off the premises before reporting back to Clayton. With no cover and next to no chance of creeping up undiscovered, Simon started to walk up the street towards him, ready to run the moment he was seen. He had hardly gone five yards before Page spotted him, hesitated fractionally then darted off, pushing between a street seller and a couple of maidservants and disappearing round the corner.

Simon tore after him, reaching the next street in time to see him dodge under the tail of a delivery cart and into an alleyway, and followed as Page wrenched open the high rickety gate in the wall at the end, slammed it behind him and shot the bolt. Hardly checking his pace, Simon turned sideways on and rammed the gate with his shoulder. The rotten timbers creaked and gave. Simon kicked at them with the heel of his boot and part of the gate splintered away. He reached a hand through and undid the bolt, and found himself looking across a small, untidy back yard to where Page was shinning up a lean-to shed to make his escape over the wall. Three long strides and he had Page by the ankles and dragged him back. The man yelped, twisting and struggling as he fell, reaching for his knife the moment he hit the ground, but Simon was too quick for him, pinning him to the ground with a knee on his chest, crushing his wrist until he was forced to let go of the weapon.

Aware of curious eyes at the windows above him, Simon snatched up the knife and jerked Page to his feet, holding him in a half-nelson.

'Move,' he ordered, and pushed the man out of the broken gate and into the narrow alleyway beyond. 'Now,' he said, bringing the point of the knifeblade up under Page's throat, 'you're going to take me to your Mr Clayton. Where does he hide in this town?'

Page refused to answer. Simon jabbed the blade up a further inch, forcing Page's neck back as far as it would reach, pricking the stretched skin of his throat.

'Talk,' he hissed, 'or you're done for. I'm not afraid to use this.'

To underline his words, he twisted the point, opening up a cut.

Page's eyes rolled wildly and he gave a hoarse croak of submission. Simon let his chin down an inch to enable him to speak.

'Off Colegate Street,' he grated.

'That's better,' Simon commended. 'Now listen. You are going to take me there, and get me in without giving any warnings, understand? One foot wrong and I shall not hesitate to slit your worthless throat. You follow?'

Page reluctantly admitted that he did.

'Good,' Simon said, and lowered the knife, keeping his grip on the man's arm. 'Now walk.'

Back on the street again, Simon sent a passing boy to find Mr Oliver Brown and bring him as fast as he could. Oliver appeared within minutes, looking annoyed. When he saw Page, however, comprehension dawned.

'What's he doing here?' he demanded.

'Spying on us, I would imagine. Our friend Clayton must be getting careless, sending someone we know. Or perhaps he thinks we're too preoccupied today to notice.' Simon handed his captive over, 'Will you keep him here, out of sight, for a few minutes? I don't want to draw attention to what's going on. I'm going to fetch some reinforcements, then this obnoxious specimen is going to take us to his master. Are you game to come with us?'

'Help catch that disciple of Satan?' Oliver's heavy face broke into a grim smile of relish. 'You'll not keep me away.'

'Capital. I knew I could rely on you.'

Simon made his way back to the Crown, located Harry Cox amongst the lingering crowd of spectators and sent him to find three men known to be handy with their fists, then raced back through streets busy with people to All Saints Green. The startled housemaid, sweeping the stairs, gaped as he ran into the study, took something out of a drawer in the desk and shot out of the house again all within the space of a minute. Simon, acutely conscious of the need for speed, cursed himself for growing soft and unguarded. Time was when he always had a gun within easy reach, not tucked away in a corner.

In the yard once more, he found Harry Cox had rounded up a couple of horsekeepers and a porter. He drew them into the privacy of the inner office, and outlined as briefly as possible what they were asked to do and why. All were more than ready to avenge themselves on the man presented to them as being responsible for the deaths of Ned Shears, Amos Burgess and the Gaffer. It was an angry and implacable group of men that joined Oliver and his prisoner in Crown Lane, a fact that Simon was quick to point out to Page.

'You give the game away with so much as a blink, and I'll not be responsible for what happens to you,' he warned.

Page, without Watkins to protect him and for once unable to talk his way out of the situation, was cowed.

They split up for the short walk through the city, arriving in ones and twos in a lane off Colegate Street. Page, white now with terror at being caught between his captor's threats and Clayton's certain revenge, pointed out the entrance, a peeling, unmarked doorway in an otherwise blank brick wall.

'Is that the only one?' Simon asked. 'Any other bolt-holes?'

Page cast desperately around for a means of escape.

'No,' he said, trying to shrink away from Oliver's iron grasp.

Mindful of the fact that there might be someone listening on the other side of the door, Simon lowered his voice to a menacing hiss.

'Listen, I wasn't born yesterday. An old building like this is a rabbit warren. Show us the other entrances and we might be grateful. Clayton's day is done, so you'd be wise to throw in your lot with us.'

Page reluctantly showed them three more unobtrusive doorways, all locked but none guarded. Simon left a member of his band at each and they finally returned to the first one.

'Get it open,' he ordered. 'Quietly.'

While Simon, Oliver and Harry flattened themselves against the wall on either side, Page knocked on the door. There was silence for a moment, then clumping footsteps and movement behind the peephole just above the lock.

'Oh, it's you,' a voice said. 'What's up?'

Page's eyes slid sideways to where Simon stood poised

with the knife in his hand.

'Nothing,' he said. 'Just got a message for Mr Clayton.'

A grunt from inside, then a key turned and as the door opened Oliver and Harry burst in, silenced the guard and caught hold of Page again before he could make a run for it.

'Good,' Simon whispered. 'Now for Clayton.' He jabbed the knife in the small of Page's back. 'Lead on, you.'

They trod carefully through winding passages and up twisting stairs lit by the occasional dirty window. Simon judged that they must have left the building they had entered, and were now climbing up into another. The whole place seemed lifeless but for the occasional scuffling of rats, and he wondered what lay behind the closed doorways. Storerooms, perhaps. It seemed unlikely that Clayton would keep the entire complex of rooms and corridors empty. A pile of boxes on a landing broader than most seemed to bear out this theory, for they had strands of fresh straw clinging to them and were bare of the dust that covered the surrounding area. Incoming goods, Simon guessed, waiting to be consigned to the right place. And just as he came to this conclusion, Page stopped before a corner and pressed back against the wall.

'What is it?' Simon asked under his breath.

'Bodyguard. Outside his rooms.'

'Get him over here.'

Page swallowed, and started forward. Simon motioned to Oliver to be ready.

'Hey, Tom,' Page called softly. 'See here.'

There was a rumble of protest from the disturbed guard.

'What's the matter with you this time?'

'Come over here,' Page insisted. 'You oughter see this.'

Unsuspecting, the man did as he was bid, and was felled by Oliver before he knew what had hit him.

'Are there likely to be any more inside?' Simon asked.

'Dunno, honest!' Page maintained. 'Depends.'

Simon drew the pistol out of his pocket.

'You two take anyone else that might be in the room. Leave Clayton to me,' he instructed.

They crept along the last corridor until they came to a door very much like all the others they had passed. Simon made an enquiring face, Page nodded. Simon motioned to Oliver. 'Get him in front of you as a shield,' he breathed. He reached for the handle. 'Ready?'

There was an explosion of sound as they burst into the room. Page yelped with alarm, Simon gasped and automatically clapped a hand to his shoulder as a bullet scorched into him, Oliver found himself grappling with the formidable bulk of Job Watkins. Harry grabbed Page as he tried to dodge out, sent him spinning with a well-aimed fist and piled into the struggle with Watkins whilst Simon, recovering from the first shock, stepped clear of them and levelled his gun at Clayton.

'Call him off,' he commanded. 'I'm reckoned a fair shot, even with a hole in my shoulder, and at this range I cannot very well miss.'

Clayton, seated behind an elegant desk with his own pistol still smoking in his hand, looked back at him with cold, impassive eyes.

'Quiet, Joby,' he ordered.

With a growl, Watkins submitted to being held and having his hands tied by Oliver and Harry.

'Put that gun down and stand up,' Simon said.

Clayton did so, but slowly.

'All this dramatic posturing will be to no avail I fear, Mr Wynwood,' he remarked. 'Your wife is not here.'

For a split second, Simon's throbbing arm wavered, till he realized it was a trick.

'No, she's on the road to Ipswich, well out of your way,' he answered. 'Walk towards the door. Slowly.'

'Wrong, Mr Wynwood. Your redoubtable lady may be on the road to Ipswich, but she is not out of my way,' Clayton stated, holding his ground. 'Would you not like to know more?'

Keeping his eyes fixed on Clayton and the pistol levelled at his head, Simon stepped carefully backwards and held out Page's knife to Oliver.

'A bullet's too quick,' he said. 'I think I prefer his guts to be split.'

As Oliver took the knife, Watkins lunged forward, butting Simon from the side. He staggered and fell, the gun cracking and the shot whistling past Harry's ear to bury itself harmlessly in the wall. The coachman grabbed a chair and brought it crashing down on Watkins's head and Oliver reached Clayton. By the time Simon struggled to his feet, Clayton was helpless, with the point of the knife beneath his jaw.

Panting, Simon faced Clayton once more.

'Explain, or I'll take great pleasure in slicing you up very slowly,' he demanded.

Clayton's expressionless granite features gave way to the ghost of a malicious smile.

'Surely you did not really think that Lord Lathenbridge would permit this mis-match with a family of innkeepers, Mr Wynwood?' he said. 'Your wife will go no further than South Stonham. After that, she will meet with an unfortunate accident.'

Simon's fists clenched convulsively.

'It would be interesting to see what my company servants would do to you if I gave them a free hand,' he remarked, and for the first time had the satisfaction of seeing a flicker of apprehension at the back of Clayton's eyes. He had hit the right nerve: Clayton did not care to be torn apart by the rabble. 'Well?' he asked. 'The bridge is under repair,' Clayton said, 'and the workmen need to use explosives. A moment of carelessness, just as your Highflyer comes over the hill—'

He broke off as Simon took a menacing step forward, but the expected blow did not land.

'To take private revenge is to sink to his level,' Simon stated, speaking to Oliver. 'Take him to Mr Engleton, tell him everything you know and say we'll be producing a string of witnesses. We'll all take a day off to see him swing. Harry—' he turned to the coachman, 'come, we've a journey to make.'

After nearly four hours on the road, Stacey knew that Simon had been right when he said that driving a stagecoach was not the same as a light curricle. Her back and legs ached abominably, her arms felt as if they would drop off if she had to check the team or use the whip one more time, she was so weary that all strength seemed to have drained out of her. She was forced to admit, though only to herself, that she had not fully taken into account the effect of her pregnancy. At home if she was tired, she could rest for an hour or so during the day, or have an early night, but her capacity for work was unimpaired. The strain of helping run the company was quite different from the sheer physical effort required to drive four-in-hand non-stop for forty miles. She recognized a landmark with overwhelming relief. Only two miles now to South Stonham, and she would be able to snatch two minutes' rest whilst the horses were changed for the last stage. If she could just hold on to the lead she had achieved over Seth Pymer, all would be well.

And then she rounded a bend to find the road completely blocked by a motley herd of cattle.

'Oh no!' she cried, her voice cracking. 'That's all we want!'

'No need to take on, Mrs Wynwood,' Foxy assured her. 'Just drive your way through 'em.' Though supposedly an impartial judge, and with nothing to gain financially from the race, Foxy was completely won over to the Flyer's side. When a recalcitrant piker had seen fit to argue over the toll, he had shouted back with the rest of the passengers, and cheered encouragement when the outsiders leaped down, lifted the gate off its hinges and threw it in the ditch.

Stacey tried to take his advice, and sent out the whip to urge the leaders forward. They went on obediently enough, but the cattle, instead of parting to let the coach through, began to mill about, lowing anxiously, bumping into each other and the horses in their confusion. The coach slowed to a crawl, the outsiders yelled at the herdsman to shift his beasts, Stacey nearly wept with frustration. Behind her on the road, drifting through the racket around her, she could hear the sound of the Comet's yard of tin. Her team of partisans heard it too, and sprang into action. Climbing down once more, two of them took the lead horses by the bridles whilst the rest shoved and kicked and beat the cattle out of the way, ignoring the herdsman's protests. But even as they scrambled on board again, the Comet came rolling up the turnpike behind them. Stacey whipped her team into a trot, then a canter, but in the time needed to gain speed the Comet caught up further still. The herd of cattle, parted now into two groups, remained docilely on the grass verges while the second coach rattled past. When they finally pulled up outside the Dun Cow at Stonham, there was only two hundred yards between them.

Stacey dropped the reins and drooped in her seat, holding her head in her hands. Foxy climbed down to stretch his legs, and the outsiders argued, as usual, over who should have the honour of buying their coachman a drink. Nat ran round to the front of the coach.

'You all right, Mrs Wynwood?' he asked anxiously. 'You're not ailing?'

Stacey straightened up and gave him a wan smile.

'No, no, I'm perfectly well,' she assured him. 'Just a little tired, that's all.'

The guard was not entirely convinced. His wife was about to give birth to their fourth child, and had been horrified when told of the intended contest.

'Begging your pardon, Mrs Wynwood, but I don't know what the Gaffer's about, letting you do this,' he said. 'It's him as should be up on the box, not you.'

It took Stacey a moment or two to work out that he was referring not to her father, but to Simon. She made a mental note to tell Simon later, knowing how pleased he would be.

'But it would hardly have been a race with him driving. Nobody in their right minds would have bet against him,' she pointed out. 'And anyway, there's nothing wrong with me, Nat, so stop fussing like an old hen.'

She accepted a glass of sherry handed up by one of her admirers, swallowed a mouthful and took up the reins and whip again as the last buckles were done up. The fresh team broke into an eager trot, and Stacey prayed that they would get through the next tollgate before the Comet completed its change. If they could do so, and get the gate closed behind them, it might serve to delay Pymer a precious minute or so. But just as they drew level with the Prince of Wales, the Comet set off again with a blare on the horn and yells of derision from its outsiders, and cut right in front of the Flyer. Stacey hauled back on her horses just in time to stop them from crashing into the Comet's rear, and tried to find a gap to overtake, but space was restricted in the narrow village street. She knew that beyond the next pike a small steep valley made it impossible to do anything but keep right behind the Comet and make a break for the lead once they were on level ground again.

Fuming with impatience, choking in the dust kicked up by the leading coach, she slowed to pay the toll, unaware in the general hubbub of a clatter of galloping horses and desperate shouting behind her. The Comet set off at a hand canter up the gentle hill towards the valley, and Stacey made a sudden decision to try to get past now. It was a risk, as they might well go over the crest side by side and collide with an oncoming vehicle, but it was preferable to trailing behind Pymer for the next three miles.

'Hold tight!' she said to Foxy, and whipped the team into a canter, steering them out towards the crown of the road.

From the rear of the Flyer came a frantic cry from Nat.

'No, Miss Stacey, pull up! Pull up!'

'Hellfire, who's driving this coach, him or me?' Stacey muttered furiously, and took no notice.

But then she became aware of another voice shouting at her, and a hard-pressed pair of sweating, foam-flecked horses coming up on her offside at a flat-out gallop.

'Idiot! Madman! Get back or you'll be killed!' she raged, and then glancing back over her shoulder saw that the challenging coachman was Harry Cox, with Simon standing precariously beside him in the bucketing curricle and yelling at her to stop.

'Not now!' she cried. 'Get back and give me room!'

'Stacey, for God's sake pull up!'

The speeding curricle was level with the Flyer's team now, and edging over, forcing them onto the left-hand side of the road. As all three vehicles drew nearer and nearer the crest of the hill, nobody noticed a ragged figure spring out of the ditch ahead of them and wave a frantic warning to the valley below. Simon leaned over and caught the Flyer's offside leader's reins and Stacey was forced to fight them to a halt.

'What the devil do you think you're doing?' Stacey demanded, trembling with fury. 'How dare you? Look at them – they've got ahead now, I'll never be able to catch them – oh!' She broke off as she caught sight of the bloodstains on Simon's shoulder. 'Oh my God, what's happened?' she cried, and thrusting the reins into Foxy's hands, started to scramble down from the box, hardly aware that the Comet was trotting triumphantly into the valley. She had just reached the ground and started towards Simon when the blast of an explosion split the air and reverberated in her ears, drawing her shocked gaze back to the road ahead. At the bottom of the hill, part of the bridge had collapsed and the Comet was toppling sideways into the river amongst the screams of horses and the shouts and curses of men. Simon reached her side and, heedless of onlookers, drew her into a shaking embrace.

'Stacey, Stacey, thank God you're safe. That was meant for you.'

Around them, inside and outside passengers were climbing down and running to give what help they could to the wrecked coach.

'For me?' Stacey repeated, but the fate of the Comet faded into insignificance beside her concern for him. Pressed against him, she could now see the jagged, scorched edges of a bullet hole at the top of his sleeve. 'Darling, you've been shot! Whatever is going on? You shouldn't be chasing down the turnpike if you're wounded.'

'With you driving towards that?' Simon asked. 'Clayton arranged all this, he must have planned it from the start, and I was too stupid to see it. My God, Stacey, I nearly let you go right into it!' He was speaking without first measuring his words, his voice raw with self-reproach. 'I should have guessed, I should have seen it was all too straightforward, I should have known he would try to be rid of me through you. And he so nearly succeeded. Another two minutes – Stacey, I couldn't have lived with myself.'

Hardly daring to believe her ears, Stacey moved her head slightly to look up at his face, and found the mask of control was gone. The killing anxiety of his pursuit of her and the overwhelming relief of reaching her in time were written plainly. She reached up and touched his haggard cheek with her fingertips.

Close by, there was an embarrassed cough from Nat.

'Going to take one of the horses and ride back to Stonham for help, Mr Wynwood sir,' he said, loud and matter-of-fact. 'Nasty mess down there. Looks like a bloody battlefield. They say Pymer's bust his leg and there's others hurt worse.'

Simon closed his eyes briefly.

410

'Yes. Right. Carry on,' he said, with something like his usual assurance.

Stacey could have throttled Nat. Just as she thought they were on the brink of discovery, he had to break the moment. With a streak of feminine cunning she never knew she possessed, she let herself sag and clutched feebly at Simon's good shoulder.

'I – I think I'd better sit down' she faltered.

Simon's attention was all hers again. Instantly solicitous, he led her to the side of the road and sat her carefully on the dusty late-summer grass.

'What is it? Are you not well? Shall I fetch you a drink?'

'No, no, I'm all right. It just suddenly came home to me what I escaped.' She gripped his hand, looking up into his eyes. 'Stay with me.'

Simon knelt down beside her, studying her white, strained face with feverish intensity.

'I thought I'd lost you,' he said. 'On the journey down, you had such a start on us, I kept seeing you – my God, Stacey, I kept seeing you blown to pieces, and it would be too late, too late to tell you all the things I've left unsaid—'

The frantic scene below them as the Flyer's passengers struggled to save the injured men and beasts of the stricken Comet, Harry Cox, holding the spent horses that had pulled the curricle on its final desperate sprint, Foxy Foxwell, still in charge of the Flyer, all faded from Stacey's consciousness. The world contracted to hold nothing but the two of them. Even the bone weariness of her own body seemed to lift miraculously as she listened to his words.

'I thought you would die thinking I didn't even care enough to drive down and meet you at Ipswich when in truth – Stacey, you don't know how happy you've made me these past months. In spite of everything that's happened, all the worry, you've given me the best part of my life. I wake up each morning glad to have you by

411

me, and I come home eager to see you again, knowing that you're waiting for me, and yet I've never told you – never let you know how much I love you.'

His image swam before her as tears rose in her eyes.

'I wanted you to say that so much,' she whispered huskily. 'I've always loved you.'

'I know – it was unforgivable of me not to tell you. I think I was afraid of losing what I had found. Stacey, you said once that I take and don't give, and you were right. I can't begin to make any return for what you've given me.'

Stacey raised his hand and kissed it.

'You've just given me all I want.'

While the road became busy with carts and carriages ferrying the victims of the crash back to Stonham, they untangled past misunderstandings and planned a fruitful future. The wreckage was cleared and the bridge declared safe to cross with care, the rescue party began to drift back to the Flyer. Simon and Stacey got to their feet.

'If everyone's here, we'd better get moving,' Stacey declared. 'We're over an hour behind time.'

'Stacey—' Simon placed a restraining hand on her arm as she made to mount the box. 'You're not taking the ribbons again. Harry can complete the journey.'

She flashed a mischievous smile.

'Oh yes I am. I've a race to finish, remember? Pymer was ahead of me at the bridge; if I don't complete the course, we'll lose all those bets.'

Simon began to say that the money was well lost, but she cut him short.

'You can't stop me now, when we're almost there,' she murmured, aware of a coachful of interested spectators. 'I'm not at all tired now. I feel as if I've drunk a bottle of champagne.'

Simon gave in, handed her up and climbed up to take the seat behind her.

'No driving to the sun,' he stipulated.

'Not this time,' Stacey agreed. She gathered up the reins and whip and settled in her seat. 'All right behind, Nat?'

'All right, Mrs Wynwood.'

The whip flicked out, the team started forward, and the Highflyer set off on the last stage of its journey.

THE END